The Lords of Navarre

The Lords of Navarre

A Basque Family Saga

José Maria Lacambra-Loizu

iUniverse, Inc.
New York Lincoln Shanghai

The Lords of Navarre
A Basque Family Saga

All Rights Reserved © 2004 by José Maria Lacambra-Loizu

No part of this book may be reproduced or transmitted in any form or by any means, graphic, electronic, or mechanical, including photocopying, recording, taping, or by any information storage retrieval system, without the written permission of the publisher.

iUniverse, Inc.

For information address:
iUniverse, Inc.
2021 Pine Lake Road, Suite 100
Lincoln, NE 68512
www.iuniverse.com

Cover © Photographic Archives of the Government of Navarre

ISBN: 0-595-31148-2 (pbk)
ISBN: 0-595-66266-8 (cloth)

Printed in the United States of America

To Atxi,

who filled my head with dreams and tales about her fair and ancient land.

JML

"Some of the oldest bits of history handed down to us (come) from thrilling battle songs or anecdotes of individual prowess. The minstrels or lectors would assemble such units into groups, producing a cycle of narratives clustered around the name of a single hero…someone who had really existed, such as Sargon, the hero-king of Akkad, Helen of Troy, Moses of the Exodus, Charlemagne behind the Chanson de Roland…

The total result would be a mixture of history and fiction, which even the modern scholar cannot disentangle…It would be history par excellence, a story that was handed down and there would be no means of checking it."

The Origins of Historical Writing
Herbert Butterfield

…the novel is, after all, the most intimate, the truest history….

Miguel de Unamuno
Saint Emanuel, the Good, Martyr

Contents

Chronological Guideline xvii
Preface xxi

BOOK 1 THE DAWNING

Chapter 1:	The Early Mists	3
Chapter 2:	A Row with the Slantheads	13
Chapter 3:	Confrontation	20
Chapter 4:	Death in the Tundra	25
Chapter 5:	The Valley of Baztán	35
Chapter 6:	The Hunt	46
Chapter 7:	A Brush with the Celts	52
Chapter 8:	The Iberian Blacksmith	60
Chapter 9:	A Roman Interlude	73
Chapter 10:	The Rhine Adventure	85
Chapter 11:	The Fair and the Swarthy	94
Chapter 12:	The Moorish Yoke	102
Chapter 13:	Cantabria	110
Chapter 14:	The Hermitage	118
Chapter 15:	Prelude to Covadonga	126

Chapter 16: The Lords of the Valleys..................................133
Chapter 17: The Witches of Sorogain..................................139
Chapter 18: Roncevaux..147
Chapter 19: The True Chanson de Roland..........................158

BOOK II THE AGE OF CHIVALRY

Chapter 20: At The Dawning of Chivalry............................171
Chapter 21: A Squire's Life...184
Chapter 22: The Eve of the Tournament..............................193
Chapter 23: A Passage of Arms...204
Chapter 24: An English Dalliance.......................................212
Chapter 25: Eleanor's Brokerage...219
Chapter 26: A Hazardous Journey.......................................232
Chapter 27: A Royal Wedding...239
Chapter 28: The Knighting..249
Chapter 29: A Royal Tryst...257
Chapter 30: The Third Crusade...263
Chapter 31: A Wobbly Legacy...274
Chapter 32: An African Adventure......................................282
Chapter 33: A Nostalgic Reunion..292
Chapter 34: Navas de Tolosa...302

BOOK III THE WANING KINGDOM

Chapter 35: A Gentleman Farmer..313
Chapter 36: Crecy..321
Chapter 37: Besieged...328

Chapter 38: Nájera 339
Chapter 39: Rubbing Elbows with Royalty 348
Chapter 40: The Wages of Friendship 354
Chapter 41: Majordomo to a would-be King 362
Chapter 42: A Pilgrimage to Santiago 370
Chapter 43: The Last Act 382
Chapter 44: Querencia 389

Acknowledgements

I would like to thank several people for their support during the writing of *The Lords of Navarre*. My mother, Atxi, preserved the family stories and shared them with me, setting me on the trail of my ancestors, the Agorretas. Her–and her mother's–knowledge of family lore and the *Saltus Vasconum's* history and culture were a great inspiration. My wife, Ann, offered invaluable help with her advice and encouragement as well as with her thoughtful and enthusiastic editing of my manuscript.

A number of books and documents were helpful in developing the cultural and historical background for this novel. The following were particularly valuable:

Archives of Navarran Heraldic Records	Diputación Forál de Navarra
Dance of the Tigers (1980)	Björn Kurtén
Desciframiento de la Lengua ibérico-tartésica (1996)	Jorge Alonso Garcia
Eleanor of Aquitaine (1999)	Alison Weir
Genes, Peoples, and Languages (2000)	Luigi Luca Cavalli-Sforza
Geographica (~ A.D 10)	Strabo
Histoire secréte du Pays basque (1980)	Michel Lamy

Histories (~ 450 B.C.)	Herodotus
La Cueva de Isturitz (1995)	Xabier Esparza San Juan
Los Vascones (1986)	Ma. Jesús Peréx de Agorreta
Los Vascones y sus Vecinos	Julio Caro Baroja
Mankind Evolving (1962)	Theodosius Dobzhansky
Mitología Vasca (1983)	José María de Barandiarán
Mitos y Creencias (1980)	José Maria Satrústegui
Natural History (~A.D. 70)	Pliny the Elder
Nueva Síntesis de la Historia del País Vasco (1982)	Martín Ugalde
Nabarra, ou Quand les Basques avaient des Rois (1978)	Pierre Narbaitz
Pedro I el Cruél (1980)	Manuel de Soroa
Reyes de Navarra (1986)	Luis Fortún Perez de Ciriza
Roncesvalles (1973)	Agapito Martinez Alegría
The Borgias (1972)	Clemente Fusero
The Histories (~AD 96)	Tacitus
The Knight in History (1984)	Frances Gies

Finally, I would like to offer apologies for the liberties I have taken when relating the lives of the early Agorretas. But as eminent historians like Herbert Butterfield admit, there is much fiction in history and no way of checking what legend hands down to us.

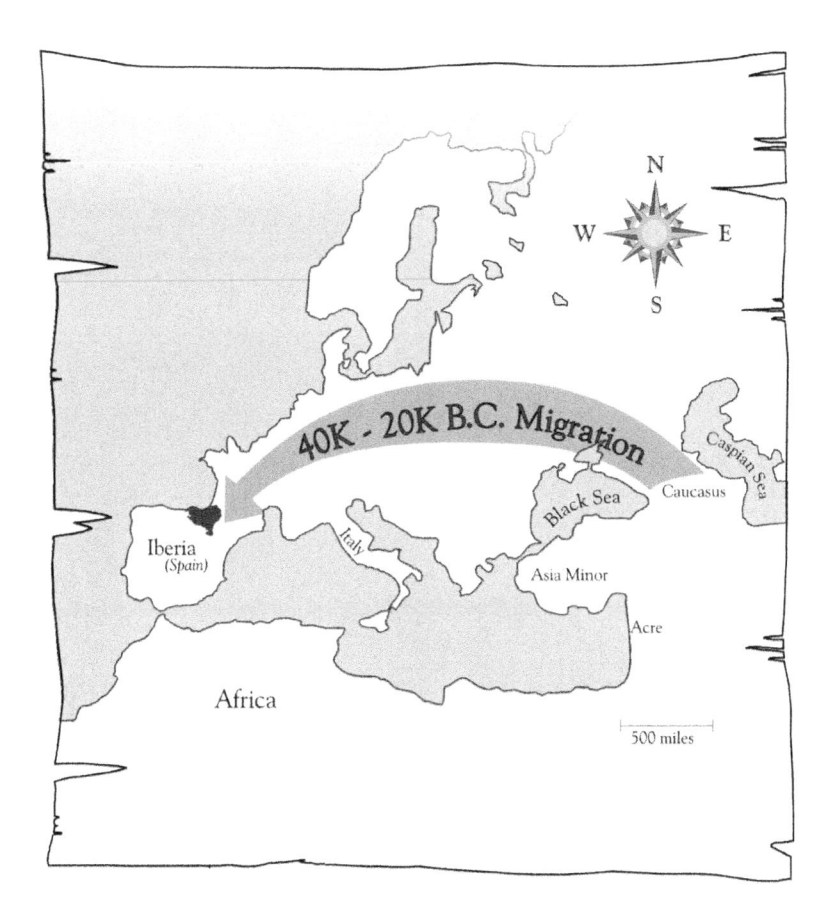

Original Basque (Cro Magnon) migration from the Caucasus to the northern tundra during a warming spell of the last Würm glaciation 40,000 years ago and subsequent retreat south, away from the advancing ice sheet during the peak of that glacial period, 20,000 years later.

Chronological Guideline

Date	Significant Event	Agorreta
B.C.		
40,000	Pandorf Interstadial, appearance of Cro-Magnon in the Middle East	Gorka
35,000	Disappearance of Neanderthals	
30,000	First cave paintings in Aquitaine	
20,000	Minimum temperatures during Würm III glaciation	Uruk
15,000	Cave paintings in Altamira and Isturitz	
10,000	Paleolithic-Holocene transition, onset of warming trend	
6,000	First Farming in Iberia	
4,000	Invention of writing	
2,000	Bronze Age, first Celtic incursions into Iberia, appearance of dolmens	
900	Phoenician colonization of eastern Iberia	
700	Celtic settlement of Catalonia, beginning of Iberian iron works	
600	Carthaginian colonies in Iberia	
500	Peak of Celtic expansion in Europe, La Tène culture	Nagusi
218	Roman legions in Iberia	
133	Romans in parts of Navarre	

75	Pamplona's founding by Pompey	
45	Julius Caesar in Iberia	

A.D.

69	Defeat of Batavians by Basque cohorts in Lower Rhine	Otsoa
415	Invasion of Spain by Visigoths	
507	Invasion of Aquitaine by Franks	
711	Moors' invasion of Iberia	Itziar
721	Battles of Liédena and Covadonga	
778	Basques' defeat of Charlemagne at Roncevaux	Ausarta
824	Crowning of Iñigo Arista, first king of Pamplona	
1125	Birth of Eleanor of Aquitaine	
1150	Crowning of Sancho VI, the Wise, King of Navarre	
1154	Birth of Sancho VII, *el Fuerte*	
1157	Birth of Richard the Lionheart	
1164	Birth of Iñaki de Agorreta	Iñaki
1170	Birth of Berenguela of Navarre	
1188	Richard the Lionheart's tournament in Pamplona	
1191	Sailing of Third Crusade for the Holy Land, marriage of Berenguela	
1199	Crowning of Sancho *el Fuerte* King of Navarre	
1200	Sancho's escapade to North Africa	
1212	Battle of Navas de Tolosa	
1234	Death of Sancho *el Fuerte*; crowning of Queen Blanca of Navarre	
1328	Marriage of Juana II to Philip d'Evreux	Fortun
1346	Battle of Crecy	

Chronological Guideline

1349	Crowning of Charles *le Mauvais* King of Navarre	
1356	Defeat of French by Black Prince at Poitiers	
1360	Treaty of Bretigny granting British suzerainty over Aquitaine	
1363	Capture of Sos by Charles *le Mauvais*	
1367	Battle of Najera	
1369	Pedro *el* Cruel's defeat and death at the hands of Trastamara	
1420	Marriage of Juan II of Aragon to Blanca of Navarre	Miguel
1421	Birth of Prince of Viana	
1450	Revolt of Prince of Viana against his father	
1452	Birth of Ferdinand of Aragon	
1456	Invasion of Navarre by Gaston de Foix	
1461	Death of Prince of Viana	
1479	Marriage of Ferdinand of Aragon to Isabel of Castile	
1482	Birth of Juan de Aguirre	Juan
1492	America discovered by Columbus	
1493	Naming of Cesare Borgia Cardinal of Valencia	
1498	Marriage of Cesare Borgia to Charlotte d'Albret	
1500	Birth of Charles V, future Holy Roman Emperor, in Ghent	
1505	Marriage of Ferdinand of Aragon to Germaine de Foix	
1507	Death of Cesare Borgia at Viana	
1512	Overruning of Navarre by Castile	
1515	Navarre's incorporation into the kingdom of Castile-Aragon	

Preface

A few segregated pockets of human populations exist in the world today whose origins have long intrigued anthropologists. The Basques, whose roots are lost in prehistoric mists, belong to one such race. Over the years, several engaging theories have been proposed regarding their origin. One of the more imaginative identified them with the lost tribe of Israel while another considered them survivors of ill-fated Atlantis.

Recent breakthroughs in linguistic and genetic investigations, however, confirm the even more startling thesis that the Basques are stragglers of the first group of Cro-Magnon to venture out of the Middle East during the middle Paleolithic to displace the Neanderthals and settle Europe. Keys to the survival of this racial isolate were the abrupt mountain valleys and near-impenetrable Pyrenean forests they chose to inhabit. The reluctance to share their gene pool with subsequent invaders helped preserve their ancestral traits and archaic morphology. So formidable were these geographical and cultural barriers, so effective their genetic isolation that the Basques managed to retain some of the vestigial traits that classify them as one of the handful of relic races remaining on earth today.

Particularly intriguing is the preponderance of the RH-negative variant in their predominantly O blood genotype, present among them in a far greater proportion than in any other living population group on earth. Equally puzzling is their language; devoid of Indo-European roots, their fossilized tongue is littered with words revealing its stone-aged origins. Current Basque words for rudimentary implements such as ax (*aitzkorra*), spade (*aitzkur*), and knife (*aitzto*) all share the common root *aitz* (stone), hinting at the material their Stone Age forbears must have once employed to fashion these tools. Equally revealing is *hortzi*, their word for either "lightning" or "tooth," a dual meaning evocative of a bygone era when tooth necklaces were worn to ward off the evil spirit of lightning. Suggestive of even hoarier origins is *karri* (ice), whose radix *arri* is a variant for "stone," a twofold meaning evoking a prehistoric glacial era when Basque hunters, caught in the open, were forced to build temporary shelters using ice blocks for building stones.

Only three other European populations speak non-Indo European languages today. However, the prevalence of blood type A and the near absence of type O among Finns, Estonians, and Magyars differentiate them from the Basques. The genotype chasm between these lingual isolates underscores the uniqueness of the Basques, a people truly set apart.

Linguists and anthropologists have long tried to solve the riddle of their origins. The mystery remained largely unsolved until recently, when a Spanish linguist[1] succeeded in breaking the Iberian hieroglyphic cipher, conclusively proving that the inscriptions engraved on Iberian vases, tombstones and lead tablets unearthed in eastern Spain represent Basque words written in archaic Phoenician or proto-Greek alphabets. This confirmation of an old conjecture underscores the intriguing hypothesis that the Basques—read "Iberians"—come from the Caucasus. Over two thousand years ago Egyptian[2], Greek[3] and Roman[4] sources identified the inhabitants of the southeastern foothills of the Caucasus as "Iberians." Strabo's and Pliny's commentaries further aver that, during Roman times, Iberian was widely spoken in Aquitaine, a vast region in southwestern France.

Combined with the ice-aged words fossilized in their language, this wealth of clues strongly supports the thesis of an Iberian ice-age migration from the Caucasus to Western Europe and their eventually crossing the Pyrenees to settle in the peninsula that bears their name today. Corroborating this conjecture is the recent genetic sleuthing[5] of Basque mitochondrial DNA, confirming that just such a migration took place some forty thousand years ago, right about the time of the first Cro-Magnon incursion into Europe.

While the vast majority of peninsular Iberians and their trans-Pyrenean kin in Aquitaine eventually lost their original ethnicity on melding with subsequent

---

1. Jorge Alonso Garcia, "*Desciframiento de la Lengua Ibérico-Tartésica,*" Fundación Tartesos, Spain 1997
2. Ptolemy *Geography* Book 5, Ch. 10
3. Strabo *Geography,* 11.1.5, Loeb
4. Pliny *Book 3,* Ch. 3, 29
5. Luigi Luca Cavalli-Sforza, *Genes, Peoples and Languages,* North Point Press, 2000.

invading cultures, quite another fate befell those who remained in fairly inaccessible pockets of the western Pyrenean mountain valleys. Inspired by a fierce spirit of independence, these few, endogamous stragglers managed to retain their archaic language, their relic racial characteristics and their original blood genotype. It is startling to realize that the Neolithic artists of those handsome cave paintings of Lascaux, Niaux, Isturitz and Altamira were Basque. It is equally intriguing to conjecture that listening to spoken Basque today may be like listening to a scratchy millennial tape recording of our Cro-Magnon ancestors.

During a recent visit to my ancestral home in the Spanish Pyrenees, I happened across a sixteenth century manuscript claiming family roots that dated back to "time immemorial." This startling discovery encouraged me to anchor this chronicle in the prehistoric past, describing a journey spanning the last glacial age to the present. It narrates the meandering of a family of Vascon warlords, the Agorretas, as they grope their way out of the prehistoric mists and into the glare of history.

The account begins during the brief warming spell of the Pandorf Interstadial, some forty-thousand years ago. A band of nomadic hunters abandons its Caucasian caves to pursue the big game, which has retreated to the northern tundra following the receding ice cap. As the weather turns cold again, during the peak of the Würm glaciation some twenty thousand years later, the big game and its pursuers retreat south, keeping one step ahead of the advancing ice sheet. The hunters seek shelter in caves at the foot of both the Massif Central and the Pyrenees and leave their artistic imprint in cave paintings along the way.

As this band of Vascon hunters finally surfaces into history, we see them rub reluctant elbows with Celts, join the Roman legions in the Rhine, tangle with Charlemagne at Roncevaux, and fight North African Muslims in battles from Covadonga to *al-Andalus,* always fiercely defending their beloved Vascon valleys in the Pyrenean uplands. Later, and now at the cusp of the age of chivalry, an Agorreta participates in jousts, takes the Cross in the Lionheart's Crusade, and woos a Moorish princess whose brother he later helps defeat in the turning-point battle of Navas de Tolosa. Later still, now in the thick of the Middle Ages, another Agorreta crosses swords with the Black Prince at Crecy and later fights under the Englishman's banner at Nájera. Finally, during the twilight years of the Vascon kingdom of Navarre, several Agorretas attain Royal Judgeships, serve as Seneschals to kings and bear brave lances under Cesare Borgia. The chronicle ends on the eve of the annexation of a once fiercely independent Vasconia to the nascent kingdom of Spain.

Although generous literary license is taken when narrating prehistoric events, actual family names and events are cited whenever historical records exist. Thus, although the early Agorretas described in this chronicle are fictional, the later characters did, in fact, leave their imprint in Navarran history as borne out in Navarre's heraldic records.

One last comment should help clarify the otherwise confusing interchangeable usage of the terms Basque, Vascon and Gascon in this chronicle. Although the term Basque is inclusive and embraces the other two, the "Vascon" designation is the most ancient, having been first employed by the Greek cartographer Strabo to identify the inhabitants of the southwestern corner of the Pyrenees. The "Vascon" appellation merely distinguishes those Basques inhabiting the southern slopes of the Pyrenees from those living in the northern slopes who are called "Gascons." Another, now archaic geographical designation frequently employed in this narrative is Aquitaine, a vast region in southwestern France extending from the Loire to the Pyrenees, once peopled by Basques. First identified by Julius Caesar as one of Gaul's three parts, this, the "watery one," was a region briefly ruled by the English centuries later during the Hundred Year War.

JML

Book 1
The Dawning

"The past is but the beginning of a beginning, and all that is and has been is but the twilight of the dawn…"

—Herbert G. Wells
The Discovery of the Future

Chapter 1

The Early Mists

~ 40,000 BC

The thin column of smoke curling above the cave's entrance was sheared by a sudden gust of wind whistling down the snow-capped mountain. Inside, a dozen men wrapped in frayed elk and reindeer skins slouched around a hesitant fire, faces rumpled, eyes downcast. The smell of refuse and unwashed bodies was barely masked by the pungent smoke of burning pine boughs. In the deeper recesses of the cave several women shuffled about their evening chores, covering the hearth embers with ashes, stashing leftover scraps of meat in the storage pit, tucking away the little ones for the night. They had more time for gossip now that there were fewer skins to scrape and tan, fewer sinews to twine.

"This warm weather has chased the big game away from the valley," grumbled Gorka. Firelight fell softly on the clan elder's weary face, his grizzled mane and creased countenance belying an inner strength and authority unchallenged for over a generation. "I wonder how much longer it will last," he added balefully, tossing a twig into the dying fire. The men echoed their leader's dire reflections with a few audible grunts. They had just finished eating a meager meal of jackdaw and rabbit, a fare depressingly common those days.

"Spring used to be such a happy season," mused the old man out loud, reminiscing on the herds of reindeer and bison that used to abandon their winter shelter in the nearby birch and elder forests just about this time of year to move north in search of the open tundra. Slowed by their young, the plodding, winter-weakened herds fell easy prey to the wily hunters. But milder winters had discouraged the big game from venturing this far down the southern slopes, near where the clan lived. It now preferred to graze in the steppes, beyond the mountain range that separated the two large inland lakes. They preferred feeding on mosses and lichen that grew along the receding ice sheet, undisturbed by pesky insects or by those cunning, two-legged hunters of whom they had grown increasingly wary.

The bitter cold of years past had given way to an unseasonable warming trend. Gorka had noticed that they could remain outdoors for longer periods of time without having to rush back to the shelter of the cave. Welcome though that rise in temperature was for those who, like him, suffered from chilblains and painful joints, the clan elder had begun to worry about the ominous implications of the big game's altered migration habits, its impact on the clan's food supply. Like an unscratched itch, the nagging worry stubbornly refused to go away. As the days wore on, Gorka began to recognize the nettle in his mind for what it really was: the clan would have to move on in order to survive.

He knew the decision would be traumatic. They had lived in that cave for as long as anyone could remember. All one had to do was count all those many scratch marks along its sooty walls to prove it. The aging clan leader had watched his father, and his father's father before him, painstakingly etch the soot-stained walls with their burins to mark the passage of the seasons. There were so many of them now that he had no way of counting them all, not even if he used all of his band members' fingers and toes, even those of the neighboring bands. Yes, he reflected nostalgically, they had been living in that cave for an awfully long time.

But shelter and comfort were not enough; they needed proper nourishment as well. He had noticed the haunted look of hunger in the women's faces and those of their children, as well. He even noticed his own ribs starting to show through his skin every time he looked at his reflection when washing in the warm spring waters at the foot of the hill. Grave decisions would have to be made soon or the clan would perish from hunger and sickness. His herbs could only do so much. It was time to voice his concern.

"When the moon grows big again in the sky," he announced in his deep, gravelly voice, "I will ask the leaders of the neighboring bands to meet with us." The unexpected announcement snapped the others out of their somnolence. The sadness in his voice surprised them, the joyless announcement portending some calamity.

"Arga," he said, addressing the adolescent squatting by his side. "Tomorrow you will go to the other caves in the valley and summon their leaders here. We will talk about the game that has left in search of colder climes beyond the mountains." Pausing briefly, he added: "I propose to follow it."

A deafening silence descended on the group. It was unlike Gorka to arrive at such a momentous decision without first consulting with them. Tribal tradition always called for consensus on all such weighty matters. But such was Gorka's charisma, his authority so uncontested, that even the most outspoken among them was reluctant to voice any reservation. Wrenching though the prospects of uprooting were, the need to move on had slipped into the collective consciousness, slowly but inexorably grown into an unvoiced expectation. There was little joy in their existence any more, gone the thrill of the hunt, the raucous celebration of the kill, the hearty meals, all now but fading memories. They had felt their strength ebbing, the cold numbing their nakedness, hunger gnawing at their entrails. Gorka was right. Something had to be done.

It was the middle of spring when the leaders of the neighboring bands turned up at Gorka's cave. The grizzled old men knew that Gorka was not one to idly call a clan council. There had to be some grave reason to summon them now, practically on the eve of the Summer Meet, the big event when the clan celebrated the longest day of the year with games and merriment, arranged the all-important mating contracts.

The five elders nodded morosely at Gorka as they filed past him, working their way to the bowels of the cavern through the smoky haze. They all sat around a crackling fire, greeting each other with grunts of recognition. Konkor, the gruff, contentious leader of the clan of the Mountain Lion, did not bother hiding his displeasure at the unexpected summons. His hunched back, a deformity for which he had been named, only added to the impression of bad-tempered strength.

When they had all settled down, Gorka addressed the assembly:

"Our band has decided to abandon the valley in search of bigger game," he announced without any preamble. Stifled gasps of surprise could be heard above the crackle of the fire. Ignoring the raised eyebrows around him, Gorka plowed on through the stunned silence: "You've all heard by now about the large herds of aurochs, woolly rhinos and mammoth that Uro and his son Arga spotted grazing at the edge of the frozen sheet of ice, just beyond this mountain range," he said, pointing behind him with a crooked thumb. "We've decided to go after the big game when the moon next waxes full in the sky."

He waited for the last murmur to die down before adding: "We would like your bands to join us."

A deafening silence settled over the assembly. Only the popping of burning logs could be heard as the clan leaders stared at Gorka, some in awe, others in disbelief. It was Konkor who finally stirred. In the fire's glare, his narrow, beady eyes burned with a fierce red fire of their own. Always at the edge of defiance, the hunchback shifted his eyes around the gathering, glaring questioningly at everyone except Gorka. His voice finally broke the silence, reverberating around the cave like a crackle of angry thunder.

"What!" he bellowed, the furrows in his brow deepening ominously, "and leave this good valley and its warm waters behind?" The cave man shook with righteous indignation. Even the tufts of hair on the lion skin draped over his humpback seemed to bristle. "Have your senses left you, Gorka?"

Gorka regarded his inquisitor with an air of calm forbearance. Konkor's unpredictable moods required tactful handling.

"It is good that we discuss such grave matters among us," admitted Gorka in a conciliatory tone. "Konkor," he added, "I will ask you to share your thoughts with the clan."

It was a shrewd maneuver. The dissenter was now put in the awkward position of having to defend his grievance before the others. Konkor looked uncomfortable, dimly sensing Gorka's cunning maneuver.

"This land has been good to us," began the irascible hunchback defensively. "It has provided food and shelter and all the flint we've ever needed for our tools and weapons. We have enjoyed the warm waters of the nearby springs for as far back as anyone can remember. Besides," he added, puffing his chest out as if suddenly discovering some high moral ground, "our dead are buried at our feet. We can't just leave their spirits behind."

The others nodded in agreement, staring at Gorka, daring him to counter Konkor's arguments.

"But, what about food, Konkor?" responded Gorka innocently. "We are quickly running out of that."

The laconic response set Konkor aback, but only momentarily. Not one to be browbeaten by the cunning clan leader, the hunchback gathered his wits about him, grumbled on:

"We may no longer have musk-oxen, or woolly rhinos, or mammoth within spear range," he said, fidgeting with the club in his hands, recalling memories of earlier hunts, "but we still have rabbits and the occasional wolf and lynx."

Sitting in a circle behind the clan elders, Gorka's men looked on impassively, settling lower on their haunches in anticipation of a long discussion, remembering that their leader had been in similar scrapes before. Gorka stroked his graying, bushy beard thoughtfully, like a hunter watching some unsuspecting prey straying into his slip noose. The wry smile that had been tugging at his lips now broke across his furrowed face in a broad grin. His men sensed that the trap was about to be sprung.

"Well spoken, Konkor," admitted Gorka equably. "They are all good reasons for not abandoning our ancestral grounds. But you forget one thing that makes all the rest unimportant: your rabbits and foxes are not putting much meat on our bones. Our children have nothing to eat these days except nuts and bulbs, roots and seeds that our women gather." Letting that thought sink in, he added: "And, in case you haven't noticed, the animal skins that cover us are all in tatters and we shiver in the night. We need bigger game to nourish and cover our bodies. Without it, many of us will perish even before the next snows."

The others looked at Gorka, their faces licked by the reflection of the flames. Gorka thought he detected the first slight nodding of heads, followed shortly after by the unmistakable murmur of approval. Their unspoken support was evidence that his proposal to move on had been accepted by the majority. The men in his own band sensed that Gorka had, once again, lived up to his nickname of 'great leader'. Even that grumpy hunchback, they thought, had to accept the simple, shattering wisdom in their leader's words.

"I am forcing no one to join us," concluded Gorka. "You do not have to decide today. But if you and your bands want to join us, you must come when the next moon waxes full in the sky again. It is then that we plan to leave the valley."

Squatting uncomfortably on the dirt floor, Konkor shifted his weight from one side to the other, the furrows in his brow deepening visibly. He had always begrudged Gorka's ability to anticipate trouble, his clever solutions to the tribe's knottiest problems. Particularly grating to him was the time Gorka successfully lured the slantheads into a trap, first feigning a retreat, then swooping down on them to push them over a chasm. It was that long-ago exploit that had earned Gorka the undisputed leadership of the tribe. The feat had festered in a corner of the hunchback's narrow mind ever since, smoldering envy raising hackles in his shriveled soul.

"It is too short notice" harrumphed Konkor, his face furrowed like cracked earth. "Besides," he scowled, "you haven't even explained how you plan to climb the frozen peaks with women and children in tow. Not even hardy young men can do that without risking death!" Casting a dubious scowl in Uro's direction, he added: "Some among you claim to have done it," he sneered. "But I notice that they still have all their fingers and toes!"

Uro, who caught the drift of the snide remark, had difficulty keeping his peace. The implication that he and his son had fabricated their last winter's mountain exploit was too hurtful to leave unchallenged. One's manhood was not called into question with impunity.

"Perhaps the faint of heart should remain behind!" Uro blurted out with righteous indignation.

"Enough!" snapped Gorka, glaring at Uro. He had to nip this useless argument before it escalated into ax blows, which it usually did and easily could again. "We have not gathered here to argue and fight."

Pausing to let tempers simmer down, he turned to Konkor: "We propose to travel along the valley, towards the big lake where the sun sets. Halfway up its boreal coast these great mountains above us melt into mere hills." Pausing, he added: "I know; my father traveled there once." Having cleared up that issue, he continued: "After crossing them, we will proceed towards the edge of the ice, where the spirits dance in the heavens at night, wrapped in their flowing, many-colored robes. There, we will hunt the big game we used to hunt." Pausing briefly, he regarded each clan leader before adding: "We hope to see you here when the moon grows big again in the sky."

Still nursing his pique, Konkor stood up abruptly and groped his way out of the cave without bidding farewell. As if responding to an unspoken signal, the other clan leaders followed him out, one at a time, without having reached a decision. Sullenly, Gorka and his men watched them file out of the cave along the narrow ledge to disappear around the bend.

"That Konkor is a bitter root!" groused Uro. "I hope he decides to stay behind. He will bring nothing but grief!"

"We need for everyone to come," replied Gorka firmly. "It is not just for hunting big game that we'll need their help. The slantheads still lurk in the tundra. They seem to stand the cold better than we do. I'd hate to have to confront them in the open by ourselves." There was a note of concern in his voice. Powerfully built and more numerous than they, the people with the sloping foreheads and the beetle brows had always been a cause for worry to the tribe. It was only through cunning that Gorka's clan had prevailed so far.

It was midsummer when four bands, almost a hundred strong, abandoned the valley. Only three of the clan's four other bands turned up on the appointed day. Gorka was disappointed to notice that Konkor's was not one of them. He may have been a source of discord but he was a good fighter, and they would be needing men like him in the days ahead. Following the river of warm waters that flowed along the valley floor, the hardy group advanced towards its source far away in the western mountains. The men carried wooden stretchers on their backs, heavy with flint cores, weapons, animal skins. The women's knapsacks bulged with skin-wrapped gourds, birch barks brimming with nuts, berries, roots. What little cured meat they carried would soon be consumed. Then they would have to live off of the land for a while.

Pervading the group's consciousness was a nagging premonition that they were jumping off into the unknown, exchanging cozy caves for a bleak, inhospitable land inhabited by predators, trolls and other evil spirits. As if that were not enough trouble, there were the 'other' people slinking in the mountains, waiting to avenge their last humiliation at the clans' hands. One had to be on guard whenever they came skulking around the valley, eyes darkly glowering, always looking for trouble. They seemed to have difficulty with language, barely able to communicate with guttural grunts. Their hostile, unpredictable reaction to any friendly overture had always been a cause for worry. This ingrained distrust had led to endless skirmishes, even all-out warfare between them over the years. Mothers gathered their young around them, warning them to beware the broad-necked people with the dangling arms and the sloping faces. The children were quick to pick up on such sinister warnings.

The clan made good progress under Gorka's leadership, plodding on with single-minded resolve, following the river ever westward, always hugging the great mountain range's southern foothills. On days when they could find no caves or rocky overhangs for shelter against the night frost, they erected lean-to's and lit fires to keep at bay hyenas and tigers lurking in the background, constantly peopling their nightmares.

Gorka had taken Uro's son under his wing and was determined to teach him his stone craft, pass along his arcane knowledge of medicinal herbs. Arga exuded self-confidence, a trait unusual in one so young. He was adept with his large hands, swift on his long, sturdy legs. His nose always reminded Gorka of an eagle's beak, which was why he started calling him *moko arranue*. His Adam's apple was no less prominent, unusually large for an adolescent. His unruly, sun-bleached hair reminded Gorka of an empty sparrow's nest, but it was that wide, generous grin of his that made one forget all the lad's other physical oddities. His steady blue eyes already revealed the man inside the adolescent. Gorka had noticed certain subtle changes in Arga's bearing lately, the way he had started holding his shoulders back, his head a little higher, as if he had suddenly discovered something new and good about himself. Someday, mused Gorka with almost paternal pride, Arga would take over as clan leader and medicine man. The thought made the old man's chest fill out with a strange, pleasurable warmth.

One evening, during early fall, having gathered enough roots and herbs to replenish his dwindling medicinal supplies, Gorka looked up at a wan moon rising over the horizon, trying to find his bearings.

"Moko," he said, addressing Arga by his nickname. "Do you know how one can tell whether the moon is growing or dying, just by looking at it?" he asked idly.

"Sure!" responded Arga without hesitation. "If her arms and legs are raised above her hollow belly, it's a sign she's already given birth and will soon die."

Gorka listened with bemusement. "I'd never heard it put that way, but you're right!" Arga's perceptiveness never ceased to surprise him. He had seen only seventeen winters or so, and yet, he already knew almost as much as he, who had lived at least forty! Perhaps the young chap could answer something that had been worrying him throughout the march. With barely enough game to sustain them during their long journey, hunger was a constant companion. Awkward against small game, their long spears and stone axes were utterly useless against wild fowl or scurrying hare. Being constantly on the move, there was little time to set traps and wait for the game to spring them. They had to devise some way to bring down small, elusive game. The need was growing more pressing as the days wore on.

"You know, Moko," said Gorka. "We must find some way to hurl stones faster and more accurately than by hand."

The adolescent's face lit up. Looking at his mentor, he remarked brightly:

"I can throw pebbles faster than a rabbit runs." Goaded by Gorka's doubtful regard, Arga continued: "I learned how to do it when I was alone in the mountain." He was referring to his ordeal in the wilderness, where he had lived alone for two full moons, during his rite of passage into manhood. "I'm still not very good at it," he admitted, "but I'm getting better at it every day."

Gorka regarded the young lad with renewed interest. Maybe, just maybe, he thought, Arga had come up with something the clan sorely needed in this journey. "Show me," he said, trying to hide his mounting curiosity.

Arga needed little prodding. Undoing the leather strap wrapped around his jerkin, he grabbed both ends in one hand. Then, picking up a smooth pebble from the riverbed, he laid it snugly in the strap's fold and started whirling the makeshift sling, all the while scanning the surroundings for a target.

"See that tree stump across the creek?" he said, pointing with his free hand at the base of a fallen tree, some twenty paces away. Just as Gorka turned to look, Arga let fly the projectile with a loud, cracking sound that reverberated in the forest clearing. Seconds later, the pebble crashed into the rotten stump, in a sunburst of splinters.

Gorka stared in amazement. He had just witnessed the demonstration of an invaluable device. Savoring the moment, his mind flitted over the sling's countless possibilities. Not only would Arga's contrivance bring down fowl and other sorely-needed small game, it could serve as an offensive weapon, as well. With it, they could fight from a distance farther than 'the others' could hurl their spears. If a well-aimed pebble could bring down a fox, he reasoned, it could do serious harm to a slanthead, perhaps even incapacitate him long enough to be overpowered.

A hint of a smile broke across Gorka's kindly face. He liked the quickness of this young man's mind, the strange and wonderful things he could come up with sometimes. Not only could he remember with clarity all the things he had seen earlier, he could also juggle them in his head and repeat them in a way that others could understand. He could, with equal ease, reach backward or forward in time with his thoughts, so that he could foretell, from how things once were, how they would be in the tomorrows to come. The young fellow would definitely make a good clan leader someday. The thought had crossed his mind before.

"How long has it been since your trial in the mountain?" asked Gorka, trying to figure out how long it would take the men in the clan to become proficient in the use of this astonishing new weapon.

"These many summers," answered the adolescent, showing Gorka all five fingers of one hand. "I have only killed a few mountain fowl with it but I'm sure I could take down a rabbit, even a fox!"

The men of the clan were soon slinging stones at different targets, occasionally hitting one another when accidentally unleashing their projectile at the wrong moment. That was how Begibakar lost an eye one day, a misfortune that would seal his fate as the clan's future shaman. Arga, who had devised the newfangled weapon, excelled in its use, always managing to return from hunting forays with more game than any of the others. Almost overnight, he had become the clan's leading hunter and provider.

The mountain clan plodded toward the westering sun, relentlessly following the broad river of warm waters to its source, never losing sight of the chain of mountains towering over their right shoulders, hoping to one day negotiate them and leave them behind. The river had narrowed to a meandering brook by the time they clambered up the slopes of the last, westernmost mountain in their path. From its snow-capped heights they gazed down upon a huge body of water glistening in the sun. Gorka's stories had not prepared them for the grand spectacle now before them. Their awed silence was shattered by the vacant calls of seagulls carried on the shoulders of a clean, sun-warmed wind. It was sheer joy to have come this far and behold such a wondrous sight.

Without anyone's prompting, they all rushed down the mountainside in gleeful excitement, racing towards the shores of the majestic inland sea. When they finally reached them, they were puzzled by the blackness of its waters, the little white, wind-blown caps of foam dancing across its face, something they had never seen before. They saw fish jumping in the water, like the ones in their river, only larger. But they were frustrated at not being able to wade into these deep waters to spear them with their pronged harpoons, as they had done back home. And so, for the time being, they would have to make do with clams and limpets and the occasional beached sturgeon, all seasoned with the seaweed strewn along its shores.

Chapter 2

▼

A Row with the Slantheads

After a short stay by the shores of the dark, wide lake, the clan resumed its westerly journey, always hugging the lake's northern coastline. As the days grew shorter, Gorka became increasingly uneasy as he noticed their path growing ever narrower, his clan now practically hemmed in between towering cliffs on one side and the deep black sea on the other. Mostly, he worried about the slantheads, fearing they would return to avenge an earlier humiliation on the cliffs above the fair valley of warm waters.

Of disparate character and disposition, the two people seemed incapable of living in peace with each other. While the slantheads begrudged the newcomers' edge in cunning and resourcefulness, the latter had grown increasingly wary of the squatters' hostile demeanor. But mostly it was their brutish appearance, guttural speech and nasty behavior that set them apart, disparities that only reinforced their differences. The slantheads' hefty build, stout legs and dangling arms gave them an almost simian appearance. Their skin, fairer in color but coarser in texture, seemed to have adapted to life in the colder, sun-starved regions they preferred to inhabit.

It was their deep-set eyes, glowering under beetle-browed ridges rimming their sloping foreheads that were the most startling feature in an already fearsome visage. Though known to protect their young and care for their old, even bury their dead, there were few other intimations of human-ness about them. One needed only to listen to their grunts and throaty utterances, observe their sour disposition and quickness to anger to conclude that these were a different, other-worldly lot, belonging more in trees than in savannas. Gorka's people had long despaired of ever befriending them, sensing that the 'others' and they would never get along.

As they advanced along the increasingly constricted passage, Gorka's apprehension turned to alarm when he became aware of strange noises in the night coming from the cliffs above them. Uruk, who understood the ways of animals, assured him that the sounds were neither those of mountain lions nor hyenas, whose growls and eerie, cackling laughter would have given them away. These noises, he said, sounded more like twigs being accidentally snapped, rocks displaced by careless, hurrying feet. And, from the sounds of it, there had to be more than just a few creatures up there growing bolder with every passing day, increasingly unconcerned about stealth. Whatever it was lurking behind the cliffs, said Uruk, was evil and meant them harm.

More compelling evidence came one evening, several days into their march along the lakeshore. They had just finished eating the lynx and jackrabbit Arga had brought down that morning with his sling when they heard a deep, rumbling noise coming from the cliffs above them. Looking up to investigate the disturbance, they were dismayed to see a huge boulder bouncing down the slope at an incredible speed, headed straight for them. Without a moment's hesitation, Gorka ordered everyone to seek shelter under the narrow, overhanging ledge nearby. They didn't have to be told twice; having long worried about an attack from above, the clan scrambled to safety with astonishing speed. Even the aging Gorka managed to leap out of harm's way with an agility that astonished young Arga, who had been eating by his mentor's side.

They stood under the shallow overhang for what seemed a long time, relieved to discover that the only casualty had been Uro's wife, who had suffered a sprained ankle in the mad scramble to safety. Having ruled out an earth tremor, which no one had felt, they were still mystified by the rockslide. Then they heard a second boulder thundering down the mountainside above them. It landed practically at their feet seconds later splintering into a thousand shards. After the din of shattering rock had subsided, they distinctly heard guttural voices from above sounding very much like taunts and whoops from the perpetrators of the rockslide.

Frozen into inaction, the men started to speak in whispers, hoping to hide their exact location from the attackers. They looked at each other helplessly, wondering how they would get out of their predicament. Uncomfotable at being so shamefully pinned down, they turned to Gorka for guidance and reassurance. Gorka, who had by now regained his composure, asked the leaders of the several bands to gather round him for a council of war. It was time to share the thoughts that had been crowding in the back of his mind. Bold and risky ventures, like the one he was contemplating, needed to be brought out in the open, discussed with the group, approved by consensus.

"We are in an awkward position," he began, with characteristic understatement. "I've been expecting this assault for some time now. I could smell an ambush the moment our path began to narrow. Now we must figure out a way to slip out of this trap. It won't be easy. The others are up there, watching our every move. We'll need a good plan to outwit them." Pausing briefly, he added: "We've done it before. We can do it again."

They watched their leader expectantly, hanging on to his every word, puzzling whether this man's canny mind would show them a way out as he'd done so many times before. Tensions grew with Gorka's prolonged silence. Finally, unable to stand the strain any longer, the leader of the Clan of the Panther spoke out:

"Gorka," said Abiu, bravely trying to appear calm, "many moons ago, you showed us the way to defeat the slantheads. It was a skillful maneuver, everyone remembers. But that time, we surprised them from above. It is different now. They control the heights while we are down here, simpering like old women. How can we hope to overcome them from below?"

There was a general nodding of heads, grunts of agreement confirming the group's shared fear. They had trusted Gorka with their lives when they started out on this risky adventure, willingly accepting the trials and dangers it entailed, blindly believing in his judgment, his guidance, his leadership. Their trust in him remained undiminished. He was still their leader, but could he show them a way out?

"Yes, Abiu," replied Gorka evenly. "We swooped down on them from above that time. This time we will meet them on a level fighting field."

The others looked puzzled, awaiting details of their leader's enigmatic tactics. Enervated by another of Gorka's maddening, protracted silences, they fidgeted, waited for him to speak.

"When it turns dark," he said with deliberate calm, "I will send someone, the most nimble among you, to scale the heights. He will survey the terrain with great stealth, count the enemy's number and observe their places. When he returns, he will tell us what he saw. And when night falls again, he will show a group of warriors how and where to climb the heights. Once up there, they will surprise the enemy and overpower him."

A stunned silence greeted Gorka's observations. First in hushes, then gradually in audible comments, the tribe leaders began discussing their leader's bold stratagem. Its soundness and simplicity appealed to them and, although some remained skeptical, the majority eventually approved of the plan. Abiu, the usual dissenting voice in these gatherings, did not long remain silent.

"What if there are more of them than us?" remarked Abiu, skeptically. Though not quite as contrary and outspoken as old Konkor, the hunchback of bygone days, Abiu had taken on the contrarian's role in the group's discussions. Seldom idle, always pithy, his probing questions invariably kept Gorka on his toes.

"We'll know that before our men scale the heights," responded Gorka calmly. "We will not do anything foolish."

Abiu remained skeptical. Hemming and hawing in his usual, disgruntled way, he pressed his inquiry: "And who have you chosen to be our scout?" he queried, still trying to find some flaw in Gorka's plan. "He'd better be one agile, clever fellow! He'll have a lot of lives riding on his shoulders!"

Gorka regarded Abiu with mild condescension. He was used to his dissent, had even grown to appreciate his prodding remarks; they always helped him hone his reasoning, come up with a better solution to knotty, unanticipated problems.

"I will send Arga to investigate the heights when it turns dark," he said simply, without emphasis.

The disclosure required none. Everyone was familiar with the young fellow's ability, his judgment sound beyond his years. They were well aware of his earlier daring exploits, his valuable contributions to the clan's survival. Yes, they agreed, he was the right person for the job. Even Abiu grunted his approval.

The moon was almost fully pregnant, as Arga himself would have described it, when he started off on his scouting mission. Heading east, he hugged the side of the mountain, availing himself of what scant cover the shallow overhang provided. Almost an hour later he came upon the geological feature he had been hoping to find: there, slicing down the length of the granite cliff, was a narrow, ragged fissure. It was the only way up.

Using pressure grips and toeholds, he started scaling the sheer rockface. His progress was slow at first, sometimes excruciatingly so. It was hard enough climbing cliffs this sheer in broad daylight, but attempting it in the semi-darkness made it doubly difficult. But having done it before elsewhere, he knew he'd gain the heights before first light. As he grunted his way up the cliff with slow, deliberate movements, he was comforted by the thought that he was far enough from the original rockslide, and those who had induced it, that he did not have to worry about the occasional clatter from the small rocks he accidentally dislodged during his ascent.

The first hint of dawn lightening up the white peaks above him came as an unpleasant surprise. He had to gain the heights before the full light of day betrayed his presence and compromised his mission. With one last prodigious heave, he finally pulled himself up over the last rocky outcropping and breathed a deep sigh of relief. He was crouching on a broad, rubble-strewn ledge overlooking the black sea far below. Somewhere down there, he reflected, pressed against the side of the cliff, his people cowered in fear, threatened by someone up here not far from where he now was. He had to find out who they were in a hurry before the creeping light of dawn revealed his presence.

With a stealth honed by years of stalking prey, he inched his way, crouching and crawling from one boulder to the next, working his way slowly westward, eyes and ears keenly taking in every obstacle, every sound, every object ahead of him. Surely, he thought, the perpetrators of the rockslide had still to be around if they planned to conclude their deadly game. That would place them somewhere near the cliff's edge, not far from where he was.

As he peered past the last large boulder on the broadening ledge, his eyes began to make out several recumbent figures huddled around a smoldering campfire. There were ten or twelve of them in all, deep in slumber except for a lookout, who sat impassively by the cliff's edge, watching for any movement down below. In the uncertain light of dawn Arga had trouble telling whether they were slantheads or kindred folk. He would have to wait until someone stirred, to confirm his suspicions.

It was a tense, unbearably long wait. Every minute spent waiting for one of them to stand up and be recognized reduced Arga's chances of getting out of there alive. He was spared further agony when one of the men finally stood up to relieve himself. The individual's broad, barrel-chested torso, the way he shuffled off to the cliff's edge on short, massive legs, arms dangling by his side, were all a dead giveaway. They were slantheads; there was no mistaking them, no doubt now about who had provoked the rockslide. Having obtained the information he had come looking for, he had to retreat at once.

Arga slunk back to the cleft in the cliff as stealthily as he could. With infinite care, he began clambering down the now better-illuminated fissure. Gravity and familiarity with the cleft's subtle indentations and toeholds helped him reach the bottom of the cliff in a far shorter time than it had taken him to climb it. With a spring in his step and a lightness of heart born of an accomplished task, he sped back to where the others waited, always hugging the rockface, careful not to reveal his progress to the lookout above.

They were all impatiently expecting his arrival when he turned up. The information he provided was characteristically succinct.

"They're slantheads," he remarked laconically, as if that were all they needed to know. Prodded for more information, he added: "From what I could tell in the early light of dawn, there must be about these many of them," he said, showing them all ten fingers. "Probably all men. They're resting on a broad ledge just above these cliffs," he said, pointing to the crags above him. "The ledge extends between this rockface and some higher cliffs beyond."

Gorka smiled with unrepressed pride, listening to his ward's brief, concise report. "Nice work, Moko!" he said with undisguised enthusiasm, patting Arga on the shoulder. "Now tell us, how hard was the climb? Will the others be able to climb the cliffs without any trouble?"

"Yes," responded Arga, without hesitation. "There's only one spot that may be a little tricky near the top, but I can show them how to get over it."

Refusing to remain silent any longer, Abiu cut in: "How wide is this ledge they're on? How high are the peaks beyond them?" The first question was sensible enough but the second puzzled Arga. Was Abiu thinking of swooping down on the slantheads from above?

"The ledge is as wide as from here to there," responded Arga, pointing to a large rock less than fifty paces distant. "It's strewn with large boulders, which may help conceal our approach but could also provide cover for them, if they're awake." Arga paused before addressing Abiu's second query. "As for the peaks beyond the ledge, they're twice as high as from here to where the slantheads are. An attack from above would be unwise. The cliffs are too steep and rugged, would take too much time to climb."

Gorka could not repress a smile as he observed Abiu's deepening frown betray his frustration at the young fellow's unsolicited lesson in tactics.

Soon after Arga had concluded his account, the group began making arrangements for that night's raid. A total of twenty men would be picked for the assault, five from each band, all chosen for their strength and agility. Noisy trappings, such as clicking tooth necklaces and other beads were to be left behind, stealth being of the essence. Arga suggested that the warriors travel lightly armed, perhaps only a hand ax slung to their belts, for ease of climbing. There was, he assured the clan leaders, an abundance of pebbles strewn about for sling ammunition should it be needed. He volunteered to carry a rope of sinew twine slung over his shoulder in case anyone required rappelling. He suggested, finally, that they start out well before dusk to make sure they dropped on the enemy while they were still asleep.

Gorka listened to his ward with pride and admiration. He had spoken like a seasoned warrior. Gorka warmed to the recurring thought that, someday, Moko would, indeed, become the leader of this tribe.

Chapter 3

▼

Confrontation

Late that afternoon Arga led a group of twenty men, closely hugging the rockface to avoid detection from above. Gori, a brash young man with broad shoulders and a prominent, jutting jaw, commanded the group. Abiu, his band's elder, had proposed that Gori lead the expedition on the merits of his proven leadership skills and unquestioned courage. Gorka had known Gori since he was a child, had seen him grow in strength and wisdom over the years, remembered his fearlessness during the clan's last confrontation with the slantheads. Observing the fire in Gori's eyes and sensing his eagerness to lead the group, Gorka laid a hand on Gori's shoulder and designated him leader of the risky mission.

They had started out at a reasonably fast pace but the onrushing darkness soon slowed the group's progress to a crawl. It was almost dark when Arga came upon the familiar fissure on the cliff. Motioning the group to a halt, he pointed the ascent route to Gori. The leader stared at the sheer cliff in silence. The spires of gray rock rising defiantly above him reminded him of a wolf's canines snapping at a rising moon. Quickly brushing the thought aside, he fixed his attention on the crack in the cliff. He noticed that the fissure, no more than a foot wide at the base, gradually tapered to a thin slit at the high reaches of the slick rockface. He couldn't help wondering how Arga could have possibly scaled it.

"It was a good thing you suggested leaving early," he remarked wryly. "This cliff must be at least three elder trees high! It'll be dawn before we can get all our men up there." After a prolonged silence, he turned to Arga and asked, this time in hushes: "Are you sure there's no other way up?"

"There is no other," responded Arga with conviction. "The ledge we need to reach begins right up there at the end of this crack." As if to stress his point, he pointed to the gash, adding: "Straight up! There's no more ledge farther on down, nothing but sheer cliff." Noticing Gori's concerned look, Arga persisted: "It's up this crack or not at all."

The conviction in Arga's voice left little room for doubt. Gori was left with a tough decision. He knew that some of the men had never climbed a cliff this sheer before. Some could easily slip and fall to their death and he would be held responsible. And yet, he reflected somberly, it was either their or the clan's demise. He had been entrusted with the mission of taking out the slantheads and he could not go back on his clan's trust. Leaders had to take risks, he reasoned. This was one decision he could not shirk.

"Lead the way, then," he ordered Arga, glumly. "Go slow so those behind you can watch your every grip and foothold."

Familiarity with the crevice allowed Arga to scale it with ease this time. With slow deliberate movements, he shimmied up the cliff, occasionally looking behind him to make sure the others followed close behind. It did not escape him that this was a risky way to attack a mountain, one climber so close to the one above him. Anyone's misstep could cause him and the trailing climbers to fall to their deaths. But there was no other way. In the moonlit murkiness, they had no option but to be close to the one ahead to observe and copy the proper grip and foothold. Despite his concern, Arga was surprised and pleased with their progress so far. At this rate, he reflected, they would reach the top well before dawn.

Several hours of stressful climbing followed. Arga could hear the men behind him grunting and groaning, gasping for breath more insistently now, clinging onto the gray, granite walls as if to dear life, slowly, painfully reaching for the sky. It was late into the climb when he began to discern the familiar protruding boulder looming up above him in the moon's wan light, signaling the approaching end of agony. Although the men were scaling the cliff reasonably well, he knew that the true test of their mettle still lay ahead. He remembered that last heartbreaking effort at the very top, knew it would try their spirit. He, himself, was dreading that last, final stretch. Though relieved by the thought that there had been no mishaps so far, he could not brush aside the recurring nightmare of having to confront the slantheads with only half the original group if anything went wrong.

He drew a long, deep breath when he finally pulled himself up onto the familiar ledge. The stillness around him was strangely comforting. The faint mountain breeze on his face felt almost as if some earth spirit were hovering over him, softly whispering approval of what was about to take place on that ledge. The spell was broken by the grunts of relief from the men behind him as they slowly heaved themselves up onto the ledge, one after the other. There was an anxious moment when Ugo, the next to youngest in the group, appeared to lose his nerve just as he was about to negotiate the last protruding boulder. Sensing his predicament, Arga quickly slipped his sinew rope around the large boulder and dropped the other end to Ugo, then hoisted him up. To everyone's relief, Gori, who was bringing up the rear, finally popped into view. It was still one hour before dawn.

Crouching from one boulder to the next, Arga led the group, noiselessly slithering westward. There were enough large rocks strewn about the broadening shelf to provide cover for every man. Hand axes now drawn, blood rushed through their veins in anticipation of battle, the age-old thrill of the hunt keening every nerve, tensing every sinew. When the faint glow of a campfire's embers finally loomed into view, they began to make out the slumbering enemy's recumbent figures. There were a dozen of them in all, lying in groups of four, huddled together for warmth in the chill night. Farther on, nearer the ledge, a wakeful lookout sat, picking at his nose, gazing impassively at the big black sea below.

Taking in the scene at a glance, Gori quickly devised a plan of action. He and Arga would sneak up on the lookout and dispatch him before he could raise the alarm. With equal stealth, the rest of the men would split up into three groups of six each, quietly spread out and at his signal pounce on the dormant figures. He was counting on his men's numerical advantage and the enemy's sleeping for his plan to succeed.

After whispering his final instructions, he motioned to Arga to follow him as he slithered up toward the lookout. They covered the few yards separating them at an excruciatingly slow pace, freezing in their tracks every time the sentry yawned or moved restlessly. When they were finally behind him, Gori drew himself up to his full height and in one incredibly fluid motion, muzzled the lookout with one hand as he brought his ax down hard on the sentry's sloping head, knocking him senseless. The others, who had been watching their leader's swift motion from a distance, heard the sickening blow. That was the signal to move out smartly from their cover and fall upon the slumbering enemy.

Never knowing what hit them, most of the slantheads succumbed at the first blow. Some, however, managed to dodge the initial assault, squirmed out of harm's way and stood up to face their attackers, letting out fearsome shrieks.

Confronting an aroused slanthead face to face augured ill for the unfortunate assailant who had missed his first attempt. His chances of surviving the ensuing struggle unscathed were now considerably reduced; the difference in size and strength between them could be telling. Complicating matters, the slantheads' keener eyesight seemed better adapted to the dark. Worse yet, they were better armed.

The three slantheads who managed to survive the initial assault put up a fearsome fight. Wielding wooden spears, they inflicted grievous wounds on several of Gori's men who, armed only with hand axes, were fighting at a distinct disadvantage. A cacophony of sounds filled the dawn air with the warriors' battle cries, the shrieks of the wounded mingling with the groans of the dying. While two of the three surviving slantheads eventually succumbed to their foes' superiority in numbers, the last survivor, who happened to be the burliest and strongest of the lot, remained standing. Despite having been severely wounded, he continued to jab and whirl his spear around like a man possessed, cutting a deadly swath around him. Thus kept at bay, Gori's men swung their axes ineffectually at the surrounded survivor, trying to stand clear of the deadly scything motion of his spear.

By now, dawn had crept surreptitiously down the cliffs towering above them, spilling its rose-gray light on the embattled shelf. Arga, who had been observing the determined standoff from a distance, decided to join the inconclusive face-off. It was now light enough for him to pick out the bulky figure of the beleaguered slanthead, gyrating in threatening circles, desperately trying to ward off his attackers. Picking up a smooth, fig-sized pebble, Arga secured it snugly in the hollow of his sling and approached the fray with measured step. Twirling his sling above his head in ever quickening circles, he took aim at his target's sloping forehead. Carefully gauging his target's rotating movement, he released his missile with such uncanny timing and accuracy that the projectile struck the slanthead squarely on the temple. With a startled look in his beetle-browed eyes, the giant fell to the ground with a thunderous thud, face first. The others converged on him to finish him off. The fight was over.

Nodding at Arga in silent approval of his timely intervention, Gori let out a ringing battle cry of victory. His joyous, trilling *irrintzi* rang out in the young morning, reverberating off the whitening cliffs behind him. Its echo was clearly audible even to the anxious clan members far below, who took it as a sign that something good had happened on the high shelf above them.

Victory had come at a price. Of the twenty warriors who had managed to scale the heights, Gori counted seventeen men still standing, two dead, one seriously wounded. Even with the element of surprise it had been a costly victory. There was sadness in his heart when he realized that some of the clan families would not see their men again. He could not bring himself to toss the lifeless bodies over the cliff for one last look and a proper burial by their loved ones down below. He decided, instead, that they would be buried where they fell. He ordered rocks gathered to build individual cairns for the two fallen men. Picking a few arctic gentian buttercups pushing up between the rocks, he strewed them over the two inanimate bodies. After the rocks had been carefully piled up on top of their dead comrades, the men stood around the cairns, grieving in silence, mentally adding to their long list of grievances with the slantheads.

It was almost noon when the group started climbing down the ledge. Leaving their dead behind, they now worried about the wounded man's descent in his weakened condition. It was challenging enough for the uninjured to retrace their steps down the fissure of the slick rockface. After all the able bodied men had reached the bottom, Arga secured his sinew rope under the wounded man's shoulders and carefully lowered him past the troublesome protruding rock at the very top of the descent. Gori, who was preceding the wounded man, helped guide his feet from below, ensuring a secure foothold. The threesome's slow, painful progress almost ended in tragedy when, grown faint from loss of blood, the wounded man once nearly lost his grip. After a brief rest, his dizzy spell overcome, they continued the slow descent until they finally reached the bottom.

It was late afternoon when they joined the rest of the clan. Relieved to see that most of the men had returned safely, the clan was glad to abandon their cramped quarters under the protective ledge. Two of the families grieved the loss of their dead men but were consoled by the news that they had fought bravely and died an honorable death trying to save the rest of the clan.

The day's exploits grew increasingly heroic with the recounting but it was Arga's feats that drew the highbest praise. His talent as a guide, decisive intervention with his deadly sling, and adeptness with his rappelling rope, earned him the clan's praise and gratitude, a eulogy of pluck and bravery that he would cherish for the rest of the journey.

His father, Uro, walked among his peers as if in a happy trance, expressing his good fortune at having sired such a stout-hearted son. Gorka, the boy-man's mentor, was more circumspect with his praise for his ward. He merely patted him on the shoulder, repeatedly whispering:

"Well done, *moko arranue*!"

Arga was slightly embarrassed and overwhelmed by all the attention. Only the occasional bobbing of his prominent Adam's apple betrayed his emotions.

Chapter 4

▼

Death in the Tundra

The clan abandoned their shelter under the ledge after a muted victory celebration, proceeding on their westward journey. They had learned the hard way that overhanging bluffs provided little protection against slantheads bent on avenging earlier drubbings. Gorka sensed that they had still a way to go before the lofty mountains dwindled down enough to allow for an easy passage to the boreal regions where the wooly mammoth roamed. Warily now, they plodded along the narrow route, casting occasional upward glances, reflexively quickening their pace.

Coming around a bend one day, they detected a suspicious movement far off in the distance. Afraid of having blundered into yet another gathering of slantheads, Gorka sent Arga ahead to investigate. It was not the place he would have chosen for a confrontation, outnumbered as they were, weakened by malnutrition and wearied by the long journey and the grim recollections of their recent encounter. Arga returned presently with welcome news: the strangers were people like them, slender, long-limbed, with prominent jaws and tell-tale upright foreheads. Stumbling on kindred folk after all those many moons of unremitting march was cause for great rejoicing.

Approaching what appeared to be a settlement, they noticed a collection of odd, beehive-like mud-and-wattle hovels, snuggled up against the foothills. Gorka conjectured that the temperate, maritime climate of these big black waters allowed these people to live outside caves, something he found remarkably quaint and wonderful.

As they came near the settlement, they adopted a non-threatening demeanor, concealing their weapons under their packs, raising their hand of killing in sign of peace. The lakeside dwellers watched them approach with a mixture of curiosity and quiet reserve. Calling his clan to a halt, Gorka raised his voice in salutation:

"*Kaixo!*" he cried out in greeting. The lake dwellers' faces suddenly lit up, relieved and surprised to recognize their own familiar salutation, welcoming the strangers in turn with their own heartfelt "*Kaixo!*" The ice thus broken, the two clans began to intermingle, their first shy gestures of greeting soon turning to warm exchanges of fellowship. Gorka's clansmen were quick to notice that though the lake people's language was not quite like theirs, there were enough similarities to bridge the awkward communication gap with hand signals and a little earnest guesswork of the others' equally gnarled language.

The chance encounter between the two clans turned out to be a joyous occasion. It was uncommon to come across a friendly band in the vast, empty spaces of their sparsely populated land. The unexpected arrival of kindred folk called for a celebration. Festivities were quickly improvised to mark the happy occasion with ritual exchanges of food and prized tokens, followed by a ceremonial dance around a large bonfire lit in the clearing in the center of the settlement, each clan taking turns singing and dancing to their own homespun melodies. The warm, uncontrived camaraderie was catching and, since partners were hard to find in that thinly populated land, the young men and nubile women of the different clans eyed each other, unabashedly expressing their individual preferences.

Arga was the first to notice the tall, lissome young maiden solicitously waiting on an elderly woman sitting outside her hovel some distance from the revelry. From the shadows he watched her, transfixed by the young woman's beauty, her graceful movements reminding him of a gazelle's. Her raven-hair and pale blue eyes slowed his breath, gripped his soul. The noise all around him seemed to suddenly die down, hushed by the spell that she had cast over him. He was puzzled by the strange pounding in his chest. That only happened when he chased after game. Yet there he was just standing there, absorbed by this woman's every feature.

A strange, pleasurable warmth began to spread inside him when her eyes accidentally met his and returned his smile. In that simple, innocent exchange there came to him a knowing that reason could not explain nor time weary. He saw in that smile all the beauty that he had ever seen in his young life, rolled into one person. All the brilliant bird feathers, the dusk-stained skies, the dancing auroras, nothing could even begin to compare with this one delectable woman. In one quick survey he took in all her feminine features, from the curve of her young breasts to the gentle roundness of her hips, from the finely wrought mouth to the delicately upturned nose, and then back again to those haunting blue eyes of hers. He was eighteen and the miracle of love had finally touched him.

The young woman straightened herself up to meet the stranger as he approached. When they finally came face to face, they stood there for a moment, looking deep inside each other's eyes. It was as if they were alone in the world, just the two of them, in the company of the life-giving Earth Spirit who, Arga thought, surely must have planned this magical encounter. Deep down, he knew that he had found the mate he had been looking for. There was no doubt in his mind that the two of them belonged to each other. There would be no need for Uro to talk to this woman's father to strike a deal for the union. The matter was already settled.

"I am Arga," he said presently, still lost in the limpid pools of the maiden's blue eyes. "And you?"

"I am Nere," she answered, lowering her eyes modestly, a hint of a blush coloring her cheeks.

Raising his right hand, Arga pointed his forefinger first at her chest and then at his own. Without hesitation, Nere repeated the gesture, laying an open palm first on Arga's chest, then on hers, blushing a little as she did. No words were exchanged but in that simple, universal gesture of attraction, their union had been proposed, their troth sealed. That was all it took for the young couple to propose and accept the basic, uncomplicated contract of a lifetime's union.

The grandmother, who had observed the brief, elemental rite from the hovel's entrance, smiled approvingly. She had been their sole witness and would later attest to the troth before the clan leaders. Slipping briefly into her hovel, the girl emerged with a token: a tiger's tooth dangling from a leather thong. Slipping the totem over his head, she said, smiling broadly:

"My father gave this to me as a gift when I was a little girl. He had just killed that tiger," she said, fondling the large ivory fang. "It is yours now."

Arga was overwhelmed. Only the brave sported such talismans. He had to live up to the challenge. Pressing himself against her, he brushed her forehead with his lips. "*Eskerrik asko*," he said, voicing his gratitude. There was no need to say anything else, no further ceremonial commitment required. Two people had found each other's lifetime mate.

The old woman, who had been watching them silently all this time, spoke out in a feeble voice: "May the spirits of nature smile upon you and may your seed people this empty land."

Lost in a world of their own, the young couple was startled by her unexpected utterance. Recognizing the profound feeling in the old woman's blessing, they both turned to her with a grateful smile. "Thank you, Amatxi," whispered Nere to her grandmother. The sweetness in her voice enthralled Arga. If he had any lingering doubts about his choice of mate, they were now forever dispelled. Turning to her, Arga confessed:

"In our language, *Nere* means 'mine'," he said, pleased by the happy coincidence of attraction and sudden ownership.

"As in ours," responded the young woman, delighted that she would now, indeed, belong to him.

There was great rejoicing among the clans as the news of the betrothal spread. Gorka was particularly pleased, could not stop patting Arga on the shoulder. From that simple gesture, the old man seemed to draw a sudden strength coming out of Arga, like warmth out of sunlight.

"Well done, Moko!" said the clan leader, his eyes misting in the firelight. His ward, his boy-man hero, had chosen well.

The happy event caused the festivities to last late into the night. The gourd containing the potion of fermented roots and honey-water was passed around by the revelers huddled round the fire, the 'happy brew' lifting spirits even more than they already were. Arga and Nere were plied with the potent potion and goaded to dance around the fire in a pleasant stupor. The men made lewd remarks and gestures at them while some of the women wept for joy, others from envy.

It was past midnight when the fire finally died down and the celebration came to an end. Arga led Nere to the shores of the black sea, away from the others. There, by the light of the full moon, Arga deftly built a lean-to from dead branches and driftwood that littered the lakeshore, lit a small fire by the entrance of the shed. He handed his bride a necklace of wolf's teeth interlaced with bright amber beads that he had threaded together some time ago for just such an occasion. She accepted it with a warm smile, rubbing his nose with hers in a sign of affection.

"*Nik maite zaitut,*" she whispered softly in his ear, professing her love.

When all was ready, Arga took his young bride inside the shed, let her gently down into the cavity he had hollowed out in the warm sand for the two of them. Easing himself down next to her, he pulled his buffalo skin over both of them and, with a joy as ancient as man, they became one. In languorous contentment, they listened to every small sound of night around them, the sudden slap and withdrawal of little waves on the beach, the sleepy complaint of birds confused by the aurora's false dawn. Through an opening in their thatch roof, they could see the moon hanging limply in a star-beaded firmament. Above the simple hiss of distance, Arga thought he discerned the presence of Mari, the Mother Earth spirit. He knew that she was smiling, as she watched over them.

Life by the lake was simple and uncomplicated, the weather mild, survival not the pressing issue it had been in their land. Some of the mountain clansmen briefly considered sinking roots there. There was much to be said for a carefree existence in a benign climate. There were enough nubile women to go around for the young men. Then, too, there was the unspoken matter of safety in numbers; they could stop worrying about the 'others' for a change.

But the first flush of novelty soon began to wear off. They found the lake people's lassitude slightly enervating. The lethargy with which they went about their chores started to grate on the mountain people, who wondered whether so much torpor was worth the price of the big lake's temperate clime. A man not only had to feel like a man, he had to live like one. They had never known a bland existence before and were now starting to look upon all this languor with mounting contempt. There had to be more to life than lolling indolently about the lakeshore, tantalized by fish they could hardly catch, subsisting on crayfish and mollusks, complemented by the occasional stray hare or ptarmigan. Their spirits would wither away without the thrill of the chase and the roar of an enraged mastodon to make their hearts pound again with the joy of the hunt.

They had not abandoned their mountain valley to exchange red meat for crayfish and limpets. Memories of the thundering herd grew more vivid and insistent as the days went by. And so, when spring finally arrived and the first snow runoffs turned the brooks into raging torrents, the mountain clan decided it was time to strike camp and head for the tundra. They would cross the westernmost foothills of the now-subdued mountain range and head for the steppes and the tundra beyond, in search of big game. This was the reason they had abandoned their valley of warm waters almost a dozen moons earlier. They were going after the big game again.

On the day of their departure, the lake people stood by, wondering what strange prickle crawled under these mountain folks' skins. Why would anyone want to jump off into the unknown and inhospitable regions of the north in search of big game, when they could stay and enjoy the gentle weather along the banks of their big black sea? Their attempts to convince the others of their folly were fruitless. Ever since they arrived at their settlement, the lake people had suspected that these mountain folk were a driven lot, their suspicions now confirmed as they watched them strike out for the hills. They worried about Nere and the other women who had chosen to follow their mountain men into the boreal wilderness. There was nothing they could do to hold them back.

It was already the middle of spring when the hardy mountain clan negotiated the last low-lying hills of the mountain range. Even from their modest elevation, they could already see the wide open savanna spreading out before them for as far as the eye could see. To those clan members who had never seen such broad, flat expanses of land before, the vast plains looked uninviting. But there was the familiar chill in the air again, and that was reassuring. Big game favored foraging on lichen and moss at the very edge of the ice sheet, and that was where they were headed.

As they worked their way north, the thinly-forested grassland country gradually turned into bleak tundra, temperatures, even in late spring, hovering just above freezing. The terrain grew rugged and fractured, the vegetation gradually changed from grassland to saprophytes, toadstools and dwarf birches, all growing in a gray land. The clan had to go back to living in caves wherever they could find them, hanging animal skins over their entrance to keep the cold wind out. Bleak and hostile though the new landscape was, they knew they would soon come upon the herds of reindeer and woolly mammoth, rhinos and ibex that they had come all this way to hunt. Meanwhile, the odd fox or stray hare would have to do for sustenance.

It was early summer when they first saw the reflection of a yellowish sun shimmering in a broad band of flowing water that cut across the tundra like a wet knife. Having lived near a river all their lives, they instinctively headed for it, knowing that game would not be far away. As they approached it, they started noticing spoors of large game. Gorka's heart gave a start when he recognized the telltale indentations on the wet ground; it had been a long time since he had last seen the unmistakable footprints of the giant aurochs.

"There must be a small herd grazing about a day's journey from here," he announced presently. For the first time in many months, there was excitement in his voice. "I don't believe we'll find bogs around here to drive them into. It'll have to be the river. We will concentrate on the yearlings of the herd this time. We'll approach them from downwind, first one band from one side of the herd, then the other, working in relays until we wear the herd down, always pushing it towards the river. In the confusion of the crossing, we will come in for the kill."

"Make sure your spearheads are sharp and properly hafted," he advised them that evening, as they sat around the fire. "And don't forget your hand-axes and scrapers. It's going to be a long way back to camp." The anticipation of the approaching hunt kept them awake late into the night, recounting stories of old hunting forays, discussing tactics for the morrow. They had not felt such excitement in years and it made for a night of fitful sleep, despite the sound of the nearby river's timeless lullaby.

The men struck out early the next morning, leaving the women and children behind, huddled in their makeshift shelters. It was not until early the next day that they first spotted the herd of aurochs grazing not far from the swollen river that sliced across the open tundra. A huge black bull was guarding the herd of a dozen cows and heifers, all grazing placidly on lichen. As they drew nearer, Gorka called his men to a halt. He split them up into separate groups, ordered them to spread out in a large semicircle. They would remain downwind of the pack for as long as they could, slowly surrounding it, then pushing it towards the river. Aurochs swam sluggishly and they'd be easy prey in the water.

"I will watch from here," said Gorka, pointing to a mound nearby. "When you are all in place, I will give the signal for the final push."

It took them the better part of the morning to work their way around the herd, crouching stealthily through the scant underbrush, avoiding snapping twigs, making no sound. The hunting skills, on which their survival as a tribe depended, rested squarely on the element of surprise; they had become masters of the art.

Gorka stood motionless atop the mound, surveying the landscape around him. He had a clear view of the herd, could occasionally see the tops of his men's heads bobbing stealthily as they moved from one bush or rocky outcropping to the next. They were within a hundred yards of the herd when Gorka first noticed the large male aurochs starting to fidget, making low snorting noises, occasionally pawing at the ground. The sudden shrill chirping of two tick birds on its rump warned it of impending danger. Several of the cows in the herd now started bobbing their heads up from their grazing, in jerky, nervous movements. The rest of the herd soon followed suit, craning their necks and keenly sniffing the wind.

Sensing that their cover was about to be compromised, Gorka knew it was time for the men to close in. Taking in a deep breath and cupping his hands around his mouth, he let out a shrill, high-pitched trilling cry that carried across the tundra, startling birds into flight, driving hare and rodent scurrying into their burrows.

The aurochs had stopped bobbing their heads and were now looking in the direction of Gorka's mound. They remained motionless until the sound of several dozen men, all echoing Gorka's piercing *irrintzi*, closed in on them from all sides, as they waved their wooden spears on high. Emitting rumbling distress signals, the herd tried to move out toward the open and away from the confining river. But the sound of men closing in on them from all directions except the river finally forced them to turn around and head toward their only watery escape route. On reaching the river's edge the male aurochs defiantly stood its ground while the cows and their young tentatively waded into the river and clumsily started to ford its deep, running waters.

Arga, who was the first to arrive on the scene, spotted a yearling that seemed to have lost its mother in the gathering confusion. It was darting about on the shore aimlessly, terrified by the rushing water on the one side and the strange sounds behind it. Closing in on the disoriented heifer, Arga hurled his spear at it with such force and accuracy that it sank into the animal's tender flesh, penetrating the full length of its midsection, its bloodied tip protruding from the side opposite the entry wound. The shaft must have sliced through some vital organ inside because the startled animal crumpled to its knees, without so much as a whimper. Arga rushed over to his fallen prey to finish it off. With one deft stroke of his stone ax at the base of the heifer's skull, he mortally wounded the animal which slumped over on its side, legs stiffening in one final death twitch.

In his eagerness to claim his prize, Arga failed to notice the large male aurochs standing only a few paces behind him, eyeing him with bloodshot eyes. Snorting ominously, the big bull lowered its head and thundered towards Arga, its sharp horns leveled at the young man's lower back. Before Arga could turn around to identify the rumbling noise behind him, the ox had overtaken him. Straddling Arga's body with its two sharp horns, the enraged aurochs jerked its massive head skyward, tossing the young man high up in the air. The animal just stood there, watching the body's lazy trajectory with beady eyes, waiting for it to drop. The angry bull caught the limp body a second time, and then a third, before finally letting it drop to the ground with a sickening thud. Not content with its deadly sport, the aurochs persisted in goring Arga's now inanimate form on the ground until its limpness finally convinced the angry bull that the tormentor of its herd had ceased to be a threat. Seeing the other men closing in on it, the large bull retreated into the river and swam to join the rest of the escaping herd.

When the men finally reached Arga, his body lay motionless. A pool of blood was slowly spreading on the white pebbles under him. Gorka stooped over and placed his ear next to the young man's gaping mouth. Not detecting any breath, the old man shook his grizzled head forlornly. He placed his hand on the young man's bloody chest to confirm what he already suspected: Arga was no more. That was a heavy price to pay for a heifer, Moko, he thought bitterly.

"He was too young to die," said Uro pitifully, kneeling by his son's inert body, slowly realizing that something dear and close to him was lost forever. The others watched in silence, not quite understanding why the young—especially this one, with such high promise—had to die when others older than he should have gone before him. Dazed, at an utter loss for words, they stood around the body, swaying listlessly from one foot to the other, not knowing what to do. Gorka noticed the tiger-tooth token resting on Arga's chest under his torn jerkin and thought of Nere. Their union had been so sweet and so brief! He could barely contain his emotion.

Finally, he spoke:

"Death is just another celebration," he said bravely. "A sad one, but a celebration of bravery, no less."

He had to say something. They had been standing mutely around the dead man-boy for what seemed a long time, grieving inside, not knowing how to manifest it, nor quite understanding the tingling in their eyes, the tightness in their throats, the heaviness in their chests. Gorka's eyes were now swimming in tears. It was not manly to shed them in front of the others, but he had to show the rest of the men how he felt about the loss. This youth had been someone special, had wormed his way into everyone's heart. His memory now came swarming back with a sense of terrible loss. They would all miss him sorely.

"We shall bury Arga where he fell," said Gorka, his voice breaking ever so slightly. "We shall honor him as the leader he could one day have been. We shall not eat the heifer that he killed. We will burn it on his grave for his journey to the spirit world."

Picking a few berries off a nearby dwarf juniper, Gorka spread them over the dead man's body. The others followed suit, strewing petals of grape hyacinth and hollyhock over the lifeless form, in the clan's final ritual of parting with one of their brave and loved ones. Then, with infinite care, they erected a cairn of rocks over the inert body to keep the wolves and hyenas away. Piling deadwood around and on top of the mound, they laid the heifer on the firewood, set fire to the pyre and watched the holocaust in grieved silence.

"Only the brave deserve a death mound," remarked Gorka, eyes still blurred with tears. "Moko earned his handsomely."

Chapter 5

The Valley of Baztán

~20,000 BC

Uruk regarded the dozen men hunkered around the fire with an air of bemusement. Wrapped in their grease-stained fur skins, they reminded him more of a gathering of old bears than a council of hunters, their mood about as disgruntled. The tribe elder had despaired of ferreting out the real source of their unrest, sometimes wondering if he truly deserved to be their leader. That honor had been passed down from a long line of Agorretas, one of whom, legend said, had led the tribe out of the shores of an inland lake of black waters and into the northern tundra in pursuit of the big game. Uruk's tribe was still shadowing its prey, only this time trying to keep one step ahead of the ice sheet inexorably creeping over the land, instead of receding from it. For some time now, he had led his tribe ever southward, steering clear of the forbidding ice of the Massif Centrale. It had not been easy. The climate was growing too bitterly cold to stray far from the foothill caves, now so essential to survival.

"We've tracked the big game since Mari knows when," bemoaned Uruk. He liked conjuring the Mother Earth's spirit in times of trial, the mere mention of whose name helped to avert any argument. "But now," he admitted sullenly, "we have to wander farther and farther afield to find it, spending altogether too much time out in the open, chasing it down. I don't have to tell you how cold it gets out there, even inside those *karri* shelters we build," he added, referring to the 'ice-stone' refuges they had to build when tracking down game far from their caves.

"Too many nights under the stars can numb one's fingers and toes," he droned on, poking dispiritedly at the embers with his spear. "And when they turn red and sore and puffy, the feeling in them is soon gone and they begin to turn black and blue and start smelling ugly." Pausing for emphasis, he added: "The moaning and the pain and the putrid death soon follow." He need not have evoked such vivid imagery, gangrene being all too depressingly common to many of them.

"And Nare can do nothing about it," he concluded, turning to the clan's shaman who was sitting next to him. Startled by the sudden, unsolicited attention, the medicine man averted his gaze, distressed by the all-too-familiar feeling of helplessness.

The baleful looks around him convinced Uruk that the drama he had conjured was approaching its climax. "We can hardly coax the big game to come any closer to our caves," he said resignedly. "And since we cannot stray any farther from our caves ourselves," he reasoned, "we may just have to make do with smaller game from now on."

Having been lulled into somnolence by his droning monotone, the tribe elders were startled to wakefulness by their leader's unexpected conclusion. They knew that chasing after smaller game would imply drastic changes, not the least of which would be abandoning their caves. The thought of yet another uprooting depressed them. The muted groans that followed were suddenly drowned by Kote's petulant objection.

"You mean bison and deer?" sniffed the clan's strong man, distressed by the prospect of having to give up the thrill of hunting bigger game, a skill in which he excelled.

"Yes, Kote," admitted Uruk evenly. "And wild cows and horses, too." One always had to explain the implications of the clan's decisions to the muscle-bound Kote, who, though big on brawn, was somewhat short on wit. "They may not provide the food and the clothing of larger game but there are more of them farther south." Noticing Kote's disappointment, Uruk tried to mollify the brute: "As you know, many 'smalls' make a 'big'," he said, reverting to child talk for Kote's benefit. "It is the price we'll have to pay for not straying too far from our caves."

Kote nodded in dubious understanding. The thought of giving up the thrill of thrusting a spear into a mastodon's side distressed him. He dimly sensed that life would not be the same from here on out, that for him the future would hold only small joy.

"And, in case you haven't noticed," pursued Uruk, now addressing the others, "the farther south we travel, the less bitter the cold seems to get."

The men watched Uruk's furrowed face with keen interest, trying to fathom the mysterious workings of their leader's mind. Its unexpected twists and turns, its uncanny insights into things still to come never ceased to amaze them. Reflecting the flames of a hesitant fire, Uruk's piercing blue eyes were like windows to a nimble mind. He was always playing games with them with seemingly trivial remarks only to jump them with some thunderous, unexpected proposal. They could sense one in the offing now.

"Perhaps," said Uruk, fingering his grey, tangled beard pensively, "we should start looking for a warmer land farther south even if it means leaving the mastodons and the wooly rhinos behind."

There it was, a shaft of bright sunlight shimmering at the edge of a fertile mind's cavern. Uruk had stripped the issue clean of argument, leaving only a stark, inescapable conclusion. The men turned to each other as if testing the communal resolve, but there was no need for that; they all knew in their heart of hearts that Uruk, as always, had spoken truth. Judging from the silent nodding of heads, Uruk sensed that his proposal had carried, to a man. He had convinced them that they had to distance themselves from the advancing ice sheet, even if it meant leaving the big game and their caves behind. There was some consolation in the thought that in the warmer, southern regions they were soon to inhabit, there would be no need for heavy woolen skins anyway.

It would turn out to be a momentous decision for the clan.

Leaving the western slopes of the Massif Centrale behind, they trudged towards the southwest, always searching for caves in the hills to provide temporary shelter against the numbing cold. As the days wore on, they were gratified to discover that the land ahead had gradually grown devoid of ice and, just as important, it had come alive with small game. Warmed by the occasional sunny interval, the less forbidding climate convinced some of the tribe's clans to settle in the handsome caves they found along the river valleys of the Dordogne and the Garonne. The rest continued on their southerly trek, determined to find an even warmer clime ahead.

They did not travel long before the snow-capped Pyrenees loomed up ahead, promising to thwart any further progress south. Awesome to behold, the frozen peaks of the forbidding barrier stood squarely between them and the warmer regions they sought. Despondently, they worked their way west along the ragged foothills of the muscular mountains, always following the sunset, hoping to find a passage through the uninviting barrier. It was like a reenactment of an ancient march out of the land of warm waters, millennia earlier, the Promised Land to the west, still beckoning.

Their unflagging search for an opening in the chain of mountains took them farther and farther west until, one day, quite unexpectedly, their journey came to an abrupt end. Another barrier, this one a watery one, brought them face to face with a boundless sea. Standing at the edge of the continent, awed by the huge expanse of water before them, they were utterly humbled by the grandiose spectacle of the Atlantic.

"*Ur-handia*," whispered Uruk, stunned by the immensity of the sea before him, for it was, indeed, a 'Big Water'. Tribal legends of the Baltic waters their forefathers had abandoned a millennium earlier did not prepare them for this majestic sight.

The temperature, which had turned perceptively warmer, was enough to convince some of the clans to sink roots along the shores of the big ocean and travel no farther. It was not, however, a unanimous decision. The more adventuresome clans elected to proceed farther south now that the Pyrenean barrier had offered them the long-sought passage. Uruk's clan, like their ancestors who had preferred red meat to mussels in a long-ago hiatus along an inland sea, decided to double back and hunt the bison and the red deer that grazed in the Pyrenean uplands they had just overshot.

The tribe was breaking up.

The night before the parting, they gathered around a huge bonfire by the shores of the big water near where the continent's south-seeking coastline turned abruptly west, to follow the peninsula's northern coast toward the sunset. It was the summer solstice, an apt occasion to celebrate their last night together as a confederacy of clans. Being the tribe elder, Uruk addressed the assembled crowd:

"For countless generations now," he began, in his deep, stentorian voice, "our tribe has flourished. It has grown in numbers and overcome many obstacles along the way. We have survived the rigors of endless winters together and have grown in many ways, improving our tools and our language, grown stronger as a tribe." He paused to lend emphasis to what he was about to add. "Now the clans have decided to part ways and settle in different lands. I have tried to hold the tribe together for countless moons, but perhaps Mari, who knows best, is trying to tell us that it is all right for each of us to go our separate ways." His eyes had turned misty but his voice remained strong and unwavering. "I wish that each of you will find your own good hunting grounds."

"*Agur.*" he said in farewell. "May Mari be kind to all of us. *Gora Euskaldunak!* Long life to you, Basque-speaking people!"

It was a simple, stirring message. Uruk's forebears would have been astounded to see how far their progeny had groped out of their early mists. They would have marveled at their descendants' new powers of reasoning, at how expressive their language had grown since the days of grunts and hand signals, at how de-burred of brutishness their feelings had grown.

In that night of celebration and farewell, the clan had no way of knowing that the descendants of those who chose to remain behind in the Pyrenees and those who would venture farther south to settle the vast peninsula beyond and give it its Iberian name, would one day meet again and surprise each other upon recognizing their shared language and heritage. By choosing to remain behind in the remote upland valleys, Uruk's clan chose to shun all foreign influence, following an instinct of self-preservation so fierce that it would one day almost lead to its extinction.

Shortly after the more venturesome clans spilled over the Pyrenees and into the heart of the peninsula, Uruk's tribe retraced its steps, searching for game in the nearby mountain valleys. They followed the mighty Bidasoa toward its source, sensing that it would eventually lead them to the hunting grounds in its uplands. They followed the river south, past where it veered abruptly east, near its confluence with two large tributaries. There, they came upon a lovely valley nestled in the southwestern folds of the Pyrenees. They were delighted to notice that its relative proximity to the sea endowed the vale with a delightfully benign climate, the snowy mountains brooding over it teeming with bison and deer. The abundance of handsome caves pocking the piedmont finally convinced Uruk to settle in the fair and gentle valley.

Being the tribe elder, he got to choose the most strategically located cavern in the region. The large, limestone cave he finally chose dominated the landscape with its commanding view of approaching unsuspecting game or unfriendly bands. Warmed by the feeble sun, the south-facing cave sat atop a promontory flanked by deep gullies overlooking the churning waters near where the two tributaries flowed into the Bidasoa. Protected by jutting walls and an overhanging ledge, the large clearing at the cave's entrance would be ideal for clan gatherings.

When he first set foot in the cave, Uruk noticed that he was not the first to inhabit it. Millennial rains had unearthed several human skulls from a shallow grave near the cave's entrance. Picking one up, he discovered, with something of a start, that it had belonged to one of the 'other people'. Its broad face and flattened dome, receding forehead and heavy brow ridges were a dead giveaway, as were the large nasal passages and the massive, chinless jaw. Equally revealing were the telltale stumpy fingers and thick leg bones he found strewn about. Though the slant-faced ones were now but a dim tribal memory, his people still referred to them as the *bogy men*, incubi still crowding their collective tribal legends, demons to threaten misbehaving children.

At first, Uruk had reservations about moving into a cave once inhabited by the slant-faced ones; it felt like treading on unhallowed ground. But the need for a dwelling soon overcame his squeamishness and he ordered the bones removed and cast into the river below. Other telltale signs of earlier habitation intrigued him; lying about in one of the deep recesses of the cave was a collection of shards and flakes of chert and flint discarded by some ancient tool maker. Uruk summoned his clan's shaman and chief weapons maker to show him the lode.

"Look, Nare," exclaimed Uruk, picking up a discarded two-edged scraper of crude workmanship. "The others worked their stone like you."

"Not really," sniffed Nare, offended by the comparison. "These tools look coarse. I can tell from these flakes alone that they knew little about knapping stone. Notice the crude edges of this scraper here," he said, picking one up and pointing to the coarse serration on its edges. "They didn't know how to strike fine notches at the edges of their tools. They certainly wouldn't know how to make the sharp, narrow blades and curved, leaf-shaped points I make," he retorted, still smarting from Uruk's thoughtless comment.

"These people probably never even learned how to use split-based stone tips for their spears," he commented contemptuously. "And forget about spear-throwers," he added, referring to the foot-long bone implement hunters now used to extend their throwing arm and their spear's range. Tribal tradition was littered with stories about pitched battles between their ancestors and the slant-heads. The others' dimmer wit, legend had it, was no match against their own cunning. Even though 'the others' once outnumbered them, they were easily outmaneuvered and outflanked, undone by the sly hit-and-run tactics that Vascons had perfected and put to good use in those long-ago battles.

Several caverns radiating from the large central chamber were parceled out to the four families in Uruk's immediate circle. Allocated according to status, Uruk had first choice. Having lost his mate during childbirth, years earlier, he chose the small enclosure nearest the cave's entrance. It would suffice his meager needs.

Kote, the strongest and most successful hunter of the band, picked the large nook opposite Uruk's, sharing it with his mate and three young children. Named after his brawn, Kote relied on it to compel the others' respect. A man of few words and even fewer ideas, his brute strength had been an invaluable asset in the harsh reality of big-game hunting, as it was in combat with unfriendly intruders. Most of the other males in the clan envied and admired Kote's imposing physique, although some secretly worried that all those rippling muscles attracted too much of their own mates' attention. The light-brained giant was, however, unaware of this unsolicited attraction. Indeed, it was because of his self-effacing nature and dubious lights that he had never been considered the dominant male in Uruk's immediate four-family band.

That distinction fell to Gargar. Unlike Kote, Gargar was gregarious and outspoken. His father had been the tribe's leader before his untimely death, trampled by a rogue mammoth while hunting near the piedmont of the Massif Centrale years earlier. Gargar, was being groomed to inherit his father's leadership of the clan, but he was still an adolescent when his father's accident occurred. That was when Uruk, the clan elder and wise man of the tribe, had taken over its leadership role. Gargar never resented this turn of hierarchical events because he knew that he would, one day, be the leader of the clan. Everyone knew and accepted that.

Gargar's mate, Enie, was a tall, graceful woman, now in her twentieth winter. Like Gargar, she too was descended from a family of clan leaders. She adored Gargar, as was evident from the way she looked at him and touched him every chance she got. They occupied an ample recess in the cave next to Kote's, and one could always hear the young couple's love noises in the night.

They had two sons. Though still at the edge of puberty, Aris, the oldest, was already showing unmistakable signs of leadership among his peers. Clever and quick of wit, he had already contributed to the clan's quality of life with his ingenious fishing technique. His bare-hands approach had provided the clan an invaluable source of food on meatless days. Fish may not have been as tasty as red meat but in days when hunters came back empty-handed, Aris could always be counted on to scare up a batch of handsome brown trout, which the clan soon learned to appreciate. It did not take much prodding for Aris to hold forth on his fishing technique:

"All you have to do," he'd lecture, "is find a large rock in the river with two openings under it. You then cover the escape hole with one hand, carefully probe the hollow under the rock with the other. When you feel the fish inside, you stroke its underbelly ever so gently until you lull it to sleep. Then, ever so slowly, you work your fingers back towards its tail and when you get there you close them tight around it and pull it out." Grinning broadly, he would add, "Simple!"

The technique was an instant success with the men.

The deepest recess of the cave went to Nare, the shy and retiring middle-aged clan shaman and toolmaker. Working with the slow, purposeful movements of a master craftsman, he struck delicate blades out of a core of flint with his bone hammer. Sometimes, when he felt inspired, he'd carve delicate needles out of water-soaked deer antler splinters with his smallest burin. The women found these indispensable for sewing skins together to make clothes for the band.

Nare was too sensitive and artistically inclined to understand the thrill of the hunt. He preferred to remain behind in his dark corner busily chipping away at flint stones or carving figurines on deer antlers. The others knew Nare was different. He was definitely not a hunter and not much of a warrior, either. The long delicate fingers of his small hands were a dead giveaway to his artistry. But they accepted him the way he was. His thrills lay elsewhere. Somewhere deep inside him, hidden in the dusky recesses of his mind, he would sometimes admit to himself that he should have been born a woman. But he would never admit that to the others. They would have drummed him out into the cold without a second thought. Nature had, after all, not equipped him to be a woman.

Nare had been born with a clubfoot and would never be a hunter, but he turned his manhood to good effect elsewhere, trying mightily to convince himself and the others that he was still a man despite his physical handicap and unmanly sensitivity. His mate, Esi, was a bit of a shrew. She even looked like one, with her sharp, hooked nose, beady eyes and straggly hair, always smelling of animal fat. She was forever whining about her mate, complaining that he was a useless man who never brought home any meat, making them live off of the others' hand-outs. She had given Nare three sons, the fourth now well on its way.

While the others were out hunting one wintry day, Nare, in one of his dawdling moods, used his burin to carve several small holes along the length of a discarded hollow deer antler. Wrapping his lips around the antler's jagged edge, he blew into it and was surprised to hear shrill, half-melodious notes emanating from the opposite end of his instrument. Experimenting with his finger placement on the different holes, he discovered, much to his surprise, that he could transpose the melody inside his head into actual sounds. His first faltering attempts at harmony on his *txistu*, as he had begun to call the gadget, were quite cacophonous, raising groans of disapproval from Kote's quarters next door.

Slowly, with practice, his musical attempts grew increasingly melodious and soon the rest of the group was enjoying his faltering ventures into harmony. His *txistu* became the musical instrument for the clan's impromptu dances. Gargar, who would lead these dances, asked his mate Enie to come up with a rhythmic beat to Nare's tunes. Not to be outdone, Enie devised a noise-making instrument of her own. Wrapping a wet deerskin tautly over the opening of a hollow gourd, she anchored the skin with a wet thong that tightened upon drying. The rhythmic cadences of her *tamboril*, as she called it, provided the beat to Nare's catchy strains in a faltering duet that was soon to enliven the clan's festivities.

But all was not music in Nare's corner of the cave. The cold outside and his cramped, gloomy quarters made Nare's existence dreary and devoid of joy, a concept that had only recently started pushing into his consciousness. Deep down, in the warm labyrinths of his brain, Nare became aware of his joyless existence. There were the fleeting pleasures of sex, admittedly, but it was depressing to watch the unremitting grip that hunting had on the others. That was all they thought and dreamed and talked about. He, on the other hand, couldn't care less.

Ever so dimly, Nare was beginning to sense that there had to be better things in life than chasing after game in the numbing cold, always tempting fate, life forever threatened by a quick thrust from an irate elk or being trampled underfoot by a rogue bison. Of course, there were worse fates, he mused, like living past one's prime, slowly dying of some lingering disease or even of hunger when one's teeth finally came loose and fell out. And if one managed to survive all those indignities, there was one fate even worse than all the rest and that was living to a useless old age in a clan of hunters and having to live off of their largesse.

One of Nare's problems was that he had too much time to think while chipping away at flint. Besides the imperceptible improvements in his tool and weapon designs, the growing ability to reason was rousing other more subtle stirrings in his mind, building on the epiphany that had once, long ago, startled him in that wondrous moment of discovery when he first knew that he knew. It was like a prayer rising above the humdrum noise and tedious chores of daily existence, an elevation to a higher, more rarefied rung of consciousness. It was as if something deep inside him had finally succeeded in touching the untouchable face of Mari, the all-pervading earth goddess, the maker of all things good—and some of the bad ones, too.

Shortly after Nare moved into his new quarters, he had lovingly carved a female figurine out of a smooth river pebble. He uncannily matched her ample bosoms and enormous hips to the pebble's natural convolutions, coming up with a statuette even more lifelike than the one he had once carved on a cave wall. The misshapen female figurine was special because it was the way he pictured Mari, the life-giver herself. He kept it hidden inside his grass-stuffed deerskin pillow, and liked to fondle her round protruberances at night before falling asleep. It was comforting to know that her spirit would be watching over him when he was in that world of dreams where each night one died a little.

Esi, his mate, was big with life again and her discomfort only seemed to heighten her moodiness. Her mate's infernal *txistu* sounds did not help. It was barely a moon after they had moved into the big cave in the pleasant valley of Baztan when her time to deliver was at hand. At the first hint of dawn, her pains began to come with the regularity that she had learned to associate with the imminence of childbirth. Stuffing a few old deerskin rags into her knapsack, she dragged herself down the hill to the edge of the river. Wracked by sharper, more frequent birth pangs, she waited stoically until her bag of waters finally broke. Squatting down awkwardly until her bottom almost touched the ground, she strained with one gigantic effort after another until she finally pushed the baby out of her, deftly catching it as it emerged. It was another boy, she noticed. Her first thought was that Nare would be pleased; her second, that it would be yet another mouth to feed.

Severing the umbilical cord with her teeth and adroitly knotting it, she wiped the baby clean of the dark, slippery matter with which it had been born, and then swaddled it in a warm buffalo skin she had brought along for that purpose. Laying the wailing infant down on the ground, she straddled two flat rocks that jutted out into the current and washed herself clean in the cold, rushing waters. Ablutions thus concluded, she climbed back up the hill to the cave and handed the infant over to Nare, who accepted it without comment.

"It's a boy," she said, without emotion, sounding very much as if she would have preferred a girl this time.

Lying down on his bison skin, Nare rested the proffered baby on his chest. It was the way of the clan; a son was held by his father for one whole day, the day it was born, until its mother's milk started to flow and she was ready to suckle it. It was the first important bonding between father and son. A woman may give birth to a son, tribal wisdom maintained, but it was the father who would nurture him into manhood. And these first hours after birth were critical to this transfer of manly vigor.

Every one in the band had heard the baby's wails when Esi brought it into the cave. The men all approached Nare's quarters in the farthest hollow of the cave, to welcome the latest addition to the clan.

"*Nola dago haurra?*" asked Gargar solicitously, wondering how the child was. Since Nare didn't answer right off, he asked again: "Does it have all his fingers and toes?"

It was not an idle question. Such traits were important in determining the child's future role in the clan. Unusual signs like missing or additional toes, being born cross-eyed or hair-lipped, all predestined a child to a life of special treatment. Indeed, it was Nare's clubfoot that had sealed his fate as a shaman. He would have, otherwise, been a mere hunter like the others.

Lying under the folds of his buffalo skin, Nare held the newborn child awkwardly on the crook of one arm. The shaman started making whimpering sounds, feigning post-partum discomfort, acting out his role in the birth ritual to the hilt.

"*Gaizki egin dut,*" he finally admitted with a grimace. "It's getting harder every time," he said, facial muscles contorted in pretended distress. "*Bai,*" he affirmed as an afterthought, "he's got all his fingers and toes."

The men around him commiserated with the artisan's travail and tried to comfort him. Gargar's son, Aris, handed him a smooth core flint as a token of his sympathy. Grousing in the background, the light-brained Kote remained aloof. Even through his fog, he could see through the pretense. "It's not as if he'd been trampled by a bison or anything," he mumbled audibly, scoffing at the performance. "After all, it's only a simple, ordinary childbirth." The others disregarded the brute's insensitive comment.

Standing just outside the niche's entrance, the newborn's mother was busily splitting firewood with one of her mate's hand axes. "Somebody's got to do the work around here," she muttered under her breath. The commiseration being dispensed inside her own lair brought a disgusted smirk to her face. Like Kote, she could not understand the need for all this production. But she was smarter than he and was not about to let on.

Tradition was, after all, tradition.

Chapter 6

The Hunt

The clan was growing weary of eating rabbit and mountain fowl which they had been hunting with their slings and *makila* boomerangs. They had even tired of the brown trout that Aris and the others fished by hand with increasing dexterity. The tubers and the roots which the women dug up in the valley were just as unappetizing. It had been a long time since they had eaten any red meat and they were eager for some serious hunting. But there was still the matter of finding a special sanctuary in the cave in which to conduct their sacred hunting rites. There had to be a hallowed niche, preferably in some hidden, barely accessible recess of the cave to ensure some sort of privacy for their arcane pre-hunt ceremonies.

"I know of just such a place in this cave," volunteered Nare, brightly. "Come," he motioned. "I will show you."

Living in a niche adjoining a narrow passageway deep inside the cave, Nare had discovered the perfect labyrinthine enclosure. Since he never ventured out to hunt with the others, he had ample time to explore the maze-like complex of tunnels at his leisure. Half ducking, half squeezing through the crawl space, he led the men into the maw of the cave, each bearing a torch to light the way. The narrow passage dead-ended quite abruptly in a small circular chamber. The ceiling was high enough for a man to stand up, but just barely. Growing out of the center of the circular enclosure was a large outcropping of smooth limestone rock shaped like a slightly domed table resembling an outsized mushroom. The protruding rock restricted all movement inside the niche except along the narrow walkway encircling it.

The men were stunned by the discovery. They stood around the smooth rocky mound, leaning over it, talking excitedly to the others standing across the rock from them. The air was heavy with the smell of burning fats, their dancing flames casting unreal shadows on the walls and vaulted ceiling. The very snugness and inconvenience of the place made it the perfect recess for their rituals. They were delighted.

That evening, after supper, the men gathered in their new meeting place. Now in his domain, Nare, the shaman, took charge of the proceedings. Pulling out his *txistu* from under his belt, he proceeded to play on it, its weird notes sounding doubly shrill in the tight enclosure. Kote squirmed under his skin but concealed the discomfort in his ears. The others, meanwhile, had started shuffling around the central rocky mound to the rhythm of the high-pitched *txistu*. When he tired of playing and the dancing ceased, Nare produced a small leather pouch he carried around his neck; it was his badge of office. Pulling at its drawstrings, he extracted several smaller pouches, which he carefully laid on the rock-mound. Each contained ochre pigments of different colors that he himself had carefully ground up and mixed.

There was tension in the air. No one spoke. With mounting curiosity, they watched the shaman perform a ritual they had never seen him do before. Pressing his hand against the ceiling to test for moisture, Nare started to paint the outline of the animal they had talked of hunting. In a blur of masterful strokes, he began to apply subtle layers of yellow, brown, red and black ochre pigments to the natural contours and undulations of the ceiling directly above him. Slowly, as if by magic, a strangely realistic three-dimensional rendition of an animal began to emerge before their very eyes, complete with swelling muscles, sharp horns, distended nostrils, startled eyes and pounding hoofs. Even in the dim light of the cave everyone could see that Nare had succeeded in capturing the spirit of a deer, endowing it with lifelike realism. It was beautifully symbolic of energy and looked almost as if it were ready to jump out of the ceiling and land in their midst.

When he had finished applying the last stroke with his ochre-stained fingers, Nare performed the last and most important ritual. Invoking the earth spirit Mari, he asked for her intercession:

"*Mariuak dizuela egun ona,*" he intoned, entreating the goddess of the underground realm to grant them good hunting on the morrow.

Mari was the bountiful nature-goddess, the Mother Earth spirit, provider of food, giver of life. They knew that the subterranean spirit inhabited the interior mansions of the earth, but exercised dominion above ground as well when she emerged from the caves of Euskalherria, the land where Basque was spoken. Though she inhabited the depths of the earth she could, just as easily, ride the wind and dance in the clouds. One knew when she had emerged because the trees would shake with the breeze of her passing. She was equally adept at unleashing tempests, attracting rain, producing drought. Nothing ever happened without her approval. She ordered the birthing and the dying of all things. Generous with her gifts and seldom angered, she could be a force to be reckoned with when displeased, for she was the mother of lightning as well and could hurl her deadly thunderbolts about, bringing swift retribution to the wayward and the unbeliever.

Uruk's sonorous voice snapped them out of their reverie:

"Gargar and Kote have explored the hunting grounds nearby. They have seen a large herd of red deer grazing in the lower elevations of the snow-capped mountain over where the sun sets."

"Yes," confirmed Gargar, self-importantly, "at the foot of the mighty Abalegui. It is only half a day's walk from here. We should leave here early on the morrow before the herd moves on. We'll have to ford the Bidasoa to get there," he explained, adding that he knew of a place where they could safely cross the river.

Dawn was breaking when the men of the clan left the cave the next morning. Uruk loved this time of day when the birds were just starting to break into song and nature yawned and stretched herself awake. This was going to be a good day for hunting, he sensed. There'd be meat by nightfall. As always the broad-shouldered Kote led the way. Occasions like this were his small intervals in the sun, when his burly strength was most valued and he could dispense it amply. He rested two long spears on his shoulder and in a leather scabbard dangling from the belt around his buffalo-skin jerkin, he carried the sharp cutting knife Nare had chiseled especially for him. The small group was made up of three men including the aging Uruk, who plodded along, bringing up the rear. Gargar's oldest son, Aris, who had been allowed to join the hunt, was flushed with the joy of his first real outing with the men. He stuck by Uruk most of the way.

No one spoke for long stretches of time as they walked along the banks of the Bidasoa. Gargar led them to a crossing where the river narrowed enough to be fordable. The men walked across, two at a time, facing each other, arms interlocked to help keep their balance in the slippery footing. Uruk began to have second thoughts about proceeding across the onrushing current. Noticing his hesitation, Kote picked the old man up bodily and carried him across the turbulent waters, depositing him safely on the opposite shore. He did the same with Aris on a subsequent crossing.

As he stepped out into the clearing, Uruk saw the mountain just ahead of him, for the first time up close. *"Mendi bat ikusten dut,"* he whispered in awe.

Bathed by the morning sun, its lofty, snow-covered peak jabbed proudly at the Pyrenean sky. No wonder, he mused, they called it 'the tiresome one to climb'. Abalegui, he thought, was a beautiful mountain in whose shadows it was good to live.

Aris, with his keen eyesight, was the first to spot the half dozen red deer grazing along the edge of a depression in the high valley. The light breeze on the hunters' faces ensured an upwind approach to the herd. They would have to crouch stealthily all the way in and sneak up on the animals undetected.

"We will approach them quietly until we have encircled them," whispered Uruk to the hunters gathered around him. "When I give the signal, we will push them into the gully near where they graze. After we trap them in there, we'll be able to kill as many as we can carry back."

It was a sound plan. They usually tried to corral these animals into pens before picking them off at will, one at a time. They would sometimes lasso a few and drag them back alive for a longer supply of fresh meat. But the fortuitous location of the herd at the edge of the subsidence would make the hunt that much easier this time.

When the hunters got close enough to the unsuspecting herd, Uruk gave the signal. The men, who had by then almost completely encircled the small herd, dashed toward it, letting out wild hunting cries, waving their spears on high. The startled pack panicked. Though one or two managed to break through gaps in the hunters' ever-confining circle, the rest followed the path of least resistance, rushing down the sloping walls to the bottom of the depression, unaware of the trap they were rushing into.

"We've got them!" exulted Kote. At the bottom of the hollow were four red deer frantically trying to escape. But the slippery walls and the presence of the shouting men on the lip of the depression made them eventually give up.

Among the trapped animals was a female deer with her week-old fawn. The moment he first laid eyes on the young animal, Aris was gripped by an insane desire to spare the fawn and keep it as a pet. He knew that the idea was outlandish; no one had ever owned a pet before. But the small animal prancing about the floor of the trap was irresistible to the young lad.

"Don't kill the fawn!" he shouted out in a high-pitched voice that reverberated around the walls of the shallow depression. The men, who were about to hurl their spears at the animals below, stopped in mid-stride and stared at the young lad in disbelief.

"Why?" asked several voices, stunned by the impudence of Gargar's boy. What could possibly have gotten into the boy's head, they puzzled.

"I want to keep it for myself," Aris answered in a voice that was almost, but not quite, a plea. It was as if, all of a sudden, he no longer was a youth and had spoken with the authority of the clan leader he would one day grow up to be. The brazenness of the proposition surprised everyone, coming from the lips of someone who still had 'the afterbirth stuck to his navel,' as Kote would quaintly phrase it any time one of his own children uttered some impertinence.

"And what would you do with it?" asked his father, who was just as perplexed as the others. "Do you intend to eat it all by yourself and not share it with the others? Is that what you want?" There was a note of bewilderment in his voice. Aris had always been a thoughtful, generous boy. What had caused this sudden change in him?

"I do not wish to eat it at all," answered the adolescent, defensively. "I just want to keep it, something to play with."

"To play with?" growled Kote, growing exasperated with Aris' impudence. "You have lost your senses! Animals are not for playing. They're for eating! That's why we're here today!"

Uruk, who was standing next to Aris, intervened. Resting a hand on the lad's shoulder, he said, in a calm, reassuring voice: "I can understand your wanting to keep that small fawn as a playmate. I'd like to cuddle it myself, the same way I like petting a baby. But babies need milk to live on and you cannot give him that. He would only die of hunger after a few days. That is no good."

Mulling over that bit of wisdom, Aris relented. "You are right, Uruk," said the lad, crushed by the leader's logic. "Probably one day we can capture the mother along with the fawn."

He was, of course, way ahead of his time. Domestication of animals was still several millennia away. But stepping out of the norm would mark Aris as an eccentric, someone at whom the rest would, henceforth, look askance. In a tribe struggling for survival, there was little room for extravagance. Gargar looked at his son with a pained expression on his face. Aris had not done himself any favor with his daft outburst. He would pay a heavy price for his sensitivity, he suddenly realized. He had probably forfeited his chances of becoming the clan's leader. Perhaps, at best, he would one day grow up to be its shaman. Gargar felt bereaved.

"*Handitzen zarauean ikasiku duzu,*" he whispered to his son, reminding him that he would learn with age, a fatherly advice that failed to mitigate Aris' pain.

The young lad averted his eyes as the trapped deer were speared one by one. But he could not avoid hearing the plaintive squeals of the mortally wounded fawn. They would stay with him for a long time.

CHAPTER 7

A Brush with the Celts

~ 500 BC

Coming at the heels of the long glacial night, the warming trend had encouraged the Vascons to abandon their caves and live outdoors. Old habits were discarded slowly, new ones adopted grudgingly. Once dug up for roots and tubers, the land was now tilled for crops. Animals, once hunted down for clothing and sustenance, were now bred and domesticated. Better suited to pasturage than farming, the rolling meadows and dark forests that dappled the abrupt mountain valleys of Vasconia soon came alive with bleating sheep, their numbers proudly proclaiming their owners' currency and standing. Grazing on the sweet upland greens during the spring and summer months, the flocks were herded to winter pasturage in the lush, more temperate ultra-Pyrenean lowlands. The yearly transhumance helped strengthen the ancient bonds between the Vascons and their northern brethren, the Gascons, from whom they had grown estranged over the years.

Erne and Sen always looked forward to overwintering their flocks in the verdant plains of Labourd, only a stone's throw away from the Pyrenean passes guarding their own valley of Baztan. For the two cousins, the yearly pilgrimage was a welcome change from the dreary winter chores at home. Even more alluring than the succulent pastures awaiting their sheep were the lovely *neskatxas* that inhabited these lush, northern valleys, lasses whose ready smiles and inviting ways never failed to turn a young man's head and fill it with dreams. Equally open and friendly, Gascon shepherds were always willing to share their rich lowland pastures with their southern mountain kin. Years of convivial contact had made them each familiar with the other's quaint Basque idioms and odd turns of phrase. The northern lowlands, with their rolling hills and kindly inhabitants, had become a home away from home for the two cousins.

But all was not well in Labourd these days.

Sharing bread with a Gascon friend while tending sheep one day, the shepherds' attention was suddenly drawn to a commotion at the far end of the meadow below them. A clutch of burly, half-naked horsemen had clattered up to the edge of the tree line and were surveying the scene before them. Sporting drooping mustaches and disheveled hair, lime-dyed to an improbable straw-blonde hue, the strangers were festooned with solid-gold bangles and heavy neck torques. Their haughty carriage appeared to clash with their bizarre state of undress. The motley group looked definitely foreign and out of place, like something out of a bad dream. Brawny muscles rippling in the sun, the horsemen started to gesture agitatedly, pointing at the flock of sheep before them. The Vascons' initial bafflement turned to concern when they first noticed the long spears and hefty broadswords the strangers brandished. Their loud hoots and raucous laughter carried across the field, boding mischief. When they began looking around for signs of the sheep's guardians, the two Vascon cousins quickly ducked behind a fallen tree, following the Gascon's prompting.

"*Wildenmen!*" whispered the Gascon hoarsely, a note of alarm in his voice. "We must not let them see us."

"Why?" murmured Sen, puzzled by their friend's obvious distress. "This is your land. They intrude in it." Always one to tout his rights, especially where his flock was concerned, Sen poked his head above the fallen log and said testily, "I don't like the way they're looking at our sheep. I think they mean them harm." Before the others could respond, the edgy Sen proposed: "Let's let them know we're here. That should scare them away."

The Gascon regarded Sen with alarm. "That would be foolish, my friend," he advised in a muffled voice. "We don't call these barbarians 'wild men' for nothing. They're a brazen, untamed lot, always looking for trouble, always finding it. They're quick to anger, too, especially when they're drunk on that mead they drink." Pausing to let the thought sink in, he added: "Judging from their hoots and hollers, they've had a little too much of that already."

Sen remained skeptical. Erne could now sense his cousin's unease; he always fidgeted with his staff when he was agitated, the way he was doing now. Suddenly, Sen sat bolt upright from his crouching position, stuck his head above the fallen log, in full view of the *wildenmen*, almost daring them to detect his presence. The nervous Gascon reached over and pulled him down forcibly. "I've watched them fight to the death just to settle some petty quibble," he warned

Sen, hoarsely. "The winner lops his opponent's head off, stabs it with his spear and gallops around the settlement, flaunting his grisly prize." After a brief pause, he asked Sen, pointedly: "How would you like your head paraded around like that?"

The disquieting thought dampened Sen's ardor. Prudence momentarily edged out foolhardiness. "There's too many of them," he admitted sheepishly. "Easy to be cocky when you're armed and mounted like that!" Then, peeking over the log once more, he asked, "What kind of weapons are those they have, anyway? They look different."

"They are," assured the Gascon. "Those swords can slice ours in half without even denting. They call the metal 'iron'. It's a lot tougher than the brass ones we use, I assure you. We wouldn't stand a chance in a confrontation with them." After a few seconds, he added: "These barbarians from the north are slowly taking over our grazing pastures. And there are more of them coming every year. They've already crossed the Garonne in force. Our land will soon be completely overrun."

The ominous admission unsettled the two Vascon shepherds. It was so unlike Gascons to roll over meekly and play dead. They used to be so fiercely independent! "I wonder what killed their spirit," puzzled Erne to himself.

A clatter of hooves and harsh yells interrupted Erne's thoughts. Peeking over the fallen log, the three men watched the burly barbarians galloping out into the open, blonde manes streaming behind them, spears leveled at the grazing sheep. Startled by the thunder of approaching hooves, the sheep scattered in all directions, bleating nervously. Trying to control the dispersing flock, the two frantic sheepdogs turned to confront the source of the disturbance. It would be their last call to duty. Two of the lead horsemen turned to the barking dogs and deftly ran them through with their lances. Yelping dogs thus impaled on their spears, the two horsemen galloped around in circles, flaunting their prowess. Howling in approval, the others galloped into the flock, wantonly trampling and skewering the bleating animals.

Outraged by the mayhem before him, something snapped in Sen's mind. Before his comrades could stop him, the young Vascon leapt out from behind the concealing log and rushed down the hill toward the meadow where his flock was being butchered. His friends looked on in helpless disbelief as Sen waded into the mêlée, wildly swinging his shepherd's staff, howling at the barbarians.

Startled at first by the raving presence, the *wildmen*'s reaction was swift. Peeling off from their sheep-lancing sport, two of the horsemen galloped toward the crazed shepherd, broadswords swinging. Sen's attempt to evade their blows proved futile, the contest far too lopsided. The duel came to a quick end when with one blinding sword stroke, one of the horsemen neatly severed Sen's right arm at the shoulder. The grievously wounded Vascon slumped to the ground without a whimper. The two horsemen cantered their horses over to where their victim lay, now bleeding profusely. They stood over him, admiring their handiwork, watching the shepherd slowly sink into unconsciousness. Leaning over his horse, one of the barbarians neatly skewered the severed arm with the point of his lance and rode off with it on high, braying of his feat to the others.

A light *sirimiri* drizzle was falling when they buried Sen in the valley of Baztan. A dozen men stood around the dolmen, heads bowed against the waspish wind, grieving the loss of a comrade. They had lowered the shepherd's body into a pit lined with upright stones and were getting ready to slide the heavy granite slab across the top of the family tomb. The corpse had been laid head facing east to insure that the rising sun would illumine the spirit's flight to the afterlife.

"*Harrapatu zenidaten!*" the dead shepherd's father kept moaning during the burial, bewailing that the gods had snatched his son away from him. After his grief had abated somewhat, he instructed the others: "Make sure to leave enough of an opening above his head. Mari must have enough room to see him off."

Though they had been living outdoors for eons now, their sense of awe for their erstwhile caverns and the earth spirits that inhabited them remained undiminished. With the advent of agriculture, the earth goddess Mari, once a nondescript deity in their crowded pantheon of spirits, had adopted the trappings of a supreme numen, had taken on the role of sole provider of life-giving rain and sunlight. No social activity took place without invoking her spirit, no bounty too small to attribute to her largesse.

The group's elder stood over the open tomb, wiping the cold rain misting his vision with the back of a gnarled hand. Memories of his young nephew flooded over him, leaving a hollow sense of loss.

"*Zu gaztea zara!*" You were so young, he whispered, bemoaning the loss of youth. Tossing a handful of sodden hyacinth leaves on the broken body lying in the open cavity at his feet, he added mournfully: "He was a good man"

The young man's untimely death at the hands of the Celts had been only the last in a growing number of incidents that had beset the mountain community for several generations now. Inferior in numbers and hopelessly outclassed in weaponry, their Gascon neighbors were being slowly overrun by waves of foreign invaders. Tales of human sacrifice only added to the outrage. Particularly gruesome were the rites conducted recently in the nearby settlement of Toulouse during the *wildenmen's* New Year's festival of Samain, where Druid priests were said to have set fire to a huge, wooden and straw effigy of a warrior, stuffed with half-a-dozen live Gascons.

Such appalling behavior had become a cause for mounting concern among the Vascons. Their valley's vulnerability to hostile incursions made Nagusi realize that it would not be long before the barbarians would come knocking at their door and try to subjugate his people, the way they had the Gascons. And there was little they could do about it except, perhaps, escape to more inaccessible country. It would be futile to stand up and fight in the open against a better-armed, more numerous horde.

Sen's death had shaken the community to its roots. His death became the spark that finally ignited the group's decision to abandon their ancestral meadows of Baztan and move to higher, safer ground. Nagusi was chagrined by the very notion of retreat; it ran against his grain. Legends still abounded of an ancestor of his who had sworn to sink roots in *Euskalherria* and move no more. But those were bygone days when foes were evenly matched and stoutheartedness sufficed to determine the outcome of battle. Someone had since changed the rules of engagement and tipped the balance against them. Until such time as they could face the enemy on an equal footing, they would have to fall back on terrain advantage to survive. It became clear to him that they would have to seek more inaccessible heights, trust the crags to balance the odds.

After many sleepless nights and much heart-searching, Nagusi finally chose to move to the remote mountain valley of Esteribar, farther east. Sparsely populated and fairly unapproachable, the dale he chose was nestled in the abrupt southern folds of the Pyrenees, deep in the heart of Vasconia. He would name the settlement *Agorreta*, an appellation he and his forebears had carried since time beyond memory. This would be his home in perpetuity. He would defend it to the death, vowing to let no *wildenman* set foot on his mountain lair.

Several hardy families accompanied Nagusi to his wild and remote eyrie. They would have followed him to the underworld, had he but asked. His leadership was legendary, his primacy undisputed. His forebears had been leaders of the Vascons ever since anyone could remember, had taught them survival in the brutal winters of long ago, led them into many a battle, helped them prevail against all odds. His wisdom was celebrated in the land, his word was law. They understood the reason for moving. Esteribar may not have been as lush and inviting as the lovely valley they were leaving behind, but the remoteness and inaccessibility of the deep gullies and forested glens of Agorreta would discourage foreign incursions. They would be safe there.

Shortly after moving, Nagusi realized that although he and his followers would survive a determined assault by the *wildenmen*, the rest of Vasconia remained at risk. Something had to be done. Wracked by these troubling thoughts, he sensed that if the other Vascon warlords could only see these rugged hills of his, they, too, would realize how easy they were to defend, might even be talked into retreating to similar terrain. To achieve this, he had to invite them to his retreat, show them its strategic advantages, discuss with them the pressing matter of survival. With this in mind, he summoned the warlords of the neighboring mountain valleys to his new lair in Agorreta, suggesting they bring along their counselors to offer sage advice on how best to solve the knotty problem of survival facing them.

"We are being pressed by the barbarians from the north," began the lord of Agorreta, addressing the dozen warlords who had gathered for the meeting. They had assembled under the sacred oak growing in the middle of the settlement, where important councils were always held. "Our Gascon brothers have already succumbed to the *wildenmen*," Nagusi explained. "More troubling, still, our own southern brothers in the Ebro river valley are starting to buckle under this foreign threat."

"They both face the same problem," offered the perceptive Arai. A robust, middle-aged man with graying hair and weathered, aquiline features, Arai had been named leader of the clan that chose to remain behind in the rich but exposed valley of Baztan. "They both live in fertile lands that others covet. Flatlands are hard to defend. Although you've recently moved to higher ground," continued the lord of Baztan, "you, too, may one day be in harm's way if the *wildenmen* ever decide to come traipsing over the mountains. Our bronze weapons are no match against theirs."

"We can defend our mountains far easier than others can their lowlands," responded Nagusi, reminding Arai of his valley's vulnerable position. "Besides," he added, "our hearts have always been stouter than our southern brothers,' or the Gascons', for that matter."

"Perhaps," remarked Unei, skeptically. The lord of the Arga valley had always been wise in the ways of war. Usually taciturn, his infrequent remarks carried the heft of experience, everyone always seeming to nod assent when he spoke. "But it would help," he continued calmly, "if our swords could cut as well as thrust like the *wildenmen's*. We've got to learn how to make tools and weapons out of that hard metal they use."

"The Iberians know how to," interrupted Arai, excitedly. "The traders that ply the Inland Sea have taught them how to work the hard metal. They may be willing to share their knowledge with us. We happen to have the same reddish ore that the Iberians use to make these hard tools and weapons. 'Iron', I think they call it in Lanz. That's a small village south of our valley, at the foot of Belatemendi, where the mountainsides are stained red. But the swords they make there are too brittle for striking. Perhaps the Iberians can teach us how to make them stronger. I know the *wildenmen* won't!"

"We'll need all the help we can get if those barbarians ever take a liking to our mountain valleys," admitted Nagusi dejectedly.

"So, who shall we send to talk to the Iberians?" asked Aimantor cagily.

From the way he posed the question, Nagusi knew that Aimantor was not volunteering for the arduous assignment. Vascons seemed to have lost the taste for far-flung adventures lately. Even a short trip to the nearby Bidasoa River for salmon was planned far in advance. And the Iberian settlements were at least a moon's journey away, as they had heard from the traders who came visiting occasionally. Besides, having to traverse *wildenman* territory to get to the Iberians would be hazardous.

Arai's suggestion had been inspired. It opened up possibilities where once there were none. The traveling Iberian tinkers he had met over the years seemed like a friendly lot. For all the good-natured fun his people poked at the itinerant salesmen's strange Basque patois, their craftsmanship was admittedly superior. They had a definite knack for working metal. Perhaps they knew something about this 'iron' that the Vascons now so desperately needed. The idea was well worth a try.

The deafening silence that had followed Aimantor's query told Nagusi that nobody in this group was going to volunteer for the perilous journey. But Arai's suggestion was too good to ignore. It had to be acted upon. After brief deliberation, Nagusi spoke:

"I will send my eldest son, Erne."

His proposal caught the assembly by surprise. "He is young and strong," his father added. "And he has a keen sense of direction. He can find his way anywhere. He should be back here before the next moon waxes full."

"Excellent!" exclaimed Arai. "We'll make spears and swords if someone can only teach us how to work that red ore in Lanz. Probably it's as easy as mixing it with something else to harden it, the way they blend tin with copper to make bronze."

"It is agreed, then," concluded Nagusi. "Erne will leave on the morrow."

There was much excitement among the warlords. They would finally be able to confront the *wildenmen* on their own terms. More to the point, the other lords would not have to pull up stakes and climb up to some inaccessible mountain like Nagusi's Agorreta stronghold. One mountain goat in the group was enough.

Chapter 8

The Iberian Blacksmith

Erne's boundless energy, a trait that had earned him his moniker, would stand him in good stead in the days ahead. The lanky, auburn-haired six-footer had the unmistakable hawk-like features of an Agorreta. His natural tact and artfulness made him the ideal ambassador for the risky and arduous assignment. The young man accepted the task with characteristic enthusiasm and was elated at the important mission his father had entrusted to him.

There were, besides, certain matters in Erne's heart that needed closure. All those winters of shared hardship and camaraderie in Labourd had developed a close bond between him and his cousin Sen. Memories of their last trip there were particularly poignant and painful. Sen had died in his arms and his parting words would haunt him for the rest of his life. "Be strong, Erne," the dying man had whispered. "Our people must prevail, no matter what." Now, the chance to avenge his friend's senseless death promised to bring Erne untold comfort and solace. When his father offered Erne that opportunity, the young man knew that Mari had smiled upon him and would finally put an end to his personal grief.

Not one to tarry, Erne was on his way the day after accepting his commission. He chose his father's best steed for the journey, knowing that its brisk, happy gait would make short shrift of the long trip ahead. He caught his first glimpse of the fertile Ebro River lowlands several days into the journey. It was early June, the hills a vault of jade, red poppies and wild lilacs carpeting the landscape in a riot of color. The land here was so much more fertile than in his uplands, he was quick to notice. The rich river valley seemed drunk with sunlight, lush with fields of cereals and vegetables, all pocked by a boggling variety of fruit trees and lovely vineyards. Life in this rich land must be sweet and easy, he reflected, with none of the harsh winters that gripped his mountain valley.

He soon became aware of several *wildenman* encampments scattered among the Vascon settlements dotting the countryside, the little earthen mounds strewn around them a dead giveaway of their identity. He had seen them before while wintering his sheep in Labourd where the barbarians in the Gascogne buried the ashes of their dead in similar urnfields. He gave the foreign encampments a wide berth, trying to avoid any contact with the quick-tempered foreigners.

The southern Vascons he met were friendly and hospitable. He was particularly taken by their women's dark, haunting eyes and ready smiles, their tanned complexion bespeaking life in a gentle, sun-drenched land. But most of all he was beguiled by their friendliness so unlike the shy, retiring womenfolk he knew. But something he noticed troubled him: these southern Vascons seemed to be slowly adopting the attire and mannerisms of their new overlords. He even noticed strange barbarisms creeping into their language. He was saddened by the realization that, like the Gascons beyond the mountains to the north, these southern brethren were, slowly but surely, succumbing to the *wildermen's* sway.

Much as he would have liked to linger among his southern kin, he had to press on. Leaving the bounteous Ebro lowlands behind, he soon noticed a dramatic change in the scenery. Almost overnight he seemed to have stumbled onto a sere wilderness, lost in endless stretches of a desert that shocked his upland-green sensibilities. At noon, the sun flared like a white scream, its heat thick and heavy on the brain. There were moments when he experienced eerie mirages. Light falling on distant rocks of far-off hills seemed to enhance their surreal blight. It was a place Mari must have surely forsaken.

After days of traveling through the harsh and savage beauty of the land, he was one day rewarded by a familiar scene when he once again gazed upon a landscape of open pastures, rippling with scented green. A deep sense of relief soaked his soul. After journeying for several more weeks along rolling hills and verdant valleys, he finally caught his first glimpse of the mighty Inland Sea he had heard so much about. Its shimmering immensity awed him as he stood on a rocky promontory overlooking the mighty expanse of water. Though it appeared as broad and deep as the large ocean near Baztan, the climate here seemed balmier, slightly oppressive. Even the smell of the sea, pungent with its scent of ripe fish, was different, unpleasant almost. The stunted sea pines, too, looked strange with their small, perfectly rounded, slightly comical tops.

Cantering his mount at a brisk gait, he presently overtook the flock of sheep he had spotted from a distance, grazing on a slanted meadow. As he approached, he caught sight of a man resting under one of those quaint pine trees. He had seen a few other men far off in the distance during his journey, but this was his first close-up encounter with another human being since leaving the Ebro lowlands. He was suddenly struck by the thought that he was starting to miss the warmth of human contact, that it was not good to be alone for such a long stretch of time.

The shepherd, who had been eyeing him with a mixture of curiosity and apprehension, stood up slowly and leaned on his staff. Erne noticed that the man was gripping it as if he were expecting to use it presently. Erne dismounted and flashed him a broad grin, raising his right hand in sign of peaceful greeting. Hesitantly, the shepherd returned the sign.

"*Kaixo!*" they both mumbled in cautious salutation, almost in unison. Half expecting the other to speak a foreign language, they were both pleasantly surprised and relieved to discover that their mutual salutation was in Basque.

Hitching his horse to the solitary pine, Erne turned to the shepherd and said: "*Gose naiz,*" admitting he was hungry. The shepherd promptly pulled out a piece of hard tack from his gunnysack and offered it to Erne along with a slab of young sheep-milk cheese. Watching him wolf it down, the shepherd in turn said: "*Egarri naiz,*" acknowledging that he himself was thirsty.

"*Ardua,*" offered Erne extending his wine sack to the man in return for the shepherd's friendly gesture. The sharing of food and drink instantly broke the awkwardness between the two.

"Are you Iberian?" asked Erne tentatively. He had always heard stories about a splinter group of Vascons that had continued south while his ancestors had chosen to remain behind in the Pyrenees. He could not get over the fact that his own Vascon language was so far-flung.

"I am," replied the shepherd, self-consciously. "You must not be from around here. You talk funny." Then he inquired: "*Non bizi zara?*" wondering where Erne lived.

"I come from a far away land," said Erne, explaining how long he had been traveling. "I come to meet your people and the seafarers with whom you trade."

"We trade with many different people," answered the shepherd self-importantly. After a brief pause, he added: "First, there are the Phoenicians. They come from across the sea in tall ships," he said, pointing toward the large, inland sea. "They live in settlements all up and down this coast. Then," he added, "there are the Greeks, who do the same except they settle farther up the coast from here.

They too come to trade their wares for ours." After another pause, he added: "Then, there are the fair-skinned ones from the north. They came last but don't trade at all. They simply move in with their flocks and take over our pastureland."

"*Gaizto!*" he said, labeling them "evil". "The Greeks call them 'Keltoi'. Their language sounds a little like Greek but there is much bad blood between them."

"And what do your people trade with these men from beyond the sea?" asked Erne, trying to steer the shepherd into more meaningful conversation. The concept of trade with foreigners was new to him, having only bartered chickens and pigs for wheat and barley with his own neighbors.

"Many things," answered the shepherd, trying to appear knowledgeable. "We make fine jewelry and pottery with fancy designs. There are also many kinds of ore under the ground which the foreigners need and trade for."

"What kind of ore?" asked Erne, his interest suddenly piqued. The stories they had heard about these people and their hard metal tools and weapons could indeed be true. Perhaps his trip had not been in vain after all.

"I don't know much about these things," admitted the shepherd sheepishly. Loath to reveal gaps in his knowledge, he added: "But I've heard of silver mines and lead mines, even gold mines." A hint of a smile crept over his tanned, furrowed face. "They also make bronze artifacts here," he added.

"What about this hard metal they call 'iron'?" pursued Erne, trying to home in on the objective of his trip.

"That, I do not know," admitted the shepherd with a shrug. "I think they do, but I'm not sure. All I know is that the Phoenicians work it. I believe they taught some of our blacksmiths how to work it, too."

There it was! Erne had stumbled on invaluable information. Things were suddenly starting to look up. "What else have these Phoenicians taught your people?" he pursued.

"They engrave stick signs on lead and bronze tablets. My master says it's magic. Why, they can actually put down their thoughts on them! Then, many moons later, they can look at them and the thoughts are still there! So they can no longer forget such things as how long ago the moon was full and when it's time to plant again, or how many sheep were traded for one's wheat, that sort of thing. It's witchcraft, I say!"

Erne was impressed. He had never heard anything like it before and it sounded like a strange and wonderful idea. His admiration for these Phoenicians was growing by the moment.

"How can I get to talk to these Phoenicians?" he inquired. "I'd like to find out more about this hard metal of theirs. I'd also like to see these tablets with their stick signs."

"There is a big settlement not far from here. See that village down there by the sea?" he said, pointing at a large colony sprawled out along the coast. "That is Kart-Hadasht. The Phoenicians live in it."

"But how do I talk to them when I get there? Do they speak Basque?"

"Basque?"

"I mean Iberian," corrected Erne, bemused at having to describe his own native tongue by some other name.

"The foreigners have learned a little Iberian over the years, doing commerce with us. It is not easy to understand them sometimes, but you can figure out what they're trying to say if you think hard enough. I sell them my cheeses sometimes."

"Do you suppose they'll share the secrets of their trade with me?" Erne asked hopefully. Noticing the shepherd's puzzled look, he clarified: "I mean teach me how to work this new metal."

"I couldn't say," admitted the shepherd diffidently. "Probably not," he ventured, after an awkward pause. Then, mulling over Erne's query, he added: "You'll probably have to sneak up on one of those Iberians who've learned the trade of working iron. They might share their knowledge with you."

Now, that was a good idea, thought Erne. Bidding the shepherd farewell, he struck out in the direction of the Phoenician colony. Its size awed him the closer he got to it. He had never seen such a sprawling settlement before. As he approached, he started noticing ships plying the incredibly blue waters of the large inland sea with their large, gaudy sails taut against the wind. Erne puzzled at how such enormous vessels could float at all or sail so fast. Next to them the little rowboats floating down the Arga back home looked like hazelnut shells.

As he approached the colony, he started noticing differences in the dwellings' construction. The ones along the fringes of the settlement were drab, honeycomb-shaped habitations strewn along potholed, randomly-traced dirt paths. Farther down, nearer the center of the settlement, he discerned taller buildings surrounded by substantial, whitewashed dwellings made of mud-brick and thatched roofs. It almost seemed as if the settlement were inhabited by two different groups of people, some better off than the others. He was not far off the mark.

Erne approached the first group of hovels on the outskirts of the settlement with some trepidation. People milling about the place showed little interest in the tall, oddly-attired stranger who had just turned up in their midst. Swarthy in complexion and of medium build, they seemed to have the same sharp, aquiline features as his shepherd friend. They were attired in homespun clothes, shuffled about in heavy leather sandals, leaned on long, crooked staffs. No one seemed to be in much of a hurry. Presently, a dog of nameless breed began barking at him. Several children, who had been teasing a disgruntled pig, suddenly looked up, noticed him, scurried off to their homes to warn their parents of the stranger's presence. Moments later, a paunchy, bowlegged man emerged from one of the outlying hovels to investigate. The leather apron draped around his jerkin and the awl he was gripping told Erne that he was looking at the village cobbler. The man eyed Erne with a look more inquisitive than challenging.

"*Kaixo!*" hailed Erne, raising his hand in salutation.

Now surrounded by a gaggle of noisy children, the middle-aged man stepped forward, hand outstretched in welcome. "*Ongi etorri!*" he said in a pleasant, friendly voice. Erne was relieved to hear the familiar Basque welcome. "I am Aznar," the man announced in way of introduction. "I am the village cobbler." His rotund face and ready smile reassured Erne. He couldn't help reflecting that his own mountain people would never have opened up like this to a stranger.

After introducing himself, Erne explained his presence, speaking slowly to make sure the Iberian understood him. His interest in ironwork soon became apparent to the Iberian. Though he was having some difficulty deciphering Erne's quaint turns of phrase, Aznar listened attentively. During a lull in Erne's conversation the Iberian remarked:

"We only work with bronze in these parts," he admitted, almost apologetically. "We have plenty of copper around here, you see. Only the Phoenicians work the iron. My friend Bua, who lives clear across town, used to work for them in one of their foundries in Kart-Hadasht. That's the name of this big settlement we live in," he added, making an encompassing motion with his hand. "My friend did mostly granulation and repoussé work for their vases and coins. Occasionally, though, he smelted silver and lead from Tarshish. He may even have worked with iron. We can go ask him if you wish."

"It is my wish, indeed!" replied Erne without hesitation, excited at the prospects of talking to a knowledgeable artisan. He didn't know what repoussé meant but didn't bother asking. He felt he was slowly closing in on the objective of his quest.

"*Etorri,*" said Aznar, inviting the stranger into his abode. He wanted to share a drink with him before starting off to his friend's home. The air inside the hovel felt close, its windowless interior lit by the scant light filtering in through the glass bead curtain that hung from the entrance. Aznar's cobbling table occupied almost half the living area, the remaining space taken up by a smallish oven and a single, solitary cot. Erne was appalled by the Iberian's squalid living conditions. But the cobbler appeared content with his lot.

After searching through an untidy cupboard, Aznar presently came up with two ceramic cups, handing one to Erne after wiping it on his jerkin's sleeve. He then reached for a small wineskin hanging from the wall and squirted a long spurt of stale red wine into Erne's cup before filling his own. The two men took sips from their cups after spilling a few drops on the clay floor as a libation to the spirits. As he put his cup down, Erne noticed the elaborate whorled patterns on its glazed ceramic.

"*Ona*!" he exclaimed, admiring the design on the cup. "*Nola egin duzu hori?*" he inquired, curious about its workmanship.

"It is handsome, indeed!" agreed Aznar. "Pure Iberian design," he added, wiping his lips with the back of a callused hand. "We trade our ceramic wares all over the known world. Greeks and Phoenicians can't seem to get enough of them. That," he said, "and *garrum*."

"Garrum?" puzzled Erne.

"It's a food preserve we make from fish heads, the consistency of molasses. People all over the Inland Sea consider it a delicacy, especially the Greeks. It's quite nourishing, you know. Would you like to try some? *Gustatuko zaizu!*" He assured his guest he'd enjoy it. Erne apologized for refusing the delicacy. Fish-head paste was not his idea of a treat.

Having finished their wine, Aznar led Erne out of the cramped abode and into the sunlight. They would have to cross the length of Kart-Hadasht to reach his friend's house. The settlement's wide thoroughfares bustled with people, all looking as if they had important chores to do. The men's wool-lined jerkins and snug breeches seemed inappropriate in the warm, muggy weather. They'd be more comfortable in the winter, he thought. The women, on the other hand, appeared more suitably dressed, their ankle-length linen tunics snugly fitted around the waist with elaborate belts. Fetching though he found their bronzed skin and sharp features, it was their whimsical hairdo that caught his attention. The huge, intricately coiled bun covering each ear provided an extravagant frame for their handsome features but must have greatly hampered their hearing. Topping the outlandish arrangement was a veil that hung down the back of their heads, attached to a fan-like comb. The overall effect was striking.

"It must take them half a day to get coifed!" commented Erne, amused by the elaborate hairdo.

"The well-to-do women have all the time in the world," observed Aznar. "Being the wives of *andis*, they can afford to have slaves do their work for them."

"In my land," commented Erne, "*andi* means big."

"As it does here," said Aznar. "That's what we call the noblemen who sit in the Council of the Elders. 'Kinglets', you might say."

"We have those, too, where I come from," remarked Erne. "They are the Council of the Elders, as well. My father is one of them. But they're no different from the rest, really, just older and wiser. However," he added, "we do not have slaves in our land."

"You don't know what you're missing," remarked Aznar smugly. "It's a great institution, you know. We didn't have them here, either, until we learned about them from the Greeks."

"Are the Greeks smarter than the Phoenicians?" asked Erne, intrigued by all these foreigners he kept hearing about.

"Perhaps," responded Aznar. "In some ways, anyway. They're both hard-nosed traders. The Phoenicians are probably better sailors. The Greeks are a little more learned, sometimes a little more warlike, too. But nothing like the *Keltoi*. Both the Phoenicians and the Greeks appreciate our Iberian metals and our handicraft. They also claim we make great warriors. They're always recruiting Iberian mercenaries."

"Who do they fight?" asked Erne, after being enlightened on the concept of fighting for pay. These people were not only good artisans but, from what he could gather, brave warriors, as well. He was starting to see certain similarities between them and the Vascons. Not in vain, he reflected, were they once related—and continued to share the same language, or at least variations of it.

"Just last year their king's nephew, some general by the name of Alcibiades, decided to take the city of Syracuse in Sicily away from the Spartans. Those are another kind of Greeks, you know," he added, trying to enlighten the puzzled young Vascon. "Anyway, he sent one of his other generals to recruit Iberian mercenaries from around Saetabi and Sagunto, even Tarraco, up the coast, a ways. So, off they went to fight the Spartans. A cousin of mine joined the expedition. That's how I know."

Erne was impressed that his distant brethren, the Iberians, were so highly regarded by these mysterious Greeks. Both he and Aznar would have been greatly surprised to learn that Iberians would, two centuries later, follow a Carthagenian general across the Alps with a herd of elephants to invade Italy in a daring military operation, the likes of which had not been seen before.

The two men walked the length of Kart-Hadasht past potters' shops and silversmiths' foundries displaying gaudily adorned clay pots and intricately-wrought jewelry. But it was the figurines of polychrome glass and ceramic ware with painted figures that caught Erne's attention.

"Who buys these articles?" he asked, taken by so much beauty.

"We export them all over the Inland Sea," responded the Iberian with undisguised pride. "We still barter with the Phoenicians and the Greeks but we have just recently started minting our own coins. It makes trade so much easier." Erne, who was barely aware of the concept of trade, was at a loss to understand the significance of coinage. Unwilling to display any further ignorance, however, he kept his curiosity to himself.

Weaving their way through a maze of streets, they presently arrived at a large square in the center of the settlement dominated by a huge building several stories high. Supported by enormous columns and arches, the imposing edifice was topped by a huge domed roof. Erne gaped at the structure, overwhelmed by its size.

"This is the Phoenicians' temple to Ashtarte," volunteered Aznar, pointing at the outsized building.

"Ash...who?"

"Ashtarte," repeated Aznar. "She's their goddess of love and fertility, their Mother Earth spirit."

"We have one like her in our land as well," remarked Erne brightly. "We call her Mari."

"Fecundity seems to be an important thing everywhere," remarked Aznar. "It also happens to be a good thing," he added knowingly. They both chuckled at the remark.

The wide thoroughfares of the busy central section of town soon turned into a warren of dirt footpaths as they approached the settlement's southern suburbs, the dwellings starting to resemble Aznar's own mud hovel. Negotiating a tangle of side alleys, they finally arrived at Aznar's friend's abode. It was similar in layout to Aznar's, complete with its potter's clay floor, windowless, lime-plastered walls and a domed beehive-shaped roof. Ducking under the lintel of the curtained entrance, they found themselves in a round, dimly lit enclosure.

"*Kaixo*!" called out Aznar cheerily, announcing their presence.

An old man was reclining on a threadbare mat in the center of the hut's single room. The figure remained recumbent, did not acknowledge the salutation nor made any effort to get up. He was staring at the domed mud brick ceiling above him with vacant gaze. The old man was blind, Erne finally realized.

"Hello Aznar," said the man presently, recognizing his friend's voice. *"Zer ekarri duzu?"* he inquired, asking what brought him there.

"There is a young man here with me who wants to talk to you. He comes from the mountain country far away to the northwest, but he speaks our language, sort of. He has traveled far to get here."

"Well?" said the old man, with a slight edge to his voice, still staring blankly at the ceiling above him. His eyes having adapted to the gloom by now, Erne noticed the scar that cut across the bridge of the old man's nose, extending from one temple to the other. That must have been the cause of his blindness, Erne surmised.

"My name is Erne," said the young Vascon, introducing himself. "I am the son of Nagusi, lord of Agorreta. We live in the high mountain country north of here, about a moon's walk away towards where the sun sets. My father sent me here to learn the ways of your people. We are curious about the way the traders from the Inland Sea make iron tools. I believe you call them Phoenicians?"

"And what would you want with ironware?" asked the blind man gruffly, almost as if someone were trying to steal the sacred fire from his hearth. "Don't you already have bronze ware?"

"Indeed we do," answered Erne, pleased by the opening the query had afforded. "We are farmers and shepherds living peacefully in our mountain valleys. We never bother anybody. But recently some newcomers from the north have tried to move in on us and have been trying to nudge us off our farmlands and our pastures. We have tried to fend them off but their weapons are stronger than ours. Theirs can slice ours in half."

"We've also been visited by those people from the north," admitted Bua somberly. "The Greeks around here call them Keltoi. They are big men with wild hair and strange customs. They burn their dead and stuff the ashes into urns, which they bury under little mounds in urnfields around their settlements." He paused a moment before adding, "We don't like them, either. They are far too quick to anger and make altogether too much noise. We call them *arrayuandi*."

Erne chuckled at the Basque term for 'big noise', a sobriquet with which loud, obstreperous people were tagged in his own land. Relieved that the blind Iberian shared his feelings about these Keltoi, he pressed his advantage. "So, will you teach us how to make these new, stronger weapons of theirs?"

"It is not hard if you have the right ore to make them with," responded the old man. "We call it iron. I have made a few iron *falcatas* in my time, when I worked in the Phoenicians' foundry. They make a formidable weapon." He paused, turning his unseeing eyes towards the young man for the first time. "Do you have this reddish ore in your land?"

"Our brothers living in a nearby valley have it. They dig it out of some reddish hills not far from Baztan," answered Erne, excitement mounting in his voice. "They've tried to work it like they work the bronze, mixing copper ore with some other ore they pan out of rivers, then melting them together. It doesn't seem to work with this 'iron' ore."

"Cassiterite," said the blind man enigmatically. Aware of Erne's puzzled silence, he explained: "That's what we mix copper with to make bronze ware." After a brief pause, he added: "You are right. It doesn't work with the iron ore. You've got to use coal instead. Do you have coal in your land?"

"Coal?" asked Erne, puzzled. "Sure! Lots of it! Some people use it to light fires in the winter. Some even cook with it."

"Good," said the blind man. "In that case you can make iron just as well as the Keltoi and the Phoenicians." After a pause, he added: "You sound like a young man with a good head on his shoulders. Listen carefully to what I am about to explain for this is the way you'll have to repeat it to your blacksmiths. Ask as many questions as you wish but I will go over this only once. And when I'm through, you will never reveal who taught you the art. The Phoenicians would be displeased and cause me harm."

Bua then proceeded to explain the metallurgical process of making iron while Erne listened intently to the blind man's every word. He would have to repeat every subtle nuance, every step of the process, to the blacksmiths back home if they were to achieve their goal. He knew this art was crucial to their survival against the *wildenmen*. He interrupted the blind man several times during his lesson but Bua didn't seem to mind.

"What keeps the melting ore from dripping into the fire while you're heating it in the kiln?" asked Erne.

"We use a container made out of fire clay. If your people melt copper, they must already know how to make crucibles out of this clay. It's a whitish clay that can hold molten copper or iron until one is ready to pour it onto a mold or a cast."

"You said that hammering hardens this spongy metal that comes out of melting iron ore with coal. Is the resulting sword hard enough to withstand cutting blows?" Erne asked.

"Hard enough for thrusting but still too brittle for cutting," answered the blind man, surprised and pleased by the young Vascon's probing questions. "One has to repeat the melting process several times, each time adding a little more charcoal dust. One must not cool the iron too quickly after pulling it out of the fire, like dunking it in water or anything like that. That makes it harder but even more brittle. Just let it cool down slowly. We sometimes add a little sand in subsequent heatings. That makes the metal tough enough for anything."

"And one more thing," he said at the conclusion of the lesson. "Once you've made your sword you must test its quality. You do that by bending it, like this," he said. Getting up, he started groping for one of the short *falcata* swords hanging from the wall directly above his stove. Grabbing its handle with one hand he started bending its tip with the other. The weapon bowed almost to its breaking point before he released it with a twanging sound. "If the sword recovers its original shape as this one does, then it is well made."

The lesson had obviously come to an end when Bua, curious as to whether he'd been of any help, asked: "*Lagundu zinzustedan?*"

"*Bai!*" responded Erne in the affirmative, adding: "*Oso ongi datorkigu!*" assuring Bua that the lesson would come in handy, indeed. "Sounds simple enough," quipped Erne. "Well," he stuttered, suddenly realizing the insensitivity of his remark, "what I meant is that it sounds simple once you've explained it. It would have taken us years to figure it out by ourselves. I and my people are very grateful to you for your help."

"It is nothing," said Bua with a casual wave of the hand. "Anything to put those Keltoi in their place. We are giving them our birthright, the same way we gave it to the Phoenicians and the Greeks before them. I don't know what changed when our ancestors split off from yours. We speak the same language but we are now a different people. I wish we had stood up to these foreigners like you say your people have."

"It is not all that bad," interjected Aznar, listening to Bua's self-lacerating remarks. "These Phoenicians and Greeks have taught us how to work the metals, how to sail, even how to write! Granted, they never were as pushy as the Keltoi who have barged in on our lands and brought us nothing but grief."

"But even the Keltoi have brought us something good," commented Erne. "It's because both you and we resent their presence that you have shared the secret of the iron with us."

"Use it wisely, young man," said Bua with a hint of a smile.

"We will, my friend," answered Erne, rising from the dirt floor he had been sitting on all this time. "My people thank you for your generosity. Someday I will come back to let you know how much all this has meant to us." So saying, he grasped the blind man's hand in farewell. "*Eskerrik asko!*" he said, expressing his gratitude in their common tongue.

Bua and Aznar were sorry to see the young man leave so soon but sensed that he was pressed for time.

"*Agur!*" said Erne, turning as he ducked out the entrance. "Next time I come you'll have to teach me about this 'stick writing'. We might need that, too, someday."

They smiled at the young man as they watched him leave. They knew their iron secret would be put to good use.

Chapter 9

A Roman Interlude

69 AD

It was only summer but the year was already shaping up to be a tumultuous one for Rome. Nero's recent death at his own hands had left a vacuum in the Roman leadership that the Senate seemed incapable of filling. At the periphery of empire powerful generals rallied their legions for a march on Rome to claim the coveted title of *Princeps*. They would not have shown such eagerness had they known the untimely end awaiting three of the imperial pretenders.

"We'll need many legions if we're to enter Rome with any authority," Governor Galba remarked to his friend and protégé, Antonius Primus. "The Senators and the Praetorian Home Guard will only bow to force." A shrewd politician, Galba was trying to lean on stalwart native sons like the Aquitainean Primus to do his local recruiting.

Sulpicius Galba had sown many political favors during his lengthy governance of Hither Spain. He was now ready to call in his dues from his Legion commanders and rally their support for the long march on Rome. His generals could hardly refuse the call to arms, considering the choice assignments awaiting them on their triumphal return to their homeland. To earn those perquisites, however, they would have to ensure that their Commanding General was named *Princeps*.

"I think I know a way to beef up the Seventh," said Antonius Primus. Now in his early forties, the handsome Legate from the Aquitainean *oppidum* of Toulouse had just recently been appointed commander of the Seventh Legion. It was a plum assignment for, of all of Galba's units, the VIIth was his very favorite. He had taken personal interest in building it up over his years as Governor of Hispania Tarraconensis and was immensely proud of the title by which it was known, 'The Seventh Galban Hispanic Legion'. He hoped that it would one day pile as much glory on its standards and its eagles as any other legion in the empire.

"I propose to recruit several native auxiliary cohorts from the mountains of Vasconia," continued Primus. "They're excellent *equites* and formidable warriors, to boot. I may even consider letting one of their own lead them into battle."

Primus knew that the auxiliary cohorts attached to its legions were the driving force of the Roman fighting machine. Led by Prefects and manned by non-Roman provincials, these highly mobile, five hundred-strong cavalry units were usually deployed around core Legion formations, protecting their flanks or acting as shock troops. Antonius Primus was well aware of the Vascons' fearless spirit in battle. He had read his Caesar, was familiar with their deft handling of their short *ezpata* swords and the peculiar but deadly accurate way they hurled their *güecia* spears. They were a frugal lot, not inclined to drunkenness or dissipation, used to sleeping on the ground and given to manly, competitive games. More important to his plans was the way they rode into battle, two astride each horse. This tactic, Primus believed, effectively doubled their offensive capability, a point which did not escape the Legate's keen, calculating mind, given the hectic recruiting schedule ahead of him.

"Have you already forgotten Vindex?" asked the Governor, concerned about granting too much authority to native commanders. He was referring to the Tribune of an auxiliary Gallic cohort which had recently deserted from its Roman Legion. Their desertion, compounded by that of several other mutinous Roman legions in Gaul and Germany, was threatening Rome's downfall.

"I'll vouch for them," answered the Legate without hesitation. "Remember, I am a Gascon by birth! I know how Vascons think. We may be able to pry an invaluable alliance from them by exploiting their age-old animosity against our mutual enemy, the barbarians from the north."

Primus visited Pompaelo in the early summer of 68 on a recruiting swing through Hither Spain. He planned to contact several mountain warlords, try to talk them into joining his VII Galban legion on its upcoming march on Rome. He soon discovered that the man he needed to convince was one Otsoa, overlord of several high Pyrenean valleys. Like most warlords of the *Saltus Vasconum*, this Otsoa held power of life and death over his clan. Antonius sent emissaries to Otsoa's fortress home in Agorreta, requesting the honor of his presence at the Roman citadel in Pompaelo, which the Vascons called Iruñea and considered their capital.

Pompaelo had been named after Pompey the Great, who had fortified the *oppidum* almost a century earlier, during the Sertorian wars. The town had become the nerve center of Vascon activity. Its location midway between the mountain valleys and the Ebro lowlands made it the ideal meeting place of Vascon cultures, blending the northern *Saltus Vasconum's* distrust of foreigners with the more congenial Ebro lowlanders in the *Ager Vasconum* to the south. But it was the northern *Vascones* that Antonius Primus was interested in at the moment. He was willing to travel to the *vicus* of Agorreta to meet with its warlord, should he refuse the invitation to come to Pompaelo, which is precisely what transpired several days later.

The meeting was cordial. Primus turned up at Otsoa's stronghold in Agorreta accompanied by half a dozen Tribunes, all smartly attired in their military regalia. Joining Otsoa's reception committee were warlords of several of the nearby mountain valleys. They convened under the sacred oak growing in the small square below Otsoa's fortified manor house where important deliberations were always held. Otsoa, as the Romans were soon to discover, was *primus inter pares* among the warlords present.

From their very first arm clasp, the Roman Legate was impressed by the unpretentious nobility of Otsoa's bearing. Uncommonly tall and broad-shouldered, the graying Vascon looked down on Primus with composure, as one equal to another. The Vascon's serene eyes and furrowed face exuded the confidence of one used to command. Even before the other warlords had raised him on his shield to elect him lord of the twelve Vascon mountain valleys, he was already known as *Otsoa,* 'the bear.' His steely blue eyes' penetrating look and a feral power that seemed to emanate from him warned Primus that he was standing before an uncompromising defender of a people that had never been subjugated by outsiders. He also knew that there were no Roman settlements in these mountain valleys, only necropoli. The two men sniffed each other out like two lions, aware of each other's power. Antonius could see why tough Vascons would follow this man into battle. This was going to be a lengthy discussion, he sensed.

"*Erromatarrak izango bagina latinez hitzengingo genuke,*" said Otsoa, at the outset. He was apologizing for the fact that, not being Roman, he could speak no Latin. Fortunately Primus' own mothern tongue was Basque, and so the deliberations were conducted in their common language. Short on small talk, the two leaders soon got down to essentials. Both parties agreed that the Germanic barbarians to the north, like the Celts that preceded them, were a menace to the Roman Empire–and, by extension, to Vasconia. Shrewdly weaving his arguments around this sore point, Primus tried to convince the Vascon warlords that it would be to their advantage to help the Roman legions neutralize the common enemy.

"Perhaps," responded Otsoa noncommittally, "but my people never go into battle led by foreign commanders. They only obey the orders of their own Vascon warlords. It has been thus long before Rome was Rome and remains so today."

Primus mulled over the unexpected resistance. He admired the spunk of this Otsoa, laying down conditions on Rome. But, by such men were great military units led, he reasoned. He could ill afford to lose them now on some petty technicality. After all, were there not auxiliary cohorts in other Roman legions led by their own leaders? He had been reminded of the risk of naming foreign commanders such as the Gallic Vindex. But, perhaps, this was a gamble Rome would have to take to control and Romanize her sprawling empire.

"You, and whomever else you choose, will lead your own cohorts," offered Antonius Primus. They had been discussing the possibility of raising two such units. "You will be given the rank of Prefect and will report only to me, your legion commander. Each of your two cohorts will be led by a Tribune of your own choosing. You will live in separate quarters if you so desire. You will share the booty of war and when your tour of duty is over, I will personally see to it that you and your troops are granted Roman citizenship with all the rights and remunerations pertaining thereto. Best of all, you will have played an active role in the elimination of the enemy that threatens your homeland."

It was vintage Primus, a smooth, convincing delivery of a seamless set of arguments almost impossible to argue with. Or so he thought.

"We will leave Vasconia undefended," ventured Arai, lord of the neighboring valley of Salazar. It was a shattering argument from one aptly nicknamed 'wolfhound', capable of sniffing through the Roman's glowing promises.

"We will defend your land against the barbarians, as we always have," responded the Roman general weakly.

"Only Vascons defend Vasconia!" retorted Kontzo, lord of Aezcoa. All of a sudden it seemed as if Primus' logic were beginning to unravel in the face of simplistic, primitive reasoning. Just when he seemed to have run out of arguments, Primus offered: "We have a massive army in Hispania. The mere presence of half a dozen legions will deter any barbarians from ever attacking here. You can leave your lands without a care." Sensing that he had not yet turned the Vascons around, he added: "You will march into the greatest city on earth as victors. When Galba is named Emperor he will personally shower you with honors and award you the same land grants awarded other Roman legionnaires. You will return to Vasconia as men of substance, awash with glory."

Otsoa and the mountain warlords retired to his house to discuss the proposition in private. Although the majority was agreeable to support the Romans, Kontzo held back.

"Our men have fought with foreigners before," argued the impetuous Lord of Aezcoa, his hirsute beard fairly bristling with contempt. "Remember that Carthaginian, Hannibal, our forefathers fought with?" There was a general nodding of heads. "That alliance didn't amount to much, did it? Only a few of them returned. They bragged about riding elephants over snow-capped mountains and all sorts of nonsense, but, in the end, they came back with their tails between their legs and empty-handed, didn't they?"

"You forget that it was the Romans they fought against," Otsoa reminded the recalcitrant Kontzo. "Don't fret about victory this time, my friend," he continued soothingly. "Romans are invincible. We will return with laurels and riches as the Legate promises. Think of all the sheep you'll be able to buy!"

"Who'll tend to the animals and the fields while we're away?" insisted Kontzo, sensing he was losing the argument.

"Not all men will leave," said Arai. "Besides," he added with a wry smile, "the women can help with the chores. They do it better than we men, anyway!"

Kontzo's reservations thus assuaged, the lords agreed to the alliance. Arai, lord of Salazar and Zezen, lord of Baztan, each agreed to lead a cohort, with Otsoa as Prefect, in overall command. But first, they had to iron out certain minor details such as the choice of weapons, cavalry, even battle attire. It was agreed that, unlike their Roman counterparts, the Vascons would not wear helmets or battle dress. They would wield their own *güecia* spears and *ezpatas* swords, and ride their own Pyrenean horses, both on parade and in battle.

Unusual though the conditions were, the Roman Legate accepted them and vowed that others under his command would also honor them. Otsoa promised within the month to round up his men and be ready for military training as full-fledged auxiliary cohorts of the VII Galban Hispanic Legion, then bivouacked on the outskirts of Pompaelo.

Antonius Primus had taken a sudden liking to these Vascons. Their primitive spirit touched something ancient in him, a once-fierce sense of independence, which his own Gascon forebears had lost long ago. He vowed to keep a close personal watch over their training to ensure that their primal fighting spirit remained intact during their Roman service.

Several weeks later, two astride each horse, Otsoa's Vascons rode into the Roman training camp under the ramparts of Pompaelo. It had distressed their families to see their young men leave their land to fight someone else's battles. But the promise of spoils and the lure of a Roman citizenship allayed their loved ones' fears.

The Roman officers who watched them arrive in camp stifled a chuckle. They couldn't wait to tame the wildness out of the ragged group of misfits and knock them into proper legionnaires. Primus deterred them, however, ordering his tribunes and centurions to limit their basic training to the bare minimum required by unit cohesion, no more. The officers knew they would have their hands full with these "primitives". Indeed, all attempts to whip them into a carbon copy of a Roman fighting unit failed miserably. Worse yet, they started noticing a strange role reversal: the traditional integration of malleable foreign auxiliaries into the Roman fighting machine took the unprecedented turn of having the veterans ending up copying the recruits!

Their group spirit was so catching, their enthusiasm so contagious that the legionnaires of the Seventh were soon mimicking the spirit of the two Vascon cohorts, down to their cunning tactics and weird, unnerving war cries. Though the officers at first muttered their displeasure, Primus himself was secretly delighted. Before long, the Seventh Galban had developed a fierce esprit-de-corps, unmatched in the Roman army of the west. It was to stand them in good stead in the months ahead.

The march on Rome turned out to be a giddy affair. Some of the Vascons had been impressed by the size of their own *oppidum* of Pompaelo, but they were not prepared for the grandeur of the enormous buildings and splendid avenues of the Roman metropolis. They could not understand why all those people lining the avenues cheered so wildly when their unit rode past in the triumphal parade. The puzzlement was mutual; the spectators were intrigued by the two oddly attired cavalry units riding with the Seventh Galban legion. Despite their ragtag appearance and the stumpy horses they rode, there was a certain unstudied nobility about their equestrian bearing, heads held high, eyes meeting the Romans' stares with unblinking self-confidence. The Romans had noticed a similar hauteur in the princely prisoners the legions sometimes dragged back from their foreign battles to parade in their triumphal marches. But the oddly attired men of these two cohorts were not prisoners, their humble attire contradicting the regal bearing of the proud lot.

The legions set up camp on the outskirts of the city, their soldierly activities soon reverting to humdrum chores of guard duty, kitchen patrol, and the occasional parade. On their days off, they flocked to the chestnut-lined avenues along the Tiber, past old temples of a Republican Rome that died with Julius Caesar. Like children out on a sunny afternoon stroll, they ogled the monuments, the basilicas, the marbled temples lining the wide avenues. They gaped at the *Forum*, the small city within a city, and the *Curia*, where wise men deliberated and made laws for the empire. They walked past the temple of Romulus and laughed when told the story about a wolf nursing him. For all their might and power, these Romans were a little naïve, they mused.

Walking past the basilicas of Julia and Emilia, a friendly passerby casually pointed out to Otsoa the house of Julius Caesar, the once Pontifex Maximus. Otsoa came alive.

"I recognize the name!" he blurted out excitedly. "He came over our mountains in my great grandfather's day. Marched right past our house, chasing after Celts! This was a great man, my grandfather used to always say." And now here he was, walking on the same flagstones the man's sandals once trod. The very thought overwhelmed him.

The Circus Maximus was the Vascons' favorite diversion. Everything about the games entranced them, from the opening parade, with its priests, magistrates and charioteers marching to the music of splendid bands, to the acrobatic feats of trick-riders riding elephants and camels, even lions–animals they had never even heard of before. The gladiatorial combats and wild beast fights, sometimes with humans, were a spectacle that made them cringe a little. Afternoons, they would watch chariot-racing events with unalloyed delight, the magnificent horses so much larger and swifter than their own. They marveled at the way the charioteers controlled them, sometimes four or six in a team, deftly blocking and fouling the rival chariots' progress. People around them laid bets on the races, a practice that sometimes led to altercations and bloodied noses. The word *circences* took on a new and wonderful meaning for the Vascon bumpkins.

Several weeks into their Roman interlude, Antonius Primus invited Otsoa to spend the day with him. A growing friendship and mutual respect had developed between the two men during their shared hardship in the field. In appreciation of the Vascon's efforts, Primus offered to show Otsoa a good time while in Rome. Sensing that the rustic and unkempt appearance of the Vascon Prefect would clash with the polite company he was about to keep, Antonius took him to a barber, where he was given a proper haircut and beard-trimming. The next stop was at the tailor's, where he was fitted with new sandals and an elegant toga.

"This," explained the Legate, "is the badge of a Roman citizen, which you will shortly be."

Grinning broadly as he donned the garment, Otsoa remarked in faltering Latin: "*Civis Romanus sum!*"

"Very good!" replied Antonius, pleased by the Vascon's stab at Latin.

Otsoa was amused by his friend's concern for propriety, but prematurely donning a Roman toga made him a little queasy. Deep down, however, he felt immensely proud of it. After all, had not the emperor himself promised to grant his men Roman citizenship one day? It was only proper to start getting used to it, early on.

The two men spent the rest of the morning at the public baths of Agrippa, lolling about from one *tepidarium* to the next before ending with a bracing cold one. The massage that followed was quite pleasurable but the perfumed oil they rubbed on him smelled effeminate, and he was all too glad to put his clothes back on when they came around to the room where they had disrobed. As he walked out into the sunlight he was pleasantly surprised by the strange sensation of total relaxation, something he had never felt before. These Romans were quite the sybarites, as Antonius sometimes described their refined tastes. The Legate had tried to explain the word to him before but now Otsoa could finally attach a meaning to it. It was a bit decadent, he had to admit, but also luxuriously pleasurable. He could see how one could get used to this sort of pampering.

The streets outside bustled with people rushing about, talking loudly, gesticulating endlessly. Performers, singers, clowns, jugglers and diviners filled the street corners and open-air squares. The two men stopped briefly to watch a snake handler charm his reptiles, a magician perform his disappearing tricks. They walked past puppet shows and people playing dice on the street.

"These are a happy people," commented Otsoa, observing the joyful flurry around him. Thieves, butchers, actors, all seemed to punctuate their incessant talk with animated gestures, especially those playing *morra*, a raucous, digit-guessing game.

"*Panem et circencem,*" remarked Primus. "The emperor keeps them happy and out of trouble by plying them with food and entertainment. It seems to work."

"I guess that's what happens when you have all these many people living in the same place. We don't need these distractions in Vasconia to live in peace," commented Otsoa, wryly.

It was mid afternoon when they arrived at Primus' home, a lordly residence in an obviously affluent neighborhood near the foot of the Capitoline hill. As they walked in, they were greeted by the soothing sound of cascading water from an ornamental fountain in the middle of an open courtyard. The walls of the handsome atrium were painted with frescoes of marine motifs with cool blue and green sea colors.

Beyond the vestibule, the walls of the central hall were lined with ancestral busts, tucked away in niches. The lofty halls and magnificent courts, the mosaic floors, the mural paintings all bespoke the Legate's high station. Presently, they entered a courtyard filled with flowerbeds and statuary, water-basins, even a shallow pool with a central fountain. These Romans really loved the sound of water, observed Otsoa.

A tall, swarthy man dressed in a rough dark tunic appeared at the living room door. Without uttering a word, he relieved them of their white togas and sandals, leaving them with their more comfortable tunics and the proffered slippers. He was, Otsoa learned presently, one of a dozen slaves Primus owned and kept in his house, a cadre that, in the society of important Romans he consorted with, ranked him as an upper middle-class nobleman.

Without notice, a woman of stunning good looks glided into the room. Probably in her early forties, the lissome matron wore an elegant white shawl draped around her shoulders with the same casual grace and insouciance as her husband wore his toga.

"You must be Otsoa," she said cheerily, offering him a limp hand that he took in his and clumsily kissed. "I am Octavia," she said brightly. "I have heard a lot about you." Her voice was that of a much younger woman. Her sharp, aristocratic features, the way she held up her head and shoulders, her serene, commanding look, all bespoke nobility.

"I am he," answered Otsoa diffidently. He had spoken to many women in his life but never to a noblewoman like this before. "I hope that what you heard was good," added Otsoa, taking a stab at the unaccustomed art of small talk. And in fractured Latin, no less.

"You fish for compliments, my friend," she said mockingly. Her easy way with words and comfortable, open manner with a perfect stranger struck Otsoa. Women in his land were far shier and considerably more circumspect than this one, and it surprised him a little.

"Come, let's make ourselves comfortable. You've had a long day," she said, leading the way to the dining room. The two men lounged on separate sofas at opposite ends of the low dining table, while a slave helped Octavia recline on a chair between them. Two other slaves helped the men slip out of their sandals, and offered them a bowl of water and a towel to wash and dry their hands before starting the repast.

A prayer to the gods preceded dinner. Primus invoked Genius, protector of family continuity, while his consort appealed to Juno, her favorite deity. Invited to invoke his gods, Otsoa called on Mari, the earth goddess of his people, the life-giver.

During the meal that followed, Otsoa watched Antonius before proceeding, making sure he committed no gaffe of etiquette. There were, he noticed, no individual plates and the only utensil was a spoon. Even that, he soon discovered, would be unnecessary, the soup sopped up with chunks of bread.

The boggling variety of dishes that followed amazed Otsoa. After the appetizers of oysters and pickled fish, the slaves served several platters of meat and fowl, carved to finger-sized morsels. A dessert of cakes and an assortment of exotic fruit followed. Otsoa had never tasted pomegranate or almond-peach before, not even figs this sweet. Watered-down wine with a touch of honey was served in moderation throughout the meal. Inquiring why it was diluted, he was informed that only barbarians drank it straight, a response that embarrassed Otsoa for having even asked.

"What do your people eat?" asked Octavia, curious of these primitives' culinary taste.

Otsoa's gastronomic explanation was brief and to the point: "We make bread from acorn flour, mostly, sometimes millet. Lamb and mountain goat are our main staple, occasionally, *jabalina* ham. We frequently eat trout and, on very, very special occasions, we'll bring in lobster from the shores of Labourd. That's always a treat. As for drink, there is little wine grown in our land so we drink mostly cider."

"What about your laws?" inquired Primus. "I understand you're pretty harsh with felons in your country."

"Our traditions are ancient, our laws clear. Crime in our land is severely punished. Those who have committed serious crimes are flung over the precipice. The really heinous criminals, like those guilty of parricide, for instance, are entombed alive, far from the settlement, so as not to desecrate it."

Octavia's eyes bulged perceptively at the lurid description. *Lex Talionis* seemed alive and well in the hinterlands, she mused, flustered slightly.

"What about your pastimes, your distractions?" she asked, trying to steer the conversation to more civilized subjects.

"We enjoy dancing to the music of the *txistu* and the *tamboríl*. You have to be lithe to dance a Basque dance. It's…athletic," he added, after hunting for an appropriate description of the *jota*. "We also enjoy performing feats of strength, weight-lifting competitions, wood chopping by our *aitzcolaris*, that sort of thing. We also enjoy horseracing. Our breed of horses is second to none. Not big, but swift and strong."

Primus wanted to probe deeper into the Vascons' traditions. "What about your religion, your customs?"

Otsoa regarded his hosts for a long time. He was starting to feel that he was being grilled for information merely to keep the conversation alive. He need not have. These were curious, intelligent people.

"We have always been a deeply religious people," he said, turning serious. "Our pantheon of nature gods is even larger than yours. Mari, our Mother Earth goddess, rules over all of them. We sacrifice animals to her during the full moon, especially during the summer solstice. We have special priestesses who conduct rites of divination and make auguries in their circles of stone, which we call *arrespil*. Our religion commands us to be kind to the sick. We present them to the tribe so that those with similar ailments can come forward to offer advice and help."

"What is your men's worst fear?" asked Primus, trying to plumb Otsoa's warrior spirit.

"For a Vascon there is nothing worse than growing to a useless old age, reduced to living off of others' hand-outs."

His succinct response passed Primus' test with flying colors. He knew then what he had suspected all along: these Vascons were the quintessential warriors. Julius Caesar's description of them was right, after all.

Lively and entertaining during the first courses, the conversation after dinner drifted towards politics, the gist of which escaped Otsoa.

"I hear from Flavia that Galba has named his son to be his successor," commented Octavia during the second tables. "Otho is hopping mad! As are the Praetorians, I understand."

"As well they should!" remarked Primus philosophically. "Otho was promised the succession to power as the price for joining Galba in our march on Rome. He left a nice governorship in Lusitania to follow Galba here. Now he's left in the lurch. I think the advocates have a name for that; I believe they call it 'false pretenses'."

Otsoa was starting to feel uncomfortable with the rarefied drift of the conversation, being, as he was, a complete innocent on subjects of high politics and

Curia infighting. He was a man of few words, to begin with, and, to make matters worse, those few were in Basque. Besides, he had had his fill of talking for one day. Though he enjoyed the company and hospitality of his friend and lovely wife, he was starting to feel ill at ease, knowing he did not belong in that setting. It was turning dark outside and that gave him a pretext to excuse himself. Thanking his hosts for a memorable day, he begged his leave and was off to camp to join his troops on the city's outskirts.

All in all, he mused as he walked back to his barracks, it had been an exercise in sensuous excess, all quite foreign to him. He knew that he would never want to live in Rome when his tour of duty was up, Roman citizen or not. Although he was the highest-ranking warlord in his land, he knew that he was a plebeian at heart, and, when all was said and done, quite happy to be one. Sophisticates, with their flowery language and subtle innuendoes, made him a little uneasy. He much preferred the straightforward, down-to-earth ways of his own people.

Chapter 10

The Rhine Adventure

The pomp and circumstance of Galba's investiture as Emperor had hardly receded into the background when an uneasy Senate started grumbling about the large military presence in their midst. To allay their concern, Galba made the mistake of relocating his armies to the frontiers, where they were most needed. The Seventh Spanish Galban Legion was displaced to Pannonia, in the Dolomites. No sooner had he denuded himself of power, however, than Otho summarily disposed of him and took over the reins of power.

Not to be outdone, other generals stationed at the periphery of empire, had themselves named *Imperator* by their own troops and started marching on Rome to grab the reins of power. First to cross the Rubicon was Aulius Vitelius, commander of the battle-scarred legions in Germany. Crushing Otho's forces, he swooped down on Rome and was named *Imperator* in short order. Ignoring Galba's lessons of history, he, too, furloughed his Gallic and Batavian cohorts, thereby weakening his precarious hold on Rome, while, at the same time, unwittingly sowing the seeds of rebellion in Lower Germany.

Vespasian, leader of the Roman armies in the Middle East, had himself named *Imperator* by his troops, and marched on Rome to challenge Vitellius. Leading his Danubian armies was Antonius Primus, now commander of five battle-hardened legions, among which was his crown jewel, the Seventh Spanish Galban, with its stalwart Vascon cohorts, all itching for their first real military engagement. There was great excitement in the ranks.

"Si vis pacem, para bellum!" was Primus' warcry to his embattled troops. "If it is peace you crave, prepare for war!"

Sweeping down the Julian Alps, Primus' hosts took Verona by storm and proceeded to confront Vitellius' forces, bivouacked in and around Cremona. The Seventh Galban spearheaded the night attack on the enemy's fortified camp on the outskirts of town. During the assault, the legion's eagle bearer was mortally wounded. In a gallant action, Otsoa picked up the fallen emblem and led his men through the camp's gates, overwhelming the defenders. Cremona fell shortly after and was put to the torch.

Rumors of disaffection among Vitellius' officers in the legions stationed in the Rhine had reached Primus. Eager to exploit this unrest and turn the mutinous factions against Vitellius, Primus devised a clever scheme: he would send Alpinus Montanus, an old comrade-at-arms and commander of one of the defeated Vitellian legions, back to the estranged legionnaires in the Rhine to relay the news of Vitellius' defeat at Cremona. He decided to send his two battle-tested Vascon cohorts to escort Montanus to Mogontiacum-on-the-Rhine to ensure that an undiluted version of the victory at Cremona was reported.

It was late October and time was of the essence. The cold weather was about to set in and the snows threatened to hamper operations, making an already difficult crossing of the Alps impossible. Primus summoned Otsoa to a meeting.

"You will cross the Alps at the Great Pass, traverse Helvetia in a forced march and head for the Rhine. There you will board your troops on Roman navy barges waiting for you near Vindonissa. Your two cohorts will sail down the Rhine until you reach Mogontiacum, where the core of the Roman legions is stationed. I want to preempt any rebellion of the northern legions against us."

"What's the rush?" queried Otsoa, puzzled by the sudden urgency of the mission. "The news of Vitellius' defeat at Cremona will reach them soon enough."

"Vitellius has been beaten at Cremona, but one battle won does not a victory make," replied Primus. "We have to follow it up. You have two missions: first, you must make sure Montanus faithfully relays the details of our victory at Cremona to his fellow officers in Germany. Second, and perhaps more important, you will try to discourage any residual allegiance to Vitellius among the legionnaires in the Rhine. I know that the officers there favor Vespasian but the soldiers remain loyal to Vitellius. You must try to shift these troops' allegiance over to us."

"How can two cohorts do that?" asked Otsoa, skeptical of the mission's growing complexity. "It is not going to be easy." He could speak to his commander with total frankness, without fear of sounding disrespectful or insubordinate. "Only uncertainty awaits us at the end of this arduous journey."

It was a complaint from one not accustomed to look for excuses. Primus knew that he had assigned the Vascon a difficult, perhaps impossible task. Courage was needed, but it was now diplomacy he was demanding from his loyal Vascon.

"Your wits have stood you in good stead all this past year," said Primus. "Your comportment in Pannonia was superb, but what you and your men did in Cremona these past few days beggars belief. You have crowned yourself and your unit with glory." Primus paused to give further emphasis to what he was about to add. "You will need more tact and acumen in this mission than in any other. You must test the waters before committing your men. It will be tricky because you'll have to reach the officers loyal to Vespasian without alienating their subordinates, who still favor Vitellius. I have no doubt that you will find the right moment and the right way to go about it. There are troubled waters up the Rhine but as your own people aptly put it, 'Troubled waters, fishermen's profit'."

Smiling at the Roman's grasp of Hispanic lore, Otsoa retorted: "You Romans also say: *'Qui amat periculum in illo peribit'.*" They both laughed at the friendly parrying of witticisms. Primus knew, then, that the challenge had been accepted.

The Vascons were off to an early start the next day. They clearly delighted in the unexpected mission. They were exhilarated by the prospects that this could be their last mission before heading for home. "*Querencia!*" whispered Arai to Otsoa, who rode by his side. Otsoa smiled. Like Arai, he too was familiar with the happy gait a horse acquires on sensing the proximity of the barn. Soon to be appeased, this homesickness could be the best goad for his weary troops. Cremona had been a brutal ordeal; he had lost a good many men in that fray.

Filled with skepticism for the unsavory mission, Alpinus Montanus, the reluctant Vitellian messenger, dourly observed the almost joyful comportment of troops that had, only a week earlier, been up to their thighs in gore. These Vascons were a truly amazing lot, he reflected dyspeptically. He had heard of their military exploits in Cremona but watching them now at close quarters, cutting up with their cheerful, almost adolescent pranks, and listening to their earthy songs and lively banter, only exacerbated the tribune's irritation. He was of two minds about delivering the message to his old comrade Officers in the Rhine legions. They would welcome the news about Vespasian's victory over Vitellius but it would be at the expense of having to admit his own Legion's defeat. One, after all, seldom bragged about one's own failures. But at least, he morosely reflected, he got away with his life after his legion's debacle in Cremona. Things could have been worse.

The Alpine pass was still open when they finally reached it. The first snow flurries had not completely obliterated the path and, though it was tricky, they managed to negotiate it without serious mishap. The forced march had been strenuous but they made good time negotiating the Pennine Alps. The weather had been ideal for the crossing and, save for a few foggy patches at dawn, the sun was out most of the time, making for excellent traveling conditions.

The Alpine foothills beyond the peaks reminded the Vascons of their Pyrenees, nostalgia only quickening their gait. Fording the Rhone river near its source, they proceeded across the plains of Helvetia and made for Vindonissa, the large *oppidum* near where the west-flowing Rhine abruptly turned north in search of the sea. After several weeks of forced marches they finally reached the river. They bivouacked near the crook in the river and supervised the loading of their horses and equipment onto a dozen large barges docked in slips jutting out into the river.

The next several days were to provide a much-needed rest. River navigation was relaxing. The scenery along the riverbanks was placidly bucolic except where small groups of hostile Germans burst out into the open to taunt them, shooting spent arrows and harmless spears at them as they glided by. The Vascons watched them in silence, wondering what made the natives so restless. Sooner or later, they would have to confront these savages again in hand-to-hand combat. They had clashed with Vitellius' Batavians in Cremona, knew they were a hardy lot, perhaps a bit awkward with their long unwieldy swords, but good, stouthearted warriors, nonetheless.

"How much farther to Mogontiacum?" inquired Otsoa of the barge captain, several days into their trip.

"Mogontiacum?" replied the puzzled Roman old salt, adding a few wrinkles to his furrowed brow. "We have already sailed past Mogontiacum. I have orders to deliver you to Novaesium. You are to join up with the Sixteenth and Twenty Second legions at Gelduba, near there. It's some sort of training camp, I understand."

"Training camp?" remarked Otsoa suspiciously "We don't need any training! Who gave the orders?" He hated last minute surprises and would certainly not take orders from anyone but Primus.

"General Flaccus, the governor and Commander-in-Chief of Upper Germany, headquartered in Mogontiacum. He was the one who provided these barges for you. He is having trouble with some turncoat Batavian Tribune named Civilis, who's managed to stir up the Batavians, the Cannenfates and the Frisi all along Lower Germany. They mauled Lupercus' Fifth and Fifteenth legions pretty badly near Vetera recently. That's a little further upriver. Gallus' First Legion was also cut to ribbons around Bonn by some mutinous Batavians. Last I heard, these rebels were converging on Vetera. Flaccus was talking about sending his Sixteenth and Twenty-Second legions to reinforce the undermanned Vetera defenses, but they're pretty green troops so they've been sent to Gelduba instead, for training. And that's where you're to join them."

"Who's commanding these legions at Gelduba?" interrupted Alpinus Montanus, the reluctant messenger of the Cremona disaster. It was he who knew the lay of the land and was supposed to suggest the overall plan of action.

"Well, there were really two commanders at Gelduba: Vocula leading the Twenty-Second and Gallus the Sixteenth," replied the barge Captain. "From what I gather, their troops are pretty restive. Don't much care for their commanders, I hear."

"Sounds like a hornets' nest we're sailing into," interrupted Otsoa, worried now about the unsettled state of affairs awaiting them, the Germans threatening from the outside, the malcontents stirring up the pot inside. "Not very promising prospects!"

"We've got to look at the big picture," volunteered Montanus philosophically. "Think of the Empire! It is the officers who must prevail at all cost. The rabble under them will come to heel once we stiffen their officer's resolve. What we cannot tolerate is the German threat. Rome has no use for barbarians. We must fight them with vigor, push them back beyond the Rhine, no matter what."

Well spoken, thought Otsoa, for one who had just recently backed a usurper of the seat of Empire. But he knew that it was an unfair judgment the moment the thought crossed his mind. After all, this Montanus, like many of his brother officers in the Vitellian army at Cremona, would rather have been fighting for, not against, Vespasian, honoring an allegiance that dated back to Galba and Otho, who had granted many of them their field commissions. From the very beginning, it had been hard for them to stomach Vitellius' opportunistic pretensions but they were hamstrung by their military oaths and code of honor.

"So if we land in Gelduba," summed up Otsoa, "we join Gallus' Sixteenth and Vocula's Twenty Second, and then proceed with them to relieve Lupercus' Fifth and Fifteenth at Vetera. Did I get that straight?"

"That was the situation two weeks ago," admitted the barge Captain peevishly. "No one knows what it is today! That's why I think it'd be wise for you to land at Novaesium. Even so, I suggest you approach the training camp at Gelduba with care. If they're in trouble, like the others at Vetera, you can help them. If they've already left to relieve Vetera, it'll only be a short hike to that other camp. As for me, I'll have my men pole the barges back up the Rhine to our base in Mogontiacum."

"Makes sense," said Otsoa. "How far is Novaesium from here?" It was getting on late afternoon and the Vascon Prefect didn't relish the idea of getting embroiled in any military action on unfamiliar terrain, especially in the dark. They had had enough of that at Cremona already.

"Just a couple more hours, I'd say," responded the Captain. You can order your men to start gearing up and saddling the horses. They'll have to wade ashore. There's not much of a landing at Novaesium. Puny little *vicus,* that's all it is."

It was almost dark when they landed on a spit of sandy shore off Novaesium. The inhabitants of the small village were used to the comings and goings of Roman troops but the latest arrivals' un-Roman like attire and strange, guttural language stirred their curiosity. They watched them from afar, pitching tents, gobbling down a quick meal, turning in for the night. The soldiers' stealth intrigued them. They lit only a few fires, none of them big enough to keep them warm in the cool November night. From the occasional soft neighing of horses, the locals sensed that the guards were up and about all night.

The Vascon cohorts struck camp even before the first cock crowed the next morning. They spoke in hushes, even went to the trouble of padding their horses' hoofs to cut down on the clatter as they followed the narrow trail bordering the western shore of the Rhine. With only a dozen-mile march to Gelduba, Otsoa felt that they would get there well before noon. That was a good time to arrive for either a friendly or hostile reception.

Even before negotiating the line of hills overlooking Gelduba, the Vascon vanguard became aware of strange noises that grew in intensity as they approached. The dull roar reminded Otsoa of drumbeats and horn blasts, even the unmistakable clangor of steel on steel. There was no mistaking it; these were the sounds of battle.

"Reminds me of the Batavians whooping it up back in Cremona!" commented Otsoa to his two tribunes, Arai and Zezen, who were riding alongside. Pulling his mount up short, he held up his right hand signaling the marching columns behind him to a halt. Turning to one of his centurions riding a few paces behind him, Arai sent him to reconnoiter the terrain beyond the next hill. The centurion came galloping back shortly after with disturbing news; the Germans had surrounded the Romans' camp and looked as if they were getting ready to overrun it.

Their worst fears were confirmed when they gained the ridge. A cohort of German horsemen was galloping around the post, howling insanely, displaying tribal emblems and captured Roman standards. The Vascons had never seen a Roman legion in direr straits. In the middle of the mêlée, standing on the slopes of what appeared to be a hastily built rampart, was a ragged group of legionnaires fighting for their lives. It was an odd situation, almost as if surprised out in the open by the Batavians, the Romans were desperately trying to put up a fight outside the ramparts. The legion commander was paying a terrible price for not having deployed his men in proper battle order. It was a scene of carnage, bodies of wounded and dying littering the slope all around the legionnaires. The hand-to-hand combat was desperate, the slaughter of the two Roman legions predictable.

Clustered in a ragged array along the southern flank of the central core of harried legionnaires, a Nervian auxiliary cohort suddenly bolted in the face of a determined Batavian assault. Seeing an opening in the Roman flank, the Batavians and Germans poured into the gap left by the fleeing Nervians, penetrating the legion's core defenses. Otsoa watched the ensuing butchery with dismay.

The Romans, who had been caught out in the open, were jammed up against their own palisades, with no room to maneuver. Naked to the waist, the Batavians swung their lethal axes and cutlasses against the Romans, keeping up a steady rain of murderous projectiles. Bunched up and unable to even raise their shields for protection, the Romans could barely defend themselves. Hundreds fell without even a chance to throw their *pila* or draw their swords. The survivors were desperately trying to reform their maniples on the bodies of the dead, locking shields, all the while trying to clamber back up into the safety of the palisades.

The onrushing barbarians hacked at the terrified legionnaires, capturing standards right and left, even taking prisoners. They would have finished off the bewildered Romans had their General not had the presence of mind to give the order to retreat behind the ramparts.

Otsoa knew it was time to intervene. Dissension in the Roman files between officers and legionnaires was now a secondary consideration, the barbarians about to annihilate them both. Raising his right hand, he pointed at the beleaguered camp and barked out the order to attack.

"*Aurrera!*" he shouted, waving his *ezpata* sword on high. Leading the charge, he galloped down the hill, letting out a blood-curdling *irrintzi*, the haunting Vascon shout of war. Helmet-less, his grizzled hair blowing in the wind, arms bare, chest covered only with a padded leather jerkin, Otsoa rode into battle on his Pyrenean horse, the very image of a fearless leader. His troops followed suit and the eerie clamor of a thousand throats trilling the wild battle cry struck first, surprise, then terror in the hearts of the Batavians.

As they reached the bottom of the hill, the two Vascon cohorts split up in a wide encircling movement, their unexpected cavalry charge catching Batavians and Germans completely by surprise. Adding to their bewilderment was the ungodly din of *irrintzis* coming from the strangely clad horsemen swarming all around them, two men astride each horse. Unnerved by the fearsome commotion, the Batavians and Germans fell easy prey to the determined charge of the Pyreneans. The Batavians who managed to survive the horsemen's ferocious *güecia* thrusts had to contend with the dismounting horsemen and their lightning *ezpata* strokes. Otsoa's men, who had fought other Batavians only a few weeks earlier, knew how clumsily they wielded their long swords and how their cumbersome shields weighed them down and got in their way. The blonde barbarians were far taller than the Vascons but that only turned out to be to their disadvantage. Deftly parrying the Batavians' sluggish sword strokes, the Vascons wriggled out from under and around their foes' shields with astonishing ease.

By mid afternoon the Vascons had succeeded in stopping the Batavians and the Germans in their tracks. There was gore all around the base of the ramparts, men, mortally wounded, moaning, begging to be put out of their misery. In utter amazement and disbelief, the Romans behind the ramparts watched the Vascons turn the tide of battle. Believing that a whole legion had arrived from Mogontiacum to relieve the Gelduba siege, the beleaguered legionaries took heart, came spilling over the rampart's slopes to help the Vascons finish off the hapless German infantry. Only a few units of the Batavian cavalry managed to escape, galloping off to convey news of their defeat to their general, Civilis, then commanding the siege of nearby Vetera.

Otsoa's men were too exhausted to pursue the fleeing Batavian cavalry. They had accomplished enough for one day and would shortly be joining the battered Sixteenth and Twenty-seventh legions to lift Civilis' siege of Vetera. The reward for the Vascons' gallantry in the field of battle was not long coming. The Legate Antonius Primus himself turned up several weeks later in Mogontiacum to lay the laurels of victory on the Vascon units.

"I knew you had it in you all the time, Prefect" he confessed to Otsoa at the ceremony. "I, personally, commend you for your comportment and gallantry above and beyond the call of duty. Emperor Vespasian sends his salutations. In his name I am authorized to confer Roman citizenship upon you and your Vascon warriors."

Otsoa was deeply touched when Primus laid the olive wreath on his head, pronouncing: "*Civis Romanus es!*" It was the highest honor for a provincial to be named a citizen of the greatest empire on earth. Besides, he thought, it was not everyday one received special commendations from the Emperor himself. Now he could, without reservation, wear that toga he was given in Rome so long ago, it seemed. And, if he so fancied, he could even have a narrow purple ribbon sewn around its neckline to denote his noble station. He was, after all, the lord of Agorreta.

"I will ask you one small favor, my friend," said Otsoa. "We have been away from home for a long time now. I request that you grant us leave to return to our families in the upland valleys of Vasconia."

"Request granted!" replied the Legate without hesitation. "But on one condition: you must come to Rome again one day soon. Our Emperor Vespasian has ordered the construction of the biggest circus in the Empire. He's going to call it the 'Colosseum' since it's being built on the spot where Nero's colossal statue now stands."

"Agreed," said Otsoa, smiling at his friend's thoughtfulness. He would never forget the hospitality he had shown him when he was in Rome. "But I also want *you* to visit me in Agorreta the next time you come to see your relatives in Toulouse. It's only a short hop from there, you know."

They clasped arms and went their separate ways, one to his giant columns, the other to his upland meadows.

Chapter 11

The Fair and the Swarthy

711 AD

Itziar poked dispiritedly at the turnips boiling in the copper kettle hanging from the hearth, checking to see if they were done. She could hear the wind moaning outside, drawing the smoke up the chimney in short, fitful gasps. The kitchen was the only place in the house cozy enough for her to shed her heavy woolen shawl without discomfort; there would be enough shivering later that evening, when she crawled under bed sheets so cold they would feel wet. Agorreta was such a misty-cold place in the winter, she reflected moodily. But there were more disquieting problems than the weather to worry about these days. The inhabitants of the hamlet's half dozen *caserios* huddling round the square hoped that the remoteness of their village would provide some refuge against the latest invasion threat.

"Father Lucas says life used to be so placid around here during Roman times," remarked Itziar distractedly, repeating something from her pastor's latest sermon.

Sitting at the other end of the hearth, lost in a blur of knitting needles and mumbled prayers, Doña Inés appeared to pay little attention to her daughter's grumbling.

"He says even a secluded village like this would be at risk if the Muslims decide to keep pushing north," rambled Itziar, trying to catch her mother's attention. "I wonder why things always have to change for the worse."

"Empires tend to grow soft after a while, then drop of their own weight, like ripe figs," observed her mother pithily.

Wrapped in a charcoal-gray shawl, graying hair done up in a bun, there was a sober, dignified elegance about the lady of the manor that Itziar had always envied and admired. Patrician, that was the word she was looking for to describe her mother. After all these many years, her mind still clicked away as nimbly as her knitting needles, her remarks always brief and to the point. "Even from the beginning the Goths were disorganized," she continued. "They get so tied up in their own sophisticated laws that the first barbarian that happens along topples them over with a mere sneeze. Look what's happening to them now!"

"Yes," admitted Itziar balefully. "At this rate they'll last even less than the Romans did!" Itziar's frown revealed her displeasure at her own unguarded admission. "My fiancé, Edilbert, always worried about his king's weakness. That half-hearted attempt of his to subdue the pagans in Baztan was pitiful. All he managed to do was anger the natives. Now the good king's gone and disappeared!"

An army of North Africans had landed in the southern tip of the Iberian Peninsula scarcely a month earlier, soundly thrashing King Roderick's Visigoth army at the embarassing battle of Guadalete. Rumors of treason among the Goth generals failed to explain the shocking defeat at the hands of an undisciplined Moorish rabble. The Goths may have been caught napping this time, acknowledged the stunned citizenry, but, even off guard they were still a foe to be reckoned with. Compounding the military disaster was king Roderick's mysterious disappearance after the turning point battle. Battered and bereft of leadership, his army left the peninsula wide open to the invaders.

Itziar's beau, Edilbert, was an officer in the Visigoth palace guard in Pamplona. Her father, Andoni de Agorreta, still rued the day he asked her to accompany him on one of his calls on the Visigoth Administration in the capital to settle yearly fiscal accounts with his overlords. Having met casually, the young couple had fallen madly in love, their attraction blossoming into nuptial plans at a pace far too unseemly for the lord of Agorreta. Now hardly a week passed without Edilbert's stopping by at her father's mountain manor to pay court to his beloved. Andoni de Agorreta had serious misgivings about the upcoming nuptials, reluctant to accept the inevitable union between his daughter and a foreigner. "He's a nice enough fellow," admitted Doña Inés, when they were alone. "Tall, strong, always a pleasant smile, everything one expects from a lovesick Visigoth."

Sternly pursing his lips, Andoni grumbled: "But he's still a Goth!"

Throughout the ages, the Vascons had managed to stave off every invading army that had come tramping over the Pyrenean passes, stubbornly refusing to be subdued. When all else failed, they would retreat to their jagged heights, where, in the hush of their communal gatherings, they would revive memories of a promise made long ago by their ancestors to maintain their sacred independence. The Visigoths, like all the other preceding invaders, despaired of ever subduing the recalcitrant lot. Exasperated and at wits' end, they had resigned themselves to leaving the unfriendly mountain folk to their own wiles, warily avoiding their inhospitable uplands.

Unlike the unruly inhabitants of the *Saltus Vasconum*, as the Romans described the Pyrenean high country, their brethren in the southern flatlands never greatly minded mingling with foreigners. They had been doing it for generations, bowing and scraping to Celts and Romans, or anyone else who happened to take a liking to their fertile river valley. From such unseemly dalliances a generation of half-breeds had sprung up to control the rich Ebro lowlands, some even rising to positions of prominence in the Visigothic administrations of Tudela, Jaca, even Pamplona. Such indecorous fraternization had started to make inroads even in the inviolate mountain uplands. Indeed, for Andoni de Agorreta, it could not have hit closer to home; he was about to lose a daughter to a Goth! And it rankled more than he cared to admit.

"What will become of you and Edilbert if the Moors succeed in beating back the Goths and, God forbid, take over our land?" asked Doña Inés, looking up briefly from her knitting.

"They will not be defeated!" retorted Itziar huffily, with more hope than conviction. "The Goths beat the so-called 'invincible' Roman legions once, didn't they?" she offered limply. "How can a ragtag horde of North Africans possibly best them?"

Being on the verge of marrying one, she could not abide ill rumors to be spread about the Visigoths. Their four century-old rule over Iberia had been a benevolent one, she replied to anyone who cared to listen, despite anecdotal stories about their early barbaric comportment. They had shown only kindness and fairness to her people. Her coming marriage to a Visigoth would prove her people's animosity towards them unfounded.

"Settle down, young lady," counseled her mother in her soothing voice. The fire in her daughter's cerulean-blue eyes mirrored the passion in her heart. Outrage, reflected the old woman, only seemed to enhance her already-striking beauty. Itziar had always been her favorite offspring, admired for her grit and determination. She was like her in so many ways, sometimes headstrong, occasionally docile, never willful. Tact had not been one of her daughter's strong suites, never having quite learned to smother her dislikes, always saying it as she saw things, sometimes at the price of peace and harmony. Her tall, imposing figure had intimidated local prospective suitors. It was fortunate that she had met one even taller than she, reflected her mother, even if he was not one of them. But Itziar was a woman of strong convictions and there was little doubt in Doña Inés' mind as to who would rule the roost in her daughter's home when she married.

"Your brother Gori disapproves of your friend, you know," said Doña Inés, trying to deflect the predictable barbed response. "He doesn't think much of the way King Roderick laid into those poor Baztanese."

"What does Gori know about such things?" snapped Itziar, chiding her mother for bringing up a sore point. "You named him appropriately enough, you know. He *is* a firebrand, through and through! Someday they'll find him in a ditch with a *güecia* through his heart."

"That was unkind and uncalled for," admonished her mother. "You must admit, the Goths have been a little heavy-handed with the Baztanese."

"Pagans!" retorted Itziar petulantly, her face flushed with irritation. "They deserved their comeuppance, with all their witches and trolls and forest genies. Anyway, they won't have king Roderick to kick around any more. From what I hear, he may have disappeared for good. Now those Vascon heathen will have to worry about the Moors instead. That should keep them busy!"

"That'll keep *all* of us occupied," remarked her motherly prophetically.

It was snowing the day Father Lucas joined the young couple in holy matrimony. The small family affair was held in the hamlet's tiny chapel, with only a handful of close relatives in attendance. Marrying a foreigner, even if he were a friendly Visigoth, was not an event to brag about to their proud Vascon friends and neighbors. The fewer bells rung, the better, mulled Andoni morosely. Itziar would leave for Pamplona with her husband after the ceremony and the whole unpleasant affair would soon blow over, be forgotten. She wasn't going to inherit his lands and his flocks, anyway, reasoned the lord of the manor. Her older brother Gori was in line for that honor, as tradition prescribed. She would get a handsome dowry and that would be all. That was the law of the Vascons.

Itziar looked radiant in her wedding gown, its white train trailing along behind her as she walked up the aisle to the altar. A simple tiara of winter hyacinths held a veil to her gold locks. Her oval face reflected a hint of nobility, the proud legacy of her father's lordship of all the neighboring mountain valleys. She was nineteen, a ripe age for these undertakings but she was not going to worry about that any more. She had skirted spinsterhood, snagged a perfectly marriageable man, and that, in the end, was what counted. Besides, he was as devout a Christian as she, and those qualifications were hard to come by in her land these days.

Standing at the foot of the altar, decked in military regalia, the bridegroom smiled broadly at his approaching bride. The red sash draped across his white Palace Guard tunic and the sheathed ceremonial sword hanging from his belt gave him a certain panache. His gray-blue eyes and tow-headed locks spilling over his robe's fur collar proudly proclaimed his Germanic ancestry. But it was his broad, serene forehead and square jaw that revealed his inner strength and resolve. After all, it took nerve to snatch the wolf's daughter from its very lair. But Itziar was well worth the trouble. He had never met one like her before and knew, from the very beginning, that he would marry no other.

Itziar's parents knelt on the front pew, at the foot of the altar, attired in their Sunday's best. The lord of the valley of Esteribar sternly looked on with bruised pride while his wife, Inés, wept silent tears of joy, convinced, despite her husband's reservations, that love transcended all, politics, ethnic differences, everything. Deep in the warm folds of her heart, however, she felt a twinge of sadness for her daughter's insecure future, plunging, as she was, into a maelstrom of uncertainty.

"God help us all!" she mumbled in silent supplication.

It was a brief, uneasy honeymoon for the newlyweds. They had returned to a Pamplona still reeling under the news of the Guadalete disaster as mauled units trickled back every day confirming the magnitude of the debacle. The Visigoth Empire was crumbling under the heels of a swiftly advancing, largely unopposed Moorish cavalry, spreading over the land like an ugly stain. The southern half of the peninsula had already been overrun by the North Africans, now pounding at the gates of Toledo, the once-proud seat of the Visigoth Empire in Iberia. King

Roderick's death had been confirmed, as was the treasonous comportment of one of his generals during the battle.

War psychosis was rampant in the Vascon capital. The shrewd Tarik was trying to talk resisting Visigoths into peaceful submission. Those who put down their arms were allowed to keep their lands, albeit at the price of onerous taxes. Despite the inducement, many abandoned their possessions and streamed north, fleeing the Islamic yoke. There was talk of retreating to the northwest, there to regroup with other Visigoth units to fight another day from the impregnable mountains of Cantabria.

"It's ironic, isn't it," commented Itziar, as they sat in front of the fire one evening, fretting over their uncertain future. "The Visigoths may even have to adopt our Vascon hit-and-run tactics. We may have to retreat to Agorreta and fight from there. It'd be a shame to have to forego these fine, comfortable Palace quarters in Pamplona, though."

Her stoic comment reassured her husband, more for its pluck than its military insight. "We'll need more rugged terrain than Agorreta to keep this horde at bay," commented her husband. "From what I hear, their cavalry is superb. They would make short shrift of our defenses there if they drove up from the south, as one would expect them to."

Edilbert had been only recently elevated to the rank of Tiuphate, in command of the elite Regiment of the Royal Guards. Only a month earlier he would not have been able to visualize a Visigoth army in retreat. Defensive tactics were foreign to his men. They had ruled this land for four centuries running, adopted the natives' Roman ways and religion, even intermingled with the natives, although mostly with the friendly southerners. But even the more independent mountain people had grown used to their presence despite the Visigoths' occasional incursion into their pagan, unredeemed hinterlands.

"Besides, I'm not so sure your people are ready to fight shoulder to shoulder with us Visigoths," he added.

"Perhaps the threat of a common enemy will unite us all," remarked Itziar hopefully. "We have a common foe now. True Christians would never dream of renouncing their faith. You must never forget that. Our faith will bring us together against the Moors."

Morale among his elite troops was high at first, despite the fact that there was no longer a monarch to protect. But determination was fickle and the best laid plans had ways of unraveling under pressure. For all the tall talk of unflagging resistance against the North Africans, news of their advance elements' cavalry approaching Pamplona was received with paralyzed indifference by the populace.

Incredibly, muted strains of celebration could be heard wafting out of the Juderia district. The local Jews were anticipating that the Moors would end their miserable existence in the ghetto and stamp out pogroms once and for all. Adding to the malaise among the Visigoth troops stationed in the Pamplona citadel was news of a peaceful and uncontested incursion of Tarik's Berbers in the Ebro river valley. Rumors were rampant about one of their own Visigoth noblemen, Count Casius, lord of Borja, shamelessly consorting with the enemy, even toying with the idea of abjuring his Christian faith and converting to Islam.

"There is talk among my superiors about moving out to the Cantabrian Mountains to the west. Duke Fávila is gathering the remnants of the Visigoth army there and plans to retreat to the craggy heights of Asturias. They are rugged people, the Asturs. The Duke thinks he can recruit their warriors and lead them into battle to retake the peninsula. He proposes to fight the Moors from the heights."

Itziar leaned over and kissed her husband softly on the forehead. A sense of pride and admiration welled up inside her, rejoicing at her husband's recent promotion to *Tiuphate*. But even more important to her was his devout Christian faith. She knew he would be willing to die for it, if it came to that. The first glimmer of a Crusade was dawning in the consciousness of both Visigoths and Vascons. Itziar was immensely proud of the fact that her Edilbert would spearhead that Crusade, push the heathen back to where they came from.

"If my unit has to abandon Pamplona to fight elsewhere, it would be best if you returned to Agorreta. You'll be safer there than in Pamplona. I'll send for you as soon as things simmer down."

The peremptory tone of his voice surprised her. It sounded almost like a military order, something she was not used to hearing. In a way, the abruptness of his decision gratified her. A Tiuphate, after all, was supposed to be forceful, sound martial. But she couldn't help feeling a sudden pang of sadness and alarm on realizing that she and her husband could part ways. Despite having married a soldier, she had never considered that possibility. She had, after all, taken an oath to be at his side in sickness and in health, had she not? Besides, she had been hoping to become pregnant by now and separation would not help bring that about.

"I will go wherever you go," she said with a finality that surprised him. Her pursed lips and steady gaze told him that she was not dissembling. "Others will bring their families with them," she reasoned. "I will be no trouble, I assure you. Besides, I can wield a spear like any man. You know that." Itziar had once shown him the way upland shepherds flung their *güecias* at wolves threatening their flock, whirling the barbed iron staff around before releasing it with deadly force and accuracy. He had been awed by the demonstration, as by her ensuing comment: "They spear enemies the same way, you know."

"I do not want to risk your life in this adventure," he answered firmly. "Women do not belong in the battlefield. You will be safer in Agorreta. Please don't make things harder for me, I implore you."

"For me it is not an adventure," she answered with grim resolve. "I will fight for my faith and die for it, if need be. I have no business in Agorreta any more. Wherever you go, I follow."

Edilbert had never seen this facet of his wife's grit and determination before. The fiery conviction in her eyes reflected the steely resolve in her heart. Stories were still rife about Christian martyrs calmly facing the lions at the Roman games in the Colosseum. They must have looked just like his Itziar did now, peaceful, determined, almost looking forward to the dreadful encounter. It became clear to him that she was not to be denied. After a long, thoughtful pause, he said:

"You cannot even imagine military hardship, my beloved. It is not just the agony and the glory of war that you hear from the lips of returning warriors. What remains unsaid is the weariness of endless marches, the foodless days, the cramped quarters, the lack of privacy. Mercifully forgotten are the sleepless nights on the hard earth, the cutting wind, the remorselessly bitter cold, the terror of battle. War, my dear, is no picnic," he added, mindful of the tough road ahead. "It will not be an easy life for you, my love."

Hearing no response from her pursed lips, he added resignedly: "I will make arrangement for you to accompany me if you must."

"Whither thou goest…" she murmured softly in his ear, turning biblical. "It seems like it was only yesterday we promised to be with each other 'till death do us part.'" Raising herself up on an elbow, she looked him straight in the eye and added: "When we said 'in sickness and in health' we should have added: 'in war and in peace.'"

Edilbert held her tightly to his breast and whispered: "So be it, my love."

Chapter 12

The Moorish Yoke

A clatter of hooves outside her window awoke Itziar with a start. The stream of harsh commands barked out in some foreign tongue alarmed her, despite her husband's reassuring presence close by. Stirred, likewise, to wakefulness, Edilbert voiced his worst fear:

"Muza's Berber cavalry!" he groaned in disbelief. "They must have breached the city's defenses!"

For several weeks now rumors had been flying about Moorish hordes overrunning the nearby Visigoth stronghold of Zaragoza. Pamplona was their next obvious objective. Their scouts had been seen reconnoitering the hills around the city, sizing up the defenders' strength and resolve with desultory probes. "It was only a matter of time," the Tiuphate had admitted dejectedly.

Edilbert's speculation had proven all too prescient. Hours before first light, the North Africans had overpowered the guards at the Citadel's southern gates, spilled into the city's labyrinthine alleys, swiftly suppressed all resistance and took control of the city's key strong points. The suddenness of the operation bewildered Edilbert. Long touted to be impregnable, Pamplona had fallen to the enemy, like the rest of the Visigoth enclaves in the peninsula, with barely a struggle. In a flash of memory, he saw before him the fair land his ancestors had wrested from the Romans, a mere two and a half centuries earlier. It had been ripe for the plucking then. Now, and just as effortlessly, it had fallen under another's sway.

"*Sic transit gloria mundi,*" he muttered under his breath, wryly imagining what the Romans themselves would have remarked, faced with similar disturbing events.

The sounds of fighting in the streets had died down by the time day broke over Mount San Cristobal. Warily at first, the townsfolk ventured out of their homes into the streets to get their first glimpse of the fabled Africans they had been hearing so much about lately. Their worst fears had now turned to reality. Overcome by curiosity, the citizens ogled the swarthy soldiers standing nervous guard at strategic street corners, unsheathed scimitars at the ready. Their flowing, cream-colored *djelabas,* elaborate turbans and red-tasseled *fez* caps gave them a whimsical, almost comical air. It was their leers and lewd remarks that first alarmed the women. Suddenly reminded of the ugly rumors of rape and plunder that had preceded these Africans, the men hurriedly herded their women and children back indoors, away from the sinister looks. Shopping and other outdoor activities would have to wait until things settled down.

The Royal Palace was one of the first buildings to be commandeered by the occupying forces. Summoned to the guardhouse by the Captain of the Guard, Edilbert confronted the dark-complexioned squadron commander with all the hauteur a Teutonic Tiuphate could muster, suspecting all along that it was only a futile gesture. He tried, at first, to pretend not to understand his counterpart's orders until a bookish aide translated them in broken but unequivocal Castilian: Edilbert and his staff were to abandon the premises by noon, surrender their arms and submit unconditionally to the new Islamic order.

Edilbert was stunned by the suddenness with which misfortune had struck. Coming from a warrior caste for which the notion of defeat was anathema, indeed nonexistent in their lexicon, he was now being forced to swallow that most bitter of pills for a military commander: surrender. In the dark recesses of his mind he had reluctantly considered the possibility of a Visigoth defeat but it had been far more sudden than he had expected.

Evacuation orders still ringing in his ears, he was now swept by a wave of shame and anger at his men's feeble resistance to this new occupation. He could only attribute their shameful behavior to the psychosis that had gripped the land ever since their king's shocking defeat at Guadalete almost a year earlier. Morale seemed to crumble after that debacle, the troops never recovering from the shock. Time only seemed to magnify the disaster and the enemy grew twice as formidable as it really was.

Having complied with the abject ceremonial transfer of powers, he now had to face his eviction from the royal palace and start looking for lodgings elsewhere. It was a thoroughly humiliating experience, having to shed his military trappings and change to nondescript civilian garb. His sudden fall from power would elicit pity from friends and family alike, something he was not looking forward to. Just as unpalatable was the scorn his deposition would evoke among both old subordinates and new overlords. Humility, a new and bitter taste in his mouth, would have to be stomached for survival's sake. For Itziar's sake, if for no other, he would have to pretend obsequiousness, revolting though the prospects were.

The harsh occupation measures imposed by the North Africans soon gave rise to a severe malaise among the population. Public meetings were banned, curfews imposed, suspects detained and seldom heard from again. Rumors of torture were rife. Bearing false witness was punishable with forty-nine lashes while calling someone a son-of-a-whore earned him ninety. Though Christian cult was tolerated, the faithful felt the eyes of Moslem surveillance upon them. Many quietly abandoned the city and headed for the hills, leaving behind shuttered businesses and vacant dwellings. For those who chose to remain, food grew scarce, commodity prices soared, basic services evanesced. City life came to a standstill. Save for a few Moorish soldiers strutting about sniffing for trouble, the streets were deserted. An eerie quiet had descended upon the capital of the Vascons.

The option of scurrying off to Agorreta, a defeated man, was unpalatable to Edilbert. He would remain in the city for as long as he could and wait for developments to unfold. He had visions of quietly pulling his old Regimental staff together. They and the stragglers from the southern armies may have been demoralized but a few encouraging words would stiffen their resolve. He was convinced that a credible resistance against a weak occupation force could be cobbled. But those plans would have to wait. There were other more pressing things to do now.

Thanks to his loyal adjutant's connections in town, Edilbert was able to find a vacated flat in the once-teeming district of Navarreria. The dank attic apartment perched atop a dilapidated tenement building was a far cry from the palatial quarters he had just vacated, but it would have to suffice. With characteristic zest, Itziar rolled up her sleeves and plunged into the daunting task of cleaning up the appallingly dingy abode.

"*Eskoba bat euriko banu zenbat gauza eskobatuko nuke!*" she said, bragging about the clean up job she could accomplish had she but a proper broom.

Edilbert observed her with mounting respect for the way she lent meaning to her favorite adage about how work ennobled, never demeaned. Her genteel birth had not exempted her from menial chores around the house, a habit that would now stand her in good stead. Her brief hiatus at palace had not dulled her old workaday habits. Edilbert recalled, with some bemusement, the impish delight she took in shocking her stuffy Visigoth acquaintances with stories about her stints as milkmaid's aide and cook's assistant when she was growing up. Any woman who looked down on such earthy errands, she liked to remind her stuffy friends, was but half a woman, a statement that had raised not a few eyebrows among her pretentious women acquaintances.

Edilbert, in contrast, had always lived the life of leisure. Born in the lap of luxury, he had never wanted for anything. There was always someone ready to do the work for him. He had been coddled by a succession of servants, from nursemaids and preceptors to lackeys and adjutants, all handsomely paid to do his bidding. His father had drummed into him the lofty notion that he was a born leader, not a follower. And though his forebear had, so far, been proven right, the Moors had suddenly changed all that, pulled the rug from under him, so to speak, even robbed him of his career. For the first time in his life he had to worry about the future's vagaries, agonize about where his next meal would come from.

"Perhaps you could try your hand at teaching," Itzibar suggested cheerily, as she wiped some cobwebs from the ceiling. "You're good with children and you have so much to teach them."

"Yes," he remarked sardonically, "martial arts! Our African friends would just love that!"

The bitterness in his voice saddened Itziar. She had never seen him this despondent before. Men were so sensitive about their maleness, she reflected. So deeply ingrained was their need for assertiveness that they felt emasculated if their authority were ever questioned. The instinct had to be as primal in them as motherhood was to women. Perhaps that was as it should be. After all, she thought, it was only yesterday they were hunting mastodon and wrestling with cave bears!

Hoping to distract him from his despondency, she suggested he help fix leaks, mend a door hinge, replace some broken windowpanes. Frustrated at first by his unfamiliarity with such menial chores, he soon rose to the challenge and actually began to enjoy the novelty of fixing broken things with his own hands, delighting in being useful around the house for a change. Immersed in their separate chores, they happened to look up to see the other involved in domestic activity. The stark contrast with their pampered existence at Palace made them break out in shared laughter.

"We've come a long way, haven't we?" mocked Edilbert, casting a sharp glance at a mouse scampering under a kitchen cabinet. "I only hope your father doesn't come visiting any time soon!"

Itziar chuckled at the thought, happy to note her husband's recovering sense of humor. "Look at it this way, my love," she said. "The place may be wretched but it will provide the anonymity an ex-Tiuphate needs in these unsettled times. Nobody will come looking for us here!"

She had reason for concern.

The skittish North Africans had begun to worry about their tenuous hold on the city. Tarik had not been forthcoming with his promised reinforcements. Muza's undermanned squadron could barely control the natives' growing unrest, their numbers swelling daily with the steady influx of Visigoth stragglers drifting into Vasconia and Cantabria from the south. Some proud Goths had preferred eviction from their lands in *al-Andalus* to servility under the new Moorish order and had fled north, hoping to escape the heavy North African yoke. The ferment of discontent already brewing among the Vascons was only stirred up by the new arrivals' grumbling.

"The only thing this seething rabble needs to boil over," commented Muza morosely to his second in command, "is for a leader to whip it into shape and start an insurgency right here under our very noses."

Sharing his superior's concern about the brewing mischief, his lieutenant replied: "They may have surrendered their arms," he remarked, "but the seditious lot remains haughty and stiff-necked. They need their self-esteem knocked down a few notches."

Muza nodded in agreement. Mulling over his officer's suggestion, he shortly arrived at a series of draconian measures: "Order their taxes redoubled," he said. "Also," he added, with a gleam in his eye, "hangings will henceforth be conducted in the public square." Finally, with a devilish smile, he concluded: "Special surveillance units will be established to monitor all subversive activity. Any incipient rebellion will be nipped in the bud!"

The lieutenant regarded his commander dubiously. "Those are excellent measures, Sir, but they'll require twice the manpower we have available," remarked the concerned officer. "There's barely enough troops to control the population, as is."

"The Jews will help," responded Muza, stroking his goatee thoughtfully. "They're already doing it elsewhere."

Capitalizing on the 'outsider' status they shared with their new overlords, the Jews of *al-Andalus* had wormed their way into positions of prominence in the new Moorish Administration, were delegated tax-collecting authority, assigned undercover intelligence responsibilities. The diligence and assertiveness with which they were carrying out their new mission had turned them into effective

Moorish allies, arousing no small ill will among the Christian population. The Visigoth elite, in particular, had attracted the unwelcome attention of those who, only yesterday, had suffered pogroms and ghettoes at their hands. Tables thus turned, the new bureaucrats were eagerly exacting the loathed *jaray* taxes levied on their erstwhile overlords' property, without forgetting the even more onerous *yizia* income dues. "Yes," concluded Muza, "they will help us too. There are plenty of them in the Juderia district of town who'll jump at the opportunity."

It was a month into Edilbert's forced retirement when his savings were finally depleted. Itziar had kept busy keeping house, earning pocket change knitting socks and sweaters, altering clothes for her acquaintances, while her husband had lain about listlessly, growing increasingly depressed by his inactivity. Planning rebellions was a worthy cause but even that was turning out to be an exercise in futility. His friends and old associates agreed in principle with his seditious project but were fearful of conspiratorial meetings. It was time to put those schemes aside and start looking for a new job, Edilbert decided. He had mulled long and hard over his wife's suggestion that he turn to pedagogy, concluding in the end that it was the best of his few remaining options. It would not only put food on the table, it would provide a good cover for the subversive activities he was planning to pursue.

Schools in the city had remained closed since the occupation. Parents, anxious for a respite from their restive wards' increasing unruliness, were eager to find any docent center willing to take their boys off their hands, knock some learning and discipline into them. A teacher with established military credentials fit their requirements to a tee. It did not take Edilbert long to gather under his wing a clutch of keen, restless adolescents from well-off families, eager to go back to the joys of male camaraderie, despite the related agony of Latin and Mathematics, Geography and Religion.

The highlight of their scholastic day was the supervised sports and drills held in an abandoned back lot nearby, playing soldiers far from view, or earshot, of curious Moors or their minions. His school would serve as the training grounds for a new generation of future patriots, fancied Edilbert. He could not command a Regiment these days but he would surreptitiously train the future officers that he would one day lead into battle against the Moors. It was a devilishly clever scheme, he admitted to himself.

Shortly after dinner, several months into the academic year, there was a knock at the door in the Navarreria attic apartment.

"I am Ibrahim Sidonia," rasped a hunched-over old man with rheumy eyes and a thatch of mousy hair. Two other men of equally disreputable demeanor stood behind him, looking on threateningly. "We are from the Civilian Enforcement arm of the local Constabulary, here to conduct an interrogation."

"Yes?" replied Edilbert icily, towering above his three visitors. He had heard of this nefarious group and knew, right off, that he was in some sort of trouble.

Signaling with a frown his displeasure at not being asked in, the old man rasped officiously: "It has come to our attention that you have recently organized a school for children of the well-to-do." Observing Edilbert's assenting nod, he continued: "We've also been apprised of the fact that you are indulging in subversive activities with these children."

"Since when has teaching the Classics been considered a subversive activity?" replied Edilbert sheepishly, eyebrows raised in feigned surprise.

"There's nothing wrong with the Classics," replied the old man. "It is the military drills that are proscribed. We have heard the children marching around the compound to the cadence of martial fifes and drums. These activities must stop immediately or there will be serious consequences to you and to your family," he barked shrilly. Without waiting for a reply, the three unsavory characters turned around and disappeared into the night.

The incident stunned Edilbert. His wife, who had been eavesdropping on the conversation, was thoroughly shaken by the exchange. Henceforth, he promised her, he would limit his martial arts lessons to theory. Instead of all those drills, he would teach them how to play chess; that should drill some stratagem into those young minds. And, yes, in future, he would have to be careful with the snoops from the Constabulary.

They would not be his only tormentors. There were Vascons, as well, who regarded Edilbert with jaundiced eye. Still smarting from King Roderick's military forays to smoke out pagans from their Pyrenean hinterlands weeks before his Guadalete disaster, some firebrand mountain warlords were still rejoicing at the Visigoths' fall from power. Edilbert suspected that even his own father-in-law might be among those. He had always sensed a certain aloofness in Andoni de Agorreta's dealings with him, the condescending way with which he treated him, giving him his daughter's hand, but only grudgingly, never ever dropping a kind word about the Visigoths. They would always remain anathema to the mountain warlord of the Valley of Esteribar. Old habits died hard with old men, mused Edilbert resignedly.

Thankfully, there were other more discerning Vascons who realized that he had been sympathetic to their cause, all along. After all, had he not married one of them? Sooner or later, he would be useful to their cause against the Moors. He was not only a devout Christian, he was also a professional soldier. They would need his talents to fight the common enemy, someday. They would have to reel him in into their inner sanctum. And while they were at it, they would also conscript some of his students' parents. They would need all the help they could get when hostilities broke out.

But they would have to be circumspect about the way they approached the estranged Visigoth Commander. They were aware that he was being watched by the Moors' sinister Intelligence Branch.

Chapter 13

Cantabria

June 721

Trailing behind a column of Visigoth soldiers marching along the road to Donostia were a dozen rickety carts teetering under the weight of refugees and their few precious belongings. Rumors of the devastation wreaked by Abd-el-Raḥman's hordes in their advance north weighed heavily on their minds, pressing them on at a brisk pace. They knew they would not be safe until they reached the precipitous heights of Cantabria, still some distance away.

Led by Itziar's brother, Gori, a clutch of Vascons from the upland country had decided to join the Visigoth expedition weary of the harsh occupation measures the Moors had imposed on their land. After centuries of vacillation, they had converted to Christianity and decided to link reluctant arms with the Goths to confront the Moors under the emblem of the cross.

It was an improbable alliance from the start. Their joint guerrilla operations against the common enemy had only succeeded in riling up the North Africans, who now harassed them with a vengeance. The abrupt Pyrenean barrier that had kept Celts, Romans, even Germanic barbarians at bay all those centuries past, was now suddenly ineffective against the latest threat. Its gentle piedmont slopes offered scant protection against the new southern menace. Edilbert had long advocated the need for more mountainous terrain to neutralize the Moorish cavalry. He now volunteered to lead the embattled group to the lofty bluffs of Cantabria, a good hundred miles to the west.

The rebellious Goths and Vascons were not the only burr under the Emir's saddle. Just beyond Cantabria, the querulous, still-to-be subjugated Asturians, posed an even more nettlesome challenge to Abd-el-Rahman's dream of a *Pax Musulmana* in the peninsula. For several months now, he'd been toying with the idea of mounting a military operation against the Franks to extend his dominions beyond the Pyrenees but could ill afford to embark on any such adventure while his back remained unprotected. The revolt festering in his own backyard had to be squelched first.

"So, where exactly are we headed?" inquired Itziar distractedly, tilting her broad-brimmed straw hat low against the noonday sun. They had skipped lunch to speed up the march, trying to put all the distance they could between them and the pursuing Moors. But the column of refugees was starting to grow weary and fidgeted for a rest stop. The luscious grapes hanging from the vines along the roadside were particularly tempting that time of day. They would have provided such a lovely snack, thought Itziar, smacking her parched lips in anticipation.

"To the land of the Asturs," responded Edilbert, who rode alongside her. He had not revealed their exact destination to anyone, for fear loose tongues would betray their position to the enemy. Noticing her puzzlement, he elaborated: "Remember how Count Pelayo was apprehended a few years back for refusing to give his sister's hand in marriage to Muza's minion in Asturica Augusta?" Noticing her nod, he continued: "Well, ever since Pelayo's escape from the emir's jail in Córdoba, he's been trying to organize a rebellion against the Moors in the rugged mountains of Asturias, just beyond Cantabria." After a brief pause, he added: "We will join forces with him there."

Pelayo's misadventures with the Moors intrigued Itziar. "I don't understand why the emir has to mount such a powerful expedition just to avenge a jilted lover," she remarked, with feminine sagacity. "I didn't think Moors were *that* touchy about such things, what with their harems, and all."

Edilbert regarded her complaisantly. "After Duke Fávila was murdered," he continued patiently, "Count Pelayo assumed his father's mantle of leadership. The Moors believe that if they can nip his rebellion in the bud, they'll finally control the northern country. Pelayo, you see, *is* the reason for Abd-el-Rahman's campaign, not Munuza's lovesickness."

Itziar remained skeptical. From the very start she had questioned the junket on which they were now embarked. Even an innocent such as she could see that the force her husband had mustered after years of secretive meetings and furtive confabulations in the backstreets of Pamplona, was woefully inadequate against the powerful, well-trained Muslim force now nipping at their heels.

"What can this sorry lot offer Pelayo?" she pursued, waving her hand at the ragtag group of no more than a hundred soldiers her husband was leading. She had not been one to shy away from pointed enquiry before and the oppressive heat was not now conducive to civil niceties. "Are we all going to end up as sacrificial lambs?"

Edilbert detected a hint of reproach in her voice. It was not in his wife's nature to beat around the bush, always going for the jugular of the matter. She should have been born a man, he reflected amusedly; she reasons like one, even expresses herself like one, he ruminated. Only a week earlier, she had questioned the wisdom of their abandoning Pamplona, leaving Casius to run around town, free to plot its take-over. "It's like leaving a fox in a hen house!" she had remarked, darkly auguring that the turncoat Visigoth would end up consolidating the Moors' tenuous hold on Pamplona.

At the time, he wished she hadn't brought up the subject of Count Cassius. It was a sore point with him, seeing that the Count was indirectly responsible for his having lost his teaching job and, with it, his meager income and livelihood. The Count's defection from the Teutonic ranks and subsequent apostasy did not sit well with the Visigoths, mortified as they were by the egregious behavior of one of their own noblemen. His abjuring Christianity to embrace Islam and sidle up to the Moor irritated Edilbert almost as much as his having adopted the ridiculous Arabic surname of "Banu Qasi", just to curry favor with his new masters. Delighted by all the groveling, the Moors had bequeathed him lordship over some choice real estate in Tudela and Pamplona. Not satisfied with the windfall, the impudent Qasi had started angling for the title of "King of Pamplona". Was there no end to the man's gall?

"This ragtag lot may look sorry and bedraggled to you, my dear," acknowledged the Tiuphate after a long hiatus, "but it's what's in their hearts that counts. They're determined to remain free and fight to the death for their freedom and their faith." After another pause, he continued: "As for your sacrificial concerns, I would have you know that there is not a single lamb among these men. They're brave warriors, every single one of them, and they'll make a fine showing in Pelayo's army. He'll be glad to see us join him."

An ineffable feeling of pride slowly welled up inside Itziar. She loved it when her husband got up on his high horse and waxed eloquent like that. A certain gravitas seemed to come over his voice, touching it with a deep, warm resonance that discouraged all argument. Every army, she thought, has a spirit that flowed down from the man the warriors considered their leader. And he had been a good leader, which was why all these men and women had decided to follow him into the unknown, leaving their land and all their worldly possessions behind. She knew that she would always feel safe by his side, even if it meant having to share his pallet in the middle of a battlefield.

"I, too, will be brave when the time comes," she confessed. "I can wield a *güecia* like the best of them," she boasted, referring to the barbed spear shepherds in her land wielded to ward off wolves. Smiling impishly she added: "And I can belt out as ringing an *irrintzi* as any of them!"

"I know your mettle, my love" he said, turning to her, eyes filled with love and warm admiration. Reaching for her hand, he added mockingly: "That's one of several reasons I chose you for a wife. The other is the way you trill those war whoops."

Detecting the teasing in his voice, she quickly withdrew her hand, shot him a furtive glance and broke out in mirthful laughter. She could take it as well as she could dole it out. That, it turned out, was another thing he loved about her.

They had been hugging the Peninsula's northern coastline for several weeks now, traveling through an amiable country of verdant glens and peaceful dales, sheltered by gentle, low-lying hills. Dotting the countryside were seigniorial *caserios*, similar in architecture to theirs back home, except for those *horreo* granaries in their backyards. The structures were built on stilts, Celtic versions of their own *sabaiao* haylofts. The proud, fiercely independent people who inhabited this land spoke a quaint, Cantabrian version of Celtiberian, laced with a few Basque idioms. It did not take Edilbert's men long to realize that these flinty folk despised the Moors almost as much as they, a shared dislike that quickly strengthened bonds of friendship between them.

They first sighted the estuary of the Deva through the haze of a late summer drizzle. The river flowed in placid majesty before funneling through the gauntlet of two truncated hillocks, to rush into the ruffled Atlantic. Puzzled by the enormous iron rings dangling from the outermost rocks of the breakwaters, they were informed by some locals that Roman galleys used to moor there long ago, when they came for blende and cassiterite for Augustus' metal works. The countryside, the locals warned, was crawling with Moors. They were advised to stay clear of their stronghold in Gijon, a fishing village farther up the coast from where patrols occasionally sallied forth in shows of force to "pacify" the countryside. The Devans suggested avoiding any encounters with them in flat, coastal terrain.

"Seek the heights," they counseled. "Their cavalry doesn't do so well up there."

All was not alarms and bad news in the land of the Devans. Edilbert was glad to learn that Abd-el-Rahman had stopped chasing them, unexpectedly veering north with his force to do battle with the Franks beyond the Pyrenees. He had left the mopping-up operation of Pelayo's rebels to Alqama, one of Munuza's trusted lieutenants. This Berber was said to be gathering his forces in Asturica Augusta for a final assault on Pelayo's eyrie.

His more pressing threat thus allayed, Edilbert headed for the sinuously rolling dunes and pine forests that bordered the Devan estuary and gave the order for his Company to set up a bivouac along the banks of the delta. They would remain there the next few days to replenish supplies and get a well-earned rest. A dip in the Atlantic provided the recreation they all sorely needed. Just as welcome was the rare delicacy of fresh seafood and shellfish, so rare farther inland. They danced around the bonfires and played games along the watery coastline of the delta, slept under the starry skies, listened to the hooting of owls, the snorting of deer, the grunting of wild boar, all the night sounds around them. It was a pleasant, restful interlude.

After a few days' rest by the sea, they struck camp and headed south, following the Deva towards its high watery reaches. Edilbert intended to follow it to its confluence with its main tributary, the Cares, a dozen miles farther south, then follow that river westward to its source, high up in the Asturian mountains. Rumor had it that Count Pelayo was holed up somewhere up there with his band of hardy Asturs preparing for the inevitable confrontation with the North Africans. It would be the first determined encounter with the Moors since the disaster at Guadalete a decade earlier.

Snaking along the banks of the Deva, they caught occasional glimpses of vales hidden among the foothills of spectacular, snow-capped mountains, made doubly intimidating because they would soon have to scale them. A friendly shepherd approached them during a lunch break at the fork of the two rivers. The young lad had gone out of his way to greet them, screwing up enough courage to barter several rounds of his fresh goat cheese for a *güecia*. Hoping to gather information about the terrain ahead, Edilbert invited the friendly chap to break bread with them after his business with the troop's quartermaster was concluded. Between mouthfuls of hardtack and *chorizo* sausage, the congenial lad described the lay of the land ahead. He laced his account with snippets of gossip and local lore. Among the bits of information he shared with them was a nugget that perfectly riveted Itziar's attention. There were, he claimed, certain sacred relics hidden in a hermitage not far downriver, brought there for safekeeping from the Moors.

Devoured by curiosity, Itziar asked: "What kind of relics?" A Benedictine friar in a monastery near the delta where they had bivouacked days earlier had mentioned the existence of certain sacred relics tucked away in an ark kept in a hermitage in the valley of Liébana, not far from the foothills of the Picos Range. Among them, he had whispered conspiratorially, was a piece of the cross on which Christ was crucified. Also in the ark, he had heard, was the *sudarium,* the mortuary facecloth with which the Lord's face had been covered when he was brought down from the cross. The shepherd's news seemed to confirm the monk's information. More exhilarating still, the relics were only a few miles away!

"They say it's one of the beams of the Holy Cross," explained the shepherd in hushes, looking around furtively, as if checking for eavesdropping Moors. "People around here say it's the real thing. Some Bishop from Asturica Augusta named Toribio apparently brought it to Toledo from the Holy Land centuries ago. Then, just before the Moors entered Toledo, someone decided to move it from there and bring it here for safekeeping."

"Is the *sudarium* kept there too?" asked Itziar, reasoning that the sacred facecloth deserved equal safekeeping.

"I wouldn't know," replied the shepherd. He had never heard of a *sudarium*, just the piece of the cross. Itziar's insistent questioning had started to make him nervous. Somewhere in the back of his simple mind, the lad began to suspect that this whole subject was too shrouded in secrecy to be shared with perfect strangers, Christians or not. Sensing he'd already revealed enough, the young shepherd stood up abruptly. There were sheep to tend, he said lamely. Clutching his newly acquired *güecia,* he made to leave. With a wave of the hand, he bade the company farewell. *"Bidaia on!"* he exclaimed, wishing them a safe journey.

"*Agur!*" waved Itziar in farewell. "May God be with you."

Even before she spoke, Edilbert knew what his wife's next request would be.

"Please," she implored, "let's follow the Deva for a few more miles. There'll be plenty of time to double back and pick up the Cares later. Pelayo can wait."

Edilbert knew that nothing would keep her from viewing Christendom's holiest relics, especially since they were so close. Christianity may have bided its time sinking roots in her upland country but the fervor with which her people had finally embraced the new religion was probably unequaled among Christ's followers. There would be no denying her this small favor, particularly now that Abd-el-Rahman was no longer nipping at their heels. Besides, he wryly admitted to himself, she would go there by herself, if denied. Itziar was one determined woman, he knew full well. It was best not to tempt fate.

Leaving the Cares tributary behind, they plunged into a deep Deva gorge, which stretched several miles south. Fed by the rains of some high-mountain storm, the turbulent, fast-flowing river spawned mists that coiled upward into the clouds, bowing tree branches with their wet burden, matting grasses in the nearby meadows. For mindless eons, the clamorous, fast-flowing Deva had snaked and twisted through these sheer granite walls, cutting an ever-deepening chasm through them, tearing the Picos range from the sierra of Peña Sagra. Silvery salmon flashed upriver, tempting some of the company to spear a few hefty samples for supper. Worried that the precipitous mountain gap could be the perfect place for a military ambush, Edilbert spurred his mount to a trot. It was not safe to tarry in such a place.

Almost as abruptly as they had plunged into it, the narrow gorge suddenly opened onto a pleasant valley, swaddled in a cirque of majestic mountains, the sylvan scene all wrapped in a profound silence. Except for the riot of poppies dotting the fields of thistle, everything was draped in a vibrant, emerald green, made even more intense by the gentle rain that had started to fall in a soothing patter. Farther on, in the middle of the magic valley, loomed a sleepy hamlet, its slate roofs glistening in the rain. Granite steps lifted the huddle of houses above the cow dung and the soft muck choking its alleys. There was not a soul in sight.

"It must rain here a lot," commented Itziar. "Just like back home, except it isn't even winter yet."

There wasn't a sound anywhere. The village appeared abandoned, yet Itziar felt someone's eyes fixed on her from behind a shutter, just before the shy observer dodged out of sight. Reaching the first house, they climbed its rough-hewn stone steps and knocked on the door. There was a soft shuffling sound inside before the top half of the split level door opened with a teeth-gritting squeak. A man's face loomed out of the dark, eyed them suspiciously. Then, quite unexpectedly, he invited them in, out of the rain.

Accepting the stranger's invitation, Itziar and Edilbert groped their way into the house. As their eyes adapted to the gloom, they noticed a young woman huddled by the fire, an infant suckling at her breast. Still clutching her baby, she rose from her stool and approached them with a mumbled salutation. Noticing Itziar shiver under her wet clothes, she offered her a seat by the fire and a cup of *orujo*. Itziar looked at her husband questioningly. She had never heard of *orujo*.

"Residue dregs for the ungodly," whispered Edilbert in her ear, trying to describe the proffered rustic liquor. Noticing his wife's frown, he clarified: "It's distilled from skins and seeds of grape, after the first pressing." Taking a sip, himself, he whispered hoarsely: "The rotgut cuts like a knife!" Aware of her admonishing look, he added: "We give *orujo* to soldiers in the winter, for breakfast. Fastest way to thaw them out." Itziar was displeased by her husband's insensitive remarks, worried that their hosts would overhear the interchange and take offense.

"We're looking for the hermitage of Liébana," announced Edilbert, presently. "We come from afar to join forces with Lord Pelayo in his struggle against the Moors. We have come out of our way to pay our respects to the holy relics kept in the hermitage."

The couple regarded their visitors in troubled silence, distrust plainly written on their faces. Outsiders weren't even supposed to know about the sacred relics. And yet, these strangers didn't look heathen. Indeed, they claimed to be Christian, like them. They spoke with a strange accent but referred to the holy relics with due reverence. More to the point, they had come from far away to fight the unbelievers. Those were good enough credentials for them.

After a brief, whispered consultation between them, the husband finally said:

"The hermitage you seek lies three hours away from here, up those mountains," he said, pointing west with a crooked thumb. "The road is steep, the climb perilous in the rain. You must be careful!"

That was it! They had stumbled upon the information they were seeking. Downing the rest of his *orujo*, Edilbert rose to leave. "You wouldn't happen to know where we could find Lord Pelayo, would you?"

The man's rheumy eyes darted over to his wife, again seeking counsel. Noticing her nod, he volunteered: "Last we heard he was holed up in the mountains overlooking the Cangas valley. That's west of the Picos," he explained. "That range over there," he added, pointing to the high mountains overlooking the hamlet. "Your easiest way there would be to double back up the Deva gap whence you came and follow the Cares west."

Edilbert thanked him for the information and clasped the man's arm in farewell.

"I wish you luck, my friend," said Edilbert.

"Say a prayer for us at the shrine," answered the peasant's wife. "*Vayan con Dios!*"

Chapter 14

▼

The Hermitage

August 721

Only a handful of men accompanied Edilbert and Itziar on their side trip to the hermitage. A glance at the daunting peaks was enough to discourage the others from joining them on their mystical errand, choosing, instead, to remain behind and wait for their commander's return. There would be plenty of time for prayer on the battlefield in the days ahead.

It was not a leisurely climb. The wind had turned waspish, tugging and irritable, cold one moment, benign the next. The distended skies failed to shed their burden of water, dripping an occasional tear or two, no more. Clambering up the forbidding goat path, Itziar tried to avoid looking up at the heights for fear she'd lose heart and desist in her attempt. She struggled up the slippery trail, breathing in the dank coils of mist swirling around her, certain at times that she could hear the rocks groaning under her feet. But it was only the surrounding silence she heard, the stillness so intense she felt it would shatter at any moment.

A magnificent view awaited them at the top. The skies above had suddenly cleared, sunlight dancing on the shoulders of a clean, scented wind. A snow-powdered plain stretched out before them, shimmering in the sun. Beyond it, lofty peaks punched through to a sky so utterly azure Itziar could find no words to describe it. And, there, sitting self-consciously in the middle of the glistening plateau, was the hermitage they had come so far to visit. The sober elegance of its stark, rectilinear lines proclaimed its sanctity to the uncaring emptiness around. The masons who had chiseled its rough-hewn granite stones were mere peasants, glad to abandon the glebe for a few crumbs of bread to build a simple edifice that would proclaim their uncomplicated faith, like a quiet voice sighing in the wilderness.

They approached the main door with a sense of trepidation. The knocker's loud clap reverberated in some inside corridor, followed shortly after by a muted shuffling of feet. Hesitantly, the heavy oak door swung open, its hinges groaning in rusty complaint. The young, peach-fuzzed face of a postulant appeared, squinting against the light. Attired in brown sackcloth, the tonsured novice did not look a day over twelve.

A bright smile broke over his innocent face, reflecting his unalloyed joy at seeing other human beings come visit their solitary abode. "*Pax vobiscum,*" he said, in a small voice. Anticipating their request, the young brother invited them in and led them through a dark, narrow corridor to his prior's cell.

"Ah, yes, the holy relics," exclaimed the rotund friar almost jovially, sounding like someone delighted by the unexpected visit of old friends. "Few come to venerate them any more," he lamented, "what with Moors prowling around, trying to destroy them." Holding Itziar and Edilbert by the arm, he ushered them out of his confining quarters, said: "Come, I'll show them to you." The young apprentice who had welcomed them had been waiting dutifully outside the prior's cell door. "Beatus," said the Abbot, addressing him, "lead us to the crypt and give me a hand with the lock."

Groping their way tentatively down a spiral staircase, they followed the firebrand-wielding Beatus to the bowels of a murky basement. The stale air inside had the unmistakable smell of cobwebs and dank age. Ducking under the low ceiling, they wove their way around stunted columns, each capped by its unique capital, adorned with phantasmagoric figures of goblins and satyrs, sculpted by some whimsical artisan, centuries earlier. A stark, solitary stone altar stood in the center of the dank crypt with a large wooden ark resting on it. Its dark, moth-eaten oak boards, corroded hinges and primitive lock all spoke of a bygone era. Its archaic workmanship reminded Itziar of something Joseph, the carpenter himself, would have lovingly crafted to hold his adoptive Son's mortuary mementos.

The thought of seeing, perhaps even touching, the sacred relics, made her come alive with anticipation. Lost in a mystic spell, she bowed her head in abject humility, dropped to her knees and whispered in awed reverence: "The Holy of Holies!"

"Yes," echoed the Abbot, touched by the woman's faith. Fumbling with the lock's mechanism, he said: "Bishop Toribio brought this ark from Jerusalem to Toledo several centuries ago. Then, just as the Moors were about to overrun the

Imperial City, one of his priests brought it to Monte Sacro, near Oviedo, for safekeeping. When the Moors caught wind of it, we had to find a safer place. That's when it was brought here."

Edilbert and Itziar peered inside the ark when the lid was finally pried open. Lying on the bottom, was a plain, two foot-long cedar beam. It didn't look like much at first, but when it dawned on Itziar that she had been redeemed by the One who'd been nailed to that very piece of wood, she was dumbstruck. Peering intently at the beam, she thought she detected a ruddy stain around a deep indentation near one of the ends of the beam. An ineffable wave of love and compassion swept over her. This was not the blood of so many sacrificial consecrations, she reflected. This was the real, the original thing! An irrepressible desire to run her fingers over the stained hole gripped her, but a soft, inner voice told her that it was too holy an object to touch. Someone had once been struck down for laying unclean hands on the Ark of the Covenant, she vaguely remembered. The sobering thought dampened her urge, stayed her hand. If it was not right then, she reasoned, it would still not be right today.

Edilbert's voice snapped her out of her reverie. "What is this cloth?" he was asking the Abbot, pointing to a frayed linen rag, carefully folded at the foot of the ark, tucked next to the wooden beam.

"That is the *sudarium*," responded the Abbot, almost reverently. "Jewish custom prescribed that the face of the deceased be covered soon after death, as a sign of respect. Jesus' was no exception. This was his mortuary facecloth. You can distinctly see his blood stains on it."

Itziar leaned over for a closer look. As her eyes grew accustomed to the dark, she detected a stain of variegated hues of russet and old ivory imprinted on the coarse linen cloth. They were, the Abbot assured them, emanations from the mouth and nose of the recently crucified Lord. Several small, rust-colored spots above the large central stain caught Itziar's attention. "Might these be the imprints of the wounds from the crown of thorns?" she asked, pointing at the small pinprick stains.

"We haven't figured those out yet," replied the Abbot, with refreshing candor, "but they could well be what you suggest."

After the viewing had concluded and the ark was locked back up, the group knelt before it to pray a *paternoster* before parting. An indefinable sense of peace flooded over Itziar. This may not have been the promised Second Coming, she reflected, but it was close enough. The young apprentice friar kneeling next to her was absorbed in other, more apocalyptic reflections on Second Comings. For some time now, and unbeknownst to his Abbot, he'd been having recurring visions of searing fires and raining brimstone, of the pestilence and the hunger and the ruin that would precede the return of the One whose blood they had just venerated. Beatus would one day write about it, famously, in one of the carrels of the monastery his Abbot was just then planning to erect on the very grounds of that hermitage.

On the way out, Edilbert asked the Abbot if he happened to know of Pelayo's whereabouts.

"We've noticed a lot of military activity in the valley lately," said the friar, noncommittally. Sensing that no harm could come from sharing the information with a Visigoth Tiuphate, he added, less diffidently, now:

"If you keep walking east along the high valley of the Deva, the road eventually comes to an end at the foot of Peña Vieja. That's the tallest mountain around here. You can't miss it." Lowering his voice conspiratorially, he whispered: "I've heard that Pelayo likes to hang around there."

Edilbert thanked the Abbot for the invaluable information. The mystical detour they had taken would, fortuitously, lead them to Pelayo! Now, they wouldn't have to double back up to the Cares, on a wild goose chase. Realizing that he had Itziar to thank for this piece of good luck, he bent over, on the spur of the moment, and kissed her lightly on the cheek. Flustered, at first, by his unexpected public show of affection, she acknowledged it with a graceful smile. Edilbert was always surprising her with his impulsive gestures of endearment.

Bidding the Abbot and brother Beatus farewell, they slipped back down the mountain path to the awaiting company. *Orujo* had been flowing freely during their absence and the men were feeling no pain or discomfort, giggling unsteadily under the soft drizzle. Annoyed by the breakdown in discipline, Edilbert had to be mollified by his wife, who teasingly reminded him that he had no clay tablets to break, this time around. The Mosaic simile made him chuckle. Though hating to admit it openly, he knew that this woman was an unmitigated blessing, that he couldn't have come this far without her moral support and irrepressible sense of humor.

The troop struck out at first light the next morning, heading west along the high Deva valley, in search of Pelayo. Halfway up the trail to Peña Vieja, just this side of the tiny hamlet of Cosgaya, a band of unfriendly Cantabrians bristling with crossbows, jumped out of the bushes, cutting off any further progress. The pack of apparent outlaws demanded an explanation for their presence there. Edilbert's calm, soothing ways defused the rude militiamen's belligerence, assuring them that they were all on the same side of the fence in this conflict against the heathen. The crusty mountain men thus momentarily appeased, Edilbert asked them about Pelayo's whereabouts.

Gruffly, and still on the defensive, the band's leader retorted that Pelayo's whereabouts were none of his concern. Besides, he admitted, the Count had not been in this neck of the high valley for quite some time now. Noticing Edilbert's disappointment, the Cantabrian chieftain relented.

"I have disturbing news for you," he said ominously. "A Moorish reconnaissance patrol has been sighted riding up the Deva gorge early this morning. They're headed this way, could be here before sundown." Peevishly, he added: "At first we thought you were they."

"We came through that gorge only yesterday!" Edilbert blurted out, recalling, with a shudder, his premonition of an ambush in that dreadful chasm.

Itziar, who had overheard the exchange, interrupted: "What about the Ark?" she exclaimed in wide-eyed alarm. "We've got to rescue it!"

The band of rude mountain men turned to the woman, irritation plainly etched on their craggy faces. One could almost read their thoughts: women didn't give orders in Cantabria, they remained quietly in the kitchen. Just as they were about to voice their contempt, their tall group leader raised his hand to stifle the grumbling. In a voice clearly accustomed to command, he said: "The woman is right. We can't let the Moors get their hands on the holy relics. We've got to do something before they get to the hermitage of San Martin."

Edilbert knew he had to take control of the situation, being the senior—and only—military officer in the odd gathering. Groping for the right words, he addressed the leader of the agitated Cantabrians: "We need better intelligence about the approaching force," he said, calmly. "I'll send scouts to reconnoiter. In the meantime, my force will double back to the hermitage and await developments there. If the Moorish scouts turn out to be an advance party of a larger force, we'll have to retreat to Peña Vieja, perhaps even beyond." Then, as an afterthought, he added: "With the relics, of course."

The flinty Cantabrians exchanged bewildered looks, still trying to figure out the chain of command. Only recently, they had acquiesced and let another glib Visigoth lead them in their uprising against the Moors. They had second thoughts about letting yet another foreigner give them orders now. And yet, though this tall Visigoth lacked Pelayo's blue-blooded credentials, he seemed to be a professional soldier. What he proposed made perfectly good sense. After another round of shifty looks and mumbled deliberations, the Cantabrians finally agreed to let the Visigoth commander act on his proposed plan. Left unsaid in all their hand-wringing was that they had precious few other options, their puny force being hopelessly outnumbered by the Visigoths'.

Edilbert's company fell back toward the hermitage, trudging past the same tawdry hamlets they had left behind earlier that morning. A few grubby Cantabrians stood outside their hovels, suspiciously eyeing them as they marched by. As she watched them, Itziar felt a sudden pang of compassion for the utter dearth of joy in these people's existence, their grinding poverty, their inability to even wonder why civilization had passed them by. Why, she pondered, would anyone want to live in this misbegotten place, anyway? As if to add injury to insult, the poor devils now had to worry about marauding Moors.

The white, muffled call of the snow-capped mountains beckoned more insistently now. But it was pointless to hurry the ascent with women and children in tow. Carts and wagons would have to be temporarily abandoned. Someone even suggested leaving the weak and the infirm behind with a detachment of soldiers. Edilbert promptly stifled the idea; there would be no splitting up of the group. They would all survive, or die, together.

Darkness had fallen by the time they reached the hermitage. When Beatus opened the door, he was surprised by the unexpected return of the Visigoths. So many mouths to feed, he fretted. But it was the news about the approaching infidels that truly worried him. The friars had always lived in dread of such a possibility. God, who had always provided solutions to their problems, would do so again, reflected Beatus with simple, innocent logic. Indeed, this army of Goths *was* the solution! He had sent them to defend His relics! Now, if He could only repeat that trick about the loaves-and-fishes to feed these many mouths!

After sharing the friars' humble repast of cheese and dark bread that evening, Edilbert stepped out of the hermitage to check up on the troops bivouacked in the hermitage grounds and offer them encouragement. Appealing to their deep religious convictions, he reminded them of their holy mission. They were there, he reminded them, to defend the sacred relics from falling into the hands of the Moors. He forewarned them of the momentous struggle in which they were about to engage, of how destiny had picked them to be the shock troops of the very first Crusade Christendom had ever embarked on. Not having heard the word before, the men listened as Edilbert explained that 'Crusade' simply stood for 'saga of the Cross', the very object they had been called to defend. The notion of fighting for the supreme symbol of one's faith took on a new and poignant meaning for the soldiers. Their faces suddenly turned resplendent on realizing that they were now, literally, the defenders of the Cross.

The promised saga was not long coming.

As the first blush of dawn lit the peaks above them a messenger came galloping up the hermitage hill. Awakened by the clatter of hooves Edilbert wrapped his tunic around his shoulders and stepped out into the brisk dawn to hear the scout's report firsthand. The Moorish patrol, he was informed, was the spearhead of a squadron of Moorish cavalry bivouacked around the hamlet of Liébana, just this side of the gorge.

"It's hard to tell," volunteered the scout, when queried. "They could well be headed toward the upper Deva valley, in search of Pelayo."

The scout's conjecture was so obvious as to be improbable, reasoned Edilbert. There was something odd about this incursion, he thought. The very size of the enemy's force puzzled him; a squadron was too large for a simple scouting mission, too small for an attack in depth, especially in abrupt country, deep in hostile territory. What was this force doing here, in the middle of nowhere, so far from its base? Thus lost in thought, it suddenly occurred to him that the force's size was just about right for a quick, in-and-out operation, not large enough to challenge a determined enemy in a frontal attack, not too small to set up a feint and sneak around entrenched defenses. Were they looking to abscond with something of value, some hidden treasure?

"That's it!" he exclaimed, slapping his forehead with the palm of his hand, at the sudden revelation. "They're after the holy relics!"

His mind was now racing. Unlikely though it was for cavalry to negotiate abrupt terrain, mounted units were known to dismount when fighting in craggy ground. Edilbert had to reach a decision in a hurry: should he hold the high ground and confront the Moors there, on the high plain, or should he take flight with the ark and join the Cantabrians to the west. His dilemma was settled on realizing that he had no way out of there except by punching through the Moors' positions. Although their forces appeared evenly matched, forcing his way through would be foolhardy. Such a confrontation went against every one of his military instincts.

The tactic to follow soon became clear to him: he would defend the pass that the infidels were planning to come through to reach the high plateau, and the hermitage. He would deploy his men to good effect, deny the enemy passage through the funnel. Floating up from some long-ago lecture in his Academy days was a lesson on how a small determined force defending a pass could hold off an enemy ten times its size. Thermopylæ! That was the pass those brave, outnumbered Spartans defended over a millennium earlier. It was now his turn to prove the theory's soundness, perhaps even repeat history.

Running out of time for further planning and preparations, he called reveille, ordered a quick ration of *orujo* distributed to the troops; it was time to prove the potion's usefulness. Splitting up his company into three platoons, he dispatched two to defend the pass, holding back the third, his elite guard, to defend the hermitage and its precious contents.

Charged with ministering to the wounded, Itziar rolled up her sleeves and set up a field hospital in the hermitage's refectory. Her medical staff consisted of two company barbers, who would double as medics, and a dozen refugee women who busied themselves rolling bandages and collecting jars of honey and wine for antiseptic uses. The friars bustled about the refectory, piling up spare blankets, laying down straw bedding on the ground, rounding up wineskins of *orujo* for anaesthetic uses.

There was electricity in the air.

Chapter 15

▼

Prelude to Covadonga

August 721

Standing on the narrow ledge of the hermitage landing, Edilbert gazed on the pleasant valley below him, nestled in the shadows of the towering Picos mountain range. Soaring, deep-green poplars stood guard over patches of lush meadows, telltale signs of water nearby. He couldn't quite see it from his vantage point but knew that, somewhere down there, the young Deva purled along, already yearning for the sea. Wisps of smoke curled heavenward from the chimneys of several sleepy hamlets dotting the valley, heralding the imminent breaking of the fast. Farther away, a faint-yellow path snaked its way resolutely westward, wending its way up the dale to disappear, finally, in the low cotton mists swaddling the piedmont of Peña Vieja, the majestic peak that lorded it over everything in sight.

The breathtaking scenery brought a smile to the Visigoth's face. "Shame," he sighed wistfully, "having to fight a battle in such a lovely place!"

But there was little time for aesthetic musings now. Returning to his now-alerted troops, Edilbert outlined his deployment plans to his officers. The success of his overall strategy, he instructed them, hinged critically on stealth and timing. For his plan to work, the troops would have to remain perfectly still in their hiding places, until the very last second.

"Wenceslas," he said, addressing his First Platoon officer, "your men will conceal themselves behind those boulders over there," he said, pointing to a tumble of rocks strategically strewn along the steep slope, just below the small tableland on which they were standing. "As for your men, Leovigild," he instructed his Second Platoon officer, "they will remain hidden in that copse of trees over there, crouching low in the undergrowth. Position them along the shallow gully to the left of the pass leading up to this ledge." Turning finally to his brother-in-law, he said: "Gori, you and your handful of Vascons will remain inside the hermitage and await the arrival of the enemy scouts. Keep your *ezpatas* sheathed until they start storming the chapel door. Then, and only then, will you strike."

Saluting smartly, the officers hurried to their respective platoons to relay their orders to the anxious foot soldiers. The deployment orders were carried out with efficiency and stealth. Lookouts were posted, men went prone behind their cover, weapons at the ready. Sweat trickled down their jerkins as the sun rose in the sky, white heat pouring down on the recumbent men. There was not much talk, the only sounds a nervous cough, the snap of a hangnail bitten in anxiety, a mumbled prayer—the usual muffled sounds that precede armed conflict. Utter silence eventually descended upon the field of impending battle. Reassured by the stillness, crickets soon resumed their chirping.

They didn't have long to wait before the lead enemy scouts materialized, struggling in single file up the narrow path. They approached on foot, sweating profusely, scimitars flashing in the sun. Their cream-colored *djellaba* tunics fluttered conspicuously in the breeze, loud, profane chatter pinpointing their exact position. Edilbert watched in disbelief at such unprofessional deployment. For a moment, he suspected that such disregard for stealth could only be some ruse to draw his men out into the open, prematurely. The Tiuphate soon realized, however, that these troops had never been trained in the basic rudiments of covert action. A long string of unbroken victories must have made any stealthy precaution superfluous. Edilbert's face suddenly broke out in a broad smile, worry lines around his eyes vanishing. For the first time in a very long time, he could smell victory.

The unwary Moorish scouts proceeded uphill, unchallenged. Crouching in ambush of the main force, the Visigoths remained undetected by the scouting party, which advanced past them, unsuspecting. Edilbert's uncanny tactic required exquisite timing. Any premature engagement between the advance scouts and Gori's Vascons hiding inside the hermitage would alert the main force of an impending ambush. Losing the element of surprise would make any subsequent attack harder to repel. An enemy alerted was twice the enemy, military textbooks taught. It had to work the first time or not at all.

By dint of sheer luck the unsuspecting scouts crested hermitage hill just about the time the main force tagging along behind them came into full view of the Visigoth platoons lying in ambush, farther down the hill. Oblivious to the danger lurking within, the squad of advance scouts tried to force the hermitage doors with a makeshift ram. As they were getting ready to assault the oak door a second time, they were surprised to see it fly open, Gori's men irrupting from the dark hallway, howling ungodly *irrintzis*. Overpowered by the Vascons, the surprised attackers quickly succumbed, invoking *Allah* as they fell. The Abbot and his trusty aide, Beatus, stuck their noses out into the dark hallway, blessing both the living and the dead with repeated signs of the Cross, thankful that the butchery had not taken place inside their sacred precinct. That would have been an 'abomination of the desolation', a biblical quote that had always intrigued and bemused Beatus.

Farther below the hermitage landing, the two Visigoth platoons defending the pass broke out from their hiding positions to engage the surprised Africans. After letting loose a deadly cloud of arrows and *ballista* darts, a fierce hand-to-hand combat ensued. Above the din of battle cries and frantic commands, the soldiers' invocations could be heard, Moors imploring *Allah*, Christians calling upon *Santiago Matamoros*. Abiding religious hatreds fed the ensuing battle, surrender an unacceptable option for either side. The hope of martyrdom in their holy *Jihad* animated the Moors while a back-to-the-wall anxiety drove Goths and Vascons alike with fighting fervor. It was a fight they could not afford to lose if they were to recapture their homeland from the North Africans. Edilbert's earlier explication of a Crusade burned bright in their hearts, fed their fighting frenzy.

Noon brought no decisive turning point in the battle, the struggle see-sawing back and forth in unrelenting fury. They could see hatred in the others' eyes as they slashed away at each other, grunts and imprecations raising the clamor to a pitch audible even in the hermitage plateau above them. A patch of ground, dearly bought with blood and sweat, had to be relinquished, shortly after, to a determined counterattack. The toll of dead and wounded grew with every passing hour, both sides now decimated, the battle raging on inconclusively, with unflagging intensity.

Edilbert had been in the front lines practically since first light, buried in the thick of the mêlée, his broadsword cutting fearsome swaths among the determined ranks of Africans. The Tiuphate's gallant figure stood out provokingly in the fray, flowing tow-haired curls gleaming in the sun, a target clearly visible to every Moor in the field. Tirelessly, he searched for pockets of resistance, moving in with swinging sword, shouting encouragement to his men, his stentorian bellows of "*Santiago y cierra España!*" booming over the din. Fearful of his commander's bravado, his aide tried to keep up with him. The man was lost in a drunken joy of battle, completely oblivious to assaults now increasingly focused on him by an enemy determined to put an end to the Christians' fearsome leader.

Edilbert had always suspected that foolhardiness was a label faint-hearted men affixed to a courage they themselves lacked, who had never experienced the joy of battle nor watched others cringe before one's swinging sword. One had to be convinced of one's invulnerability, know with certitude that the woman had yet to give birth to the man who'd best him in battle, that the sword that would pierce his flesh was yet to be forged. One had to feel as invincible as the God for whom one fought.

But hubris was merely biding its time for retribution on the heights above Cosgaya. For, just as Edilbert was drawing his sword from a fallen foe, an arrow struck him squarely in the chest. For a flitting instant, his gray-blue eyes stared in disbelief at the quivering shaft firmly imbedded in him, surprised to see his invulnerability so rudely challenged. Overcome by shock moments later, he slowly swayed forward, lost his footing and fell unceremoniously to the ground with a thunderous thud. His men, who saw him fall, came rushing to his aid, fending off a clutch of Moors who had started to swarm around him, trying to finish him off. His helpers shook their heads when they noticed the thin stream of blood trickling down the side of their leader's mouth. It was an ominous sign. With infinite care, four of the men lifted him up onto a makeshift stretcher and carried him up the hill to the hermitage. Behind them, the battle raged.

Shocked at first by the sight of her wounded husband, Itziar quickly recovered her composure. She summoned her most senior barber-surgeon, calling out at the same time for bandages and hot water. After plying Edilbert with *orujo* to sedate him, the short, balding medic proceeded to cut open his tunic, pulling aside the bloody linen jerkin, baring the wound. The shaft had barely missed Edilbert's heart but must have pierced a lung, judging from the blood trickling down his mouth after every anguished cough. It did not look promising.

"You have to do something!" whispered Itziar in the barber's ear. The desperate plea moved the medic-apprentice into reluctant action. Gently, he tugged at the protruding shaft but had to stop, shortly after, when the clumsy attempt only brought groans from his patient. The arrow's barb appeared to be firmly lodged somewhere inside his rib cage. His subsequent attempt to twist it loose only evinced an even more pained response.

"The arrowhead," he finally whispered to the anxious wife in an aside, "appears to be firmly embedded inside his chest cavity. I don't think it can be extracted," he said, admitting defeat. An attempt to push it through would only inflict more grievous internal damage.

The look of hopelessness in the barber's eyes told the whole story. With a pang of sudden understanding, Itziar realized that her husband's fate was sealed. More to assuage his patient's mental distress than his health, the barber performed one last rite of mercy: waiting for his patient to lapse into unconsciousness, he severed the protruding shaft, with infinite care. Edilbert, who had passed out from the combined effects of *orujo* and loss of blood, remained mercifully unaware of the clumsy procedure.

When Edilbert awakened from his stupor hours later, his situation had visibly worsened. His head throbbed from the effects of the crude anesthetic, his chest heaving with every shooting pang. A raging fever consumed him and the blood on his lips, once only a trickle, now gushed forth freely every time he coughed. He was barely conscious in his torpor, slipping in and out of delirium.

Gori, who had earlier led his Vascons from hermitage hill to the main fray after disposing of the advance scouts, returned to his brother-in-law's side with news to cheer him up. The two Visigoth platoons that had come close to foundering after their Commander was wounded managed to regain their bearing when they saw the platoon of Vascons sweep into the fray, turning the tide in one last effort. They had stopped the Moors dead in their tracks, sending a few survivors packing. Terrain advantage, combined with more effective weaponry–the Moors' clumsy scimitars a sorry match to the Vascons' short *ezpata* swords and the Visigoths' double-edged axes—helped the Christians carry the day.

A faint smile appeared briefly in Edilbert's ashen face when he heard the good news. "There won't be any need to move the relics to higher ground, after all," he whispered faintly. "They'll be safe in the hermitage, for the time being," he added, now barely audibly.

"We've questioned a wounded Moorish officer at length," reported Gori. "He admits they'd come all this way from Gijon to get the relics, which is what you suspected, all along." Edilbert ruminated on that thought briefly, nodded. It was good to have anticipated the Moors' little stratagem and nip it in the bud, he mused feebly.

"He said they're mounting a full-blown offensive against Pelayo's hosts," continued Gori. "The Count has apparently abandoned the Cangas valley and is holed up in the Picos Mountains, somewhere beyond Peña Vieja." Gori's enthusiasm mounted. "If his Visigoths and Asturians fight with as much *cojones* as ours did today, the Moors won't have a chance!"

Edilbert frowned in disapproved of the coarse language but refrained from reproving his brother-in-law. Gori was, after all, only a young chap. He'd learn to control his enthusiasm, with time.

Several days had gone by since the 'battle of the Hermitage', as the men were starting to call it. After licking their wounds and burying their dead, the survivors marked time, nervously awaiting developments. With so many battles to be fought elsewhere, the troops were starting to get restive.

Edilbert's condition had deteriorated visibly. His wound had started to fester, hallucinations now coming more frequently, his fever raging. He was losing ground fast. Itziar remained by his side night and day, comforting him, applying poultices soaked in wine-and-honey to his wound, soaking his feverish forehead with cool, wet compresses. Behind her brave front, she grieved. As her husband's moments of lucidity grew fewer and farther apart, she decided it was time to share her secret with him. She had tried to save it for a more propitious moment, but time was running out.

"I'm expecting a child," she confessed, holding his hand in one of his moments of clarity.

His eyes opened wide, turning bright with some deep, ineffable joy. With superhuman effort, he forced himself up on one elbow and kissed her on her lips, in a gesture of gratitude. The effort provoked a fit of coughing, the ensuing hemorrhage hard to stem. Touched by an infinite compassion, she thanked him for the gesture. It was, she thought, the height of love and generosity, a bloodletting gift not unlike childbirth, which she would shortly experience.

A brief moment of lucidity ensued after the coughing fit subsided. They talked about the coming child who would, he predicted, be a boy.

"And what shall we name him?" inquired Edilbert feebly.

"How about 'Ausarta'?" she proposed brightly. She was thinking of its father now, how proud he'd be to have a son named for his bravery.

"Strange name for a baby, 'brave'," he remarked in a voice grown suddenly stronger. "But yes, why not?" he agreed. He, himself, had suddenly remembered the lord of Agorreta, a bear of a man, grumbling in his lair. "Your Aita may be a gruff old father-in-law but his grandson's name will do him proud. If the child grows up to be half as brave as his Vascon grandfather, he will go far in life."

"He'll grow up to be a good warrior like his father," said Itziar.

"And a good leader of men," he added, almost inaudibly now.

She leaned over and kissed him softly on the forehead. He had been a good husband and would have made a great father, she reflected with a pang of sadness. Now, she'd have to go back to Agorreta and take care of her son's upbringing herself. She felt in her bones that one day, her son would grow up to be the lord of all those Vascon mountain valleys and keep these Moors at bay. Perhaps even those Franks across the northern border, who were starting to get as restless and pushy as the Moors.

Edilbert was still conscious when an Asturian messenger turned up with news about a great battle that had just been waged nearby, on the Asturian slopes of the Picos, about an hour away from Peña Vieja, as a falcon flies. Pelayo's men had soundly trounced a large army of Moors, in the shadows of the Onga Mountain, the one with the gaping cave they called Cova d'Onga.

It was the second defeat the North Africans had suffered in as many days. Both victories would signal the start of a crusade that would conclude almost eight centuries later, with the Moors being pushed back to the Africa out of which they came.

CHAPTER 16

THE LORDS OF THE VALLEYS

Spring 778

The mists had started billowing down the mountains, engulfing the high valleys in their wet embrace. A dozen men sat uncomfortably on rough-hewn logs arranged around a giant oak in the hamlet's square. Traditionally, the Council of the Twelve convened only once a year but, with the neighboring Franks and Muslims growing increasingly restive, the warlords had been meeting more frequently, of late. The men were all talking at the same time, platitudes effortlessly rolling out of their mouths, hearing but not always listening to one another. Several goatskins filled with heady fermented cider were being passed around, making the men increasingly loquacious and argumentative. A rare pause in someone's exposition was quickly filled by someone else's rephrased opinion. Not by happenstance had these obstinate, strong-willed men been chosen lords of their respective Pyrenean valleys.

Sitting serenely in their midst, back resting on the sacred oak, was a venerable man, his age-furrowed face half hidden behind a white, flowing beard. Resting a weary chin on a crooked staff, Ausarta listened to the chaotic chatter swirling around him, bemused at times by the loud assertions that passed for conversation.

"*Duzu ixilik egoteak zenbat balio du!*" mused the old man, sagely ruminating on the sometimes-golden value of silence. From the increasingly contentious tone of the discussion, the Sire of Agorreta sensed that the lords were growing edgy. It was the eve of the summer solstice and they did not relish missing their summer festivals back home.

Ausarta waved his staff on high to call the assembly to order whenever the discussion threatened to get out of hand. Descended from an unbroken line of warlords dating back to the dimmest past, he had, years ago, been raised on his shield in the ancient Vascon rite of overlordship. There had at one time been some question about the Visigoth strain in his immediate ancestry but his formidable mother, Itziar, had quickly put those misgivings to rest. She reminded them that while their forebears sniveled under the Moors' heel, Ausarta's father had led a band of brave Vascons into battle in Cantabria, beating even Pelayo to the punch. Ausarta had proven his mettle many times over. The man was clearly endowed with a tactical genius and a charismatic gift for command that, together, made him the quintessential leader. Had there been a monarchical tradition in their seminally democratic land, Ausarta would have been named king long ago.

"What makes you so sure the Franks will invade our land this time?" asked Manrique. A broad-shouldered man with weather-worn features, the lord of the westernmost Vascon valley of Roncál had been arguing with Sancho, the rumpled, overweight lord of neighboring Aezcoa, about the renewed threat posed by the Franks. "They have their hands full just keeping those Saxons off their backs."

"Charlemagne is determined to expand his empire southward," responded Sancho. "He's hungry for new lands. He's even tricked that Gascon minion of his, Duke Loup, with promises of adding our Vascon highlands to his Gascon Dukedom."

The lord of Aezcoa was plowing old ground, reliving age-old differences between the mountain Vascons and their kin from across the Pyrenees, the Gascons. They had been blood brothers eons earlier, even spoken the same language at one time, until the Gascons allowed the Celts, and then the Romans, and lately the Franks to inject themselves into their Gascon affairs and dilute their Basque-ness. Squandering their identity was almost, but not quite as contemptible as the overtures their southern Vascon brethren in the Ebro river flatlands had been making with the Moors, for some time now.

"Charlemagne has promised Vasconia to Duke Loup in exchange for safe passage for his Frankish armies through the Gascogne," added Sancho. "But the Moors aren't going to sit idly by and watch the Franks come traipsing over the Pyrenees to take Pamplona and all these mountain valleys of ours. Those Moors are worried enough with just us Vascons, as is!"

"Yes," piped in the lord of Ulzama, "the Franks may have stopped the Moors at Poitiers threescore years ago, but the Africans were overextended then. Ausarta can tell you how his father and his uncle Gori harassed Abd-el-Rahman's southern flank at Covadonga, contributing in no small measure to Martel's victory over the Moors at Poitiers. But the Moors are a lot closer to home now. Their strongholds in Zaragoza and Jaca aren't that far from Pamplona."

"While on that subject," interjected Ausarta, joining in on the conversation, "Iñigo, here, tells me that the Moorish Governor of Zaragoza visited Charlemagne recently. Tell them about it, Iñigo."

The retiring, soft-spoken lord of Bidasoa was only too happy to oblige, having tried to get a word in edgewise ever since his arrival.

"We've heard," he said to a suddenly attentive audience, "that the ruler of Zaragoza, Suleiman Ibn-Yakzan Ibn al-Arabi, traveled to Paderborn to hold secret talks with Charlemagne during the last summer games in Westphalia. Suleiman has apparently been scheming to wriggle out from under his Caliph's thumb to try and carve out a small Principality for himself, with Zaragoza as its capital. He probably has an eye on Tudela and Jaca, as well." After the long-winded preamble, he continued: "Anyway, it's obvious he's groveling for Charlemagne's support of his little insurrection." Pausing for emphasis, he added: "And guess what he's offering the Franks for their troubles?"

"What?" asked several men in unison, apprehension etched on their faces.

"Pamplona and all our high mountain valleys!" responded the lord of Bidasoa. "That's why the Duke of Gascogne is so sanguine about this whole invasion business."

"I can vouch for that," rejoined the Sire of Alduides. Garcia was one of the two ultra-Pyrenean valleys represented in the council, located closer to the Franks than any of the others. "We're hearing the same rumors from our informant in Loup's camp."

Rumor and hearsay were starting to congeal into hard reality. And the gradual realization was disturbing.

"We Ultra-Pyreneans know how it feels to live under the Gascons' sway" continued Garcia. "Ever since early spring, it's only gotten worse. The Franks are literally swarming over southern Aquitaine, camped just beyond the Gascon border. They're trampling their wheat fields, eating their livestock, even raping their women. These are not the pushy settlers of old; they're a ravenous army on a war footing, armed to the teeth and ready to overrun Gascogne." He paused for emphasis, then added: "And from there, it's only a skip and a hop over the Pyrenees and into our mountain valleys."

A pall descended on the gathering. It was not the first time in tribal memory that invaders from the north had tried to overrun their upland valleys. Their peaceful way of life was being threatened anew and the prospects were now more disheartening than on previous occasions.

"How large is the Frankish gathering in Aquitaine?" inquired Ausarta, his calm demeanor belying a deep, inner turmoil.

Ausarta had been a fearless warrior and leader of men ever since any one could remember. These men revered him, respected his judgment, especially in matters of strategy and tactics. Only that spring, he had led them on a successful operation to recapture Pamplona from the Moors. The Ben-Qasi, renegade Christians turned Muslim, were frustrated by the setback, having long nursed hopes of founding a Vascon Kingdom of their own with Pamplona as their seat of realm.

"They've amassed about twenty-thousand men around Casseneuil, in Aquitaine, just in the last several weeks," reported the lord of Alduides. "We've observed their maneuvers across the Garonne. Rumor has it that Charlemagne is organizing two separate armies, each about twenty thousand strong. Duke Bernard is expected to command the eastern contingent of Austrians, Lombards, Bavarians, even Burgundians and Provençals. It's rumored that the Duke's army will cross the Pyrenees along the Mediterranean passes and then proceed west. Charlemagne is expected to lead the western army, himself, across the Garonne, through Gascogne and over the pass at Ibañeta. A pincer movement on Zaragoza appears likely."

Such detailed intelligence left the gathered lords dazed. They had feared something like this would happen one day but they were wholly unprepared for the magnitude and imminence of the invasion.

"An army that size is unstoppable!" remarked Manrique soberly. Being one of the more levelheaded members of the Council of the Twelve, the lord of Roncal's comments always carried weight with his peers. He may have been brash, sometimes foolhardy in battle, but his counsel was always staid, his advice straightforward. "Even if Charlemagne's hosts were split evenly between the eastern and western prongs of his pincer," he continued, "we can expect at least twenty-thousand armed Franks spilling over the pass, here at Ibañeta."

"Why would they need that many men simply to help Suleiman grab control of Zaragoza?" asked the skeptical lord of Salazar. "It sounds like overkill. It doesn't make sense."

"Yes it does," remarked Ausarta. "They'll need every single one of those warriors to ward off Abd-el-Rahman's armies when the Caliph finds out they're trying to snatch his rich Vascon breadbasket from under his very nose, with

Zaragoza and Jaca, thrown into the bargain. That pincer movement is not only a clever idea, it's a brilliant and necessary tactic."

His observation was greeted with a general nodding of heads. Steeped in military history, Ausarta had been in too many skirmishes with the Moors for anyone to question his judgment. He had always felt that the Moors' defeat in the battles of Toulouse and Poitiers decades earlier had only aggravated the Vascons' current dilemma. With less sprawl in their dominions, shorter supply lines and tighter communication routes, the Moors could now afford to concentrate their unwelcome attention on the mountain Vascons. Adding to that unpleasant reality, Loup, the ingrate Gascon Duke, was now scheming to incorporate the Vascon mountain valleys of the Pyrenees into his Duchy, with Charlemagne's blessing.

"How do we fend off the Franks?" asked Lope, the Lord of Arce, angrily. "We can't let them overrun our land, pillage our crops and eat our flocks! Twenty thousand troops are not easy to overlook, let alone feed!"

"We could form an alliance with the Moors and put up a mutual front against the Franks," proposed Sancho. The lord of Aezcoa had had dealings with the renegade Christians of Tudela before and was not averse to striking a deal with the devil himself, if there was something to be gained by it. Observing the raised eyebrows around him, he continued: "The Ben-Qasi of Tudela could summon help from Abd-el-Rahman to fend off the Franks," he added lamely.

"Never!" howled several irate voices in unison. "That would be an insult to everything we hold sacred!" cried Teodomiro of Ulzama. "I would rather die at the hands of the Franks than sully our honor sidling up to the Moors!"

Averting their glowering looks, Sancho lowered his eyes, stared at his hands. "I was only trying to suggest a solution to what seems an insoluble problem," he responded diffidently. "I was merely agreeing with Manrique. We cannot stop these Franks by ourselves. There are too many of them!"

"It's possible your informant miscalculated," cut in the Lord of Erro, skeptical of Garcia's military intelligence. "Sometimes it's hard to estimate numbers, especially when you're counting people from across a river."

"My informer didn't count them from across the Garonne," countered the lord of Alduides huffily. "He actually visited Casseneuil and rubbed elbows with the inhabitants there, local merchants, priests, blacksmiths, even prostitutes. They all said the same thing: 'They're crawling all over their land, at least twenty thousand of them. When the local food supply is exhausted and they've milked the land dry, they'll move on.'"

Having made his point, Garcia concluded: "And that was two months ago. They've probably run them out of house and home by now. Most likely, they're on the move, as we speak."

The gathered lords listened to that last bit of intelligence in somber silence. A sense of hopelessness seemed to have gripped the assembly. They had seen many foreign incursions before but none as massive or as well organized as the approaching menace. They had outsmarted the Celts, outmaneuvered the Romans, outwitted the Visigoths, repelled the Moors before, but how could they possibly avert this imminent deluge of Franks?

Chapter 17

The Witches of Sorogain

A chill evening breeze had started to pick up, adding to the group's discomfort. But there was another more subtle source of malaise that chilled their hearts, ancient fears that rose once again to haunt the innermost recesses of Vasconia's soul. Their people's fate hung in the balance. Ausarta sensed the mental anguish around him sapping the group's determination. It was time to stiffen the flagging resolve of the lords of Vasconia. He would have to rekindle the old fighting spirit in these men.

Rising slowly from his granite slab, Ausarta wrapped his cloak around his shoulders to ward off the evening chill. Under a grayish mane, his tanned, creased face bespoke a lifetime of outdoor living. The usual penetrating look of his steely blue eyes that had never failed to elicit awe from his peers and shivers from his foes, was now absent. In its stead, an indefinable gentleness shone through them, something one would associate with a father. Perhaps, some thought, he should have been named *Aita,* father, for he was, indeed, their father and their lord, all rolled into one. Every nation had a soul, a spirit that had to be nourished by some great commander. Ausarta had inherited that mantle.

He walked slowly around the circle of wooden logs arranged around the oak tree, looked at each of the lords in the eye. Then he did an odd and wholly unexpected thing: clearing his throat and cupping his lips with his gnarled, time-mottled hands, he let out an eerie, ululating *irrintzi* that broke the stillness of the evening. Coming from deep down in his lungs, the wild sound slowly worked its way up to his throat, his vocal chords trilling the high-pitched notes in an exultant, seemingly endless warble of defiance. The ancient call to battle came from the dimmest mists of tribal memory, a war cry that could freeze the blood of foes, instill resolve in the flagging hearts of Vascon warriors. It was the most primal, haunting call to battle ever heard in any land.

The gathered Lords looked at each other in delighted surprise, exulting in the manly battlecry. Rising as one, they joined in with their own joyous *irrintzis,* shattering the silence of the shadow-filled valley. The birds, that had already settled to roost on the branches above them, shot off in startled flight. And when the last echoing warble died down and silence had once again been restored, Ausarta spoke in a deep, resounding voice:

"A people without history are a people without roots." The old man's pithy preamble promised a memorable address. The men sat back down on their logs, listened intently. "Our history as a race is boundless. We have lived in these sweet uplands of Vasconia from time beyond memory. Nobody really knows where our progenitor Aitor came from. Our brethren to the west, whom the Romans called Vardulos and Austrigones and Caristos, all claim that he sailed onto their shores from a distant land. Our Vascon mountain memories, on the other hand, speak of a long overland trek."

After a pause, he continued: "Long before the big rain that once soaked the earth, our forefathers were already living in the land straddled by two inland lakes, far to the East. They had to abandon their gentle lands fed by rivers of warm waters, forced to follow the migrating game. They started the long trek west, leaving the inland seas behind, until they eventually reached the rich green valleys of Aquitaine."

Pausing to let his words sink in, he continued:

"But other fierce tribesmen started coveting their lands. Aitor decided to move to new, easier-to-defend uplands. Following the migrating herds, they discovered these mountain valleys where we now live. 'Let us take possession of these upland greens and never again abandon them,' he said to his travel-weary tribe. 'We shall move no more. We will die in these mountain valleys. Our bones and those of our descendants will rest in these Pyrenean highlands forevermore'."

The gathering of lords listened to their leader in awe and wonder. Not a sound could be heard, not even that of nighting birds.

"In more recent times," continued Ausarta, in his gravelly voice, "other tribes have tried to edge us out of these mountains without success. Unlike the rich lands between the inland lakes or those of Aquitaine, there is really little to covet in these pasturelands of ours, with their rugged hills and damp, inclement weather. More important, they have been easy to defend. And with the will to remain came the wile to elude and the cunning to fight back and in the end to persevere and prevail."

"And so you see, my lords, history will be no different this time around. The hordes trampling our land may be more numerous than usual but they will not long remain in our mountain valleys, nor control them from afar. Long ago, our brothers to the south gave up the rich Ebro lowlands, first to the Celts, then to the Romans and the Goths and, more recently, to the Moors. But our mountains have remained inviolate and we with them. There will be a rumble of hooves and a clangor of weaponry once again, but that too shall pass. Perhaps the Franks will do to the Moor what Martel once did to him at Poitiers. And when it is all over, the Ebro River lowlands may have found yet another master, this time the Frank. But, as on all previous occasions, our mountain valleys will remain unsullied and intact. A little bloodied perhaps, but unbowed and not the worse for wear."

As Ausarta sat down on his granite slab, the murmurs of approval turned into loud acclaim: "*Gora, Ausarta!*" they burst out in unrestrained pride. "Long live Ausarta!" The old man's simple words of wisdom and encouragement had lifted their dejected spirits once again.

"It is all good and well that Charlemagne take over our Ebro lowlands, or even Zaragoza and Jaca, for that matter," remarked Lope, lord of Arce, sounding the sole dissonant chord in the otherwise unanimous approval of the old man's words. "But what if Charlemagne decides to snatch Pamplona away from us permanently? Who'll prevent him from doing that?"

"Yes, what then?" echoed several of the others, snapping out of their complacence.

"Then we'll apply the same pressure on him that we did on the Moor," responded Ausarta calmly. "We'll simply wear him down. He will have to keep open his lines of communication with the north through the Cissa range, as have all those who came before him, including Caesar, for which that range is named. We will wait for the right moment and then we will pounce on him when and where he least expects it. He will despair and eventually leave. We own this pass and know it better than anyone else. In the end, if we use our heads, we shall prevail, as we always have."

"What must we do to prepare for the onslaught?" asked the lord of Aezcoa.

"We shall do nothing for the time being, Sancho," responded Ausarta. "We shall not shed blood needlessly. We shall watch the passes from the heights until we see the foreigners coming. Then we shall meld into the forests of these mountain valleys, away from the main route of Ibañeta. We shall let them pass through our land, unopposed. They will find our villages deserted, our crops harvested, our cattle and sheep gone. They will not remain long in these mountains; they will find little sustenance here. Leery of ambuscades, they will proceed quickly to Pamplona.

"Preferring Christians to Muslims," he continued, "the inhabitants of Pamplona and the *Ager Vasconum* regions beyond will at first welcome them. But they will soon weary of the brigandage and the excesses of an occupation army that large. They will grow hungry and start grumbling but won't be able to do anything about it. We will not act until the Frankish lion returns to its northern lair."

"Are we going to give up Pamplona without a fight?" asked the lord of Baztan, incredulous. "After all the blood and the sweat it took us to win it back from the Moors just this past spring?"

"We will have to, Txomin," answered Ausarta evenly. "An army ten times the size of a city's population has little difficulty besieging it and taking it. It is best we let them march on through without a fight. They may bivouac in Pamplona for a while but they will eventually move on. We will warn the citizenry there to remain distant and aloof, not overly friendly."

It was almost dark when Ausarta fielded the last question. The meeting's resolutions were approved by voice vote, as was the custom in every meeting of the Council of the Twelve. Although each valley's lord recognized no superior and, ultimately, voted his own conscience, some innate instinct or ingrained regard for natural law tipped their decision to the wishes of the oldest and wisest among them. And so, this time too, the vote was unanimous; they would lie low and await developments. And if some unforeseen event warranted another emergency meeting of the Twelve, they would gather again in Agorreta. Meanwhile, Ausarta urged them to gird their loins, sharpen their *ezpata* swords and double-barbed *güecia* spears and wait for their final marching orders before proceeding to their designated battle lines. They had rehearsed it many times before, knew each group's tactics and disposition by heart.

The chill mists had started to fold their limp coils round the elders, the first owl hoots signaling the approaching darkness.

"It is late," concluded Ausarta. "You will spend the night in Jaureguizar." The invitation to stay in Ausarta's home was more an urging than a request. "After supper, we will visit Sorogain. It is the full moon and the crones will be there at midnight. It won't hurt to consult the oracle. Tomorrow, after we break the fast, you can all go back to your homes and your midsummer festivals."

After the meeting adjourned, they repaired to Ausarta's manor house, a large stone building overlooking the hamlet's square where they had sat all day. Climbing the torch-lit, double-back stairs, they were ushered into a cavernous hall with a high, oak-beamed ceiling. The fire roaring in the large fireplace at the end of the hall offered a cozy welcome in the evening chill.

Burning torches hung from wall rings adding their flickering light to the fire roaring in the large hearth, where the men milled around, waiting for supper to be served. An enormous, long oak table had been set up near the fire with the care befitting the lordly company. Wooden plates and copper-rimmed drinking horns had been set in each of the twelve settings around the table. Laid out in the center were four large wooden trays, overflowing with haunches of roasted venison, wild boar and several dozen partridges and pheasant, all filling the room with their delicious aroma.

The din of the conversation died down perceptively as the men dug into their meal. Only the sound of noisy chewing and slurping could be heard, as the company made short shrift of dinner. Several hounds loitered around the table, crushing bones tossed off to them, adding to the sounds of food being consumed. Ausarta's wife, Doña Angela, watched from the sidelines, pleased to see her food gobbled up with such gusto. She whispered orders to several maids serving plates, filling cider horns, sweeping debris from the floor with green rushes.

At the end of the sumptuous meal, Ausarta stood up. Lifting his drinking horn, he proposed a toast: *"Gora Vasconia!"* It was a heartfelt wish for a long life to their small corner of the world.

"Gora!" responded the others, wobbling up from their benches to down the contents of yet another horn.

Having thanked their hostess for her cooking, all twelve men rode off into the clear night, guided by the North Star. Ausarta led the way along familiar paths, across vales and over ridges, each man bearing a torch to complement the full moon's wan light. Stumbling along goat paths, through dense beechwood forests and moonlit glens swaddled in dank patches of mist, their mounts slowly cantered their way toward Sorogain. Far off in the distance, bonfires dotted the dark hilltops with pinpricks of light. It was the eve of the summer solstice, when fertility rites were celebrated with fires lit to Mari and other ancient nature deities. Strains of Basque music played on high-pitched *txistu* flutes pierced the quiet of the night.

Crossing a shallow stream that flowed along a narrow dale, the animal path they had been following grew suddenly steeper. Looming up ahead, halfway up the rise, was a small promontory overlooking the path.

Ausarta raised his hand, motioned the others to halt and dismount.

"Sorogain!" he whispered hoarsely, cupping an ear and motioning them to tread lightly, be vigilant. As they proceeded on foot, cautiously up the rise, strains of eerie chants wafted down the slope towards them. Muffled at first by the heavy mists, the chants grew louder as they negotiated the rise. Just beyond a crook in the path, the light of a small bonfire suddenly flickered into view. Half a dozen women, garbed in white flowing robes, huddled round the fire with uplifted arms, moaning at the full moon. Encircling the bonfire and the group of women standing round it was a small circle of upright stones impaled in the ground. A kid goat tied to one of the stone posts bleated plaintively.

Dancing around the huddled group in measured steps was a large woman ululating incantations punctuated by the others' weird, maniacal cackles. Dressed in white, like the rest of them, the giant crone held up a mask of a he-goat to her face. The ponderous animality of her movements around the small fire added to the strangeness of the scene. Eerily, she scratched at the night sky with the gnarled fingers of one hand, poking at the moon with the crooked staff she held in the other.

"The witches of Sorogain!" whispered Ausarta, speaking in hushes. The lords shuddered at the unearthly scene, some instinctively reaching for their *ezpatas*, expecting to unsheathe them presently.

"What are they up to?" whispered the Lord of Luzaide. The others sensed that Garcés would rather have been elsewhere at that moment. Some of the others shared his concern. They had been flirting with Christianity for only a short time and, while some of them were still ambivalent about the new religion, the more earnest believers sensed that their priests would have frowned upon their witnessing such witchery.

"It's their full-moon ritual," whispered Íñigo of Bidasoa. "They do this every month, during the full moon, but the exorcisms of tonight's summer solstice are doubly important to them. That big woman with the he-goat mask must be the sorceress of Zugarramurdi herself!"

The corpulent old crone seemed to have suddenly caught wind of the men's whispering. Stopping at half chant, she dropped her he-goat mask and rose to her full height. Squaring her shoulders, she turned to face the lords with an arrogant, disdainful regard.

"Who goes?" she demanded in a hoarse voice that commanded everyone's attention. The witches squatting around the fire all stood up in unison, cackling weird guttural noises as if to add their own powers of sorcery to those of their leader.

"It is we, the lords of the valleys of Vasconia," answered Ausarta in a deep, carrying voice. "We are here to consult the oracle."

"Approach and be recognized!" ordered the tall witch, without a hint of surprise or concern.

Ausarta and the others clambered up the hillock until they were level with the circle of stones, standing face to face with the giant witch. Her glowering crones had by now grouped themselves behind their leader, using her as a shield. Interruptions like this were rare but requests for oracles were totally unheard of. Basques naturally shied away from witches as from something evil and otherworldly. Most caves, high in the western mountains of Vasconia, were considered taboo by the locals because of the witchcraft and strange sacrifices known to take place in them during the full moon. And this giant of a woman they were now confronting had to be the head sorceress in the land.

"I am Ausarta, the lord of Agorreta," he said with unwavering voice. "We, the lords of the twelve valleys of Vasconia, request your augury on what is to befall our land."

An eerie silence fell upon the gathering, everyone holding his breath. Slowly, dimly, through the shards of Ausarta's booming utterance, the head witch seemed to have perceived the drift of his odd demand.

"I am the sorceress of Zugarramurdi," said the tall, imposing woman, nostrils flaring like those of a laboring warhorse. Her voice was husky, her manner haughty. Unfamiliar with small talk or civilized pleasantries, she seemed to delight in the cowering impact of her brusque demeanor and rude delivery.

"You are concerned about the Franks," she continued in a hoarse, almost irate voice. She was obviously irritated by Ausarta's impassive dignity. "This much I know," she added presciently. "You have reason to worry. They will come with great noise from afar. Towns will crumble under their horses' hooves, the land will be shorn, the women violated. There will be much blood spilt when our people clash with them."

Just as she finished voicing her dire pronouncement, a single solitary cloud drifted in from the west, momentarily obscuring the already tenuous light of the moon. Suddenly, everything was immersed in darkness, save for the light of the bonfire and the lords' dying firebrands. As if heeding an omen, the witch stopped talking just as abruptly as she had begun. With a gruff grunt and a wave of her crooked staff, she signaled the lords to be gone. The oracle had concluded and the crones were to be left to their arcane rites.

Ausarta and his lords quietly began their descent down the hillock, some of them casting an occasional backward glance. Hearts heavy with foreboding, they mounted their horses and picked their way back to Agorreta.

"Don't pay any heed to that witch," said the lord of Arce. "Her warnings are always dire!"

"I'm not so sure about that, Lope," responded the lord of Baztan. "She once predicted the plague, and, sure enough, the plague came."

Having hoped otherwise, they knew that, deep down, they had anticipated the oracle. It was now only a matter of time before her terrible omen would come to pass.

Chapter 18

Roncevaux

Aug. 15, 778

The moon had waxed and waned since the night of the witches in Sorogain. The wheat had been gathered, the livestock herded to remote highland pastures when Charlemagne's armies streamed down the Pyrenean pass of Ibañeta, marching unmolested into Pamplona. The Vascon capital warily opened its gates to the northern hosts, pleased, at first, to count on such powerful Christian allies in their struggle against the Moors. But it was with a collective sigh of relief that the inhabitants of Pamplona watched the soldiery march out of town several weeks later on their way to Zaragoza. Ausarta sent his two sons to shadow the foreign armies and was pleased to learn that the Moors had shut the doors of Zaragoza on the Franks. The Caliph of Cordoba had caught wind of Suleiman's treasonous overtures with Charlemagne and had had him replaced with a trusted governor.

"Great!" exulted Ausarta, hoping that the Franks and the Moors would neutralize each other. "Let them fight and wear each other down."

His enthusiasm was short-lived. Unforeseen events were about to force Charlemagne to lift his ill-timed siege. News of a Saxon uprising in Westphalia came on the heels of his troops' mutinous grumbling, giving Charlemagne second thoughts about the siege. A tempting Moorish bribe of gold bullion finally persuaded him to lift it and return home. But he was not going to abandon the Iberian Peninsula without leaving his scent on it. The Saxons and the Moors may have momentarily thwarted his grand designs but he would insure Vasconia's future incorporation into his kingdom by stripping her capital of its fortifications.

Hopelessly outnumbered and kept at bay by the Frankish soldiers, the inhabitants of Pamplona stood by, sullenly watching their ancient fortress walls laid low by the Franks. Bare to the waist, an army of sweating engineers worked feverishly under a broiling summer sun, dismantling the city's Roman walls. Siege machines swung heavy iron rams against the ancient ramparts, sending chunks of honey-colored rocks tumbling down into the Arga River below, coating trees and bushes with layers of yellow dust. The earth shuddered with every ram blow, sending pangs of anguish through the stunned citizenry. The dastardly act would earn the Franks the Vascons' lasting hatred.

The day of reckoning was not long coming.

A long line of Vascon warriors marched up the birch-lined road that sliced through the plain of Errozabal at the very foothills of the Pyrenees, some eight leagues north of Pamplona. Having bivouacked by the spring of Jaureastegui the night before, their leading elements were now approaching the small clearing of Orreaga, the valley of thorns, at the foot of Ibañeta, the mountain the Romans used to call *Summo Pyreneo*. The men walked silently, raising puffs of dust, as they plodded along with stern resolve. The fog that lingered in the canopy of the forest was soon dissipated by a whitening summer sun. Through breaks in the forest, the peaks of the Cissa range loomed in the distance. It was going to be a hot day.

Some of the men rode stocky, honey-colored horses of hardy Pyrenean stock, others trudged along on foot, weighed down by bows and laden quivers. Strapped to their forearms were round leather shields while their hands gripped battle axes or long, double-barbed *güecia* spears which they swung to the rhythmic thwack of their sheathed *ezpata* swords slapping against their thighs. Devoid of armor or coat-of-mail, they wore sleeveless wool-lined jerkins and sheepskin leggings secured by leather cross-straps anchored to their sandals. The only color in their otherwise drab attire was a narrow red ribbon tightly wound around their foreheads. To an innocent shepherd watching the column of men from the heights of Menditxuri, the grim procession of warriors looked invincible, a people who believed in actions more than words.

Ausarta and his two sons led the column of men from the Esteribar, Erro and Arga valleys. All three Agorretas rode fiery Arabian steeds captured from the

Moors on their latest foray in the Ebro River lowlands. Except for the colorful pheasant feathers rakishly stuck to their leather caps, it was hard to distinguish them from the warriors they were leading. Several hundred Vascons from Pamplona had joined Ausarta's forces during the last few days, eager to avenge the Franks' dastardly leveling of their city walls. At the first hint of Frankish troop movement out of the city, the Iruñeans had slipped out under cover of darkness to join up with Ausarta's men, already assembling in the village of Agorreta.

The Agorreta men had just pulled up at the small clearing of Orreaga, just beyond the beech forest of Errozabal. "Nabar," said Ausarta turning to his oldest son. "You will pull out with our Esteribar and Erro forces, scale the heights of Girizu and join up with Teodomiro's Ulzama men. They should be in place by now. Spread yourselves out all the way to Lindux."

"Who's deployed farther up the Luzaide gap?" asked the tall, broad-shouldered Nabar. Now in his mid-thirties, Ausarta's firstborn had never been known to be a reluctant warrior, his outward calm reflecting an inner strength that matched his father's grit. He and his younger brother had missed the operational meeting held a week earlier by the Council of the Elders and wanted to know who was protecting his northern flank.

"Teodomiro," replied his father. "He will have closed ranks with Garcia's Alduides contingent by now. The Baztan and Bidasoa forces should be in position farther north, along the heights overlooking the gorge. Garces' Luzaide men are the northernmost anchor, west of the gap, several leagues up the gorge. They'll be looking directly down on Elizaldea."

"Yes, *Aita*," said Nabar, striking his breast with his fist, in acknowledgment of his marching orders. He had fought alongside his father against the Moors and was keenly aware of his innate military cunning. The old man may be growing too frail to wield *ezpatas,* he reflected, but there was no doubt in his mind that Ausarta would swing it to good effect in a pinch. Nabar knew that his father's keen mind and unflagging spirit more than made up for his ebbing strength.

"As for you, Antxon," continued Ausarta, turning to his youngest son, "you'll take command of the Iruñea and Arga men and follow me to Ortzanzurieta. Just before we reach the peak, you'll slip down the southern brink of the Lepoeder narrows. Make sure your men are concealed in the undergrowth just below the edge of the drop-off. You're to remain there, out of sight. You will know when to strike."

The young man looked at his father with undisguised puzzlement. The sun played in his curly brown hair, his jutting chin up, his hazel eyes still. It was a face that women loved and men followed unquestioningly into battle. Antxon knew that his father had something up his sleeve but he could not quite fathom the tactic. "That's an odd spot to be fighting a battle," he puzzled out loud.

"I have a suspicion that before the day is done you'll be engaging many a panicked Frank trying to escape Sancho's Aezcoan onslaught from Atzobiskar, just above you," Ausarta said confidently. "We will control the entire line between Girizu and Ortzanzurieta. Between your brother Nabar's forces west of the Ibañeta pass and yours to the east of it, we'll cover both the steeper Luzaide valley route and Caesar's old Roman road, whichever the enemy decides to take. From your positions, you'll be able to finish off any stragglers."

"What if the enemy decides to proceed down only one of those two routes?" asked the mystified Antxon.

"It'd be foolish to funnel forty thousand men through a single narrow pass," explained Ausarta patiently. "I fully expect the enemy to split his force up into a two-pronged retreat to avoid bottlenecks and lessen his vulnerability to an ambush. After reaching Ibañeta," he continued, "half of the Frankish force will, most likely, proceed down the western route overlooking the Subibelz gorge, and descend to Elizaldea along the Luzaide brook. They may even get as far as the village of Donibane Garazi, depending on the time of day. That gorge-hugging route is seldom traveled. Though steep and narrow the cavalry can negotiate it with ease."

"What about the other half of the army?" persisted Antxon.

"The infantry will be slowed down by its war machines and baggage train. They'll have to take the old Roman road, along the shadows of Atzobiskar, Mendi Txipi and Txangoa, before proceeding north, along the folds of Loizar-Atheca, until they reach Donibane, where they'll join up with the other column."

"But you're splitting up our meager forces on a hunch that the enemy will split up into two columns," Antxon boldly pointed out. He feared that half of the Vascons, probably himself included, would end up sitting idly by, along a route not traveled, while the other undermanned half would bear the brunt of a single massive Frankish thrust.

"I have no choice," admitted Ausarta with a shrug of his shoulders. "You could be left waiting in vain, defending an un-traveled route, while Charlemagne decides to take his whole army along the other one. But by doing it this way, we've got all his options covered."

"And you, *Aita*, where do you plan to be during the battle?" asked the young man, worried about his father's safety in the coming fray.

"I will leave you at the Lepoeder narrows and continue on to the peak of Ortzanzurieta, just beyond it. I'll be able to observe the battle from the heights. I will hold Andoni's Lauribar forces and Lope's Arce men with me in reserve."

"But *Aita*," persisted the young Agorreta, "you're too frail for these endeavors. You should remain concealed here in Orreaga and go no farther."

"How little you know me, *seme maitea*!" responded Ausarta, an edge of impatience starting to creep into his voice. The old man felt a sudden pang of sadness for having to remonstrate with his youngest son, just moments before the battle. "I may no longer be able to hurl the *güecia* as far as I used to, but I can still raise my arms, like Moses, to inspire my men in battle. So fret no more about your old father, dear Antxon. He may have fought one battle too many but this is still *his* battle, and he shall not be denied."

"Yes, *Aita*," answered Antxon in a subdued tone, regretful of having sounded overly protective of his aging father. He, like his older brother, was inordinately proud of having sprung from such noble roots, to be allowed to follow in the footsteps of such a fearless leader.

"Your men will remain perfectly still," continued Ausarta, now addressing both of his sons, "hidden behind the thorn bushes in the beech forest; yours, Nabar, on the Girizu ridges; yours, Antxon, just below the Lepoeder ledge. You will watch the bulk of Charlemagne's army march by. You may even think that you missed the opportunity to close with them, but you, Nabar, will not budge until after you hear my *irrintzi* signaling the attack."

"As for you, Antxon," continued Ausarta, "you'll remain hidden until the enemy troops literally start stumbling over you in full flight. You will fight a running battle from the brim of Lepoeder all the way down the Arranosin gap. You may probably slay the last surviving Frank on this very ground of Orreaga on which we now stand. Do it well, my sons, for it will henceforth be considered hallowed ground."

Antxon broke out in a broad grin. He had suddenly plumbed the depths of his father's military genius.

"And when the battle is over," continued Ausarta, "you will retreat in good order and fade into the forest as quietly as you came. Instruct your men not to bother collecting booty because they may pay dearly for their greed. Charlemagne's main force won't be far away and he's bound to rush back to support his rearguard as soon as he hears the clamor."

"I will say no more," concluded Ausarta, raising his hand as if in blessing. "We will meet again when the battle is over. Go, fight the good fight. *Aurrera, Euzkaldunak!* Godspeed, my Vascons!"

Ausarta embraced Nabar briefly before the two groups split up to go their separate ways. With heavy heart, Ausarta watched his oldest son take off with his men, disappearing into the high forests of Girizu. In a matter of only a dozen years, he had lost three sons fighting the Moors, two only six months earlier, taking Pamplona. He now had a rending premonition that he may be seeing his firstborn for the last time. He had always been the reckless one.

"Vasconia," he thought to himself, sadly, "you are one jealous lover!"

Vascons from the neighboring valleys had arrived at their assigned positions by mid afternoon and deployed along the Cissa range, to the east and west of the pass of Ibañeta. Through sporadic clearings in the forest north and west of where he stood, Ausarta could see his men clambering up the nearby peaks of Atzobiskar, Menditxipi and Txangoa. And when the sun was just right, he thought he detected sunlight glinting off the spear tips of figures fleeting stealthily in and out of the forests of Girizu, far away to the west, beyond Ibañeta.

When he could no longer see movement, Ausarta knew that his men were in place, ready for battle. Though he had come from farther away than any of the others, Iñigo of Bidasoa had, for once, arrived on time. He deployed his men along the western approaches overlooking the gorge of Subibelz, behind the bluffs above Gorostgaray. The Baztan and Alduides forces, meanwhile, had quietly occupied the heights farther north, overlooking the Luzaide brook, stretching themselves out as far as the hills that overlooked Elizaldea.

Andoni and Lope were unhappy at having to hold their forces in reserve under the shadows of Ortzanzurieta. But it was not for them to question Ausarta's strategy. They had to console themselves and their disappointed Lauribar and Arce men with the thought that their time to do battle would surely come, arriving, they hoped, at a crucial juncture, when glory would be theirs for the taking. Meanwhile, they had to cool their heels in the blustery heights of Ortzanzurieta until Ausarta gave the order.

By noon, a strange quiet had descended upon the forests of the western Pyrenees. It was almost as if the birds and the crickets had become suddenly aware of the unusual human presence around them. The men spoke in hushes when they did, but mostly they were quiet, their thoughts flitting back and forth, from the safety of home to the imminence of a sudden and unsung end in the ravines they now guarded. Hiding behind rocks along the northern slopes of the Cissa range, they had no way of knowing that the enemy was drawing near, far faster than anybody had anticipated.

Only Ausarta and his two reserve commanders, Andoni and Lope, were aware of the Frankish army's rapid advance. Standing among sheep droppings on the blustery clearing atop the highest mountain of the range, Ausarta and the lords of Lauribar and Arce gazed south across the sharp drop-off beyond the bald mountaintop of Ortzanzurieta, surveying the valley below. There, they beheld an awesome spectacle: for as far as the eye could see, a swarm of men and war machines advanced with deliberate speed along the old Roman road that cut across the plane of Errozabal, raising clouds of dust as they approached Orreaga, the valley of thorns. The noonday sun glinted off their metal helmets and mail cuirasses as from a sea of dull sequins, shimmering in their tens of thousands. Ausarta shuddered at the sight; he had never seen so many men lined up like that in all his long life.

"So many!" whispered Andoni, equally awestruck by the approaching column of humanity. "At that pace, they'll be over the pass before dusk."

"It almost looks like those in the lead are stepping out at a forced march," remarked Ausarta, pleased at what he saw.

"They're cavalry. They can go fast," commented Lope. "They're worried about an ambush, no doubt. The quicker they cross the gorge, the less exposed they think they'll be."

"Actually, it'll be their undoing," responded Ausarta enigmatically. Pausing a moment, he added: "At that pace, they'll string themselves out farther and farther apart, the cavalry in the vanguard advancing too fast for the slower rearguard train to keep up. You can already see it happening," he said, pointing at the carts and machines in the train starting to lag behind. "They're still way back there to the south, while the cavalry is already here below us, at the fringes of the Orreaga clearing." In its eagerness to gain the heights and cross the forbidding defile beyond, the enemy was stretching itself thin. If they kept up this pace, Ausarta reflected, the vanguard would reach Elizaldea, a score of miles beyond the Cissa pass, perhaps even Donibane, farther north, hours before the rearguard even crested Ibañeta. Nice prospects, he mused.

The cavalry spearheading the vanguard was now so close that Ausarta crouched instinctively to avoid being silhouetted against the northeastern sky and risk being spotted by the advance patrols. He could already see them trotting past the clearing of Orreaga, starting their arduous, switchback ascent of Ibañeta. From their tree limbs in the forest just below Lepoeder, Antxon's men watched the hordes of armed Franks lumbering up the mountain under the hot August sun. His brother Nabar also observed the progress from the peaks of Girizu, west of the pass. Weighed down by their ill-gotten gains, the enemy appeared sweaty and uncomfortable under their coats-of-mail and bronze helmets. It was not the proper attire for traveling under the merciless midsummer sun. The puffs of dust raised by the leading cavalry and the long lines of Percheron-drawn carts only added to the misery and discomfort of those marching behind.

Had the two Agorreta brothers been any closer, they would have detected the Frankish soldiers' apprehension at the unnatural stillness around them, wondering where the natives had gone underground. They must have sensed that something was amiss; not having seen a soul since leaving Pamplona two days earlier. And the usually raucous crickets were now silent, adding to the ominous stillness of the afternoon. Wary but deliberate, the columns pressed on. Riding powerful, large-chested horses, the first vanguard units finally crested the high pass of Ibañeta and had started their descent down the forbidding Subibelz gorge beyond. About a league behind the leading elements, surrounded by a heavily armored cavalry squadron, several horse-drawn carts with gaudily colored canopies and flying streamers rattled along on massive, squeaking wheels.

"Charlemagne!" commented Ausarta, pointing to the largest of the lumbering conveyances. "The one flying the pennants and the battle banners," he clarified.

"It would be such a lovely target!" commented Andoni wistfully. "We could finish this battle in a heartbeat!"

"Yes," responded Ausarta, "but that's not the plan. It would be foolhardy to strike the enemy at its strongest point. We will only strike at the rearguard, as planned."

Several hours after Charlemagne's showy train had negotiated the narrow road hewn out of the western slopes of the Subibelz chasm and reached the bottom of the Luzaide gorge, the main force was still just then starting to struggle up the steep southern approaches of Ibañeta. On reaching the pass, what had been a single column, suddenly split into two, one following Charlemagne and his cavalry down the Luzaide gorge, the other forking off to the east, crossing the narrow Lepoeder ridge, then veering north, along the old Roman road over the Cissa range. It was just as Ausarta had predicted. Skirting the southern slopes of Atzobiscar, the second column marched under the lengthening shadows of Menditxipi and Txangoa, before starting their long, ten-league descent toward Donibane Garazi, the old Roman *oppidum* to the north, a town whose Christian inhabitants were just then starting to call it St. Jean.

From his lookout atop Ortzanzurieta, Ausarta observed the two columns advancing northward at a cautious pace. He could see Charlemagne's cavalry trotting jauntily down the Luzaide narrows, past the Elizaldea clearing. The troops in the rearguard, however, appeared neither jaunty nor pleased. Their captains urged them on with shouts of encouragement, while the sweaty, exhausted foot soldiers, disgruntled by the unrelenting pace, swore their way up Ibañeta, limping under the heavy burden of arms and loot. There was no relief in sight. Only the fear of being left behind, trapped in the gorge, pushed them on.

All afternoon they marched along the narrow, twisting road, their commanders' shouts now clearly audible even from Ausarta's height. Andoni and Lope stood behind the lord of Agorreta, watching the old man at the edge of the mountain, arms crossed over his chest, white beard and dark cape flowing in the gusty wind that whistled over the summit of the tallest peak of the range. He observed the scene below him, transfixed by the immensity of it all, saying nothing. To the lords of Lauribar and Arce who stood nearby, Ausarta was like a vision of a biblical patriarch, driven by some inner holy wrath, wrapped in thoughts of his own private Apocalypse. They looked at him with something akin to awe and reverence, reluctant to voice their thoughts and snap the magic spell.

And then Ausarta spoke.

"The last of the Frank rearguard is halfway up Ibañeta," he said calmly. "Charlemagne is already in Elizaldea. It is time to light the fire."

"*Bada ordua!* High time! muttered the impatient Andoni under his breath.

Filling his lungs with one deep breath, Ausarta cupped his lips with his gnarled hands and let out a loud, blood-curdling *irrintzi* that rang across the peaks and valleys of the Cissa range. It gave those around him shivers of pride just listening to the strong, endless trill issuing from the old man's throat, warbling in his vocal chords before pouring forth in waves of ear-piercing ululation. It was the ultimate gesture of bravado, a gauntlet thrown with all the daring his rough-hewn gallantry could muster.

Those in the valleys below picked up the trilling signal and repeated it like an echo that reverberated along every crag and bluff of the rugged mountain range. Others, farther on, relayed the message with horn blasts and *irrintzis* of their own, until every valley of the Cissa range resounded with the joyous din. Briskly rubbing two sticks together over a handful of wood shavings, one of the men lit the mound of twigs and dry logs they had piled up earlier on the bare mountaintop of Ortzanzurieta. Tongues of flame were soon licking at the column of smoke billowing hundreds of feet above the mountaintop. For those strung out along the western ridges of the gorge extending from Girizu to Elizaldea who had not heard Ausarta's battle cry, the pillar of smoke rising from the crest of Ortzanzurieta relayed the message clearly enough.

The battle had begun.

Roncevaux 157

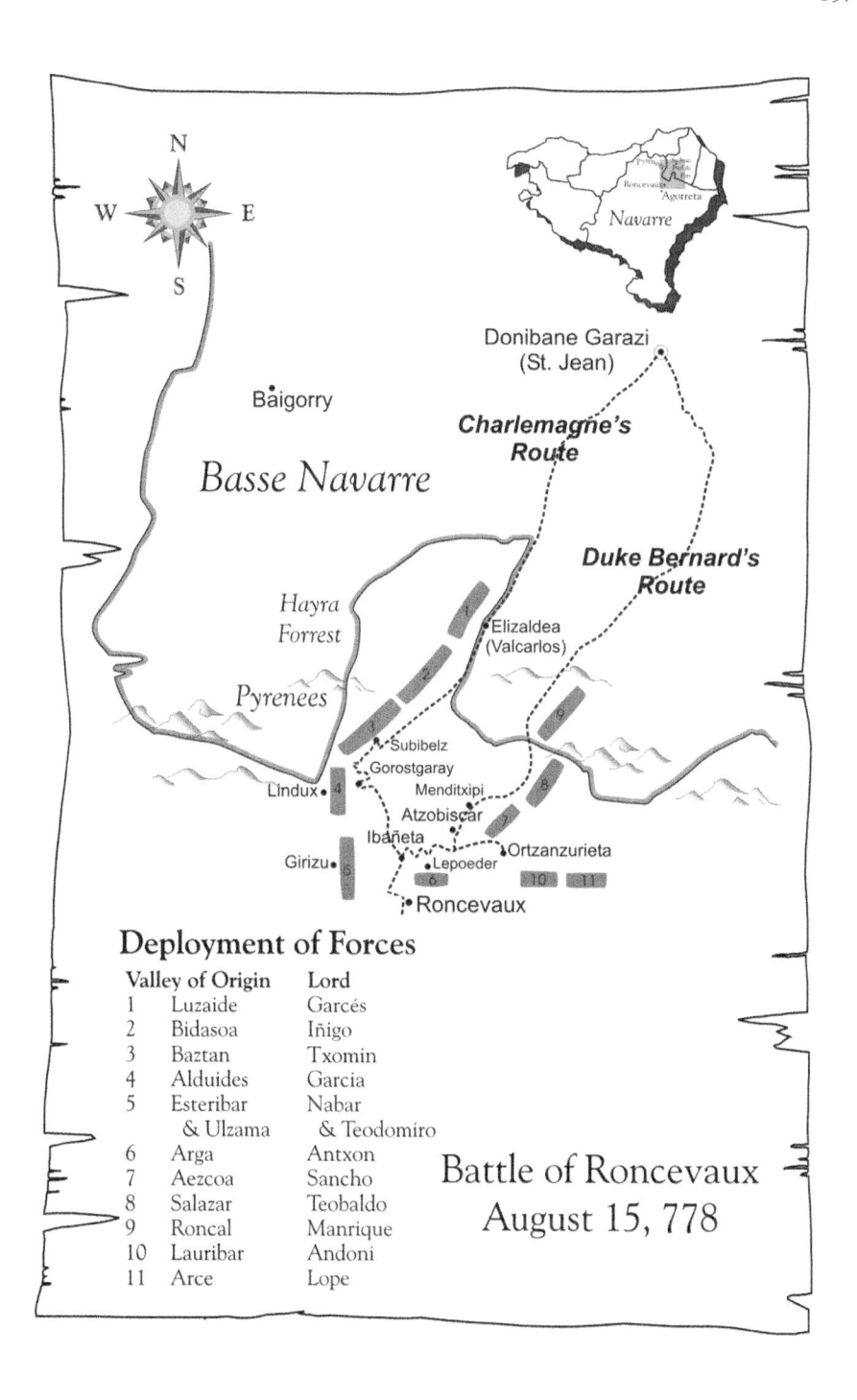

Donibane Garazi
(St. Jean)

Baigorry

Charlemagne's Route

Basse Navarre

Duke Bernard's Route

Hayra Forrest

Elizaldea (Valcarlos)

Pyrenees

Subibelz
Gorostgaray
Lindux • 4 Menditxipi
         Atzobiscar
         Ibañeta   • Ortzanzurieta
Girizu • • Lepoeder
        •Roncevaux

Deployment of Forces

Valley of Origin	Lord
1 Luzaide	Garcés
2 Bidasoa	Iñigo
3 Baztan	Txomin
4 Alduides	Garcia
5 Esteribar & Ulzama	Nabar & Teodomiro
6 Arga	Antxon
7 Aezcoa	Sancho
8 Salazar	Teobaldo
9 Roncal	Manrique
10 Lauribar	Andoni
11 Arce	Lope

Battle of Roncevaux
August 15, 778

Chapter 19

The True Chanson de Roland

The shadows lengthened, sunlight growing more feeble inside the canyon walls. The Frankish troops bringing up the rear had unwittingly created a bottleneck, despite their captains' urging to move along smartly. They had stopped to quench their thirst at the mountain spring near the sharp switchback at Gorostgaray, halfway down the path that hugged the western slope of the Subibelz chasm. It was to be a fatal breakdown in discipline, for it was precisely over that watering hole that the first boulders came tumbling down from the heights above the gorge.

At first, the rumble of granite smashing on granite sounded like thunder on a clear summer afternoon. Nobody paid much attention to the deep, muffled noise until the very ground under their feet began to shudder ominously. Looking up to explain the disturbance, the startled troops beheld a fearsome spectacle: the whole side of the mountain above them seemed to have sheared off, creating an avalanche of rocks that came crashing down on them with frightening speed.

For some, it was to be their last glimpse of the sliver of blue summer sky visible from the narrow gorge. Those who managed to escape the initial rockslide were petrified at the sight of their comrades, crushed beneath the jumble of jagged rock. It was an appalling sight. There was gore everywhere. Even the little fountain of Gorostgaray started to flow crimson with the blood of the broken bodies that had started piling up around it. Their commanders' desperate orders to abandon the path were lost in the din and dust around them, horses scattering every which way, trampling hapless survivors underfoot.

The avalanche ceased when Garcia's Alduides Vascons dislodged the last loose rocks from the high ridges. When the dust finally settled, the surviving Franks were horrified to realize that they had been cut off from the main force ahead of them by an impenetrable barrier left behind by the landslide. Survival would have been difficult enough even if the retreat had been executed in an orderly fashion. But the men were now in a full-fledged panic and it was each man for himself. Hysteria clouded any rational options the surviving Franks may have had. Foolishly, some retraced their steps toward the pass of Ibañeta. Even more reckless, others dispensed with their shields and heavy broadswords and began to clamber up the steep gorge, straight into the hands of Garcia's Alduides men. Still others rushed down the steep slope, slipping and sliding down to the bottom of the Subibelz gorge, hoping to toil through the Luzaide stream to join the Carolingian vanguard ahead of them.

Observing the tumult from and around the heights of Atxistoy, farther north, Chomin's Baztan and Iñigo's Bidasoa men proceeded to execute the second phase of the attack from the western slopes of the gorge. Rushing down the mountainside, they pursued the now-unsaddled Franks, shooting arrows and hurling *güecias* before closing with the enemy. Their *ezpatas* did the rest when they finally fell upon them.

Adroit at the cut-and-thrust tactic in dense underbrush, the Vascons ripped into the dislocated enemy, cutting it down mercilessly. Terror spread through the forest. The sound of steel crashing on helmets, cutting through bone, could be heard everywhere, screams of dying men echoing along the gorge, the little Luzaide stream peacefully flowing at its bottom, now running red with blood. Though greatly outnumbered, The Vascons fought with the cunning and tenacity of a people who understood the price of failure. There was no other option but victory, no force stronger than the conviction that they would prevail.

Several leagues farther north, just above the beech forest brooding over the Luzaide brook, Garcés had strung his small Luzaide force along the ridge overlooking Elizaldea. From his concealed position, he observed the Franks' vanguard pitching camp in the clearing near the hamlet, which would soon be named Valcarlos, Charles' vale. He noticed the troops stirring now, a detachment of cavalry saddling up, starting to head back towards Ibañeta, responding to the distress signals from their trapped comrades' horn blasts. Aware that the flower of Frankish knighthood had been bringing up the rear, they rushed to the rescue of the noble

Peers. Trapped somewhere behind the wall of rocks was the very cream of Charlemagne's court at Aix-la-Chapelle, stalwarts like Hruolandus, Prefect of the Breton marches, Eginhard, the court's majordomo, and the palace favorites, Counts Anselm and Oliver, even the crusty old Bishop Turpin. It would be a black day at Court if they succumbed.

Detecting the sudden activity, Garcés saw his chance to strike. A delaying tactic would give his Vascon comrades farther up the gorge time to inflict heavier damage on the trapped rearguard. Severely outnumbered, he knew that he could not afford a head-on encounter with the enemy in the open. Any harassing thrust had to be an in-and-out operation, lightning-quick and of the briefest duration. There was not much room for error, no great heights to fade back into once his position was exposed.

Letting out an ululating war whoop, Garcés spurred his horse into the open, leading the charge with great daring. Letting fly their arrows, his men came rushing out of hiding, howling a cacophony of battle cries as they plunged headlong into the thick of the startled Frankish support column. Before the enemy realized what was happening, the Vascons had penetrated their lines, were swarming in their midst, thrusting *güecias*, swinging *ezpatas* and axes with telling effectiveness. The resistance, at first, was disorganized and ineffective. Some Franks tried to gallop out of danger only to be cut down by flying spears. Those who survived the first onslaught tried to regroup and fend off the raging Vascons with their shields, swinging maces and broadswords at the onrushing warriors.

Although the element of surprise had taken its toll on the Frankish relief detachment, there were not enough Vascons to press their advantage and achieve a tactical victory. Noticing that the Franks were starting to regroup and that reinforcements had started to arrive from Elizaldea, Garcés sounded retreat with a blast of his ox horn. His battered force limped back into the Hayra forest where it had emerged moments earlier. Elements of the Frankish cavalry soon overtook the Vascons as they clambered up the slopes of Argaray and Ehunzaroy.

A fierce battle ensued. With their backs to the cliffs, the Vascons fought a desperate, delaying action. Their thrust-and-dodge tactics were effective at first but the massive Frankish reinforcements were too fresh and well saddled to elude or fend off. With nothing but *ezpatas* to defend themselves, the original hundred-man Luzaide force was now decimated. Garcés himself had been seriously wounded by a mace blow in the original assault and was barely able to carry on. His only hope was that the approaching darkness would allow his mauled remnants to crawl back to Baigorry without further loss of life.

It was not to be.

In one last surge, the Captain of the pursuing Franks overtook Garcés and cut him down with a stroke of his enormous broadsword. The Vascon slumped to the ground, mortally wounded. As he lay there dying, the lord of Luzaide hoped that his diversionary action had disrupted the Franks' relief column long enough for his Vascon brothers to finish off the rearguard trapped behind the original rockslide. In the never-ending struggle between valor and survival, mused Garcés darkly as he slipped closer into unconsciousness, his race had always erred on the side of foolhardiness. It was a miracle they had prevailed this long.

"*Gora Vasconia!*" he whispered weakly. They were to be his last words. The Frankish Captain, who was standing over him, stared at his dying foe, amazed that this vanquished warrior with the split skull could still manage to talk.

Matters had started to unravel behind the site of the first rockslide. The survivors of the isolated Carolingian rearguard had decided to back off from the bottleneck at Gorostgaray and retrace their steps towards the heights of Ibañeta. They were hoping to join Duke Bernard's column traveling along the old Roman road in the mistaken belief that the Burgundians and Provençals had been spared Charlemagne's column's fate.

From their positions along the commanding heights of Lindux and Girizu, the Vascons observed the Franks' retreat uphill and were quick to react. Letting out fearsome war cries, Nabar's Esteribar and Ulzama forces, heavily reinforced by the Alduides and Baztan warriors, came swooping down the mountainside, spilling onto the pass of Ibañeta. They were resolved to close the trap on the isolated rearguard and deprive it of any means of regrouping.

In the meantime, a similar drama had begun to unfold farther east of Charlemagne's withdrawing force. The trailing units of Duke Bernard's column marching along the old Roman road had met a fate similar to that of the Carolingian rearguard. On hearing Ausarta's first *irrintzi* echoing from the nearby peaks and valleys, the Vascons, deployed along the heights of Atzobiskar, Menditxipi and Txangoa, started rolling huge boulders down on the startled Franks below. Unlike the debacle at the Subibelz gorge, the slaughter here was mitigated by the absence of abrupt ravines. The consequences of the rockfall were, nevertheless, devastating. The initial rockslide had effectively severed the road, making forward progress possible only by sliding down the slopes to skirt the obstruction. Once off the old Roman road, however, the Franks found themselves ensnared in dense underbrush, nettlesome brambles hampering their progress.

The Vascons were lying in wait, ready to finish off what the rockslide had failed to accomplish. In the forests of Atzobiskar, Menditxipi and Txangoa, Sancho's, Teobaldo's and Manrique's warriors unleashed a hail of arrows on the desperate Franks. Dropping on them from tree limbs and jumping out from behind bushes, the Vascons grappled with the terrified Burgundians and Provençals. Without room to maneuver in the thick undergrowth, the Franks' cavalry was forced to dismount and fight on foot, losing, in so doing, whatever mobility and height advantage they originally had had. In the hand-to-hand combat that ensued, the Franks' long swords and maces were no match against the Vascons' short *ezpatas*.

Ill-equipped for combat at close quarters, the heavily burdened Franks were soon overpowered by the Vascons. Having fought before against enemies similarly attired and armed, the Vascons were quick to find the enemy's soft underbelly behind shield and hauberk, sometimes simply going for the unprotected jugular. Sure-footed and familiar with the terrain, the Vascons went about their task with lightning-quick thrusts, cutting Duke Bernard's ill-fated rearguard to shreds.

Unaware of the difficulties their Carolingian comrades in the western column were facing, Duke Bernard's battered rearguard, now in mass confusion, started retracing its steps towards Ibañeta, hoping to join up with Charlemagne's column and slip down the Luzaide gorge towards safety.

Both rearguard columns made the same fatal mistake.

From the heights of Atzobiskar, Menditxipi and Txangoa, Sancho's Aezcoa forces, reinforced by Teobaldo's Salazar and Manrique's Roncal contingents, descended upon the retreating Franks in full force. Vascons and Franks came to a standstill at a critical juncture in the ensuing mêlée. Observing the impasse from his Ortzanzurieta watch post, Ausarta decided it was time to commit his Lauribar and Arce reserves. Giving Andoni and Lope a nod, the two warlords led their eager men to reinforce the vacillating Aezcoa, Salazar and Roncal warriors.

In the fury of the ensuing clash, the Burgundians and the Provençals, which made up Duke Bernard's rearguard, were separated. While the former barely managed to cross the narrow land bridge of Lepoeder and reach Ibañeta, the Provençals were overcome by the converging Vascon forces and were, literally, pushed off the ridge and into the forbidding ravine of Arranosin.

Ausarta had foreseen that Charlemagne would split his forces and march them down separate Cissa passes. Even more clairvoyant, he had shrewdly timed his attack to sever both rearguard columns from their main forces, sowing such chaos that their fallback reaction was unavoidable. More perceptive yet was his positioning of his sons' forces to finish off both stampeding Frankish rearguard units. It was the lord of Agorreta's finest hour.

Approaching the fork in the road at Ibañeta, Duke Bernard's Burgundians were unpleasantly surprised to stumble upon Charlemagne's retreating Bretons, themselves relentlessly pursued by Nabar's and Teodomiro's forces. The rearguard contingent's only option was to retreat down the southern slopes of Ibañeta, toward the foot of the mountain they had started climbing only a few hours earlier.

Now on solid ground, the coalesced group of Bretons and Burgundians were able to fight a delaying action. Duke Bernard's Provençals fared worse, however, for though they were pushed down toward the same Orreaga clearing as their Breton and Burgundian comrades, they had the misfortune of having to fight a defensive action on the abrupt slopes and almost impenetrable forest of the Arranosin gully.

"An enemy in full flight is but a shadow of its former self," Ausarta had tirelessly reminded his mountain warlords during the operational meetings in Agorreta. His younger son, Antxon, who had concealed his troops under the Lepoeder narrows, now saw the wisdom of his father's words. In their eagerness to outdistance the pesky Vascons nipping at their heels, the Provençals proceeded to shed their heavy shields and cumbersome armor as they stumbled down the increasingly rugged terrain, in the waning light of day. The utter chaos of their undisciplined retreat was to be their undoing.

Remorselessly, the Vascons pressed on against the fading light, pouncing upon their prey like wolves in a feeding frenzy, all the while shrieking their eerie, unnerving *irrintzis*. The small brook running down the Arranosin gully would soon run crimson with the blood of Provençals and Vascons alike. When the wind was blowing just right, Ausarta, standing serenely on the top of Ortzanzurieta, could hear the pitiful shrieks of the dying, which reassured him that his tactics were proceeding according to plan. Even the timing had been perfect. Now only the *coup de grace* remained to be executed in the clearing of Orreaga, as he had visualized it in his mind's eye all along.

While few of Duke Bernard's Provençals would survive the dreadful pounding at the Arranosin gully, the more disciplined, better-led Bretons managed to fight a vigorous holding action against the repeated onslaughts of Nabar's and Teodomiro's men. They retreated in good order from the Ibañeta pass, all the way down to the small clearing of Orreaga, at the foot of the mountain. Inspired by the example of three of Charlemagne's fearless Peers commanding them, the Bretons continued to put up a stiff resistance, fighting desperately with their backs now literally to the Pyrenean wall.

Slowly, inevitably, the Bretons fell one by one as wave upon wave of Erro and Esteribar Vascons fell upon them. Now in the open, without the Vascons' advantage of cover or the hindrance of trees or slippery footing, the contest between the two contending forces became more even. Only the pride of place and the dim recollections of previous battles fought on this hollowed ground were enough to give the Vascons a fierce incentive to prevail.

The Franks had formed a defensive circle behind a wall of shields. Mounted, two astride each horse, Nabar's men plowed through the bristling phalanx, engaging the enemy from both sides of their mounts, in the manner of double-scythed chariots. Tearing into the enemy, they cut a clean swath through the defensive perimeter, sowing havoc among the troops inside. Once in their midst, the hind rider jumped off to grapple with the enemy, while the horseman holding the reins continued his progress through the huddled group, until he, too, was forced to dismount. The time-tested maneuver inflicted a great number of casualties among the startled Franks. Once again, the *ezpata* was to prove its mettle in close combat. Nimbly avoiding the enemy's swinging maces and clumsy broadswords, the Vascons thrust their short, double-edged swords into the enemy's unprotected groins and bared underarms. In the end, however, both equestrian Vascons paid dearly for their suicidal tactic, isolated as they were, inside the enemy's formation.

Sitting on the fringes of the fray astride his dark Arabian steed, Nabar watched his men plunge into the thick of battle with joyful abandon. While thus admiring their confidence and enthusiasm, he was suddenly distracted by a fracas in the gully directly above the clearing of Orreaga, where his own battle was taking place. Looking up, he saw a group of men fighting desperately down both sides of the brook flowing down the Arranosin chasm. Near the bottom of the gorge, he detected the brawny figure of a tall, bearded young man with a shock of brown hair. It was his brother!

The young Agorreta was grappling with a paunchy, oddly-attired Frank brandishing an unwieldy foreign broadsword in one hand and a bishop's crosier in the other, his flowing white robes occasionally getting in his way. Nabar could not believe his eyes: his brother was engaged in mortal combat with a Bishop who seemed to have lost his miter! The bizarre scene made Nabar chuckle, anticipating the ribbing his brother Antxon would get when it was all over.

Battling near his brother, farther down the gorge, now almost level with the Orreaga clearing, Nabar recognized the lanky figure of the lord of the Arga valley. Together with Antxon, Arista had harassed the hapless Provençals from the moment they were pushed off the ledge of the Lepoeder narrows. Arista was engaged in combat with a tall warrior who, like the other Peers in the Frankish army, was inappropriately clad in hot, cumbersome full battle armor. The nobleman looked as if he belonged more in the ballrooms of Aachen or Aix-la-Chapelle than in the bloody battleground of Arranosin. He had obviously been unhorsed early on and was now having difficulty moving around the slippery, moss-covered terrain, attired in his hauberk, burnished cuirass and fancy, mailed footwear.

Despite his awkward impedimenta, the nobleman was putting up a good fight, taking full advantage of his height to take out not a few Vascons with his fearsome mace. His reflexes were, however, starting to show signs of fatigue. Noticing his exhaustion, Arista jumped in for the kill. Ducking under the nobleman's swinging mace, the Vascon closed and struck at his throat with his short sword. A groan was heard as the Frank hit the ground with a sickening thud, followed shortly after by a death rattle, as blood gushed from his severed jugular. Losing consciousness must have been a blessing for the Peer after the ceaseless torment he had been subjected to for the last hour of his young life. Arista would never know that he had just finished slaying Count Anselm himself, one of Charlemagne's court favorites.

Across the gully, in the small clearing of Orreaga, Nabar now turned his attention to the fighting before him. His men, along with Teodomiro's, had been methodically suppressing the opposition. The original defensive perimeter had, by now, crumbled and the few remaining pockets of resistance were fighting their own individual skirmishes. The battle would be over before nightfall, Ausarta's firstborn predicted.

It was then that Nabar noticed the gallant horseman riding back and forth among his troops on a powerful, white charger. Waving a massive, sword on high, he rallied his exhausted Breton foot soldiers with spirited words of encouragement. The husky cavalier, who looked to be in his mid-forties, spoke with the same distinctive accent as his troops and would, thus, have to be a Breton himself, Nabar rightly surmised.

The chivalrous figure was no other than Hruolandus, stalwart lord of the Breton Marches, one of the twelve noble Peers rumored to have accompanied Charlemagne on his trans-Pyrenean adventure. Of all the noblemen in his entourage, Hruolandus was known to be the King's favorite, not only for his dashing presence and courtly demeanor but for the sagacity he had shown in the administration of his realm's affairs in Brittany. His imposing carriage and gift of leadership in the field of battle were distinct assets in the Franks' rife-torn empire. Sensing that his rearguard would be the target of a Basque ambush, Charlemagne had assigned its defense to Hruolandus. He needed his best man to defend the Vascons' most obvious target—the tempting booty train in his rearguard.

Nabar made a quick decision: he would engage the Breton leader and finish him off himself. Raising his eyes towards Ortzanzurieta, he saw the mountain ablaze with the sun's last rays. Standing on the bald mountaintop, he thought he detected the figure of a white-bearded man, cape blowing in the wind, holding up both arms on high, as if blessing his warriors.

It was *Aita*!

Nabar spurred his horse into the thick of the fray. Cutting a swath through the small pocket of Franks fighting in the middle of the clearing, Nabar challenged the chevalier with the outsized sword, sitting confidently astride his white stallion. For a brief moment, the two men stared at each other, sensing, without the saying, that they were, each, the leader of their contending forces. Their look, like a gauntlet thrown, reflected their mixed emotions of admiration and contempt for one another. One of them, if not both, was going to die as a result of this clash. For a fleeting unspoken instant of *noblesse oblige*, their eyes saluted each other.

Both horses charged at full tilt, their riders waving their swords on high, having long since splintered their lances. The thunder of hooves and the clash of steel resounded along the mountains surrounding Orreaga. For a brief instant, the warring Vascons and Breton foot soldiers held their swords to witness the awesome spectacle of their respective leaders dueling in mortal combat. Back and forth they charged the other, maneuvering their mounts, trading blows, waiting for any tactical advantage. Nabar knew that despite the hazard involved, his only hope of overcoming the reach advantage of the Frank's enormous sword was to duel at close quarters, where his short *ezpata* would have a fighting chance of inflicting damage.

Hruolandus, on the other hand, sensed that the only way of equalizing their obvious difference in age and strength was to keep the young Vascon at arm's length. Cunningly, he contrived to maneuver his horse away from Nabar's every time they closed. On one of the charges the Breton succeeded in inflicting a deep gash in the Vascon's left arm, unseating him from his mount. Time and again, Hruolandus tried to run down his wounded foe, but each time Nabar managed to sidestep the thrust at the very last moment.

Observing the disadvantage at which his wounded lord was now forced to fight, one of Teodomiro's sharpshooters standing nearby let fly an arrow at Hruolandus horse, fortuitously piercing a vital organ. Stumbling to the ground, the horse spilled the Breton a few paces from where Nabar stood. Now bleeding profusely from his wounded arm, Nabar closed with his foe. The two men exchanged crashing sword blows that Nabar painfully parried with his wounded shield arm. Now at closer quarters, however, the Vascon was more in his element. He could thrust his shorter sword faster than Hruolandus could swing his long broadsword. The middle-aged Breton had to use both hands to raise and swing his weapon, a tiresome effort increasingly apparent in his now labored breathing.

Feeling progressively faint from loss of blood, Nabar knew that he had to bring the duel to a quick conclusion. Sidestepping one of Hruolandus' blows, he stepped into the small space separating them and, with every ounce of his ebbing strength, thrust his *ezpata* into the underarm gap of Hruolandus' hauberk. Feeling the steel sink deep into the Breton's chest, he gave it one last downward pull, ripping his foe's chest cavity apart.

Hruolandus' startled eyes met Nabar's. There was no complaint uttered, no message exchanged between them other than one's agony and the other's exultation of victory. The Breton's eyes glazed over even as he crashed to the ground, Nabar's sword still sticking from his armpit at an odd angle. The few remaining Franks knew that the battle was over. Their desultory resistance was soon squelched by the Vascons' swords until not a Breton remained standing in the small clearing of Orreaga. Only their groans could be heard in the gloaming valley.

Antxon came bounding over to where Nabar stood, now increasingly faint from loss of blood.

"Well done, brother," said the young Antxon, proud of his sibling's mighty feat. He had watched the contest from afar, sensing the outcome beforehand. Strapping a leather thong tightly above his brother's wound, he lifted him up in his strong arms, propped him up on his horse and slapped its rump to start it down the road, towards home.

From the heights of Ortzanzurieta, Ausarta saw the commotion cease in the clearing of Orreaga, the valley of thorns. He also thought he heard his young son's long and joyous *irrintzi* rising from the valley below. It filled his heart with a warm, ineffable glow.

"*Aupa Vasconia!*" he whispered under his breath, dropping his weary arms.

It was already dark when the last surviving Vascons abandoned the clearing of Orreaga, carrying their wounded and their dead, nothing else, not even the spoils strewn around the valley. When Charlemagne rode up early the next morning, he found nothing but dead Bretons. The silence of so many awed him. He was surprised to find his booty trains untouched. It was that mute evidence that made him realize that the fight had been fought not for lucre but over the field of honor. He even found his beloved Hruolandus lying face up, carefully stretched out as if in sleep, his shining sword resting over his chest, hands reverently clasped around its handle's cross, eyelids respectfully shut by some thoughtful foe.

There was honor even among Vascons, thought the future Emperor.

BOOK II
THE AGE OF CHIVALRY

"There is properly no history, only biography."
—Ralph Waldo Emerson
Essays: First Series

The Lords of Navarre

Kingdom of Navarre ca. 1190

Chapter 20

At The Dawning of Chivalry

1170s

Sancho the Wise was only seventeen when he was crowned king of Pamplona. Though living in the age of chivalry, precious little of its code of honor had rubbed off on the monarchs of the neighboring Iberian kingdoms of Aragon and Castile, both loath to recognize the young upstart's right to the Vascon throne. Through cunning and dogged determination, however, the young Vascon managed to hold on to his crown and steer his young kingdom through the turbulent waters of the late twelfth century, managing to extend its frontiers to their farthest historical confines.

Basking in Sancho's magnanimity were a handful of powerful Vascon lords who, having swept him into power, now sat back to watch their seigniories prosper under their king's goodwill and largesse. High in the monarch's favor were Counts, barons and *hidalgos* who owned lands on the kingdom's frontiers critical to the realm's security. Among this favored handful was Juan de Agorreta, a *gentilhombre* whose possessions happened to straddle the main artery connecting Pamplona with the French border. Lord of the valley of Esteribar, Juan had been knighted by the king's father in the battle of Baeza, in far-off *al-Andalus*, where Agorreta had served his liege lord with distinction.

Having accumulated enough wealth through harvest dues and hearth-silver from his several fiefs, Juan now sat back to enjoy the leisurely life of a gentleman farmer. He had trained as seneschal to several Counts and had grown wise in the ways of commerce and the husbandry of his feudal resources. Now in his sundown years, he preferred spending his summers in Gasteluzar, his fortified manor house overlooking the village that bore his name, strategically located on the road between Pamplona and France. He owned large tracts of woodlands and lush, rolling meadows on which his large flocks of sheep grazed. Adding to his serfs' rent money and other pastoral proceeds were several mills he owned and exploited, all of which made Juan a man of substance.

The lord of Agorreta enjoyed the company of other rough-hewn knights and country squires who also owed vassalage to their king for their mountain fiefs. Most of them had played more or less important roles in local wars, though, unlike Juan, few had ventured to far-off *al-Andalus* to tangle with the Moors. Some liked to brag about having visited Santiago de Compostela on religious pilgrimage, others of having participated in tournaments, accomplishments all far more exciting than overseeing their serfs' planting, milling and sheepherding chores, though the former, of course, would not have been possible without the perquisites from the latter.

They all worried about good marriages for their progeny. Juan and Laura had raised ten children, most of whom had, by now, married and moved on. His daughters had led an uncommon life of refined leisure, with time to embroider, play chess, even read Ovid and the romantic *gestes* of the day from books borrowed from the well-stocked library of the nearby Collegiate of Roncevaux. Juan and Laura knew that these cultivated pastimes would one day help them land genteel husbands of good breeding, as they all eventually did.

Following time-honored tradition, Andoni, the oldest son, would inherit the family titles and possessions upon his father's death, a tradition meant to prevent the breaking up of the patrimony into ever-dwindling parcels. The rest of the brood would have to fend for themselves, the girls with their dowries, the men by their wits, their swords or their breviaries. Only the oldest and the youngest sons now remained in the ancestral manor house. Though Andoni's future was assured, the prospects of Iñaki, the youngest, remained uncertain.

Their last-born was the joy of his aging parents' waning days. Though only ten, Iñaki was already a strapping young lad, endowed with strength unusual for one so young. Remarkable for one so tall, he had about him a litheness and a hand-to-eye coordination that graced his every move. Though short in years, he already excelled at sports, of which his people were so fond. He could show the points and paces of a horse with the easy elegance of a seasoned horseman, making it dance or dash, leap or prance with the slightest of equestrian hints. It almost seemed as if he could talk to the animals. It was not only with horses that he seemed able to communicate; he could talk to the hawks, as well. He loved falconry as much as his father and had developed an uncanny ability to imitate their feral cries, which the birds seemed to understand and respond to.

His parents were inordinately proud of Iñaki. Hardly a day went by without their thanking the good Lord for this gift He had given them as solace in their old age. The lad was so full of promise that his doting parents were convinced he would achieve anything he set his mind to. They were amazed at his ability to converse in Latin with the village priest, occasionally even beating him at *Mus*, a favorite Vascon card game. And yet they couldn't help worrying about Iñaki's future, for, other than a good education, there was little else they could bequeath him. By rights, he should have followed a monastic life but the lad had no religious calling, his head already swimming thickly with dreams of knighthood.

"You could call on Count Aznarez," suggested Laura to her husband on the eve of Iñaki's eleventh birthday. "He could probably page and then squire for him. Who knows, one day he could even become a knight like you!"

She had always secretly wished to see one of her sons come riding up the hill on his white charger, decked in gleaming armor, as her husband once did when they were young. She had been so proud of him! Being a hopeless romantic, the lady Agorreta had avidly read all the outpouring of Spanish and French *chansons de geste* that happened to fall in her hands. She and her daughters were particularly fond of *El Cantar del Mio Cid* and the *Chanson de Roland*, the latter of which, Juan assured them in his usual gruff way, was pure fabrication.

"It was not the Saracens who slew the noble Breton," he'd huff. "Our very own Vascon ancestors did!" There was, of course, no way to prove that his forebears had, four centuries earlier, fought in the epic battle that took place not far from where they lived. But he could still recite strains of ancient family lore strongly hinting at such involvement. He loved to embarrass unwary French *trouvères* who happened to blunder into his manor on their way to court in Pamplona, with his own version of the chauvinistic Frankish *chanson*.

"Be practical, woman," remonstrated Agorreta, a little put out by her suggestion of sending Iñaki off to Count Aznarez' castle in Sangüesa. "It's been too many years since I served as his seneschal. He was already old and infirm then, surely dead by now."

"It may be worth a try, anyway" persisted his wife. "He had several sons, didn't he? Ramón, the oldest, may now be the new Count. You knew him well, didn't you? He was quite fond of you, as I recall."

"So he was," responded Agorreta, the edge in his voice receding. "I have to go to Tudela after the harvest to settle accounts with the king's steward. I suppose I could skip on up to Sangüesa on my way back. Nothing ventured, nothing gained." He tried to hide the gleam in his eye from his wife. There was no point letting women know how good some of their suggestions really were sometimes, particularly Laura's. She came from genteel stock and her mind had always been keen as a bear trap.

The castle on top of the hill overlooking Sangüesa looked just as imposing as when Juan had served there as seneschal, years earlier. Ramón, the old Count's firstborn, had inherited the castle and its rich lands when his father died. Agorreta was quick to notice that the young Count was running the castle much more efficiently than his old man ever did. Ramón remembered Agorreta well. Over a mug of heady Liédena wine they reminisced on his years of tutelage, recalling the lessons on the arts of war and the intricacies of the Basque language, both of which Agorreta had taught the young Aznarez. All that learning had stood the Count in good stead over the years, he readily admitted. When the subject of Iñaki came up, the Count's eyes seemed to light up.

"Why, of course!" he exclaimed. "I've been short of help all year, what with all the casualties we've sustained with these incessant frontier skirmishes with the Aragonese. I'd be more than happy to take the young lad under my wing. I'll make him go through the paces, of course. If he's as good as you claim he is, we may shorten his stint as a page. He's got to go through some of that, you know. Lots of things to learn, character to build, all that sort of thing. Who knows, one day I may even give him the arms of knighthood if he sticks with it and proves his mettle." Pausing briefly, he added: "And I promise to make him sweat at the quintain as much as you made me do, with those interminable lessons of yours!" They both chortled at the reminiscence.

A week later, Iñaki rode into Sangüesa with his brother, Andoni, astride their father's favorite stallion. It was Michaelmas, the day of the harvest festival signaling the beginning of fall, when farmers and townsfolk gathered round the main square to spend some of their hard-earned Sanchetes after a year's back-breaking work. Before heading for the castle, the two brothers tarried awhile to enjoy the festivities. The town's main square teemed with humanity, the air alive with the sounds of *txistu* flutes and tambourines playing the *jota*. Children frolicked, mingling with the dancers, trying to imitate their dancing skills. The two brothers laughed at the antics of tumblers and jugglers and were mesmerized by the way the conjurers swallowed fire, some even swords. Iñaki knew, right off, that he was going to like this place.

It was late afternoon when they finally cantered their mount up the hill to the castle's main gate. Iñaki gawked at the complex of moats, towers, drawbridges. A crenellated wall with corner towers guarded the entrance to the square keep which dominated the center of the castle grounds.

"Notice those arrow loops?" remarked Andoni, pointing at the vertical slots cut intermittently along the curtain wall, just below the battlements. "Archers shoot arrows through them." Iñaki stared at them, his mind racing, scenes of sieges and gory battles dancing in his head. Pointing at the overhanging structures protruding from the top of the wall, his brother explained: "Those are machicolations; they pour boiling oil from them on the besiegers below." Iñaki stared at them in awe.

"It sure looks impregnable," exclaimed the lad, overwhelmed by the apparent unassailability of the fortress.

"That's what the previous owners thought," responded Andoni knowingly. "The Moors owned it once, not long ago, but Christians found a way to take it away from them. Everything is vulnerable if one has the courage and the determination…and the wherewithal." His brother seemed so knowledgeable, reflected Iñaki.

As they approached the drawbridge guarding the castle's main gate, Iñaki dismounted, bade his brother farewell. "Thanks for the ride and the company," he said. "It was fun at the fair." Pointing his thumb at the castle behind him, he added: "I hope it's as much fun in there."

"Take care of yourself," counseled the older brother. "Always remember: you're an Agorreta."

"As if I could forget!" answered the youth. He waved at his departing brother as he walked across the lowered drawbridge.

A stout, middle-aged man with a crop of gray hair and a huge, jutting jaw greeted him as he reached the main gate. The wild bushiness of his eyebrows seemed to add to the fierce squint in his eyes. "I'm Sir Tomás, warden of the castle," he announced in a deep voice. The battle banners hanging from the whitewashed walls did little to dampen the sound of the warden's booming voice, as it bounced around the high walls of the guardhouse. "I've been asked to look after you," he added comfortingly. There was something avuncular about this gruff old man, thought Iñaki. He had a feeling he'd get along well with him.

"Are you a knight?" asked the lad brightly. Though he wore no armor, the man's bearing and vestments gave him the distinguished air of someone important.

"I most certainly am!" roared the man jovially, amused by the youth's ingenuousness. "Come, let me show you around the castle before we get down to business."

Leaving the gatehouse behind, they walked across the first of two concentric courtyards. Set on the outer bailey was a large wooden structure housing a hall with several adjoining rooms. "These," explained the warden, "are the garrison's domestic quarters and offices." Stepping through the doorway, they emerged into the castle gardens. Iñaki was astonished to find fruit trees and small plots of herbs and flowers, even a diminutive vineyard in one corner. In the middle of the garden was a small, circular fishpond where trout were surface-feeding on bugs. The place was like an incongruous little oasis surrounded by otherwise forbidding surroundings. Proceeding past an artesian well, they approached the castle's central keep, the distinctive square tower visible from afar.

"In a serious siege," explained the warden reassuringly, "this keep becomes the fortress' last stronghold. Everyone abandons the baileys and retreats here for a last-ditch stand." Iñaki was impressed by the casualness of Sir Tomás' remark, sounding as if the hurried retreat were a common occurrence. It all sounded so exciting!

Winding along the keep's wall was a stone stairway, which led up to the castle's upper floor. The Great Hall inside was dimly lit by tallow candles impaled on iron candleposts, rushlights hanging from rusty brackets on the wall. A small fire burned in a huge fireplace gaping from one of the walls, its projecting hood only partially capturing the smoke rising up the flue. The smoke from the candles, the torches and the fireplace's faulty draft were making Iñaki's eyes water.

"These are the Count's living quarters," explained the warden, climbing the few steps of a raised wooden dais at the far end of the Great Hall. "He and his wife are at court in Pamplona today, so I can show them to you."

Spartanly furnished, the quarters' wainscoted walls were hung with tapestries depicting saints and knights engaged in pitched battles. At the far end of the dais sat a canopied leather chair flanked by several wooden, straight-backed chairs. It was the Count's chair, Iñaki was informed, or the King's, when he came visiting.

Neatly stacked against the wall in one corner of the hall were the trestles and boards used to assemble dinner tables. The gallery overlooking the daised area was where the musicians played, he was informed.

At the far end of a dimly lit passageway, just beyond the pantry and the buttery, was a spiral staircase leading down to a storage room under the Great Hall. A door at the far end of the basement opened onto an outbuilding in the inner bailey where the kitchen was located. A cook was turning several legs of lamb on a spit over a central hearth, while red Sangüesa beans were slowly cooking in a huge pot over the hearth's fire. The delicious blend of aromas made Iñaki hungry. They reminded him of home.

After the brief castle tour, the warden led Iñaki to his administrative quarters in the outer bailey to go over Iñaki's duties and training program.

"You will join the ranks of pages," he began officiously. "There are presently only half a dozen pages in the castle, most of them younger than you. You'll have to serve several years as a page. Then, if all goes well, you'll move on to become a squire. Normally, each of those stages takes about seven years," he explained. Iñaki winced; a quick calculation making him realize that he'd be twenty-five before he would become eligible for knighthood. Surely there had to be some shortcut around this long, drawn-out process.

Iñaki adapted to castle life with surprising ease. Though a page's fare turned out not to be as appetizing as his mother's home cooking, and his quarters in the lean-to shed by the outer bailey were damp and drafty, the company he shared with two other pages made life in the cramped space passably bearable. He was determined to enjoy the challenge of this disciplined way of life. One was supposed to learn from hardship and privation because, as his father was fond of reminding him, suffering built character. In his mind's eye he associated character with calluses; they both grew slowly and painfully, and were eventually forgotten.

Castle chores were not unlike those back home. He was used to cleaning stables and feeding and grooming horses. Cows, too, had to be milked and firewood stacked up around hearths and fireplaces, soiled rushes swept from the floor of the Great Hall after dinner, fresh new ones cut and strewn about to replace them. Other chores, such as cleaning and polishing the knights' armor, were new to him, as were such dinner preparations as setting up tables and tending to knights with ewers and basins and towels for their ablutions. Only squires were allowed to serve the lord and his family during meals. Pages had to observe the squires' demeanor, the way they poured the wine, the number of fingers they used to cut the meat, the way they presented the laden trenchers, all simple, yet tedious, rituals. The novelty of it all made it look like fun.

Required to fade discretely into the background when not needed, he and the other pages would linger in the shadows of the Great Hall after dinner to hear the minstrels and the jesters recite their stories and their jokes. They listened, spellbound, to their rambling stories of El Cid and Ulysses, Caesar and Roland. It was good enticement to learn French because most of the great troubadours came from French Aquitaine, a land beyond the Pyrenees where they once spoke Basque but had long since forgotten.

But all was not work and drudgery. Parts of the day were devoted to the enlightenment of the mind and the edification of the soul. There were good manners to be learned and Latin, numbers, and astronomy to be mastered under the vigilant tutelage of the castle Chaplain. It was a poor knight, they were reminded, who could not read or write, use proper language or display good manners.

The tedium of castle life was broken by a succession of feast days that came, mercifully enough, just as the ennui started to build up. Everyone, townsfolk and castellans alike, looked forward to the good food and better drink that flowed freely during these festivities, thanks to the lord's largesse. It was on one such holiday, Whitsunday, that two of the squires were knighted. The castle simply erupted in an explosion of festivities and merrymaking. The Great Hall was decked in such profusion of herbs and flowers that the usual smell of smoke and rank sweat was masked by the sweet scent of cowslip and germander, hyssop and roses. The meals were sumptuous, with such exotic dishes as boar's head and peacocks, plovers and larks, none of which Iñaki had ever tasted before.

But it was his rare moments of leisure that Iñaki treasured the most. On such occasions, he'd stroll over to the mews, where the Count's hawks were kept. He soon befriended the falconer, talked him into letting him watch him train his birds of prey. He observed how the falconer painstakingly built up the birds' hunting skills, starting them off going after hare, then snipe and, finally, their most demanding quarry, cranes. The lengthy, year-long process went far to explain why a well-trained hawk was such a rare and valuable possession.

Iñaki soon became a permanent fixture at the mews. He and the falconer enjoyed each other's company, talked endlessly about hawks, discussed their ailments and weaknesses, learned about each breed's moods and temperament. The falconer was intrigued by Iñaki's predilection for the weakest bird in the roost, a gyrfalcon that, for reasons unknown, had refused to go beyond the hare phase of its training.

"I could teach him to go after crane," bragged Iñaki one day, much to the falconer's amusement.

"You don't even have the build of a good falconer!" chided the bird keeper. "One has to be agile and of medium build, like me, not tall and gangly like you. Besides, a first class falconer has to have keen eyesight and hearing, be alert of mind and have an even temper. Above all, he has to be patient and have good, neat fingers. Do you have any these qualities?" taunted the birdman.

"I most certainly do!" replied Iñaki testily. "I may be taller than you but I'm agile enough. And as for the rest, my eyes can spot a bird five leagues away. I can also hear bird notes nobody else can hear." He stopped for breath, added: "And talking about alert minds, the Chaplain says that I'm good with numbers and Latin." Then, with an impish grin, he added: "As for patience, I have more of that than you'll ever have."

The falconer laughed out heartily. He enjoyed the lad's spunk and sense of humor. "The Count ordered that bird from some town near the cliffs of Cantabria," he explained, referring to the defective hawk. "That's where the best hawks nest. But something happened to arrest its normal learning process. Personally, I think its brain is flawed." After a moment's hesitation, he added: "I'll give you six months to train that gyrfalcon to go after crane. If you succeed, the Count will make you a squire on the spot, believe you me! He had high hopes for that bird, once. It cost him a pretty Sanchete!"

"You're on!" said Iñaki excitedly, rising to the bait. His mind was racing with the thought of skipping page-hood altogether and moving directly on to squire-hood. He could already run circles around any of those squires in Latin and Arithmetic. He'd been watching them prepare and serve meals at the Lord's table, heard them speak their prissy kind of "court" Castilian. There was nothing to it. He could certainly beat any of them at speaking Basque! And, on top of all that, there was nothing anyone could teach him about horseback riding. That was, after all, the whole object of this long, drawn-out learning process toward knighthood, was it not? Sure, he admitted, there were still sword-wielding and lance-tucking to master but he'd already tried them at the quintain and felt he could best a few squires at the sport.

The Marshall and his stable lackeys had begun noticing young Agorreta's natural equestrian talents and uncanny way with horses. On one occasion, threatened by one of the frequent Aragonese border raids, Iñaki had volunteered to help round up the horses from the Count's demesne. Apprised of how his horsemanship had helped save the day, the Count decided to find out for himself. The approaching Mayday festivities would be a good opportunity to put him to the test.

The main event in the yearly celebration was a horserace around the town's main square. The plaza was abuzz with anticipation—and not a few giggles—when Iñaki turned up at the starting line with his sorry mount, an old swayback mare more fit for pulling a plow than for racing. Despite the handicap, however, the race turned out to be quite close. The crowd watched in astonishment as Iñaki's mount crossed the finish line in second place, a mere nose behind a magnificent Arabian stallion ridden by the Marshall's favorite squire. The Count offered his usual perfunctory congratulations to the winner, but when Iñaki walked up to the platform, the smile on the Count's face spoke volumes for his admiration of young Agorreta's unexpected showing.

That was only the beginning of the lord's many surprises. An avid falconer himself, Count Aznarez had been hearing talk about Agorreta's way with birds. One afternoon in early November, he invited the lad to one of his hawking outings, hoping to observe firsthand the young fellow's way with falcons. As they rode out to the fields, the Count was surprised to see Iñaki carrying the flawed gyrfalcon on which he had given up, long ago. With mounting curiosity, he observed the gentleness and dexterity with which the youth handled it. Holding the long-winged bird on his gloved hand, Iñaki lowered the falcon's hooded head to his mouth, began exchanging strange chirping sounds with it. The bird responded with its own muffled warbles. It was almost as if they were talking to each other, thought the Count.

At a signal from the falconer, the Count and Iñaki un-hooded their respective hawks, raised their gloved hands and released their birds at the same time. With breathtaking suddenness, the two falcons were airborne. They soared into the high sky with equal grace, each lifting itself up with rhythmic, powerful wing strokes, as if intoxicated by the wind under their wings. They rolled and spiraled in the updrafts, climbing almost out of sight.

A few minutes later, the Count and his retinue observed the gyrfalcon hunch its long, dagger-shaped wings in a tight tuck as its bullet-shaped body went into a power stoop, screeching at an unsuspecting crane which was flying near ground level. The Count's peregrine was not far behind. The Count, who had never suspected that the flawed gyrfalcon could stoop and dive with such blinding speed, watched in awe as it tore into the crane in a flurry of feathers. From a distance, the Count's peregrine watched disconsolately at its missed prey.

But the Count's amazement was just beginning. After flying around in a wide circle, the gyrfalcon dropped its prey precisely at Iñaki's feet, before coming to rest on his extended arm.

"*Mirabile visu!*" whispered the Count under his breath at the wondrous feat of falconry. It had taken his falconer many frustrating months to try to teach that hawk to go after crane, without success. Now, this young page had, with a few strange sounds, made it accomplish that feat. More wondrous yet, he had made it fly back directly to him instead of to the mock bird lure dangling from a stand nearby, as gyrfalcons and peregrines were wont to do.

Although unknown at the time, Agorreta's days in Sangüesa were numbered when his lord accepted the King's invitation to the investiture ceremony of a new Abbot in Leyre, the Cistercian monastery perched high atop a mountain, nearby. Count Aznarez knew his monarch well, being of the same age as he and having enjoyed the other's company in skirmishes against Moors, in tussles with troublesome barons, and at councils of the realm and religious investiture ceremonies. He enjoyed consorting with his royal friend because one could always count on good food and better falconry, a sport they both loved with undiluted passion.

On the spur of the moment, the Count decided to bring young Agorreta along to show him off to his royal hunting friend. That, it turned out, was a mistake, for no sooner had King Sancho the Wise observed the curious interchange between page and gyrfalcon than his curiosity was aroused. All conversation around them ceased as the king raised his hand requesting silence to better listen to the feral interchange between youth and bird. Moments later, they stood in awe, watching the hawk plummet in its deadly, unerring dive, grabbing its prey and dropping it at the lad's feet before coming to rest on his gloved hand. Gyrfalcons were not supposed to do that, murmured the gathering of lords. Only goshawks did that! What manner of lad was this?

"The chap is mine," said the king with a regal finality that left little room for argument. "I will make arrangements for him to come to Tudela." Count

Aznarez was about to voice his objection at such royal highhandedness when the king added: "Where, pray, did you find this jewel?"

It was too late to complain now. Aznarez knew it would have been churlish to show his displeasure at the loss. He quickly realized that the king now owed him a favor. For years he had been casting longing glances at the fortified town of Sos, just across Navarre's eastern border with Aragon, a mere stone's throw from Sangüesa. Perhaps, just perhaps, he could pry it loose from the Aragonese, with his king's approval and support, of course. But for that to happen he had to be in his king's good graces. The young Agorreta could just turn out to be the opening he needed. He thought he would raise the stakes by praising the lad's other virtues.

"He came to me from a petty baronage in one of the mountain valleys, your Highness. His father used to be my father's seneschal, years ago. He's a fine young chap, as your Highness can see for himself. Keen as hunger, too. Speaks Basque with a pure accent, not this adulterated version we speak around here." As if to further underscore the lad's merits, he added: "You've seen his way with falcons. You should see him ride!"

"So, why is he still a page?" puzzled the king, observing the strapping young lad appreciatively.

"I was meaning to make him a squire presently," answered the Count, lamely.

The king mulled over the boy's glowing credentials. Sancho, his son and heir-apparent, had been in sore need of learning the Basques' ways. He was, after all, going to be their next king. This young fellow, Agorreta, could teach him his future subjects' ways and language. The lad was tall and strong, like his son, whom people had started calling "*el Fuerte*," the strong one, a nickname he would one day carry into the history books. They were going to hit it off, these two, he was sure. It was a stroke of good luck that Aznarez had brought him along.

Iñaki was on the road to Tudela a week later. He would miss his friends, the falconer, the Marshall, the pages and squires who had befriended him in Sangüesa, but there were bigger and better things ahead. His parents had come to see him off. They were inordinately proud of his squiring in the King's palace. They could never, in their wildest dreams, have envisioned such good fortune for their youngest son. His mother, who had prayed for him to her Virgin of Roncevaux all these many years, now promised her a token of her gratitude; she would grant a handsome tithe to help pay for the new monastery church, just then under construction in Roncevaux.

Juan de Agorreta could not get over how quickly his son was making his way up in the world of chivalry. He knew, of course, that he had had it in him, all along. He had always been immensely proud of the youngest of his brood, but he now felt a new, more ineffable happiness about his youngest son's future.

"When I go to Tudela to see the King's Chancellor on business," he told his son, "I'll get to visit with you. You may even show me this newfangled sport they call 'jousting' that I've been hearing about. Sounds more civilized than mêlées."

That pleased Iñaki. He was, after all, only fourteen and had been prone to bouts of homesickness in Sangüesa, especially around Christmastime. Life, from now on, was going to be too hectic for maudlin feelings. He was, after all, going to live under the same roof as his king. How much more exciting could life get!

And, on top of all that, he'd always dreamed of having a prince for a friend.

Chapter 21

A Squire's Life

1180s

King Sancho the Wise much preferred spending his time in his southern Navarran castle of Tudela rather than in Pamplona, his young kingdom's official capital. It was not only warmer in the Ebro lowlands but the inhabitants of the *Ager Vasconum* were far more sophisticated than the boorish counts and cantankerous barons living in the seat of kingdom. He didn't mind rubbing elbows with the resident Christian converts to Islam, whom the locals called *muladi*, and whose learned co-religionists were keeping the flickering flame of civilization alive during Europe's dark ages, glad to share their knowledge and cultured ways with the nascent kingdoms of Christendom.

Sancho came naturally by his diplomatic skills. His great grandfather, El Cid, had displayed the same tact and political talent with the vanquished Moors in the Spanish Levant, decades earlier, ruling over them in a Mediterranean fief large enough to make any Christian duke drool with envy. Like his famous forebear, Sancho the Wise treated the Jews and the Moors of Tudela with benevolence, shrewdly forging alliances with foreign powers to keep his troublesome Christian neighbors of Aragon and Castile from whittling away at his young kingdom.

It was to this world of international politics and high intrigue that the fourteen year-old Iñaki was introduced when he first rode into the King's castle in Tudela. The royal residence in the heart of the walled, brown-brick town sat on the southern banks of the serene Ebro River. It was not the safest place for the Vascon king's residence, being only a stone's throw away from the frontiers of both Aragon and Castile. But it was a warm and bounteous land and the powerful castle, built three centuries earlier by a Moorish Caliph, was capable of withstanding any assault his two unfriendly Christian neighbors might care to mount against it.

Iñaki was shown to his living quarters in a cramped, ill-lit corner room in one of the castle's many towers. Though he had to share the confined lodgings with two other squires, Iñaki could already see a definite improvement over his earlier digs in Sangüesa. He had a proper bed, for one, and its feather mattress was far more comfortable than the bug-ridden straw pallet on the hard Sangüesan floor. He was allotted a drawer in a chest shared with the other two squires, where he arranged his tunics and undergarments and a few personal belongings. On top of the chest he placed the small statue of the Virgin of Roncevaux, which his mother had given him in parting. "She'll keep you out of harm's way," she had said, with her characteristic piety.

What he found most appealing about his new station was having left behind menial page labor altogether. He had even been assigned a page of his own to help with the humdrum chores of grooming his horse and burnishing his armor, for he was now the proud owner of his own mount and armor. His father had given him his favorite Arabian stallion as a gift the day Count Aznarez made him a squire. It was a splendidly spirited animal that seemed to resent inactivity. The Marshall had assigned him a stall for his steed in the stables and a peg on which to hang his armor, his other prized possession. It must have cost his father a small fortune to have his hauberk and armor custom-made to fit his lanky frame. He was starting to realize the necessity of coming from a family of means just to become a lowly squire. Lord only knew what knighthood would cost! But that was still too far off in the future to have to worry about now.

Convivial and gregarious by nature, Iñaki was quick to make friends with the other castle squires. Eager to learn the ways of knighthood, they all tried to outdo each other in the Chaplain's classroom, struggling mightily to translate Caesar's Gallic Wars and spot the Pleiades in the night sky. But it was at the bailey that they thrilled, sneaking in the occasional half-forbidden charge at the quintain when the knights were off drinking mead and the Marshall was taking his nap.

Iñaki's height made him stand out like a solitary oat in summer stubble. He didn't approach his friends so much as engulfed them. "Is it cloudy up there?" they'd ask, jesting about his height. They teased about his mountain accent, too, and the funny way his feet dangled when he rode his horse. But it was all in good fun. Squireship, Iñaki soon discovered, was a tight-knit brotherhood, where everyone tried to outdo the others in mastering the code of chivalry. Iñaki's strength and equestrian abilities were traits his friends openly admired and secretly envied. They even encouraged him to cross lances with the knights in practice jousts at the bailey, but he refrained from doing their bidding, afraid he'd overstep his bounds and alienate the knights. There was no point in rushing things. He knew, deep down, that he would one day joust with the best of them and be a tough horseman to unseat.

The dining room in the Great Hall was the hub of palace life. One of Iñaki's first assignments as a court squire was to serve meals to a clutch of mercenary knights in the Great Hall. Mostly of Burgundian and Breton extraction, the odd lot liked to gather at the lower end of the long table, keeping to themselves most of the time, speaking their own peculiar dialects. Compared to their Navarran and Aquitainean counterparts, they came off a bit saturnine and humorless, taking their mercenary services a little too seriously. But they were good, fearsome warriors, which was why the king, always short of local knights, had hired them. With his natural flair for languages, Iñaki soon ingratiated himself with them, addressing them in their native tongue, even exchanging witticisms with them. This won them over quickly.

Having heard of Iñaki's way with hawks, the king's falconer asked him to his mews, an invitation Iñaki was quick to accept. When not at his Latin classes or at his equestrian exercises, he was to be found in the company of falcons, talking to them, smoothing their feathers, petting them, helping to reinforce the falconer's tedious lessons in falconry.

On rare occasions, the king would bring him along on his hawking outings. Those were memorable occasions for Iñaki for, although his relationship with his monarch in the castle was respectfully stiff and deferential, they both seemed to drop their guard when thrown together in the field of falconry. A strange transformation seemed to come over them, the king stepping down from his imaginary pedestal, the young squire reverting to his adolescent ways and meeting his lord on equal, yet respectful terms. During these moments of rare intimacy, they were as one, the fifty-some year-old monarch and the adolescent squire. The regal retinue, who observed the odd transformation, was both astonished and envious of the camaraderie that had sprung up between monarch and lowly squire. Nearby, meanwhile, the falconer beamed with pride, as if he had concocted this singular chemistry himself.

Soon after his arrival at court, Iñaki was assigned to serve as prince Sancho's personal squire. The prince was bemused by his new squire's naïveté and gentle disposition, traits, he thought, at odds with his imposing stature. Though still a teenager and a good ten years younger, Iñaki was already as tall as the prince and was starting to draw envious stares from men of shorter stature in the prince's coterie.

Height, Prince Sancho had learned early on, seemed to confer something other than the physical advantage of towering above the others. One was looked up to, not just in the physical sense but in the metaphysical as well, almost as if height, if not a sine-qua-non of leadership, was at least an important ingredient of it. Lamentably, being different engendered an indefinable sense of aloneness. Both prince and squire shared the solitude of being different, set apart by their exceptional, almost freakish stature. Slowly, imperceptibly, this shared sense of aloneness began to nurture an invisible bond between the two, a tie that would draw them closer with every passing day, despite their difference in age and station. It was like a symbiotic relationship, with the prince admiring his squire's adeptness at physical feats, the squire looking up to his prince as if to an older brother, treating him with an odd mixture of comradeship and deference due a future king.

Iñaki spent a large part of his days in Prince Sancho's company, competing with him at handball and bowls, sharing equestrian training at the quintain, hawking or riding out with the hounds. On rainy afternoons they would pool their mental resources, struggle with the incunabula in the castle's library, trying to decipher the tortuous French *chansons de geste* from which Iñaki slowly gleaned the subtle nuances of chivalry. He had been instructed to speak only Basque to the prince. Though awkward at first, this new channel of communication soon became a natural thing with them, giving the odd couple a cryptic advantage over the others who could barely comprehend their gnarled tongue.

Without being disrespectful, Iñaki would tease his elder, saying: "*Handitzen zaranean ikasiku duzu,*" assuring him that he'd learn the language when he grew up. It became a secret channel of communication between them, something that, over the years, would bind them even more than their shared height, their love of horses or their unmitigated passion for falconry.

A year into his training as a squire, and already fifteen, Iñaki started casting longing glances at the royal table on the raised dais at the Great Hall, hoping to someday graduate from serving his boorish Frankish knights to attending to his royal majesties. Queen Sancha, a handsome woman of graying hair and fine, aristocratic features, sprang from royal Castilian lineage. She gazed benignly on her brood of five children, sitting round the royal couple at the dinner table. Sancho, the oldest and heir to the throne, was now twenty-five. Tall and prodigiously strong, he put his powerful physique to good use in tournaments and the occasional frontier skirmish. His father was immensely proud of his nerve and strength of character, traits he would one day need to rule his unruly land.

Next in line came the reclusive Constanza, a reserved princess strangely indifferent to her royal condition. Following her was the twenty year-old Fernando whose dour, taciturn nature was in stark contrast to his older brother's boisterous bonhomie. Bridging that gap in charm was the captivating, nine year-old Berenguela. Shy and circumspect at first, the princess with the soulful blue eyes and flaxen hair soon caught Iñaki's attention. She was like the kid sister he always had wanted but never had. Fancying his resemblance to her oldest brother whom she adored, she, too, soon warmed to the tall squire. The budding friendship that developed between the two of them both amused and pleased her older brother Sancho. Next to last of the royal brood was the seven year-old Ramiro, quiet as a church mouse, a trait that presaged the priestly career he would one day pursue. Last, but certainly not least, was Blanca, a vivacious three year-old with cheeks like roses and eyes like a painted doll's. Even at that tender age, she was already showing signs of a coquetry that would one day land her a French Count and her brother's kingdom.

Presiding over this brood was King Sancho, growing ever wiser but no younger, forever fretting over what could befall his progeny and his kingdom. The ever-present Castilian and Aragonese threat knocking at his door was starting to tell on the aging monarch's health. So far, only by dint of diplomacy had he managed to stave off the hungry wolves.

During the next several years, young Sancho had grown increasingly concerned that it would take more than mere cunning to preserve the integrity of the kingdom he was supposed to inherit, if there was, indeed, a kingdom left to fall heir to. Prince Sancho was growing weary of the Castilian damoclean sword forever hanging over them. Navarre needed some powerful ally to keep her hostile neighbors at bay. Being an accomplished chess player, young Sancho knew the value of looking several moves ahead and had hatched a plan that would curry favor with the English, who happened to control neighboring Aquitaine.

"I was talking to Count Monteagudo yesterday," commented Prince Sancho at dinner one evening. "He was telling me about the Duke of Aquitaine's troubles with his Gascon subjects in Labourd and Dax. There seems to be growing unrest over their English yoke in the Viscounties." The king, who was aware of the Gascons' unease, gnawed at his leg of lamb, disinterestedly. "And that's not all," added the prince pointedly. "Alfonso of Castile has been making overtures to lure Bayonne away from the English."

King Sancho dropped his shank on the trencher, perking up at his son's last remark. He regarded his heir with a mixture of surprise and fatherly pride. He had noticed, of late, that he'd been showing a keener interest in the administrative affairs of the realm, an unmistakable sign of his readiness to take on added responsibilities in matters of governance. The aging monarch could not help remembering that he himself was only sixteen when he inherited the reins of power. That was half his firstborn's present age! It was getting time to cut him some slack and let him try his hand at affairs of the realm.

"That would be Prince Richard, wouldn't it?" asked the king noncommittally. "The one they call the Lionheart?" he added sardonically. He knew perfectly well who the Duke of Aquitaine was but was angling for his son's opinion of the English prince's bombastic title. He personally thought the appellation a little pompous, coined, no doubt, by that overbearing mother of his, Eleanor. Sancho had never approved of the shameless hussy's *lèse majesté*, cuckolding her first husband, Louis of France, and then divorcing the poor fellow to rob the English royal cradle to marry Henry, a good dozen years her junior.

"The very same," responded the prince, ignoring the gibe. "We have known each other for quite some time now, you know. We've crossed lances at several jousts in Aquitaine. I was thinking that perhaps we should help him subdue those Gascon troublemakers. We'd get in England's good graces if we did, perhaps even get them to tilt in our favor instead of Castile's, for a change. Besides," he added with uncanny prescience, "Richard intends to take Bayonne just to pre-empt Castile. It would behoove us to help him in that military operation. We can't allow Alfonso to take Bayonne. It may be our last and only remaining outlet to the sea if the Castilians ever take Donostia."

"Good thinking, son," replied the king, pleased at young Sancho's surprising grasp of foreign affairs and their not-so-subtle power plays. "I believe such an alliance could, indeed, be useful." Turning over the different possibilities in his head, king Sancho finally agreed to back up his son's proposal. "You may go help him. Take five-hundred lances with you. That should suffice as a token of our good faith. I'll arrange to send Richard a note alerting him of our intentions."

The small army of knights and men-at-arms rode out of Pamplona's *Puerta de los Franceses* two weeks later, heading north. Prince Sancho was in his element. Decked in mail and shining armor, a huge broadsword dangling from his side, helmet plumes fluttering in the cool Navarran breeze, he was the very image of knighthood. His enormous equestrian bearing always gave the impression that he was riding a pony, even if his mounts were magnificent chargers, his weight and stature demanding nothing less. Iñaki always rode by his side, acting as his scout and messenger, attentive to his lord's every whim. The two had sallied forth on skirmishes before, had learned to complement each other's strengths and weaknesses. Both powerfully built, Iñaki's slimmer figure gave him the edge in horsemanship while Sancho's larger girth made his sword strokes that much more telling. Both at war and at peace, the two seemed inseparable, always speaking their arcane Basque language so others would not pry. Visible half a league away, their twin giant silhouettes were like guideposts in battle, ensuring that the prince's forces always knew where their leader was, even if they could only spot his squire in the confusion of battle.

They arrived at the outskirts of Bayonne several days into their *chevauchée*, only to discover that Richard's troops were already besieging the seaport. The Lionheart, whose siege had gone poorly, so far, greeted his Navarran friend, welcoming his reinforcements. Hard by the Nive River, the fortress town originally built by the Romans had, over the centuries, been fortified by the Gascons who, like their Vascon brethren across the Pyrenees, had little sufferance for interlopers. Unhappy about the way the English had been trying to muscle their way into their affairs, the Bayonnese had simply shut their city's doors on them.

Sancho was quick to assess the situation: with hardy, well-supplied defenders, the fortified town was unassailable. It would take an army far larger than Richard's to mount a credible assault. Even then, the outcome would be in doubt. Sancho had participated in a few Pyrrhic victories of his own to know, at a glance, that this one would only add to that tally. Richard had sorely miscalculated his enemy's strength and determination.

"You're in a bit of a pickle, my friend," said Sancho to his English friend that evening, as they walked under the town's ramparts, just out of projectile reach. "Your forces are inadequate to force a capitulation from these Bayonnese. They're a tough, stubborn lot, and their fortress is nigh impregnable. The curtain walls are steep and well enfiladed by many towers and anyone can see that the water approaches are out of the question. I suggest we stop and think about other options."

"Such as?" replied Richard testily. He admired Sancho's equestrian abilities—indeed, was one of his favorite jousting partners—and had always admired the Navarran's blunt, straightforward advice. But he disliked being reminded of tactical miscalculations, especially by a foreigner.

"Let me act as mediator between you and the Bayonnese. Gascons and Vascons are blood brothers, you know. They are just as eager as you to end this siege. The trick is to do it gracefully, without any loss of face on either side."

"And how would you propose to do that?" persisted Richard, skeptically.

"Well, for starters, we'll promise not to interfere in their affairs in exchange for their neutrality. We don't have to demand that they refrain from making overtures to Castile. They are, as you know, just as leery of them as they are of you. We can sweeten the offer by promising that both England and Navarre will come to their aid should Castile ever threaten Bayonne."

Richard mulled over Sancho's proposal. He could see the wisdom in the Navarran's plan. He was really not that keen on adding one more possession to his already vast Aquitanian domain. He just wanted to make sure the Castilians remained on their side of the Pyrenees. He would consider lifting the siege if the Bayonnese offered him that assurance.

Under a flag of truce, Sancho entered Bayonne the next morning to negotiate a cease-fire between the contending armies. Having agreed to the conditions of the Navarran's proposal, a pact was quickly drawn up and signed by all parties, the English relieved to lift the ill-conceived siege, the Bayonnese elated to see a bloodless end to their defensive efforts. They were, they sensed, the real victors in the test of wills; they had staved off the English threat while extracting their-and Navarre's—promise to defend them against the Castilians, if the need arose. It was a good deal, all around. England was off their backs, for the time being, and, unlike the arrogant Castilians whom they cordially detested, the Bayonnese had always looked kindly on the Navarrans, trusting their support if it ever came to blows with Castile.

There was great celebration in the English camp with the happy and bloodless conclusion of the siege. Sancho's stature as a peacemaker had been visibly enhanced in Richard's estimation. In return for his successful mediation, Richard accepted Sancho's invitation to attend a tournament in Pamplona the coming spring. The offer was not wholly altruistic. Under pain of excommunication, the Bishops of Aquitaine had been threatening to prohibit tournaments altogether because of their increasing gore. Richard, who was the doyen and leading supporter of the sport, was quickly running out of suitable jousting venues. Pamplona seemed like virgin territory for the games. Sancho, who loved tournaments himself, was elated by the prospect of his friend's participation in his games.

Chapter 22

The Eve of the Tournament

Shortly after the Bayonne expedition, Iñaki began hearing rumors about Berenguela's engagement to Richard. The English ambassador to the Navarran court had indiscreetly leaked news of the English crown's interest in the princess. Iñaki felt a twinge of impending loss on first hearing the news. After having lived under the same roof all those growing-up years, they had grown quite fond of each other. He always thought of Berenguela as a younger sister and treated her with brotherly affection. To her, Iñaki was like just another big brother, this one more affable and considerate with her than the others. She had been demanding of his time and attention, constantly begging to be taught the arts of hawking and horsemanship. On dreary winter afternoons, she would sit him by her side at the hearth and make him listen to her lute-playing, or play backgammon or chess, or simply exchange witticisms with him. Like her other sisters, Berenguela was versed in French, Latin and music but, unlike her younger sister Blanca, the feminine art of flirting did not come naturally to her.

All that began to change when Berenguela slipped into womanhood a few years earlier. Iñaki had puzzled over why the lissome princess had not yet been betrothed to some prince, when, by rights, most other princesses were affianced even before turning five, married no later than fourteen. She, on the other hand, was totally unaware of the physical attraction she had started to arouse in her brother's squire. By his early twenties, Iñaki had had his discrete flings with kitchen maids and the odd lady-in-waiting. But Berenguela was different. He found himself trying to hide his increasingly awkward interest in the budding princess, forcing himself to sublimate his longing for her into a higher, more platonic plane. He daydreamed of one day sporting some token of hers on his first joust. He would promise her his eternal loyalty and obeisance, swear to defend her honor to the death. Even squires were allowed to dream, so long as their fantasies remained chaste.

It was the beginning of summer, a time when the heart grows homesick and turns to the old haunts. It had been unseasonably cold in the Pyrenees that spring and a freak snowstorm had just dampened the vespers' festivities of St. John's in Agorreta, putting an abrupt end to the dancing around the bonfire in the village square, sending the shivering serfs packing to their homes. Iñaki had made it to his native village just before the snowdrifts closed the road to Pamplona, bringing all traffic between France and Spain to a standstill.

That evening, as his family gathered round the large fireplace in the Great Hall of Gasteluzar, they heard a sudden insistent knocking at the front door. After a serf opened it, the lord of Agorreta stood face to face with a tall, handsome man wrapped in a damp, ermine-lined coat hanging limply down to his boots. The carrot-colored hair showing under his fur cap was matted by a light coat of snow, as were his long mustache handles, drooping under the weight of icicles. Accompanying him were a dozen noblemen of equally imposing garb and mount, all equally chilled. The tall stranger's bearing and attire made Juan de Agorreta suspect that he was in the presence of some important nobleman caught in the storm, perhaps on his pilgrimage to Santiago. It would not be the first time.

"I am Prince Richard of England," announced the visitor in a deep, stentorian voice, convinced that everyone in Christendom, including this hamlet's inhabitants, had heard of the Lionheart. "And this," he continued in perfect French, casually waving his hand at the company of horsemen behind him, "is my retinue." Observing the befuddled look on the old man's face, he explained: "We come in peace and request lodgings for the night. We were on our way to visit your king but are unable to proceed on our journey to Pamplona. The snow is deep and we can make no farther progress in the dark."

Iñaki, his mother and older brother, were now standing behind the lord of the manor, surprised by the unexpected presence of such illustrious visitors. Even in the dim rushlight, Iñaki immediately recognized the English prince. He had seen him only recently in Bayonne, albeit from a distance. Everyone, including his parents, had heard of this Aquitainean's feats of valor in his many forays against rebellious barons in the Gascogne and lands beyond the Adour. Iñaki was also aware that every knight in Christendom was eager to join the ranks of the Crusade that this very prince was organizing. And there he stood, in all his princely regalia, at their very doorstep, asking for lodgings!

"*Mais, bien sûr, mon sire!*" exclaimed Iñaki's father in thickly-accented French, as he stepped forward to clasp the lord's proffered hand. "I am Juan, Sire of Agorreta and these are my wife and two sons. Please, come in," he said, ushering them into the hallway after they had dismounted.

"*Zu nere etxera etorzeak alaitzen nau,*" he said in welcome, slipping distractedly into his native.tongue. Noticing the Aquitanean's puzzled look, he added, now in broken French: "This, though ever so humble, is your home, milord. You may remain under my roof for as long as you please. We have plenty of room to accommodate your party." The old man's voice quivered with excitement. He had fought alongside kings and princes in his day and he knew a gallant one when he saw one.

"You honor me," responded the English prince. "Perhaps, if we can rest the night in your manor we can proceed on the morrow to Pamplona to honor your king's invitation. Your kindness will be handsomely rewarded."

"There will be no need for that," responded Agorreta, regaining his lordly composure. "The honor is all mine. Besides," he added, pointing to Iñaki, who was standing by his side, "my youngest son, here, can escort you to the king's palace. He serves as a squire there."

With an inquisitive look, the English prince looked up at the young squire who towered over him, trying to remember where he had seen him before. He was struck by the boyish good looks of the young giant. He could read the inner strength in the square jaw and the level, unblinking stare of the young man.

"Your face is familiar. Have we met before?" asked the prince, taking off his wet coat.

"Yes, milord," responded Iñaki. "Only briefly, last fall. I was in Bayonne with my prince Sancho."

Richard stared at Iñaki for a few seconds before finally recognizing him. "Now I remember!" he said, slapping his forehead lightly with the palm of his hand. "Sancho's tall squire!" he added with a broad smile. "Small world, indeed!" Eyeing the tall young Vascon appreciatively, he asked: "Has he started you jousting yet?"

Jousting had only recently started to gain favor in Navarre. It was considered a far more civilized contest than mêlées, where the outcome sometimes hinged more on chance than on prowess. The Church had turned a jaundiced eye on tournaments in general but was more permissive of the latest wrinkle in the noble passage-of-arms.

"Yes, milord," responded Iñaki. "Prince Sancho and I practice crossing lances now and then. But I'm still a little green at it. He, on the other hand, is quite accomplished at the jousts. He makes a good teacher."

Iñaki was proud and happy to sing the praises of his liege lord. They had grown quite close during the past few years and though, when in the presence of others, he still addressed the young Sancho with the deference and respect due a prince and future king, there were other less formal occasions when they were alone, hunting or hawking, when all barriers would come down. They would then address each other by their first names, the way any two friends would, sharing laughs, recalling youthful pranks and foibles, sharing dreams and yearnings, just being good friends.

"Yes" agreed the Lionheart. "I have crossed lances with Sancho many a time. I know his mettle. I may even cross lances with you one day. I'm always looking for a good match at the lists."

The Aquitaineans had timed their arrival just right. Laura, the lady of Agorreta, set up a sumptuous meal for them that evening. She had prepared enough food for the festivities of St. John, when their feudal vassals from the surrounding valleys were invited to the yearly free meal and revelry at Gasteluzar, the manor's castle. It was the lord's way of repaying his serfs for a year's work well done. They would come despite the freak snowstorm, and the celebration would be boisterous, as always, helped along by the hearty food and the free-flowing hard cider and wine.

Later that evening, at the dinner table, Prince Richard remarked, through a mouthful of venison: "I know your people are quite religious. Have they heard of the call to arms to free Jerusalem from the Saracens?" The Hermit would have phrased the appeal more movingly but no less bluntly.

"Yes, milord," responded the lord of the manor. "We heard how Saladin overran the Holy Land several years ago. We have also heard that you, the French and the Germans are making preparations to march there with an army of Christians to take it back from the Muslims." Agorreta paused a moment before adding: "We have our own ongoing Crusade here in the peninsula, as you are, no doubt, aware, Sire. We don't feel we have to sail to the Holy Land to find enemies of Christianity. I myself have crossed swords with him in our own backyard, so to speak, side by side with my liege lord and king, Sancho Garcés, the present king's father."

There was a moment of awkward silence among his guests; surprised at their host's outspokenness, some even finding it bordering on lack of respect. Here was this obscure Vascon knight giving them an unsolicited lesson in history. Iñaki, on the other hand, felt a prickle of pride for his father who had, in his own simple and inimitable fashion, given witness, yet again, of his people's gritty, independent streak.

"I am quite aware of the ongoing battle you call the '*Reconquest*' of your land from the Moors," retorted the Englishman, catching the drift of Agorreta's subtle remonstrance. "I myself have, on occasion, sent knights to help the king of Castile in his fight against the Moors." Feeling he had set Agorreta straight on that score, he continued: "Our Crusade, however, is of another nature altogether. We are defending the very ground on which our Lord walked and preached. We will reclaim the Holy Sepulcher from the heathen and defend it *à oultrance*."

"It is a most noble and holy enterprise, milord," responded Agorreta, still unbowed, his countenance serene and unfazed. "I am sure you will find volunteers in King Sancho's court who will be happy to join your hosts. I wish you good luck."

Without having given an inch from his original stand, his rejoinder seemed to have mollified his guest's ruffled sensitivities. Juan de Agorreta let the opportunity pass to remind the English prince that one's own soil is far more sacred than any foreign land, however holy, and that a man's chapel, like his faith, is something carried deep inside, not something to be sought in the Holy Land, which the French called *Outremer*.

After the tables had been cleared and the *txistularis* and *tambourines* sounded their fanfare, the *versolaris* made their appearance. Their Basque poems and ditties, some recited, others sung, went over the heads of the Aquitaineans, who gazed on, uncomprehending. Richard, whose mother Eleanor was the patroness and doyenne of troubadours in France, could not help comparing this feeble attempt at entertainment with the grand shows he was used to in his Aquitainean palaces. But he kept his thoughts to himself. They were, after all, guests in a petty baron's home, buried in snow in the fastness of the Pyrenees. They were lucky they'd been fed passably well and had warm bedding awaiting them.

By the time the Aquitaineans had broken the fast the next morning, the villagers had cleared a path through the snow, all the way down the hill to the village of Zubiri. Iñaki was delighted to accompany them to the king's palace in Pamplona, where they were planning to stay during the tournament. Thanking their hosts for their kind hospitality, the princely cortege rode off at a canter on their magnificent horses, gaudy banners fluttering in the crisp morning breeze. It had stopped snowing and the road from the piedmont village of Zubiri to Pamplona would make for easy riding.

They traveled south and west, along the whispering waters of the Arga, leaving behind the frowning Pyrenean hills with their grand and awesome scenery. Cantering at a leisurely pace, they followed the road that meandered along the folds of unpretentious hills, a thin coat of snow dusting the ground like white sugar on the tawny fields of a late Navarran spring. The snorting horses with their lively gait seemed to sense the approaching journey's end, an anticipation shared by their riders.

Night fell as they approached Pamplona. The guard at the Frenchmen's Gate ordered them to halt and be recognized. The drawbridge was lowered as soon as Iñaki identified himself and the distinguished company. Surrounded by several dozen knights, the lord Steward of Pamplona extended an official welcome, led them through the narrow cobblestone streets of the Navarreria district, under the shadows of the large Romanesque cathedral. Riding past the Frankish and Jewish quarters, they presently reached the royal summer palace dominating the square behind St. Cernin's church.

"I follow in the footsteps of the triumvirs," remarked Richard to one of his retinue. He was awed by the fact that two members of the famous Roman triumvirate, Pompey, after whom Pamplona was named, and Julius Caesar, then chasing after Celts, had probably walked these very stones. "That," he mused, "was over a dozen centuries ago!"

"And don't forget Charlemagne," commented the Steward, who had overheard the Lionheart's exchange.

"Yes, his too," said Richard, harking back to the *chanson* that was just then starting to popularize that famous, or, in this people's memory, infamous Frankish incursion into Vasconia, four centuries earlier.

The doors to the royal palace were flung open when they arrived. A messenger had preceded them with news of the illustrious visitors' approach. The king was standing at the top of the stairs of the Great Hall, waiting to greet them.

"*Bienvenu a mon royaum*, Prince Richard," the king greeted his guest in flawless French, giving him a hearty hug. "I apologize for not greeting you at the border. I never thought anyone could ride through those snowdrifts! You were bold to make the effort."

"Perhaps a little foolhardy, Sire," admitted the English prince, trying to ingratiate himself to his royal host. "Your squire's family in Agorreta graciously set us up for the night. Thanks to his villeins' efforts, the road was cleared enough for us to get through this morning. It looks like good weather from here on out."

The Aquitainean knights were shown to their quarters adjoining the Great Hall while Prince Richard was ushered into one of the rooms reserved for honored guests. The curtained enclosure at the end of the hall's daised area adjoined prince Sancho's room on one side, the palace steward's on the other. Elegantly appointed, its wainscoted walls were hung with magnificent tapestries, embroidered with figures of saints and local heroes. His eyes were immediately drawn to the figure of St. James, riding a white stallion, sword unsheathed, and charging a group of cowering Moors.

Prince Richard had heard about king Sancho's religious bent and his successful efforts at ensuring the safety of the Jacobean route. Pilgrims from all over Europe had started crossing the Pyrenees on their pilgrimage to Santiago de Compostela, the final resting place of St. James, one of Christ's Apostle's. This religious pilgrimage had brought with it a sudden influx of Frankish traders and artisans who, encouraged by the king's generous land grants and tax exemptions, were starting to settle all along the route, opening up a thriving commercial interchange with the rest of Europe.

Prince Richard first caught sight of Berenguela at dinner that evening. The young eighteen year-old sat primly next to her mother, almost directly across the table from him. Her softly-curved oval face was framed by a shock of blond curls partially held up by a tiara, revealing a swan-like neck indicating her noble birth. Her complexion was fair and her eyes, which he could see in the flickering light of the hanging firebrands, were of a blue so light and cerulean that he was sure some Visigoth must have left his mark in Sancho's line. Though she still had a girlish air about her, Richard was quick to notice the curves pushing against her white blouse, bespeaking nubile womanhood. She had a pleasant, quiet way about her, demure and circumspect, like all young maidens of rank and good breeding. But it was her conversation that struck him most, for it revealed a maturity far beyond her years. Though her French was faltering, her Latin was flawless, showing a familiarity with the Classics that surprised him. His mother's ambassador to the Navarran court had briefed Eleanor well.

As these thoughts coursed through his mind, he was already coldly visualizing her in her wifely role, the mother of that heir Eleanor so doggedly insisted he sire for the perpetuation of the Plantagenet line on the English throne. Well, he thought, as he munched on a tender morsel of venison, she doesn't show much spirit but that is a good trait in women. At least this one looks docile enough and will not give any trouble. More importantly, she is far more attractive than that Alice Capet he'd been betrothed to since God knew when. His mother had warned him, early on, that he'd have to dower the young and flighty Capetienne with his duchy of Aquitaine, as her brother, Philip Augustus of France, had stipulated. That prospect pleased neither Richard nor his mother. Surely, he thought, the more accommodating Navarran king would exact no such dot. Berenguela was starting to look better and better all the time.

The following weeks saw a flurry of activity at the palace, preparations for the tournament occupying many of King Sancho's and Prince Richard's waking hours. They huddled together in the king's quarters, discussing every detail of the contest. Richard, who had codified tournament rules-of-engagement in Aquitaine, was keen to update the Navarrans on the latest regulations of the passage-of-arms. He suggested starting the games with jousts rather than mêlées, arguing that the audience would observe the contest with more attention to detail. Another new format he wanted to try out was to allow two worthy squires to open the tournament in the first single-combat event. This would serve as a curtain raiser, something to whet the crowd's appetite and serve as foil to the more experienced combatants to follow. King Sancho thought both ideas excellent and granted his approval.

The tourney was scheduled to start two days before St. Fermin's, so that the winners could celebrate their victory and the vanquished drown their woes in wine on the Vascons' favorite holiday. The jousting event was to take place in La

Rochapea, a broad meadow along the northern banks of the Arga, directly under the northern ramparts of Pamplona. Palisades a quarter mile long would be set up along both sides of the lists to control the crowds expected to attend the event. The rules of engagement had been established and clearly spelled out to the contestants. The first day would be dedicated to a series of one-on-one combats in which Richard and his four Aquitainean champions would challenge any Navarran knight who chose to cross lances with the challengers. The one who unhorsed the most opponents would be declared winner of that day's joust. He would receive an Arabian horse as a price and would have the privilege of naming the festival's "Queen of the Tourney."

The second day would be devoted to a general mêlée between two bands of equal and opposing numbers of knights and their squires. This less structured, more dangerous mock combat would take place within the fields encompassing La Rochapea and the commons of the nearby hamlet of Huarte, in a free-wheeling clash of arms not unlike that of real combat. On the king's signal, the mêlée would be brought to a close by a clarion call. Every vanquished knight would forfeit his horse, saddle, weapons and armor to the victor. These would be delivered in the presence of the king's Chancellor and held for ransom by the victor. Losing a tournament was not only ignominious; it was also a costly business.

There was a frenzy of training activity in both camps the week before the tourney. Richard's knights spent endless hours practicing at the quintain set up in a meadow outside the Citadel. Observing them from a fence nearby, prince Sancho and Iñaki were amused by the antics of one of the French knights who ended up being unhorsed by the swiveling contraption. Richard, who had also been observing the exercise, frowned in disapproval. Observing the two amused onlookers, he joined them presently. Richard seemed uncomfortable having to look up at the strapping prince and his young squire, both of whom towered a full head above the English prince, who was, himself, no dwarf.

"Pretty nasty device, eh?" he remarked brightly, motioning with his head at the quintain's ball, still spining threateningly above the fallen knight's head. "Would either of you two care to have a go at it?" he offered, hoping that a nasty spill would cut short their merriment.

The two men looked at each other, surprised by the unexpected invitation. Winking slyly at *el Fuerte*, Iñaki remarked: "That's pretty tame stuff. What's really fun is jousting. Now, that's another kettle of fish altogether!"

His bravado amused the Lionheart; the young fellow had spunk. Here was a young squire already thinking about jousting. He would probably make a formidable foe someday when he added a little more meat to his bones, thought the English prince. "Does your father let you joust?" queried the prince, subtly reminding the squire of his youth.

"Yes, Sire. He's watched milord Sancho and me go at it several times. Using *armes de courtoisie*, of course," referring to the blunted lances used in friendly combat.

"Who beats whom?" pursued Richard. He was starting to like this youth's swagger. Having a good supply of that bluster himself, he knew that it had stood him in good stead over the years.

"He does, most of the time," admitted Iñaki. "He's also ten years older and a bit stronger than I. One of these days, though, I'll surprise him," he added, mockingly. *El Fuerte* smiled at the friendly taunt but said nothing. Not too long ago, barely beyond his teens, he too had been a brazen young man who had known no bounds, brooked few taunts.

"I see," said the Englishman. Something about this young man's cheekiness continued to arouse his interest. "Someday you and I will meet in some joust and you can show me how it's done," he smiled. Richard turned and headed back to the quintain. Looking over his shoulder, he said: "As for you, Sancho, I'm looking forward to crossing lances with you day after tomorrow. I don't know if you're keeping score but I think you owe me one." They both laughed.

As Sancho and Iñaki rode back to the castle, the prince turned to Iñaki and asked: "How would you like to joust in the tournament?" It was the prince's way of showing his appreciation for all their years of friendship and camaraderie, for all the happy hours of hunting and hawking his young squire had shared with him. He was well aware of Iñaki's superb horsemanship and dexterity with the lance. If any squire was deserving of the opportunity to fight in the 'curtain raiser' event of the coming joust, he was.

Iñaki's face lit up with a broad grin. "I'd be more than honored, milord!" he said, without a moment's hesitation. He was touched by the compliment his prince had just paid him by singling him out for the event. There were many others he could have chosen, but he chose him. "Someday," said Iñaki with feeling, "after I've been dubbed a knight, I would dearly like to unhorse that prince at some passage-of-arms!"

"He's a sneaky one, that one," said Sancho. "You've got a lot to learn before you can do that!"

Chapter 23

A Passage of Arms

Early morning sunlight broke through the mists that loitered over the Arga river valley. The inhabitants of Pamplona had risen early to secure places along the palisades lining the lists. Halfway along the length of the barricade, galleries had been erected, decked with rich carpets and gaudy pennons. From their cushioned gradins, the royals, noblemen and magnates would observe the feast of lances. Royal crimson-and-gold banners fluttered above the canopied dais overlooking the area where the contending knights would come together in a clash of spears.

A hubbub arose from the crowd when the first noblemen and their ladies began to arrive. The barons and *hidalgos* who came first, occupied the seats of the lower galleries. The magnates and higher nobility arrived shortly after, their ladies twitching rich silk scarfs, flashing bejeweled fingers and coronets for effect. They sat on the choicer seats of the higher gallery, with a commanding view of the games.

Banners portraying the rampant lions of England and the Aquitainean fleur-de-lis fluttered atop the pavilion on the western end of the lists. Several squires tended to splendid palfreys that twitched and snorted impatiently outside the tent. The Navarran pavilion stood on the opposite end of the lists. Its pennants, sporting the royal, two-headed eagle, fluttered limply in the fitful morning breeze. Here, too, squires bustled, cinching saddles, fitting chanfrons and peytrals, draping the magnificent chargers in emblazoned housings. Even without the banners or the blazons, one could readily identify the two camps; while the

Anglo-Aquitaineans remained inconspicuous inside their tent, the mettlesome Navarran knights stood outside theirs, spiritedly taunting and jesting with one another. For them, a tournament was more a friendly game than a mock war.

The crowd had started turning restless when a flourish of high-pitched trumpets rang out. Sancho the Wise made his entrance at the lists, followed by a group of noblemen and their attendants. The king was splendidly attired in a tunic of royal crimson and gold, a cloak of rich, ermine-collared sable casually draped over his shoulders. The mob roared in welcome, strewing flowers and tokens in his path, shouting peals of "*Gora Errege!*" with clamorous applause as their king caracoled his magnificent Andalusian steed around the lists with regal dignity, nodding and waving at his subjects.

Climbing the steps to his canopied dais, the king ensconced himself in his makeshift throne, exchanged pleasantries with the noblemen and ladies in his retinue. Moments later, he drew a white kerchief from his robe and laid it on the red velvet cloak draped over the balustrade facing him. It was the signal for the games to begin. A flourish of clarions rang out in the young morning signaling the marshals-at-arms to clear the lists for the contest.

At the second clarion call, five challenger knights, led by their champion, walked awkwardly out of the Aquitainean pavilion toward their waiting chargers. Decked in heavy, cumbersome armor, they had to be helped up to their palfreys' saddles by their squires. Other helpers stood by, each holding two tall lances, one, the cross-tipped *arme de courtoisie*, the other the *arme à oultrance*, equipped with the sharp point of a regular lance. The Aquitaineans lined themselves up in order of rank and seniority, Prince Richard occupying the champion's position on the extreme right of the row of five knights. Restraining their fiery stallions, all five turned to face the Navarran camp.

At the opposite end of the lists, the Navarran platform had been cleared of knights and squires Anticipating that something unusual was about to happen, the crowd suddenly fell silent. A blue pennon was raised atop the pavilion, announcing the choice of *armes de courtoisie* for the first joust. When a chevalier finally cantered out of the pavilion, a gasp of surprise arose from the multitude. The appearance of a single entrant was most unusual in their short memory of tournaments. Their surprise mounted when they spied the unusual coat-of-arms blazoned on the chevalier's shield—a boar athwart a thorn bush on a field of argent—a heraldic insignia they had never seen before.

The mystery contestant was plainly attired. His hauberk of light mail, flimsy breastplate and leggings of unburnished steel were all unusual, as was the lack of an identifying housing for his mount. In stark contrast to his unpretentious appearance was his magnificent Arabian steed. He sat on it as if he had been born on it, hands loosely gripping spear and shield, back straight, demeanor impassive. There was an air of coiled power about the lanky chevalier as he sat there coldly eyeing the challengers across the lists.

Topped by a plume of bright red feathers, his pot helmet's lowered visor kept his features effectively hidden from view. He was built somewhat like prince Sancho, observed the more perceptive spectators, but, though just as tall, he was considerably slimmer and the colors and blazons he sported were certainly not the prince's. At first, the master-at-arms seemed hesitant to let the unknown contestant participate in the games. He was about to challenge his right to be there when prince Sancho came out of the pavilion and gave his placet.

The murmur of the crowd rose to an audible pitch when the mystery knight, decked in his dull metal armor, cantered off the pavilion's mound and slowly rode his horse over to the King's gallery. Lowering his lance toward the king in salutation and fealty, the chevalier then deftly maneuvered his steed sideways a few paces down the gallery to rest his lance's tip on the balustrade, directly in front of princess Berenguela.

Surprised and flustered by the gallant and unexpected gesture, the young princess blushed noticeably. She knew that a damsel so honored had to reciprocate with some token; the knight was, after all, laying his life on the line for her. Drawing an embroidered kerchief from her sleeve, she carefully tied it around the shaft of the extended lance, trying all the while to recognize the tall, silent knight who had so honored her.

Almost in a whisper, she asked the mystery contestant: "Are you who I think you are?" restraining herself from calling out the chevalier's name outright.

The princess' query touched something deep inside the horseman's heart, giving him an unexpected surge of strength. His only response was to raise a finger to his helmet's grilled mouthpiece, pleading for silence. Bowing his head slightly to his lady, he trotted off to his end of the lists. Turning to face the challengers, the chevalier positioned his horse on the extreme left of the landing, directly across the lists from Richard the Lionheart. He had picked the champion's squire as his adversary.

Iñaki restrained his nervous steed, staring down the lists at his splendidly armed English contender. Richard's squire returned the Navarran's stare. Had he been a little more perceptive, he would have noticed that, though not powerfully built, his lanky opponent's legs were almost completely wrapped around his charger's underbelly, making him that much harder to unsaddle.

The two horsemen sat glaring at each other across the lists, their horses champing nervously at the bit. A flourish of trumpets and clarions suddenly rang out, signaling the start of the joust. Having cheered the end of a long wait, the crowd grew silent to better hear the imminent clangor of steel on steel. The two horsemen dug their spurs deep into their mounts' sides. With startled snorts, the two horses leaped forward, hooves thundering across the meadow. They approached each other with blurring speed, manes blowing in the wind, divots flying, billows of breath trailing behind in the chill morning air. It was a splendid sight to behold, two men charging at full tilt, lances leveled at each other's breastplate, fire of mutual defiance in their eyes.

The crowd watched breathlessly as the distance between the two horses narrowed. In the galleries, the maidens' hearts beat a little faster as they watched the two men rumble down the lists with that same flamboyance they had read about in all those thrilling *chansons* and storybooks of the day. Some even surprised themselves secretly hoping that someone would get hurt. It was all quite primitive, they realized, but oh, so very exciting! There was something of the ancient thrill of the Colosseum in it all. Only the young Berenguela feared the outcome. Here was a gallant chevalier fighting for the grace of a simple smile from her. Utterly flattered by such gallantry, she said a silent prayer for his victory.

When it finally came, the clanging of steel on steel was shuddering. The glancing blow splintered both their lances, allowing both horsemen to hang on to their mounts. Slimmer than his heavyset opponent and more lightly armed, Iñaki could afford to ride a swifter stallion than Richard's squire. He had trained it to move almost imperceptibly sideways, on a knee command, and it was that split second maneuver that had taken the edge off his opponent's thrust. The crowd cheered in astonished relief, mostly because they had fully expected the Aquitainean to unseat their "Chevalier of the Boar," as some had started calling him. Iñaki was slightly dazed by the impact; one of his shoulder plates had been jarred loose, but his armor had, otherwise, remained intact.

Both horsemen returned to their respective ends of the lists for a new set of lances and a second attempt. *El Fuerte*, who had been watching anxiously from the Navarran pavilion, walked over to Iñaki.

"He's met his match!" encouraged the prince. "Go for the jugular this time!"

Iñaki smiled behind his helmet's faceguard as he picked up the snubbed lance handed him by his page, snuggling it securely under his arm. The second charge was equally inconclusive. This time, however, Iñaki had noticed his contender's last-second parry and thought he'd figured out a way to counter the clever dodge.

He, himself, had learned a trick or two during his years of training at the quintain and was about to execute one of them.

A fraction of a second before the next impact, Iñaki raised his lance's aim from his contender's shield to his helmet's faceguard. For a split second, the clouds of billowing dust and flying debris engulfed both horsemen, momentarily hiding them from view. Even before the dust had settled, the Aquitainean squire was seen going down with his mount after the shuddering impact, hitting the ground with a sickening thud. While his startled steed struggled to its feet and dashed off towards the palisades, the squire remained on the ground, the wind knocked out of him. Iñaki wheeled his horse around and approached his contender. He lowered his lance in salute to a fallen foe and cantered off towards his pavilion. Turning his head briefly toward Berenguela, he bowed his helmet ever so slightly as he rode past her.

A collective cheer arose from the crowd, which had grown suddenly fond of the "Chevalier of the Boar". With characteristic modesty, Iñaki acknowledged their acclaim with a slight wave of the hand. But when prince Sancho himself came galloping up to congratulate the winner, the crowd cheered frantically. The prince's solicitude toward the mystery jouster made some of them finally realize that the "Chevalier of the Boar" was none other than the prince's inseparable squire. Touched by the moving scene, they cheered with renewed enthusiasm. The Chancellor of the Realm, who was standing by the king's side, explained to the puzzled king that prince Sancho had chosen his own squire to duel in the opening round.

A flourish of trumpets announced the next passage of arms. When the pennon with the double-headed eagle was raised atop the Navarran pavilion, the crowd roared; their very favorite royal was to be the next contestant. A giant equestrian figure sallied forth from the tent, trying to restrain his black, high-spirited palfrey. He was splendidly attired in gold-inlaid armor, a tall lance loosely tucked under his arm. The crowd, which did not need the royal device on his shield to recognize the powerful knight in glistening armor, erupted in deafening applause. Their prince, the pride of Navarre, would give these foreigners a taste of their Vascon spirit.

As he trotted onto the landing in front of the pavilion, young Sancho sensed that he had a tall order to fill. When the crowd saw the red pennant raised atop the Navarran pavilion, they became delirious. They were about to be treated to a bona fide contest, with *armes à oultrance*! There was yet another reason to be ecstatic; when Sancho cantered his mount to the position opposite Coeur de

Lion's across the lists, the crowd simply exploded in wild ovations. They knew they were in for a treat.

The two princes eyed each other across the lists. This would be just one more of many lances crossed between these two over their recent years of tournaments. They were almost the same age and had always enjoyed testing each other's equestrian skills, knowing that the other was the measure of his own true grit. No one was really keeping score of the number of times each had trounced the other in these equestrian duels. They simply enjoyed the sport and relished the danger involved in any passage-of-arms.

Both in their early thirties and on the eve of being crowned, they thrilled at the danger of jeopardizing a coronation with an untimely tumble. They had never dueled using *armes à oultrance* before and doing so now exhilarated them both. Seeing the folly of the challenge to a lethal combat, Sancho's parents were greatly troubled. But nothing could deter the princes' pursuit of adventure. The Englishman was a poet at heart, intent on playing the role of the romantic knight to the hilt; the Navarran, gutsy, down to earth, had the deep-rooted courage of a Vascon.

When the clarions sounded the flourish, the two knights started towards each other at full tilt, aiming their lances squarely at each other's shields. Because of their weight, both relied on the advantage of their superior momentum to unhorse the other, hoping to reap victory from that advantage. When they closed at the center of the lists, the clatter of steel on resonating steel made the spectators cringe. Queen Sancha feared for her son's life. Fortunately, the glancing blows of lance tips and the splintering of shafts on each other's shields prevented the full force of the impact from unhorsing either contestant, saving them from serious harm or humiliation. Stunned but unbowed, both horsemen retreated to their respective pavilions for lance replacements.

The second and third charges were equally inconclusive, both riders hanging on to their faltering mounts, their spears in slivers after each encounter. By the fourth trial, it became apparent to the crowd that these two cavaliers were almost equally matched. Although their *Fuerte* was a head taller and several inches wider in girth than the challenger, *Corazon de Leon* was a slightly more dexterous horseman. His artful, feinting and dodging was enough to dull the edge of Sancho's brute-force assaults. Richard resorted to shifting his spear's aim, instants before impact, from Sancho's shield to his helmet's visor but the artifice was ineffective against the seasoned Sancho, who anticipated the ruse and dodged it masterfully.

Finally, on the fifth attempt, Richard's lance tip accidentally tore into the eye-shield of his opponent's palfrey, penetrating deep into its brain. Mortally wounded, the horse collapsed, spilling its rider in a jumble of flaying limbs and dented armor. A gasp of surprised disappointment arose from the spectators. Some even cried foul, but the duel was over between these two contestants.

Richard cantered his mount over to the dazed Sancho who had, by now, wobbled up on one knee, stunned and winded by the fall, but otherwise unharmed. With the help of several squires who had rushed out to assist their fallen lord, Richard managed to dismount and offer comfort to his fallen foe. He apologized profusely for the unintentional mishap, refusing to acknowledge the ill-gotten victory. It was, he assured his fallen friend, a draw. Richard, who had written them, assured Sancho that those were the rules of the tourney. The Lionheart further promised to compensate Sancho for his mount, an offer the Navarran graciously refused. The crowd was touched by the sight of Richard offering Sancho a shoulder to lean on as the two princes hobbled awkwardly toward the Navarran pavilion. Even the queen and Berenguela stood up to applaud the noble gesture.

The games continued with their scheduled jousts. But it would be hard for the others to match the excitement of the princes' joust. By the rampant black bear blazoned on the red banner now flying atop the Navarran pavilion, everyone knew that Count Rada was the next contestant. Being the most seasoned of the Navarran contestants, the Count had drawn on his seniority to be the next Navarran to joust. He had been toying with the idea of dueling with Richard the Lionheart, despite his companions' advice to the contrary. He had known of and, only moments earlier, witnessed the prince's jousting dexterity. Though sensing that he himself was already past his prime, Rada could not bring himself to pass up such a singular opportunity. Besides, he reflected hopefully, *Corazon de Leon* would be a little tired and a bit sluggish after the last demanding joust.

Mounting his mottled palfrey, the Count ordered the blue pennant flown under his emblem, signaling his choice of *armes de courtoisie*. The crowd, that had just witnessed the real thing, was disappointed by the choice of arms and began to murmur audibly. The Count, who sensed their displeasure, shrugged his shoulders under his armor. After all, he reasoned, glory or humiliation was all right at the lists but death was a little too heavy a price to pay for a mere sport. This way, he had all to gain and precious little to lose, perhaps a bruised rib from a nasty spill, nothing more. Besides, it would be at the hands of the epitome of chivalry, and that, no matter the outcome, was an honor in itself.

Cantering his horse towards the extreme left of the pavilion's landing, he now sat directly facing the Lionheart in the Aquitaineans' camp. The crowd fell silent, partially appeased at the prospects of seeing the challengers' champion yet again. Under his plumed helmet, Richard smiled as he observed the Navarran's choice of foe and weapon. He liked Rada, a bit of a pompous fool, really, but that was all right. He himself had a good supply of that arrogance. Besides, a bit of bluster was all in character with Counts.

The outcome of that third duel was predictable. Unceremoniously unhorsed on the very first encounter, Rada slunk back to his pavilion, pride and purse slightly bruised but not, otherwise, the worse for wear. No one else chose to cross lances with Richard that day. Four more Navarran knights took the field after count Rada. Daunted by Coeur de Lion's impeccable horsemanship and lance-wielding, they all wisely chose to break lances with the other less formidable Aquitaineans, any one of whom had to be fairer game than *Corazon de Leon*. All, without exception, chose to duel with *armes de courtoisie,* a selection, which, time and again, disappointed the crowd that would have enjoyed seeing a little blood.

The young count of Lehet elected to cross lances with the redoubtable Bois-Guilbert, while count Azagra dueled with Malvoisin, leaving Count Oteiza to joust with the wily Cor-de-Boeuf. They, like Rada before them, were unhorsed at the very first encounter. But, lopsided though most of these matches appeared to be, the Navarrans never swerved from the charge. Only Count Aznarez, Iñaki's erstwhile lord in Sangüesa, met with some success. He first dueled with Fonteinac, whom Aznarez succeeded in unhorsing after the second attempt, to the crowd's ecstatic cheers. He subsequently jousted with Malvoisin, with similar results. He himself was finally unseated by the formidable Cor-de-Boeuf on their very first trial. Delighted by the Sangüesan's horsemanship and creditable performance, the crowd cheered him as he limped off the field. In the end, it was the challengers' seasoned performance in tournaments and Crusades that carried the day.

It was late afternoon when the King declared Richard the victor of the day's tourney. His price was a fine Andalusian stallion and the honor of naming the tournament's Queen. Richard cantered his mount over to the gallery to receive a laurel wreath from the king. Balancing it on the tip of his lance, he extended it to an abashed Berenguela. A roar of approval arose from the crowd. Second in popularity only to the likable *El Fuerte*, the young princess was their next favorite of all of king Sancho's progeny.

"You do me great honor, milord," said the flustered eighteen year-old, overwhelmed by the fact that she had been made the object of chivalrous attention twice that day. First, there was the courtly display of a mysterious chevalier who had broken lances in her honor, and now, only a few hours later, she was named Queen of the Tourney. And by a dashing prince, no less!

Chapter 24

An English Dalliance

Berenguela had been captivated by the gallantry and charming manner of this handsome prince. He seemed to enjoy listening to her lute-playing while she had just recently learned that he could quote whole passages of Ovid's romantic poetry. He had even dedicated one of his own romantic poems to her! She had confided to her mother that the English prince was perhaps smitten by her and that his overtures could well herald a betrothal.

"After all, *mamá*," the young princess burbled, "you were married when you were only thirteen!"

Her mother, who had also noticed the prince's courtly attentions towards her daughter, tried to sound noncommittal. She counseled Berenguela not to appear forward or overly eager, encouraging her, instead, to continue being her normal, charming, guileless self.

"Modesty and naïveté become women. They have ensnared more men than have fickleness or frivolity," counseled Sancha, dredging up some dimly-remembered Senecan aphorism, or was it Cicero? But she could not long hide her excitement at the prospects. "Who knows," she mused out loud, "you may someday end up being the queen of England! Now, how many other Navarran princesses have been given that chance?"

Her mother's indiscreet remark piqued Berenguela's curiosity. Was she really hinting at wedding bells? Was there something, some secret contract she hadn't heard about? She knew royal betrothals were arranged long before the parties involved even heard about them. Though suspicious of a court conspiracy around her, Berenguela was, nonetheless, pleasantly intrigued. This Lionheart fellow seemed a bit on the older side but he was, after all, the heir to the crown of England. She'd even heard that his father was a sick man and that Richard could be named king any moment now. How perfectly exciting!

Returning from a stroll around the palace grounds that evening, prince Sancho and his sister Berenguela found Iñaki at the palace stables, tending to his horse. Berenguela reached for Iñaki's hand, said, in her usual frank, uncomplicated way: "The English prince may have won the prize, but *you* are my real champion! You should not have risked your life for me," she said. It was her simple way of thanking him for his gallantry.

Iñaki felt a sudden shiver of delight. "I'm sorry your brother didn't win the prize," he said. "That was an unfortunate spill. Come to think of it," he added, turning to the prince, "since he didn't really trounce you, Count Aznarez should have taken the prize. He unhorsed two men, which is more than *Corazon de León* did!"

"Lionheart won the prize, fair and square," admitted the noble Sancho, not wanting to sour the tourney by questioning a fait accompli. "Besides, I think he's going to end up being my brother-in-law. One should be nice to one's *cuñado*!"

"He most certainly won't," blurted Berenguela, furious at her brother's embarrassing her by voicing her own innermost thoughts. "You know he's betrothed to the French King's sister."

"Yes, but I hear that Alice is not half as fair as you," volunteered Iñaki. "She's much older, for one thing. Why, she's already twenty-seven!"

He, of course, didn't have the slightest idea what Alice Capet looked like, but he suspected that she must have been endowed with some charm for Richard's own father to have kept her as his mistress all those many years. Even Navarran squires had heard about that scandalous liaison; it was too titillating to ignore. But it was not in Iñaki's nature to indulge in gossip.

"Now, how would you know!" asked the young princess coyly. She sensed that Iñaki was just saying that to make her feel good. They'd been friends long enough to know each other's thoughts without saying.

Iñaki ignored her remark. He would not parry witticisms with the young princess whom he had placed on an unreachable pedestal. He would retire that night promising himself and his God that he would, henceforth, serve her and defend her honor, married or not. He would even follow her to the Crusades if Richard chose to take her to Outremer. He could go as her squire. Prince Sancho would let him do that, knowing that she would need help there, more than ever before. He would be at her beck and call with his heart and his sword.

The next day's tournament turned out to be anti-climactic. It was unpleasantly drizzly, for one, and the match turned out to be as lopsided as the previous day's jousts. As had been agreed, only *armes de courtoisie* were allowed. The opposing teams had ranged far and wide along the hilly country on the outskirts of Pamplona, five Aquitainean knights and their squires pitted against five Navarran cavaliers and their attendants. They galloped their lumbering Percherons tirelessly up and down the plains of La Rochapea and into the hillocks of Huarte, trying to outfox each other.

When they finally closed, there was precious little sham in the mock battle that ensued, the encounters as realistic as in real battle. Although prince Sancho and Counts Rada, Lehet and Aznarez had crossed lances with the Moors in *al-Andalus* before, they had not parried weapons against the wily Turks in the Holy Land, as had the redoubtable Bois-Gilbert and Cor-de-Boeuf. Once again, as in the previous day's jousts, it was Count Aznarez who fought the longest and was the last to fall. The battle horns that sounded across the valley announcing the tournament's end at high noon came a little late for the Navarrans, who had long since been unhorsed by the Aquitaineans. Fortunately, only Count Azagra required medical attention for a dislocated shoulder.

The festivities that afternoon would go on into the wee hours of the morning. From her dais in the Great Hall, Berenguela, as Queen of the Tourney, presided over the celebration under the watchful eye of her parents. She looked stunning, decked in her mother's queenly robes and bejeweled tiara. The subtle eye shadow accentuating her azure eyes and the rouge on her cheeks made her look far more mature than her years. Richard was especially solicitous with her that evening, showing her a facet of his charm that enthralled the young princess. Had she previously known the thrill of infatuation, she would now realize that she was falling madly in love with the dashing English prince.

The jesters and the *jongleurs*, troubadours and *versolaris* all performed their acts and recited their pieces to the delight of the increasingly inebriated guests. Unfamiliar with the potency of the heady wines from Tiebas and Liédena, the Aquitaineans' songs turned bawdy, the verses more ribald as the night progressed.

It was only the presence of the king and queen that kept the celebration from getting out of hand.

The day after the tourney, Richard took Berenguela out for a stroll in Pamplona's hanging gardens of La Taconera, escorted by her older brother, Sancho. She had just beaten him at backgammon, a fact that quite impressed Richard, who had earlier bragged about his expertise at the board game. They were talking about falconry and hunting when Berenguela, in passing, mentioned Iñaki and his uncanny way with animals.

"And not a bad jouster, at that!" remarked Sancho, as if to remind Richard that his squire had bested the Englishman's.

Intrigued, Richard inquired: "Was that the fellow who crossed lances with my squire at the joust?" He had recognized *El Fuerte* walking out into the lists to congratulate him after the bout, appearing to know him well. But Richard had not made the connection at the time.

"That was my favorite squire, Iñaki de Agorreta," said Sancho. "You've met him before."

"Do you mean to tell me that the 'Chevalier of the Boar' was the young Agorreta?" asked Richard, incredulous. All of a sudden he remembered the horseman's tall bearing on the saddle, those long legs wrapped around his steed's underbelly, looking as if his mount were too small for him. He should have known!

"Yes," answered Sancho. "That was he."

Richard remembered being hosted by the squire's father, a crusty old mountain baron and his gruff yet charming chauvinism. His handsome son seemed to have inherited the old man's grit. "He should have been knighted by now," he commented. "And then he should take the Cross," he added. "I'll be needing men like him in the Crusade."

"We'll see," said Sancho noncommittally. He did not relish the thought of losing Iñaki to the Englishman.

Tempted by the king's gracious invitation, Richard decided to extend his visit in Pamplona several days. Unforeseen financial and logistics problems had already delayed his Crusade, and a week's added postponement would make little difference. Besides, there were other reasons for delaying his return. First, there was Berenguela; he had to get better acquainted with her if she was to become his wife. Second, and almost as alluring, was Sancho's offer to take him hunting and hawking at his renowned *Quinto Real*, a large royal hunting reserve north of Pamplona, nestled in the southern folds of the Pyrenees, known for the best collection of wild boar and cranes anywhere in Christendom. Now *that* combination was something he could simply not pass up.

The freak snowfalls and inclement weather of late spring had given way to a warm, dry spell at the beginning of summer. The deep dark forests west of Roncevaux were teeming with fowl and wild game and the royal pair enjoyed their outing immensely. Early each morning, they'd strike out on their steeds, following the yaps and yelps of a pack of hounds panting after the scent of boar. By noon they had bagged several trophies, using their bows and arrows to bring down the tuskers, which their hounds had raised and cornered. After a hearty noonday meal at the campsite, they headed for the bald heights of Lindux, falcons perched on gauntleted arms. It was hawking at its best.

"I wish I had young Agorreta here with us," commented the king on their last afternoon, after an unproductive hawking spell. "He would have bagged a few birds for us by now. Amazing fellow, you know. He talks to these birds as you and I are talking to each other. And the most astonishing thing about it is that they seem to understand every chirp and warble he tweets in their ears. Do you see this peregrine here?" said the king holding up the falcon perched on his arm. "He taught it everything it knows. You've seen how good it is with doves. You should see it perform when Agorreta handles it. It's uncanny!"

"He's also a remarkable horseman," commented Richard. "I watched his horse do a side-slip on my squire in the last fraction of a second before each encounter. That was superb horsemanship!"

"I know," said Sancho, "he also talks to horses."

The conversation turned to Berenguela. The Englishman was trying to broach a sensitive subject, one usually handled by ambassadors and chancellors, years before a troth was sealed. But Richard knew, as his mother had all too insistently reminded him, that he was running out of time.

"Your Highness," said Richard in a tone reserved for matters of grave importance. "What I am about to ask may sound forward, perhaps even a little out of place, but I will soon explain the reason for my question." After a brief pause, he inquired: "Is your daughter Berenguela betrothed to anyone?"

The king considered the question for what seemed an eternity to Richard. Finally, he answered. "She's been spoken for by one of the sons of the Count of Champagne." Then, considering the possible outcome of this conversation, he added: "Actually, there is still no formal betrothal agreement between them."

"In that case, milord, may I be so bold as to ask for your daughter's hand in matrimony?"

There, thought Richard, it was out. Not getting an immediate reply, he quickly added: "I would have gone through the proper channels to pose this request of betrothal but, as you are well aware, Sire, I am in the throes of preparing a Crusade, which is to sail for Outremer presently. I don't have much time for lengthy protocols. I would like to marry before my departure for the Holy Land, if at all possible." Richard paused a moment before adding: "I believe your daughter Berenguela feels the same attraction towards me as I feel for her. So you see, Milord, on this occasion, there is a happy confluence of matters of state and of the heart."

King Sancho listened to Richard's request with ill-repressed joy. It was almost poetic justice. For years, he had tried, fruitlessly, to have this man's father tilt in his favor in the endless squabbles between Navarre and Castile. Richard himself had, not too long ago, favored King Alfonso, his sister Alionor's husband, in the Castilian's demand to incorporate Navarre's Rioja region to Castile. Now he, Sancho, had Richard in the awkward position of having to ask favors from him. But, much as he enjoyed the sight of Richard squirming, he knew that he would never find a better match for his daughter. Indeed, by her marrying the future king of England, he, Sancho, would be assured of finally getting Castile and Aragon off his back. It was the best of all possible worlds. After all, had that not been the reason behind this whole tournament exercise? He had succeeded!

"You have my blessing, my son," said the king trying hard to conceal his emotion. "There are matters of dowries to be ironed out but, in principle, you may have her hand."

Richard was delighted. He knew that his mother would be elated by the arrangement as well. He would send her down here to pick up Berenguela later, at some convenient time, and they could marry at some prearranged cathedral, perhaps Westminster, depending on how things came along with his Crusade's preparations. His father's health was failing. Perhaps she could become the queen of England outright!

The Aquitaineans left Pamplona a few days after the hunting excursion at *El Quinto Real*. They thanked their hosts and extended them an invitation to visit

Poitiers. On parting, Richard leaned over to kiss Berenguela's hand. He had been taken by the simple grace of this handsome young princess. He had met not a few worldly, frivolous courtesans in his own court, all panting to jump in bed with him in hopes of bearing him a child that would one day make them queen. And here was this guileless beauty, looking up at him adoringly with her innocent blue eyes. If he had to marry, it would be to one such as her. Before he could repress them, his thoughts became words.

"You will one day be my queen," he whispered in her ear, convinced that, like everything else he had wished for in life, this, too, would come to pass. He had never said anything like that before to any woman and was astonished at his own words the moment he uttered them. The faint blush creeping up on the pretty oval face looking up at him absolutely beguiled him.

Berenguela herself remained speechless. She could not help suspecting that it had been more a brash statement than a proposition of marriage, something only an impulsive, lion-hearted man would utter. Perhaps, she thought, men who are strong and brave in the field of battle are terribly shy at *amours*. She had proof that he could express his feelings in poetic verse; she had received a missive from him whose ardor had taken her breath. But then, she thought, some men are glib with the written word yet terribly shy when it came time to voicing their thoughts.

Still at a loss for words, the young maiden merely bowed to the prince in a deep curtsy. The words of another virgin flashed through her mind: "Let it be done to me!"

When she snapped out of her reverie and straightened herself up, her prince was gone.

Chapter 25

Eleanor's Brokerage

1189

Henry II died the summer after Richard's escapade to Pamplona. He had been married to Eleanor of Aquitaine, a formidable woman whom the French king Louis had divorced earlier, charitably invoking consanguinity rather than infidelity. Of all the sons and daughters she gave Henry, Richard, her next to youngest, had always been the apple of her eye. Tiring of her husband's protracted absences on military forays, Eleanor had quietly slipped back to her beloved Poitiers. Accused of fomenting rebellion against her husband, she was yanked back to England to spend the next sixteen years in comfortable but dreary confinement in Salisbury castle. Only her husband's death and Richard's rise to the throne ended her forced seclusion.

Richard was crowned in Westminster Abbey with great pomp and ceremony. His subjects adored their stalwart new monarch, the paragon of chivalry who had cunningly foiled the French from usurping England's continental possessions. Richard, whose upbringing had been thoroughly French, did not requite his English subjects' adulation. Barely able to speak their language, he spent his brief island interlude raising money for his Crusade to the Holy Land. Crusading fever gripped Europe following Saladin's capture of Jerusalem. In castles across the Continent, knights could talk only about taking the Cross. Recruiting was already in full swing in France and Austria and Richard had a lot of catching up to do. He sold practically everything the crown owned to fill his war chest. Though many openly grumbled against the "Saladin tithe," Richard managed to stave off revolt by invoking his Crusade's holy mission to recapture Jerusalem from the Saracens.

Eleanor regained her old zest for life on recovering her freedom. She worried about the distinct possibility of her favorite son's untimely death in Outremer, leaving the throne without a proper heir to continue the Plantagenet line. She had made up her mind that Alice Capet—to whom Richard had been betrothed twenty-odd years earlier—would never do as his consort. Eleanor cordially detested Philip's half sister for having been her husband Henry's mistress during all those years of her confinement. Not too keen on marriage himself, Richard had confided to his mother his disgust at the prospects of marrying a woman who had not only dallied with his own father but borne him an illegitimate son.

But Eleanor had other matters of a more personal nature to worry about. Richard's indifference towards women was not half as disturbing as his alleged attraction towards men. Indeed, rumors about his intimacies with Philip Augustus, himself, were swirling around court. There had to be a simple way out of her dilemma, some way to extract a legitimate male heir from her adored Richard's loins. And it had to happen in a hurry. Searching for a solution to her quandary, she suddenly remembered Richard's passing comments about a fair princess he had met in Pamplona a year earlier. As far as she could recall, that was the only woman Richard had ever mentioned with favor.

Eleanor decided to find out for herself whether Berenguela would make a suitable queen of England. Even if an escapade to Navarre turned out to be a wild goose chase, it would serve the useful purpose of meeting Sancho *el Sabio* personally. Over all those years, she had learned that it paid to add to one's list of royal acquaintances.

Having wintered in Bordeaux that year, she felt an expedition to Navarre would be a lark, a mere intelligence-gathering exercise. She would go in and out without even her courtiers finding out about it, thus nipping the rumor mill in the bud. She would travel incognito, accompanied by a handful of trusty Angevin and Poitevin knights. They'd make the short jaunt from Bordeaux to Pamplona in a few short stages, stopping in Bayonne, St. Jean-Pied-Port, Roncevaux, then finally on to Pamplona. She had read so much about Roncevaux! She absolutely adored *La Chanson de Roland*, so much so that she expected every student in her school of troubadours in Poitiers to learn it by heart and recite it verbatim. Now she'd finally get a chance to visit the very site where the noble Breton had met his untimely end. Mixing business with pleasure would make this a fun and fruitful escapade.

It was already early summer when she set off on the Navarran spree. Richard had just recently sailed with his small armada from Marseilles, headed for Sicily, where he would join forces with Philip Augustus. If she hurried, she could catch up with him there before he sailed for Outremer. Though already a matronly sixty-five, Eleanor was still in superb physical condition, handsome enough to turn a young knight's head and make him think of the raving beauty she must have been forty years earlier. Her bearing was always regal, shoulders held back, head high, never letting anyone forget that she was the dowager Queen of England, and, of course, the Duchess of Aquitaine.

The trip from Bayonne inland was pleasant. They traveled at a leisurely pace along the plush green valleys of Vasconia, redolent of thyme and new-mown hay, its hills speckled with grazing sheep and the occasional herd of honey-colored cows. The serfs they met along the way stopped to ogle the soberly elegant lady riding her magnificent Arabian steed in the company of equally richly attired noblemen. The small cortege would stop at homely *caserios* along the way, where villeins offered them their humble fare of bread and *chorizo*, downed with hearty Bordeaux wine. It was delightfully bucolic and peaceful in the Vascon country that time of year.

Eleanor caused quite a stir at St. Jean Pied de Port, the day she arrived. Word got around that an important lady from Poitiers had arrived with her noble retinue on a pilgrimage to Santiago. Since this was not an infrequent occurrence at St. Jean, where pilgrims normally gathered before attempting the challenging crossing of the Pyrenees, they were not overly intrigued by her presence when she checked in at the Navarran king's royal residence for the night.

There was some discussion about which route to take to Roncevaux. One of King Sancho's majordomos, who happened to be visiting that week, suggested the trail winding up the Luzaide valley; it was, he assured her, steeper and narrower, but shorter. The palace's Seneschal, on the other hand, insisted they take the Cissa route, the one Caesar and his armies had taken.

"Which one did Charlemagne take?" inquired Eleanor.

"Rumor has it that he came through the Luzaide gorge" answered the Seneschal. "Duke Bernard is said to have taken the old Roman route."

"Very well, then," said Eleanor, cutting the discussion short. "We shall take the Luzaide route." She wanted to retrace Charlemagne's steps, not Caesar's.

The Aquitainean expedition left early the next morning, breakfasted and refreshed. It was a short but steep trek from St. Jean to the peak of Ibañeta. Though they could see clear skies above them, the road up the gorge was somber, the precipice to their left forbidding. Eleanor felt an inexplicable shiver as she visualized in her mind's eye the gory battle that must have taken place along that deep ravine, four centuries earlier.

"Poor Bretons!" she sighed softly. "Men and their wars are such fools!" She had conveniently forgotten that she had, herself, once prodded her two sons to do battle with their own father in the fields of Aquitaine and Gascogne.

When she finally reached the sunny heights of Ibañeta, Eleanor gazed breathlessly upon the 'valley of thorns' directly below her. It was a pretty little valley, its glens and dales no different from all the others in the Vascon country, north of the pass, all with their green, sheep-dotted slopes and patches of dark beech forests. Yet this valley was different, for there, at the foot of the mountain, was a quaint sprawl of gray buildings sidled up against a small Romanesque church and a squat, odd-looking, ogive-windowed structure next to it.

"Roncevaux!" she whispered in nostalgic wonder, recognizing the pilgrims' Hospice she had heard so much about. It had been built on the very grounds where Roland and Turpin, Oliver and Anselm and all those other noble peers of France had fallen. Memories of the *chanson's* verses she knew and loved so well came flooding over her. She spurred her mount to get to the valley below before the heavy mists roiling behind her began to surge down the mountainside, making the going that much more hazardous. Many a pilgrim had been lost crossing these mountains in the fog and the snow, and she didn't want to add to their numbers.

The Abbot was duly impressed when informed of his visitors' identity. He was delighted to host the wife of kings and mother of the most renowned chevalier of them all, the one who was just about to embark on a Crusade to recapture Jerusalem from the Saracens. Though offered the best accommodations at the hospice, Eleanor and her knights were appalled by the austere appointments in the rooms assigned them. No wainscoted or tapestried walls here, just stark, whitewashed, humble monks' cells. They consoled themselves with the thought that these, after all, were pilgrims' lodgings, where people came to willingly suffer privation and penury, flagellating their bodies and their souls, not to wallow in human comforts. A hint of a smile slowly spread across Eleanor's face as she visualized her knights' discomfort in such austere surroundings. She knew they would be eager to leave on the morrow.

The Abbot and his eleven Canons invited the regal company to honor their refectory table with their presence at supper. Frugal in selection but hearty in fare, the meal was definitely a cut above ordinary pilgrims' fare, the fish fresher, the meat of a better cut, the cheese properly aged. Eleanor engaged the Abbot in convivial conversation, delving into the subject of Roland's local debacle. She wanted to know where the battle had taken place and who, exactly, had beaten him that summer evening, a little over four centuries earlier.

The Abbot, a historian of note, was happy to oblige, having authored several learned tracts on the subject and answered that very question, invariably posed by inquisitive pilgrims.

"The battle started in Atzobiskar, up there," he said, pointing toward one of the peaks to the northeast, "and ended in this very clearing on which our Hospice now stands. As for the victors, the *chanson* has it all wrong, milady. There were no Moors in this battle of Roncevaux; only Vascons and Franks."

"But how could a handful of primitive shepherds defeat the cream of the Franks' armies?" inquired Eleanor, eager to engage the Abbot in meaningful discussion. "It had to be a relatively strong and effective force. At the time, only the Moors were so equipped." She thought her logic seamless, her arguments unassailable. She was Aquitainean by birth, in effect an ex-Vascon, but even she knew that no rabble could defeat a disciplined army.

"Roland didn't have a chance," answered the Abbot with calm authority. "It only takes a handful of brave men to trap an army in a funnel. Courage and the element of surprise have turned impossible odds into victories before. Surely, milady has heard of Horatio's stand at the bridge, and the victories at Thermopilae and Gelduba. Besides," he added, reverting to her original question, "Charlemagne's wasn't the first army defeated in these ravines and gorges. You came up through them yourselves. You know whereof I speak."

Eleanor mulled over her host's response, decided not to press her point further. She had prodded the curate enough for one evening. Besides, she knew that she wasn't going to change his mind, no matter how much logic she marshaled to trip him up. Then, again, he could be right. Roland's *chanson* had been written centuries after the fact by some jingoistic Breton monk probably more interested in his people's self-exaltation than in historical fact. One had to watch these Bretons! Besides, history had a funny way of coming down on the side of the powerful, victors or not, she reflected philosophically. She smiled as she remembered her jester's twisted rendering of the Golden Rule: "He who owns the gold gets to write the rules."

They left early the next morning, making sure they'd arrive in Pamplona before the city gates closed for the night. The trip was leisurely, unhurried. It was late afternoon when they finally got there. The king himself was waiting for them at the Palace gates when they turned up. He had heard a great deal about Eleanor over the years but had never had the pleasure of meeting her. She had been put away in some castle, accused of sedition, if memory served, the time he visited her late husband Henry's court in Poitiers. He had gone pleading for arbitration on one of Navarre's interminable squabbles with Alfonso of Castile. It seemed to Sancho that she looked no worse for wear after all those years of confinement. Indeed, his first impression of her was that she looked remarkably attractive for a woman in her mid-sixties.

Queen Sancha, too, had heard rumors about Eleanor, not all of them flattering. Being a devout Christian, the Navarran queen frowned upon over-assertive women, disapproved of frivolous marriage annulments and grimaced at the thought of sedition. Besides, it did not befit a married woman to be coquettish, especially if she was a queen, from whom only decorum and good example were expected. All else aside, it was evil to be adulterous. Long ago, when Sancha was a young lady, she had overheard scandalous rumors about this woman's illicit affairs with a relative of hers in Jerusalem during the Second Crusade. King Louis of France subsequently divorced her for it, although grounds of consanguinity were invoked. Just as scandalous at the time was that the shameless hussy lost little time marrying the king of England himself.

But all that was now water under the bridge, conceded Sancha charitably. Perhaps her years of confinement in a Salisbury dungeon had served the time and purpose of Purgatory, cleansing her soul and making a new woman of her. Still, Sancha wasn't sure; Eleanor still looked suspiciously attractive, even a little flirtatious at times. She could tell from the way the knights and squires, hers and her husband's included, hovered around her with shameless solicitousness, like bees fluttering around honey. Men were so ridiculous sometimes!

It was Iñaki's turn to serve the royal family at table that evening. Like every other knight and squire around, he was immediately taken by the presence and good looks of Richard's mother. She was the kind of woman who seemed to emanate animal magnetism—and Iñaki knew a little something about animals—someone who would attract attention even while remaining silent and perfectly still. Though understated, her attire was elegant, her manner refined and sophisticated. The Navarran court was obviously beneath her courtly element, thought Iñaki. She outclassed everyone present.

He did not fail to notice that her Spanish was grammatically correct, an almost imperceptible French accent lending it a certain gracious, cosmopolitan charm. She was witty and engaging. The way she tossed her head around and the smile that came so readily to her lips were those of a woman sure of herself, acting far younger than her years. She was a definite success at the Navarran court that evening.

Sitting across the table from her, Berenguela was equally mesmerized by the English dowager queen. She could immediately see whose good looks Richard the Lionheart had inherited. The young princess was discerning enough to recognize class and good breeding when she saw it. She had never before been in the presence of such a courtly, charismatic person, with so much *savoir faire*. She would make a formidable mother-in-law, Berenguela sensed in her innermost thoughts, someone whom one would not lightly cross. Realizing that she had caught herself sizing up her future mother-in-law made her blush.

Eleanor noticed the princess' keen interest in her. It was almost as if the young lady were sizing her up, hanging on her every word, entranced by her every gesture.

"And what do you do for entertainment, young lady?" asked Eleanor addressing Berenguela directly for the first time, during a lull in the conversation.

"After my Latin and religion classes," answered Berenguela, "I like to do needlepoint and play backgammon with my brothers and sisters. I also play the lute. I love horseback riding. Some days I even go hawking with my brother Sancho and his squire. Now, *that* I really enjoy!"

She was fair enough and of passably refined breeding, thought Eleanor. More importantly, she looked healthy, not buxom but broad-hipped enough to make a prolific mother. Yes, she thought, this one will do quite well for my Richard. Not too spirited, not too submissive, just right. She wondered why she hadn't married yet, being already nineteen.

"How would you like to come with me to the Crusades?" asked Eleanor, clear out of the blue.

Berenguela did a double take. She was puzzled by the question and, judging from the sudden silence around the table, so were the others.

"And what, pray, would Berenguela be doing in Outremer?" queried the king, pretending to be baffled by her question. Though Sancho had had a strong suspicion of the real reason for the dowager's visit, Eleanor had managed to avoid the subject altogether, until now. She had gone on about her Richard's leadership and organizational skills, his planning the logistics of the combined armies of England, France and Austria for a concerted thrust on Outremer, but she had, so far, cannily skirted the real purpose of her visit. Now, finally, she had shown her hand.

"Let's stop playing games, Milord," said Eleanor, straightening herself up in her chair. Suddenly, she herself sounded regal, talking to the king on equal terms, daring to chide him for feigning ignorance of her visit's purpose. "We all know the reason for my trip here. Though unannounced, it still remains a State visit.

Such diplomatic calls serve to arrange treaties or forge agreements, peaceful or otherwise. Others are to discuss troths. I am here to discuss the marriage arrangements between young Berenguela and my son Richard. I was led to believe that he, himself, discussed betrothal matters with you when he was here last year?"

A deafening silence descended upon the table. Berenguela's heart gave a fresh start. Even Iñaki rested his knife on the cutting table, turned around to better capture the momentous interchange taking place behind him. There must have been some urgency to the matter for her to discuss such a delicate subject in public. Matters of State were seldom discussed at the dinner table.

"He brought up the subject, indeed, milady," responded Sancho amiably enough. "And I gave him my blessing." He could have left it at that but could not abide the Aquitainean duchess' gaining the upper hand. Two could play at this game of one-upmanship, he thought to himself. "It has been over a year since we spoke last, as I recall, but I have seen no follow-through on his or his Ambassador's part." The unsubtle gibe must have sunk home for Eleanor came perceptively off her haughty stance.

"He has been a very busy man, your Highness," said Eleanor trying to placate Sancho, who was obviously wearied by the delay in finalizing the wedding arrangements, "what with the crowning ceremony and the preparations for the Crusades." One had to treat these proud Peninsulars with kid gloves, she reflected. She could not afford his antagonism now. She had come all this way to get Berenguela, not spar with her father.

"May I be so bold as to request that Berenguela and her small cortege join me in my upcoming trip to Sicily, where my son Richard waits?"

There, thought the King of Navarre, it was finally out in the open. Here, at last, was the follow-up he had been so eagerly awaiting for over a year now, to be precise. One didn't ask a young maiden to go traipsing around the countryside just to visit her son unless he had honorable intentions. But he had to nail these down.

"Am I to understand that England is offering my daughter a queen's crown?" Sancho could not have put it more bluntly. Not even the canny Eleanor of Aquitaine could wriggle out of that pointed question.

"You may so understand," responded Eleanor with equally regal hauteur. "I have been empowered by my son, Richard, King of England, to offer Berenguela the same crown that I myself have worn these many years."

It was a memorable response. The Great Hall of Sancho's palace had heard many a weighty pronouncement uttered within its walls but this proposition by the dowager queen of the island kingdom topped them all in drama and moment. Sancho was thrilled by the import of her succinct response. He had long dreamed of an alliance with England to help him fend off the hostile advances of Castile and Aragon. Berenguela's marriage would seal that alliance. The plum was ready for the plucking.

"I am pleased by your offer, milady, and honored to accept it on my daughter's behalf," said Sancho, unable to suppress the smile spreading across his serene countenance. Berenguela herself was delighted by the sudden turn of events. She had dreamed of this moment since the handsome and debonair prince had first shown interest in her. She was, after all, getting on in years, and though still nineteen, she was marrying much later than most other princesses around. Fleeting thoughts of spinsterhood had already started to cross her mind lately.

"...arrangements will have to be made and papers signed between the Chancellors of our respective kingdoms," her father was saying officiously. "Dowry agreements, wedding details, like time and place, all that sort of thing. It shouldn't take long, I am sure."

"It has all been arranged, your Highness," responded Eleanor. "I plan to sail from Marseilles shortly to visit my daughter Joanna in Sicily. She has recently been widowed and needs my comfort. Richard happens to be there at the moment, gathering his and Philip Augustus' forces for the final push on the Holy Land. It is of the utmost importance that the wedding take place before his departure."

"And what, pray, is the urgency?" inquired Sancho, puzzled by the rush to marriage. "It will take several weeks for Berenguela and her retinue to get ready. Surely the king can wait that long."

"We had best discuss this in private, your Highness," suggested Eleanor, concerned now that enough matters of State had been discussed in the open. Besides, she did not wish young Berenguela to know the real reason for the hasty marriage. The possibility of her future husband's death in Outremer was something Eleanor would rather spare her, for the time being.

Sancho agreed and the two retired to his private offices, accompanied by his Chancellor.

While they were thus engaged, Berenguela, became increasingly intrigued by her future mother-in-law's designing ways. She had a growing suspicion that the die for the rest of her life had been cast; she would, no doubt, be leaving home shortly to become the next queen of England. How perfectly exhilarating! The imminence and magnitude of the event had not quite dawned on her yet. Things were happening so fast! Her mind raced with visions of the marriage ceremony, her trip abroad, perhaps even a pilgrimage to the Holy Land. She tried to imagine her future life in England and Aquitaine. In her mind, she was already sorting out the members of her retinue for the trip. They would have precious little time to get ready. Besides ladies-in-waiting, she would need some trusted knights to come along, too. After all, there was a war going on in Outremer.

Of all the prospective members of her retinue, she was only sure of two, so far. Lady Monteagudo had been her closest friend and lady-in-waiting ever since she attained the age of puberty. To her she had always confided her deepest secrets and was closer than to either of her own two sisters, or even her own mother. As for the male escorts, there was little doubt about who one of them would be. And dear Iñaki was not even a knight yet. She had always trusted his good judgment and cherished his friendship. He had taught her to love the ways of nature and the art of falconry. He had been her loyal friend and confidant as far back as she could remember. She had even had a crush on him for awhile until Lady Monteagudo pointed out the folly of her infatuation.

"You'll get over it," she had told her. And she thought she had, until the day he promised her his eternal fealty at the joust, a year earlier. That gesture had touched her very soul. Nobody else had offered her anything like that, before or since. Not even Richard! Well, she would give Iñaki a chance to fulfill his promise to defend her honor and her life. He was not yet a knight but he would be dubbed one soon enough. Perhaps before the walls of Jerusalem itself! She would see to that.

The king and the duchess' return snapped her out of her musings.

"You will leave before the week is up," her father told her. "There are powerful reasons for your immediate nuptials with Richard, which I cannot go into right now. You must trust your father's judgment on this matter. It is imperative that the wedding take place before the Crusaders set out for the Holy Land." With the more urgent aspects of his instructions out of the way, he continued, now in a more fatherly tone: "You will travel with the Duchess of Aquitaine to Sicily within the week. She will be your guide and mentor. The details of your wedding and the matter of the dowry have been discussed to our satisfaction. Your older brother Sancho will accompany you and will represent me at the nuptials. On the morrow, you will choose your retinue and start packing for the trip. Your mother will help you."

And that was that, thought Berenguela, a marriage contract arranged on the fly, as it were. Thank God she was marrying a man she admired and, yes, had already begun to love. Few princesses were fortunate to marry a handsome and famous man, a king no less! Mostly, they were thrust into marriages of convenience, arranged for reasons of State, no more. Perhaps that was why so many regal marriages floundered these days, she reflected. But, in her case, it was different. It had been love at first sight. Besides, there was no annulling this union for reasons of consanguinity, the two not being related in any way or form. "Till death do us part," she mused, innocently.

It was a busy week at the palace. It had been decided to keep the number of Berenguela's retinue down for the upcoming trip to Bordeaux, where Eleanor was to meet them before setting off for Toulouse, proceeding from there to Marseilles, where they'd set sail for Sicily. Berenguela had asked her father that Iñaki be one of her retinue. His devotion to her was well known in court; she could not be better served if she ever ran into trouble.

Iñaki was, of course, delighted with the prospects of taking the Cross. Everyone in the palace had dreamed of being able to do just that. Sure, there was the local distraction of fighting the Moors, which some fancied a Crusade of sorts, but it was not the same. Important as it was to the local warlords, it lacked the universality and transcendence of fighting to recapture the very birthplace of Christ himself. The Pope seldom summoned Crusades against the Moors in the Peninsula; it was always against the Saracens in the Holy Land. That was the place to fight, perhaps to die. The indulgences thus earned would be plenary and definitive. A battling pilgrim! Of such were the ranks of the Orders of knighthood filled. And he was going to be one of them soon. He could feel it in his bones.

Delighted as he was at the prospects of knighthood and indulgences, he felt an equal elation at the thought of being able to serve his princess and longtime friend. He had always been fond of her, ever since he came to the palace. He was fourteen then, she only eight. They grew up and played together all those many years. She had been like a kid sister to him. Sometimes, he thought, her brother Sancho was a little jealous of their friendship, especially when Iñaki would chide him for not treating her more kindly. Iñaki had always stood up for her and, once, not too long ago, in a joust, he had even laid his life on the line for her, promised to defend her honor and her life with his own.

It was when she turned thirteen that he first noticed a change in his attitude towards her. Something new had quietly, almost surreptitiously, slipped into their friendship. It happened almost overnight. She was no longer the kid sister whose pigtails he could pull, nor the little girl with whom he could rough-house and tease. She was growing into a lovely maiden, a gentle lady with all the ingenuous attributes of new womanhood. A certain tenderness and mutual respect seemed to have crept into their relationship. Iñaki had just turned nineteen, a restless age when the thoughts of a young man hovered more over roundnesses than religious scruples. But he managed to subdue his inner turbulence and sublimate the tumult in his soul into a chivalrous state of suspended animation, building, one day at a time, an ever-higher pedestal under her feet, until she became his model of all virtue.

She, of course, noticed the change, but was noble enough not to take advantage of his inner struggle with his stilled yearnings. When with him, she went about as if they were still the friends of old, happy, innocent, carefree. She loved joining them when he and her brother Sancho struck out to hawk, or hunt, or ride the stallions. Ever since she was a little girl, she'd always been a bit of a tomboy, preferring the company of men to that of women. She'd always felt at ease with them, even enjoyed competing with them. It was no different now. She would never change that way.

"Thank you for agreeing to join my entourage," she told Iñaki in one of their brief asides, the day after Eleanor left for Aquitaine. "*Behar zaitut,*" she added, confiding that she really needed him. After a pause, she asked: "Shouldn't you go bid farewell to your parents before you part for Outremer? You may not see them again for a while, you know."

"My father passed on last year but I do plan to stop by to see my mother and brother before we leave," he answered. "It's been so long since I last saw them that I may not find my way home," he added jokingly. "And you," he said, "are you ready for this big step?"

It was the first time he'd broached the subject of her marriage. It rankled a little inside, for, gallant and debonair as her future husband seemed, Iñaki felt, in his bones, that there was something not quite right about him. His endless fighting and jousting almost seemed as if he were trying to run away from something. Even his brief courtship of Berenguela—if it could be called that—seemed a little stilted, stiff even. It seemed to lack warmth. Even the romantic verses he had addressed to her had sounded a little priggish to Iñaki. She had shown them to him in confidence, one day after Richard left Pamplona. She was so taken by them! But Iñaki had volunteered nothing. It was not his place to do so. The future of kingdoms rode on this marriage and he knew when to be circumspect, even with his dear Berenguela. Besides, it would have sounded disingenuous, a little like sour grapes. It was best to let sleeping dogs lie. Let history take its inexorable course. It would, anyway, without his meddling.

"I can't wait to marry him!" said the artless princess, exulting at the prospects of her imminent nuptials. Iñaki thought that she looked prettier than ever. Love did that to women sometimes, gave them an ineffable radiance, a special aura. "Father says that he has pledged Maine to me as dowry. That's near Anjou, in the Loire country, you know. They say it's lush and pretty. I will be the Countess of Maine, can you believe it!"

"You'll be more than that, Bery," he said, addressing her by the nickname he always used with her when they were alone. "You'll be the Queen of England!" Suddenly, he himself was stunned by the thought. Here he was exchanging pleasantries with royalty! "And I'll be there to help you if you ever need me," he added on a more serious note. "And we will speak Basque when we don't want others to understand."

"Yes!" said Berenguela impishly. For one fleeting instant, she had reverted to her younger years. Leaning over, she pecked him on the cheek, saying: "That will be our secret language!"

Chapter 26

A Hazardous Journey

1191

"It would have been so much simpler to just ship out of Marseilles," muttered prince Sancho, hunkering down by the fire. They had struggled up a steep goat path for the better part of the morning, had now stopped to rest midway up the Alpine pass, cold, hungry, exhausted.

"It would certainly have made for a shorter journey," agreed Iñaki, poking at the embers with the tip of his sword, trying to keep the flickering flame from going out altogether. "I wonder what prompted her to take this roundabout way. It's going to take us weeks to get there!" As usual, they spoke in Basque so the Aquitaineans around them would not pry.

"Remember the courier who overtook us back in Avignon, just as we were about to sail down the Rhone to Marseilles?" Sancho reminded him. "He warned against proceeding to Marseilles. King Philip's henchmen had orders to arrest us as soon as we set foot there. They intended to hold us hostage until Eleanor gave orders to set his sister, Alice, free." He paused for a moment before adding: "Eleanor had her locked up in Rouen just before setting off on this trip, you know."

"Probably didn't want the little hussy causing any trouble back home while Richard was away," remarked Iñaki sardonically. "Now it's not only the Saracens we'll have to worry about but our own allies back home as well! That's reassuring, isn't it?"

"Yes," agreed Sancho morosely. "It looks like Eleanor's been hoisted on her own petard!"

"And we along with her!" rejoined Iñaki, trying a little levity to hide his displeasure at their predicament.

The small group of knights and squires escorting the two noblewomen and their ladies-in-waiting had had to alter their original plans on leaving Avignon, electing to follow the Durance north, instead of proceeding down the Rhone to Marseilles. Crossing the Alps would make for a longer, more hazardous journey. It would have surprised Iñaki to learn that one of his ancestors had crossed those very Alps centuries earlier when Prefect Otsoa negotiated them with his two cohorts to fight the Huns in Lower Germany shortly after their victory at Cremona. But Otsoa had crossed them earlier in the year, when the snows were neither as deep nor the passage as arduous and forbidding as it was now, in the early winter of 1190.

Despite the small band's exhaustion, Eleanor had pushed them on relentlessly, fearful of missing Richard, who was to sail from Sicily to the Holy Land in the early spring, with or without his wife-to-be. They followed the Rhone's tributary almost to its source before turning east to confront the Alps. Someone suggested crossing them at the narrow pass between the Cottian and the Graian Alps. They could have traveled a little farther north for an easier crossing at the St. Bernard pass but that would have entailed traveling through unfriendly Helvetian country. It would be bad enough having to traverse the length of the Italian peninsula, with its voluble, unpredictable natives. They finally opted to cross the Alps through the less-traveled Frejus pass and spill into the wide plains of the Piedmont.

Prince Sancho was turning out to be the ideal leader for the expedition. He was not only the highest-ranking nobleman in the group but was a warrior of renown as well, second in distinction only to the Lionheart himself. Every man in his party would have followed him to hell and back, risking his life at his service. He was aware that the group was woefully undermanned to provide proper protection for the two high-ranking ladies in their entourage, one a stubborn, adventurous dowager, the other his own sister and soon-to-be queen of England. But Sancho had a knack for wresting the best out of a poor situation and he felt it would be no different this time.

Besides, it was reassuring to have Iñaki around. The young Vascon had a keen eye for country, always keeping a good lookout for trouble. From the most imperceptible bird twit or stealthy animal movement, he could sense an ambush or smell a trap some distance away. By observing the general lay of the land he could detect the presence of concealed fords or hidden passes that would get the group through swiftly, avoiding dead-ends, saving precious travel time. Best of all, Iñaki knew his animals. He could still talk to the horses in their own language, knew when halts in the journey were necessary to avoid overstressing the beasts.

His knack for dealing with peasants also paid off handsomely at day's end, when the group stopped at some village. He could always bargain for enough food and adequate quarters for the party, or find some barn nearby with enough clean straw to sleep in. Iñaki was the perfect scout, a master logistician, a born quartermaster, all invaluable assets to any company on the move. This realization had gradually dawned on Eleanor and her knights, all of whom had grown increasingly fond of the lanky Vascon squire.

They reached the Frejus pass on Christmas Eve, after climbing a steep, broken path seldom traveled that time of year. Sancho had called a halt as the group came to a narrow pass in the mountain, which offered some shelter from the bitter wintry blast. The servants and muleteers set up a windbreak in a shallow recess in the mountainside to provide a modicum of shelter. The men sat around a hesitant fire, fueled by dead kromholtz bushes, frozen hands extended towards its feeble flame. Their shared discomfort in the harsh surroundings had started to forge a cohesive bond between the Vascons and Aquitaineans, despite their difference in language, background and culture.

Inside the makeshift shelter provided by an overhanging ledge, the women huddled together under piles of sheepskins, trying hard to keep warm. Though she was, by far, the oldest in the group, Eleanor was still the life of the party, lifting the group's spirits with endless tales of youthful adventures. The older ladies-in-waiting in the group had heard a few risqué stories about her indiscretions with her uncle, Raymond of Antioch, during the previous Crusade in the Holy Land, a behavior so unseemly that it precipitated the annulment of her marriage to Louis, King of France. The ladies dared not pry, but they did not really have to, able to read between the lines the titillating truth about the dowager queen's flighty past. She could still spin a yarn merry enough to distract the women from the bitter cold outside. Not in vain was she the patroness of the troubadours in Poitiers, the alma mater of the bards.

It was Twelfthnight when they finally came to the end of a long, winding descent into the Piedmont plains. They followed the Dora Riparia east until it spilled into the mighty Po. It had taken them several weeks to get there from Toulouse. Running low on supplies and sorely in need of refitting, Eleanor and Sancho agreed to take a short break in the little hamlet of Lodi, to regain their strength and replenish their stores. Cereals, salted bacon and wineskins were purchased and fresh horses acquired. They rested there for a few days while their victuals were packed.

Eleanor wanted to reach Messina before Richard's forces sailed for the Holy Land. To get there they would have to proceed in a tortuous, roundabout way to avoid the flighty, unpredictable politics in Italy. They'd have to feel their way around, imposing on friendly hosts, skirting feuding Duchies. Richard himself had suggested they embark at Brindisi, on Italy's southeastern tip and sail from there to Sicily. The friendly Apulians would show them how to negotiate the passage around the Ionian Sea to Messina. Hopefully, Richard would still be in Sicily and would get on with this tiresome business of marriage, which had become an obsession with his mother.

"Then we should travel down the eastern coast of Italy," suggested Sancho. "It's the most direct route to Brindisi."

"Yes," responded Eleanor, "but it would entail traveling through territory friendly to the Venetians. That would be hazardous, considering those people's love for lucre, especially the ill-gotten kind. They're notorious for kidnapping noblemen for ransom. We cannot afford to take that risk."

It was this well founded concern that finally prompted them to travel down the western coast of Italy despite the prospects of having to negotiate yet another, though not so forbidding, mountain range. Besides the now familiar hardship of the climb, the Apennines were known to be crawling with "*molti banditi*," the locals warned. As a precaution, Sancho ordered every knight and man-at-arms to wear mail during the crossing.

The lush plains of Tuscany greeted them after an uncomfortable but uneventful passage over the northern Apennines. The natives turned out to be friendly and generous, eager to slaughter their sheep to feed the group. Slowly, they wended their way down to the ancient town of Pisa, where they rested for a few days before proceeding south, now at a more deliberate pace. Eleanor opted to skirt Rome altogether, despite her ladies' pleas to stop and visit the Eternal City, it being so close by. But there was little love lost between Eleanor and Rome. Pope Eugenius' denial of a prompt dissolution of her first marriage, forty-odd years earlier, still rankled. Besides, she thought, there was little time for pious frivolities now. Spring was almost at hand and, with it, Richard's sailing date. They had to press on.

Though they made good time, it was not until the eve of Candlemas that they hailed into Naples. There was much merriment in town, the lively southerners wanting to make up for the fasts and privations of a Lenten season about to descend upon them. The men in Eleanor's party were only too happy to join in the merriment. It had been a long, arduous journey and they needed relief from the many pent-up days of restraint and abstinence endured so far. Naples offered just the entertainment and distraction the men sorely needed.

For Sancho and Iñaki, part of the city's charm was being able to walk down the old town's quaint narrow streets, dance in the piazzas and frequent the many drinking establishments, unrecognized and unchallenged. Attractive young Neapolitan women beckoned them, eager for the company of the two tall, handsome foreigners, one a prince in his mid-thirties, the other his squire, ten years his junior.

Walking along the narrow cobblestone streets in the old part of town that first evening, they were greeted by sounds of revelry. A willowy, olive-skinned maiden with raven-black hair startled them when she jumped out in front of them, cutting off any further progress. Singling Iñaki out with insinuating, gray-green eyes, she slipped an arm under one of his and tugged him gently into a doorway, brazenly inviting him into her dwelling. Surprised at first, Iñaki yielded, smiling broadly at the prince as he disappeared behind a curtain of glass beads. On the wages of a landless squire, thought Sancho, he could ill afford to consort with noble ladies. He had, on occasion, gotten involved with ladies-in-waiting who had taken a liking to him but until he earned his knighthood, his dalliances would have to be limited to palace servants and town wenches.

"*Carpe diem!*" called out Sancho, smiling knowingly at his squire as they parted ways. He knew Iñaki would be able to handle the situation gracefully. He always did. His good looks and engaging ways made him irresistible to most women. Sancho had watched him go about his amorous exploits at court, managing to emerge from his trysts unattached, his code of chivalry unsullied. Sancho sometimes wished he knew how Iñaki did it. The prince had an inkling that he would not be seeing his squire again for the duration of their stay in Naples.

As word of Eleanor's arrival in town got around, invitations started pouring in but it was the Duke of Naples' invitation they finally accepted. The Duke was waiting to greet them when they arrived at the magnificent fortress-castle atop the hill overlooking the bay. Standing in the middle of a manicured garden chockfull of fountains and marble statuary, he greeted them with gracious deference, insisting they be his guests during their stay in Naples.

Eleanor was a well known commodity in every court in Europe but few had heard of the Navarran nobility in her company. Sancho's imposing stature and Berenguela's striking good looks immediately captured the Neapolitans' attention, making them the instant darlings of the court. Mindful of her imminent marriage, Berenguela remained reserved and circumspect. Her brother, on the other hand, took full advantage of his hosts' hospitality and plunged directly into the festivities, flirting with the ladies who were all too eager to seduce an unattached, eminently marriageable prince.

The Duke treated them to a dizzying round of banquets, plying them with a boggling variety of food. Squires and pages presented them with heaping trays of exotic seafood, suckling pigs and swans, peacocks and cranes, served with rich wines from Campania, Latium, even far-off Tuscany. Minstrels and harpers, actors and jesters made their appearance after the desserts. Aware of Eleanor's fondness for oratorical entertainment, some of the knights vied for her attention with ribald songs in the *trouvère* tradition. The contest perfectly delighted Eleanor who, at one point, borrowed a lute from one of the musicians and broke out in song. There was not a dry eye in the audience as she sang a sad ballad about crusading pilgrims who never returned home to have their sons tend their graves. At one point, even Eleanor's eyes brimmed with tears when she realized that her own son could meet a similar fate.

A variety of games and amusements followed after the tables were cleared. The bachelors and ladies dallied and sang carols, joining hands to dance around in circles. Others favored games, playing hot cockles and blind man's bluff, chess and dice, even bowls. Still others engaged in dart-shooting, stone throwing and lance hurling. Sancho, who was not partial to parlor games and considered them an utter waste of time, went off with the Duke to snare falcons and hunt for boar. He enjoyed the outings with his host but missed Iñaki, who could have helped him with his host's finicky falcons.

They spent several restful days in Naples, all cares forgotten, enjoying the Italians' unhurried way of life, which they charmingly described as *dolce far niente*, a decadent lassitude raised to an art form. But it was getting on late February and there was little time to lose if they were to catch Richard in Sicily before he sailed for Outremer.

Iñaki turned up at the very last moment, grinning from ear to ear. Though obviously pleased with his latest seduction, he was never one to bray his conquests, remaining, as ever, discreet about his indulgence. Only the *padre* would hear the details of his amorous dalliance in his next Confession and would, no doubt, lay a few *paternosters* on him as penance. Or perhaps the Crusader's plenary indulgence he'd earn on reaching the Holy Land would obviate that little embarrassment altogether.

"I wonder why we're going to Brindisi instead of just sailing directly to Mesina, which is just across the straits from here," puzzled Iñaki, who would have dearly loved to have tarried a while longer in the arms of his olive-skinned Neapolitan beauty. "This little detour is going to eat up a lot of time."

"The Duke of Naples happens to be at war with the Calabrese, at the moment," replied Sancho. "They patrol these waters regularly," he explained. "We would be risking capture if we tried sailing to Messina in one of his ships. It'd be a shame to be captured after having come this far. Besides, Richard has arranged for one of his ships to pick us up at Brindisi."

They rode across the ankle of Italy at a brisk pace, stopping occasionally to rest the horses. Campania was pleasantly bucolic. They paused briefly in Potenza, a town full of memories for Eleanor who, on a rest stop there forty years earlier, had learned about the untimely death of Raymond of Antioch, her uncle and paramour. Everyone in that Second Crusade except her husband seemed to have known about her affair with the Prince. She was not worried about losing a kingdom, knowing there were others to be had. Indeed, she had already been scheming to turn her charms on young Henry Plantagenet and become his wife and queen of England.

Brindisi greeted them with its warm Adriatic breezes smelling of thyme and the sea, its towers and battlements attesting to age-old anxieties of invasion from Africa and the Aegean. But they could not tarry there and promptly boarded Richard's merchant vessel already waiting at the dock for the royal entourage.

Chapter 27

A Royal Wedding

Richard was waiting for them at the wharf when they sailed into Messina, several days later. He walked up the gangplank to welcome the party in person, as soon as the ship docked.

"Hello, *maman*," he said, planting a kiss on each of Eleanor's cheeks. "I'm so glad to see you! I worried so about you!" His mother never doubted her son's sincerity. He had always relied on her judgment, even left her in charge of his kingdom's affairs during his absence. She was immensely proud of his trust. He had, after all, always been her fair Coeur de Lion. "I'm sorry you had to tramp all over Italy to get here," her son was saying. "But I'm glad you're here at last, safe and sound."

He turned distractedly to Berenguela, who was curtsying to him. A faint smile briefly crossed his eyes, his mouth remaining set. Richard bent over to kiss her on the cheek in welcome. "You were brave to come all this way, my beloved. But I will make it up to you."

Eleanor seemed satisfied with the propitious reunion. She had never seen her son attracted to any woman before, sensed that some special chemistry still existed between these two. She desperately hoped that the magic would last long enough to produce an heir. That was all she was really interested in. It was, after all, the whole object of this ghastly trip.

Richard was delighted to see Sancho, his old jousting partner and comrade-at-arms in the troubled land of Gascogne. They had not seen each other since the tournament in Pamplona. Looking beyond Sancho, his eyes came to rest briefly on the tall squire standing behind him. He immediately recognized Iñaki, this time. He and Sancho were the only two persons he had ever known to tower over him.

"Has he knighted you yet?" he asked Iñaki, turning to Sancho with a questioning look.

"Not yet, your Highness," answered Sancho before Iñaki could respond. It was strange having to address his old friend and partner with such formality. Soon, thought Sancho, they would be addressing him the same way. "But I've been meaning to," he added.

"I may have to do it myself," chided the Lionheart. "Any chevalier who can unhorse a squire of mine deserves at least that recognition." The jousting match with the mysterious Knight of the Boar in the tourney in Pamplona remained etched in Richard's memory. Iñaki smiled at the compliment. "There'll be plenty of opportunities to dub him in the Holy Land," pursued Richard. "I'll see to that myself, if you don't."

Notably absent from the reception committee was the king of France. There was little love lost between Philip Augustus and Eleanor, who had sullied his father's honor by cuckolding him before divorcing him. Compounding that old grievance, her son Richard was now, after almost twenty years, reneging on his own troth to Philip Augustus' half sister, Alice, so he could marry this upstart, Berenguela, whom Eleanor had the effrontery to drag all the way to Sicily. With all this in mind, Eleanor, with Richard's blessing no doubt, had locked up Alice in Rouen. Rather than having to confront the brassy Duchess of Aquitaine, Philip had chosen to sail from Sicily on the eve of her arrival in Messina.

It was perhaps all for the better. This way, it would truly be a family reunion, just the three Plantagenets, Eleanor, Richard and Joanna, *tout en famille*. Joanna's plight was one of the reasons Richard was glad to see Eleanor; the Duchess would know what to do with a daughter who, like herself, had become a dowager queen.

But that was the least of Richard's problems. Eleanor apprised him of the sticky situation back home. In his absence, his younger, light-brained brother, John, was stirring trouble among the disgruntled English and Norman barons, angling for the crown of England. He had started spreading rumors about Richard's bleeding the country white with his Crusade taxes, and the unlikeliness of his returning from the Holy Land alive. Richard mulled over these treasonous allegations before responding.

"I, quite obviously, cannot return to straighten out these revolting developments," he said plaintively. "I am practically with one foot on my flagship, ready to sail. I beg you, *maman*, hurry back to England and set those barons straight. You're the only one with any authority to pull it off."

"Yes," agreed Eleanor pensively, flattered by the responsibility her son, the king of England, was once again laying on her shoulders. "We cannot let this matter fester for too long. You would find yourself without a kingdom on your return."

Eleanor had been worrying about that very possibility ever since she left Bordeaux four months earlier. God only knew how far the rot had spread during her absence. She would have to return right away. It was a shame that she would not be able to attend the nuptials after all the bother. She had forgotten that in Sicily, weddings were not celebrated during Lent, a period of abstinence taken much more seriously than in France. She now looked back on the short hiatus in Naples with regret; she would have made it, without that little interlude.

"Pity I'll have to miss the wedding," she said disconsolately. "You must promise me that the nuptials *will* take place before you land in the Holy Land." There was a muffled threat in her voice. "I didn't hatch this plan and go though hell and high snows to see it fail now." Leveling him with a steely gaze, she added, "Promise!"

It was a mother's peremptory order, a stern admonition to a wayward child. There was a regal authority in her entreaty that not even the king of England could ignore. Eleanor, when determined, was a formidable woman who brooked no dissent. She had always been strong-willed and stubborn like her grandfather William, and she was immensely proud of that heritage.

"I promise," responded Richard in a subdued voice, looking very much like someone who had just had his ears boxed. His mother's next statement made him realize that there was no slithering out from under the covenant after her departure.

"You, Joanna," she said, addressing her daughter who, up to that point, had sat passively by, contributing little to the family discussion, "will accompany Berenguela. You'll be her confidante and mentor, even after she marries. You'll be Berenguela's maid-of-honor at the wedding, her escort and shadow, thenceforth. The two of you will travel with Richard to Outremer."

Richard blinked. He had briefly considered going through with the marriage and then proceeding to the Holy Land, unaccompanied by his bride or sister.

"But mother…" he started to say.

His mother's scowl cut him short. "There is no point in getting married if no issue results," she added candidly. "And that is something one doesn't achieve with just one bedding." Her reply was blunt and to the point. She'd played this game too many times to underestimate the importance of perseverance and determination in matters of procreation. Knowing her son's proclivities, she was afraid that he would consider this whole matter a sovereign chore, go through the nuptial motions, and no further.

"Richard," she said in a voice halfway between a plea and a command, "we need a young Plantagenet from *your* loins!" Then, in a more pleasant, almost motherly tone, she added: "Just close your eyes, *mon cher*, and think of England."

The meeting had ended. Assured that she had done all she could to ensure the marriage, Eleanor sailed for Marseilles two days later to try to quell the sedition back home. Berenguela and Joanna retired to their quarters in Joanna's palace, there to await developments. They had to get ready for the wedding, everything including the gown and the trousseau, the church flowers and the music, the banquet and the games, all the thousand and one things a royal wedding entailed. And there was precious little time left to make the wedding arrangements. Easter was right around the corner and that was, they thought, the earliest wedding date.

Richard, however, had other plans.

The weather that had kept them grounded all winter long was finally lifting. The seas were becalmed for the first time in weeks and the westerlies promised smooth sailing across the Mediterranean, a sea always fickle that time of year. And since one did not tempt Eolus, they had to sail promptly. The army had been ready for weeks, restless, champing at the bit, the ships stocked and made ready. Richard gave the order to sail two days after Eleanor left Messina. She would be unhappy at his breach of promise but there was nothing wrong with marrying in Jerusalem if it came to that. Now, wouldn't that be grand! A royal wedding in Jerusalem! Even Berenguela would be delighted with that prospect, he pondered.

The two women were not at all elated by the news. They had been busily preparing for the wedding and now had to call everything off. Joanna, in particular, was distraught at having to announce to her former subjects and friends that the wedding was being called off. There was discontent, as well, among the ladies-in-waiting, who had been so looking forward to the wedding.

Berenguela was the most disappointed of all. "Easter is but a few days away," she confided to Iñaki during an evening walk in the palace gardens that evening. She was distraught by the postponement, he could see. "Richard could have waited to sail after the wedding. After all, it would have delayed the sailing of the fleet only a week, no more."

Though the reproach was understandable, Iñaki knew that well-born ladies seldom married for love. Happiness, he knew, was not a sine-qua-non of royal marriages. They had to make the best of all that childbearing duty. Still, he had always had a funny feeling about the way the Lionheart treated Berenguela, this princess whose honor he, Iñaki, had sworn to defend not too long ago. He had observed their meeting at the dock and sensed a certain coldness, a strange dearth of feeling in Richard's greeting. One would have expected a more effusive welcome between two lovers. Of course, they were not lovers in the strict sense of the word, but they were, after all, betrothed to each other. Iñaki mulled these things over in his heart but refrained from expressing them for fear of aggravating Berenguela's hurt feelings. She was disappointed enough by the postponement of the marriage.

"Well," he said, trying to comfort her, "ask yourself this question: how many queens can say they've been married in Jerusalem?" He thought he'd appeal to her deep religious feelings. "It would be a Crusader's crowning accomplishment to marry in the Holy Land!" he added. Berenguela remained skeptical. The postponement continued to distress her.

Joanna, on the other hand, was less guarded about her feelings. Incensed by her brother's breaking his promise, she pestered him about it every chance she got those last days in Messina. She confronted him with their mother's expressed concern that he could die issue-less in Outremer, that he had to marry before setting foot there.

"I do not intend to get killed in the Holy Land!" he retorted, annoyed by his sister's badgering. "I have very powerful reasons to sail now. I have already issued orders for the army's departure. You and Berenguela will board the *Dauntless* and follow my flagship to the Holy Land. We will marry when we touch land."

"All these are mere words!" rejoined his sister huffily. "You promised mother you'd marry before sailing for Outremer!" Joanna spoke with the authority of one preaching from a commanding moral ground.

"All right!" Richard finally agreed, trying to put an end to an acrimonious conversation that had dragged on for too long. "We shall stop somewhere before getting there and marry. How's that? Wouldn't that serve my pledge?"

"You're in such a hurry to get to Jerusalem that you'll stop somewhere else before getting there just to marry?" she retorted mockingly. "Likely story!"

"I promise!" said Richard. But his sister did not believe him. He had broken that same promise to his mother, someone he honored and respected far more than his sister.

The twenty-five ship English flotilla sailed from Messina on the first week of April, along with a few stragglers of Philip's fleet. The crossing promised to be short and uneventful. Only two days short of arriving in the Holy Land, however, they ran into a fearful storm off Cyprus. Strewn about by heavy winds, the ships of the fleet momentarily lost contact with one another and had to seek shelter in the first available safe harbor. The Captain of the *Dauntless* managed to steer his battered brigantine into the port of Limassol, on the southern coast of Cyprus. Upon learning of the precious cargo aboard the English ship, Isaac Comnenus, the rebel princeling of Cyprus and pretender to the Byzantine throne, ordered its distinguished passengers held under boat arrest. Because he was on friendly terms with Saladin, Comnenus schemed to hand over his guests for a hefty ransom.

The rest of Richard's ships sailed into other nearby Cyprean ports, farther east. Having received distress signals from Limassol, he stormed the town, rescuing his sister and wife-to-be from the clutches of Comnenus, who managed to slip away at the very last minute. Now leery of letting a hostile warlord loose to threaten his supply lines, Richard set off to hunt down and destroy Comnenus' forces in the rugged mountains overlooking Limassol.

It was during this tedious, month-long operation that Joanna finally confronted Richard. She had the foresight to invite Sancho to the meeting. The Navarran prince, himself, was growing increasingly concerned with Richard's procrastination and delayed wedding plans.

"You promised to stop and marry Berenguela before landing in the Holy Land," she reminded him bluntly. "You now have the chance to do it."

Richard resented Joanna's dragging Sancho into the confrontation. He could hardly deny having broken his promise to his mother, and now to his sister. He had, literally, run out of excuses. They all knew it would take a while to mop up Comnenus' forces in the interior. Lent had come and gone and they were now almost into Pentecost. There was nothing holding back the nuptials. With Sancho present, Richard could hardly deny that he had been spending time hawking while his knights hunted Comnenus down. Richard was trapped by his own wiles.

"Very well," he retorted, displeased at being forced into a corner. "You may start making arrangements for the wedding. It will take place on St. Pancras' day," he said to his sister. "It needn't be too elaborate. You've already made the preparations before in Messina. Just a different church, that's all."

Joanna dared not show her glee for fear her peevish brother would interpret her smile as a moral victory and call the whole thing off again out of spite. Sancho, too, felt relieved. He was not particularly happy about how this whole affair had been handled from the very beginning. It was becoming increasingly obvious to him that Richard was not particularly keen on marrying his sister. He had hardly been with her since she stepped off the gangplank in Messina. That boded ill for her marriage. For the first time, he felt sorry for his sister.

It was a glorious day in Limassol. The sun shone from a flawless sky over Mt. Troodos, spilling its purple shadows all the way down to a serene, azure sea. Redolent of lavender and sage grass, the clean, translucent air of the cool spring morning made many a knight feel young again, wishing he could call this Mediterranean backwater his home.

The marriage was celebrated without the fanfare that would have accompanied it at Westminster Abbey, but it was a royal wedding, nonetheless. The ceremony captured the imagination of the inhabitants of Limassol who thronged around the main square, eager to take in the pageantry. A smattering of Navarran noblemen joined several thousand English and French knights to witness the marriage. Several dozen knights sat astride their magnificent war-horses in colorful housings, distinctive red Crusader's crosses stitched on their white surcoats. They lined both sides of the rush-strewn pathway leading to the church entrance, their crossed lances forming a canopy of arms for the royal couple. Heraldic shields and crested helmets gleamed in the sun.

Announcing the approach of the sovereign couple, several long horns sounded in the distance heralding the conclusion of the civil ceremony that had just been held at an old Roman villa, nearby. The royal couple approached the church to the fanfare of regimental clarions and trumpets.

It was a small, many-columned temple of honey-colored marble, its onion-shaped dome lending it a certain Middle Eastern air proclaiming its Greek Orthodox persuasion. Inside, the church had been decked with battle banners and pennants of the different kingdoms and Duchies there represented, from the English and Norman to the Aquitainean and Navarran. The church was packed with noblemen and a handful of ladies, dressed in their best finery. Among them was Joanna, Richard's sister, magnificently garbed in Plantagenet red and Sicilian green.

Richard was attired in a silk tunic of blue and white checks embossed with the rampant lions of England, an ermine-hemmed cape loosely draped over one shoulder. His shock of red hair was partially covered by a velvet cap of state, framing a strong face marked with the unmistakable square jaw of the Plantagenets. Richard nodded to the wild acclaim of the crowd. Gathered round the entrance were the Peers of the realm, among whom stood the Earl of Leicester, Sir Thomas Multon, Sir Folk Doilly and Sir Edwin Turnehan. Even the Knight Ivanhoe was present.

Several paces behind Richard, Berenguela approached on the arm of her brother, who was to give her away in marriage. The princess was tall for a woman, handsome like the long line of Aristas from whom she sprang. She looked absolutely radiant in her wedding gown of heavy natural silk, its ivory-colored train dragging a dozen feet behind her, her tunic richly encrusted with jewels and sparkling gems. She was twenty-one, slim and statuesque. No longer spilling down her shoulder as a sign of maidenhood, her golden hair was held up by a ribbon of gold, revealing a white, swan-like neck. She held herself erect, looking regal as she walked down the aisle, remarkably calm despite the knowledge that she was about to become the queen of England.

The bride and groom knelt on contiguous *prie-dieus* in front of the altar, while Berenguela's bridesmaids busied themselves arranging her veil, straightening out her long train. The Earl of Leicester stood by, holding the king's heavy crown, which Richard had worn two years earlier, on the occasion of his coronation. Iñaki was standing near a side altar in one of the transepts, leaning against the wall. He towered above the other knights, who were pushing against the altar railing. His seven-foot height gave him a commanding view of the proceedings. Turning briefly toward the throng, Berenguela spotted Iñaki behind the mass of humanity. She gave him a smile to reassure him that everything was going to be all right.

In a flash of memory, Iñaki remembered the favor she had given him during the joust in Pamplona, an embroidered kerchief he would always treasure. He remembered the countless outings with her, his daydreams about all those fantasies of courtly love and virtue. No less vivid were the times he had sighed his eternal devotion to her, the inspiration of excellence for all his martial endeavors and travails. Most memorable of all were the simple, happy moments when he had played cat's cradle with her, lingering on her fingers far longer than he should have, gazing into her blue eyes with devotion, a mere squire sighing in hopeless, courtly love to a princess. Now, this lady of his chivalrous dreams was marrying someone else. Iñaki was immensely happy for her, despite his lingering doubts about Richard.

The Bishop of Evreux concelebrated High Mass with the local Bishop of the Greek rite in an elaborate, sometimes baroque and confusing ceremony, the Canon and the Epistle sung in Greek, the Gospel read in Latin. At the end of the service, after the Latin and the Greek Bishops had witnessed their exchange of rings and pronounced them man and wife in their respective tongues, the Bishop of Evreux anointed Berenguela's forehead with the royal chrism, to the cantors' swelling chant of *Salve Regina*. The Bishop then placed a gold scepter in her right hand and a crown on her forehead. Richard lifted Berenguela's veil, kissed her briefly on her lips.

A tumultuous roar rose from the throats of a thousand Crusaders, those who had packed the church and those who had to remain outside for lack of room. After the clamor subsided, one could almost hear a general sigh of relief. Everyone felt suddenly reassured that the union of their brave Lionheart and the handsome Navarran princess would ensure the continuation of the royal Plantagenet line. Like Eleanor, they, too, had wondered if such an event would ever come to pass.

A grand feast was held after the ceremony to which every knight and foot soldier of the expedition was invited. A huge number of steers and sheep had been slaughtered and local stores emptied of their supplies of fish and black olives, figs and strong Cypriot wine to feed and quench the thirst of the multitudes. Crusaders who could not be accommodated inside the great hall of Comnenus' old castle spilled out onto the bailey. As they ate, lutes and drums vied with church bells while troubadours sang music composed especially for the occasion. Local wenches in their festive garb served the tables to the ribald jokes and prodding hands of sergeants and men-at-arms.

Inside the castle, on the dais of the great hall, the royal couple shared their table with prince Sancho and other high-ranking English and Aquitainean lords, while the rest of the knights ate on trestle tables set up along the length of the great hall. Asked to serve the royal table, Iñaki dished out a staggering assortment of food, from hors d'oeuvres of oysters and mussels, partridges and pheasants, to the main fare of boars' heads and lamb, sirloin and venison, all the while replenishing cups with rich wines from distant Bordeaux, Burgundy and Tuscany. Figs in syrup and exotic nuts, rare cheeses and local pastries were served for dessert, to the soft music of harpers, the stories of minstrels, the jokes of jesters. After the tables were cleared, actors and troubadours regaled the assembly with plays and more songs.

Spring was uncharacteristically chilly that year. The crowd outside in the bailey sat around fires after the huge meal, singing salacious songs and snickering about first-nights. Their king and commander would now put his 'first night' to good use, exercising it with a partner of the proper sex. Richard was not known for seducing women, despite the coquetry and dalliance shamefacedly shown him by the ladies of his own court. His philandering was a poorly guarded state secret, spoken of mostly in hushes: he preferred the company of boys and men. Probably, laughed the inebriated soldiery as they staggered about the bailey of Limassol castle that evening, this Navarran beauty would snap him out of his odd predilections.

Chapter 28

The Knighting

June, 1191

A frenzy of activity kept the troops busy during their final days in Cyprus. Armorers whetted swords and sharpened spears, shields were stiffened, splintered pikes replaced, halberds and maces mended. Horses were shod and fed extra fodder while the kitchen help prepared extra rations for the army. Constables urged the knights to redouble their efforts at the quintain, insisting they drill their wheeling and turning movements.

"Iñaki," said Sancho, as they rode back to the castle after their morning exercises at the quintain, "when we get to the Holy Land you will ride by my side into battle, as you've always done. We've fought together these many years and know each other's strengths and failings. We are good for each other. But this time it will be different." He paused to let the thought sink in. "You will no longer serve me as my squire."

Iñaki pulled up his horse to a halt, puzzled by his lord's statement. He had only an inkling of what his liege lord was trying to tell him but was afraid to ask. He had aspired to knighthood for so long now that he could almost taste it. He sensed that Sancho had been under some pressure from the King of England to dub him, had even heard him being chided by Richard for his procrastination. Yet Iñaki, always the gentleman, refrained from bringing up the subject.

"I do not understand, milord," he stuttered inadequately, looking at the prince with searching eyes.

"Tomorrow, at dawn, I will dub you a knight," said Sancho, smiling broadly.

Iñaki remained speechless for a long time, overwhelmed by the implications of knighthood. His mind flitted back and forth from the joy and the pride of chivalry to its awesome responsibilities. He knew the rules of knighthood by heart but he was all too conscious of his lack of means to support himself in that exalted position. It took a handsome fiefdom to pay for the steeds and the armor, the squires and the errant life of a knight. Sancho's searching look brought him back down to earth.

"Milord, you know that I am eternally grateful for your offer. But I lack the wherewithal to support that station." Embarrassed though he was at having to bring up such a sensitive subject, he had enough familiarity with his prince to bare his inmost thoughts to him, however uncomfortable or humbling. They had both been forthright with each other all these many years and this was not the time to hide any nagging concern.

"First, it was my father's generosity, then your lordship's that supported my life as a squire in your father's court. But a knight's outlay is far more onerous. I lack a fief to support my knighthood and my father is now dead. Perhaps we'll have a good war and I can pick up some plunder. I may even win at some tournament. And, who knows, someday I may even earn a fief. But now…"

"Never fret, my loyal Vascon," said the prince with his usual gallant bonhomie. "I shall provide handsomely." Iñaki's concerns were allayed momentarily; he knew that his lord's word was as good as gold. Some of his courtiers had even dubbed him "Prince Midas," so shrewdly successful was he in his financial and business dealings. "You will pick up ransom and plunder soon enough. The fief will come in due course. Meanwhile, you will be a palace knight with the handsome remuneration and the perquisites that go with that position."

"Your destrier is a good war-horse," continued the prince. "I will ask the Constable to provide you with the arms and armor befitting your new rank. The steward will see to it that from now on your garb and your quarters are commensurate with your new standing. Now, my friend, you will sit at table in the Great Hall with the other knights and you will have your own squire to serve you."

"But milord…" Iñaki started to say as they dismounted at the castle gates, still overwhelmed by his lord's munificence.

"Enough said," said Sancho, raising a hand to allay Iñaki's concerns. "I have dubbed many a knight before. Few have deserved it so much as you. So, just go out there and get ready for the ceremony. You don't have much time. In your vigil tonight, think about the oaths that you will be pledging. Tomorrow, after early Mass, I shall knight you in the castle's chapel. You shall emerge from it a gentleman of honor," he said, adding wryly, "as if you weren't one already!"

Kneeling before his liege lord, Iñaki reached over and touched Sancho's hand to his forehead. Before the prince could retrieve it, Iñaki had already kissed it.

"Thank you, my lord," he said with heartfelt gratitude. "I will never disappoint you."

Flustered by his squire's public show of obeisance, the prince hurriedly helped Iñaki to his feet. The two men looked at each other briefly and embraced. They had been friends since adolescence and it would be no different now. The rules of chivalry would only strengthen the ties that bound them. Nothing would change their abiding friendship.

There was precious little time left before the night-long vigil. After paying the armorer a visit and checking with the castle steward, he slipped into the chapel to confess his sins to the Benedictine chaplain of the expedition. He then hurried to his quarters for a change of clothes. As if to reinforce the spiritual cleansing of that afternoon's confession, he took a ritual bath in rose water that his companion squires had drawn for him with much to-do and not a little envy. After his ablutions, he tied a white belt around his loin as a reminder of the vow of chastity he was about to take. Thus girded, he slipped on clean linen undergarments and donned a white tunic with a purple lining, a hand-me-down from Sancho that he had saved for this special occasion. Donning a set of white cotton stockings, he slipped into the silver-buckled leather shoes he had won at a hawking contest. They felt a little snug but they would have to do.

It was almost dark when he approached the castle chapel. The small, musty, ill-lit place of worship was empty. He would have his own thoughts to keep him company. Walking down the chapel's narrow aisle, Iñaki knelt on a prie-dieu at the foot of the altar. He made himself comfortable knowing that he'd be spending the rest of the night kneeling there, motionless, in silent prayer and contemplation, steeling his mind, purifying his soul.

Wearied by the endless paternosters that followed, his mind wandered off to the duties he was about to embrace after the knighting. He had been thoroughly imbued with the code of chivalry, nurtured by legends of Roland and el Cid and, only recently, King Arthur. He had taken it all to heart during his years as a squire, trying mightily to live by its tenets, though the order of chivalry had been but a gleam in his eye.

He felt good about the first of those vows, the one about protecting the Church. After all, he reasoned, he was on his way to recover the Holy Sepulcher from the Saracens. As for the second vow, his impecunious condition did not yet allow him to foster the widow and the orphan, but he felt that he had already done something about the third, and perhaps the easiest vow of all, that of helping ladies in distress. Had he not consoled an upset Berenguela when her wedding in Messina had been postponed? Besides, he was eager to help his lady if she were ever in distress. He had a dreadful premonition that she would soon be in dire straits, being as she was, on her way to a war zone, married to a man who didn't seem to pay much attention to her. Poor, dear Bery! He would take care of her and defend her honor, always.

He reverted briefly to his prayers before his thoughts once again strayed from piety, this time flitting over to his Vascon highlands, to the manor house of Gasteluzar in the hamlet of Agorreta, where his aging mother still lived. She would not be able to witness the knighting, something she had dreamed of and talked about throughout his youth as she instilled in him dreams of knighthood. His father would have loved to have been there, too, having once been a knight himself. But he was gone now and so someone else would have to help him with his armor and his equipment, and deliver him the buffet to remind him always of his oath. Someday, when he returned to his green uplands, he would ride up to his family's manor on his charger, decked in gleaming armor, kiss his mother and offer her the gift of his knighthood.

He was into another rosary when he heard the first chirps of dawn. A grayish rosy blush tinged the sliver of high sky visible through the narrow slit of the chapel window above him. Moments later, as he watched the first faint shafts of light streaming through, he heard footsteps outside the chapel door. The chaplain cracked the door open and poked his nose inside the chapel. It was time for Mass, he whispered, relieved to see that his knight-to-be had not dozed off during his vigil. A page was helping the monk with his vestments when prince Sancho and several Navarran knights walked in and knelt in the front pews. There was no word exchanged between them.

The Mass was brief, the homily succinct and to the point. The monk encouraged Iñaki to defend the faith of Christ against the unbelievers, to fight for his temporal lord, to prize honor and eschew pride, false swearing, idleness, lechery and treason. He was enjoined to never forget that his noblest virtues should be those of wisdom, charity and loyalty, to be hardy and humble and to have the courage to lead a life beyond reproach. It was a fairly complete list of the duties and proper comportment for a knight. Iñaki had heard them before, knew them all by heart.

When Mass was over, Sancho approached the altar and faced Iñaki, who was still kneeling on the prie-dieu. Unsheathing his huge sword, the prince rested it, first on one of Iñaki's shoulders, then the other, saying:

"Iñaki de Agorreta, I, Sancho, prince of Navarre, dub thee a knight. Go forth, fair friend, and be true and courageous in the face of the enemy. Remember always that you spring from a Vascon race that can never be false." To which Iñaki responded: "So shall I, my lord, with God's help."

The dubbing ceremony over, Iñaki stood up, Sancho embraced and kissed him on both cheeks.

"Come," he said, leading Iñaki by the arm towards the chapel door. "They wait."

As they were about to leave the chapel, Iñaki caught sight of Berenguela standing in the shadows, by a confessional. She had quietly witnessed the dubbing ceremony. Iñaki quickly walked over to her, knelt down on one knee before her and kissed her proffered hand. His friendship with this lady had, over time, grown into a refined adoration, a relationship comparable in intensity to that of the faithful service to her brother, Sancho. An overwhelming respect touched with a special *courtoisie* had forever bound him to her service.

"Milady," he said, bursting with ineffable emotion. "I thank thee for the honor of thy presence. As a knight, I can now truly serve thee. I shall seek higher renown only for the honor it will bring thee." She gazed into his eyes with rapt devotion, smiled, remained silent. They were old friends, knew every nuance of each other's language and gesture. An almost imperceptible smile spread over the face of Sancho, who waited by the door, watching the simple, quiet gesture of chivalry. He knew the abiding friendship that bonded these two from long ago was sure to serve her well in the months ahead.

There was a sudden flourish of trumpets as they walked out of the chapel and into the bailey. The enclosure was packed with knights and squires, some bleary-eyed because of the early hour. An *irrintzi* rang out, loud and clear, above the hubbub of the crowd. Someone shouted: "*Gora Iñaki*!" His Navarran friends, who had shared his travails during this long journey, were wishing him a long life. Iñaki was choked with emotion.

Standing at the opposite end of the long red carpet was Richard the Lionheart, waiting for the new knight to approach.

"High time they dubbed you!" he quipped in Iñaki's ear, gripping his hand firmly to prevent him from kneeling in homage to the king of England. "Welcome to the ranks of chivalry, young man. You have been deserving of this honor for quite some time now."

Iñaki was deeply touched. He had never dreamed that a prince would dub him, and a king and a queen honor him with their presence at his knighting to wish him well. "You do me great honor, your Majesty. I am unworthy of your presence at my knighting."

Richard stepped aside to let Sancho take his place, facing the new knight. They waited for the squires to help Iñaki don his corselet of mail and shoe him with boots of meshed mail. It was now time for Sancho to intervene in the ritual. Bending over, he attached a set of golden spurs on Iñaki's heels, picked up a huge broadsword blessed the night before and handed it to Iñaki, who kissed the cross of its hilt reverently. Holding the heavy sword in the palms of his outstretched hands, he faced prince Sancho. After a moment of silent prayer, he uttered his oath of knighthood in a deep voice heard round the bailey:

"I, Iñaki de Agorreta, swear before Almighty God that with this sword I will uphold justice, defend the Church against the heathen, protect the weak and aid women in distress. With it I vow to serve thee, my lord, keep thy counsel and, if need be, defend thee and thy honor with my life. In all these undertakings I vow to behave nobly, according to all the tenets of the order of chivalry, which I now gladly join."

Sancho took the proffered sword, sheathed it in its scabbard and girded it around Iñaki's waist. Picking up the shield handed him by a squire, he hung it around Iñaki's neck. It was only then that Iñaki noticed the blazon on the shield; depicted on a field of argent, was a black boar leaping over a thorn bush. Iñaki had seen the familiar blazon many times before. It was a variation of the escutcheon hanging over the main portal of Gazteluzar, in the village of Agorreta.

"May this blazon remind you and all those who lay eyes upon it, of the feats of valor your Vascon forefathers carved in the granite chasms of the Pyrenees, overlooking a mountain valley named after this thorn bush. This wild boar symbolizes the indomitable spirit of your race. Wear this shield with honor and return to your country either with it or on it."

An indescribable feeling of pride welled up in Iñaki that his prince would have chosen this particular blazon for him, singing the praises of his mountain people. His father would have been so proud! A quick glance at Richard and his Aquitainean knights confirmed his suspicion that they had caught the gist of Sancho's proclamation; it was this knight's forebears, not the Saracens of their *chanson de geste,* who had defeated Roland, their countryman, at Roncevaux, the valleys where the thorn bush grew.

Richard, who was standing by, recognized the blazon he had seen in a joust in Pamplona. The "Chevalier of the Boar" they had called him then. This young man would go places, he reflected.

The dubbing ceremony was about to conclude. Facing his knighted friend standing imperturbably before him, Sancho hauled off and delivered Iñaki a resounding open-handed blow to the side of the face that almost knocked him off his feet. "May this *colée*," said Sancho, "ever remind you to keep the knightly oath you have just taken."

A flourish of trumpets signaled the conclusion of the ceremony. A spontaneous roar of approval arose from the crowd. Iñaki turned to acknowledge the acclamation with a wave of the hand, too choked with emotion to utter any words of appreciation. His squire led a fully harnessed charger to the platform where Iñaki waited. Helping Iñaki don a cylindrical pot helmet topped with a hawk's head, he guided his mailed left shoe into the stirrup and helped him mount the destrier before handing him his shield and a steel-tipped lance. Sitting fully armed on his fiery charger, the tall, broad-shouldered knight was the very image of chivalry. Several ladies in the balconies overlooking the bailey turned to one another, hoping someday to get better acquainted with the handsome young knight, perhaps even *par amours*.

The queen stood on one of the balconies of the palace, watching the proceedings. Her sister-in-law, Joanna, was standing by her side.

"He looks so dashing!" burbled Joanna. Like most ladies in the court, she had grown fond of "the Vascon," as they liked to call him, feeling that there was something irresistibly primitive and manly, almost feral, about him. Joanna was fonder of him than the others perhaps because she was a young, twenty-five year old widow, longing for companionship. Iñaki, she sensed, could provide that in spades.

"Yes," responded Berenguela guardedly. A hint of a smile spread across her lips, speaking volumes for her admiration of *her* knight. "They should have knighted him long ago."

Below them, a quintain had been set up at one end of the town square. The crowd was pushed back to make room for the brief exhibition that was about to begin. At the flourish of clarions and trumpets, Iñaki's charger first pranced around the square before starting the galloping charge at the counterweighted dummy hanging from a post, simulating a mailed knight holding a shield. The impact was shattering. Iñaki's lance ripped through the dummy's shield and mail, tearing it apart in a sunburst of steel and straw. With a quick duck of the head and a feint of the body, Iñaki gracefully sidestepped the dummy's swiveling counterweight, set in motion by his blow. The crowd cheered appreciatively, admiring his superb control of his palfrey, suspecting that he was, indeed, one of the more gallant horsemen in the Crusade.

"*Aupa, mutiko ederra!*" whispered the queen beneath her breath, bidding her fair young friend Godspeed in his knightly endeavors.

CHAPTER 29

▼

A ROYAL TRYST

1191

Several thousand men waded ashore a few miles south of the ancient port city of Acre, banners flying, spirits buoyed by the overwhelming moment of the occasion. They had waited long and sailed far to get there and nothing could dampen the pride of their accomplishment nor still the joy of their holy undertaking. Some had died along the way, others turned back, wounded or in ill health, but for those who stepped ashore and kissed the ground that day, it was the fulfillment of a lifetime's dream. They lived in an age when religion was the shining light and guiding principle of existence. The dross of sin and its wages of eternal damnation were wondrously lifted by the simple act of setting foot on that hallowed ground. By that act alone they erased from their souls all pending dues in Purgatory. The certainty that this pilgrimage was all-redeeming lifted the spirits of even the most callous and cynical among them.

Meeting no resistance at the beachhead, they unloaded their equipment unhurriedly, setting up camp a few hundred yards from the landing site. It was a desolate kind of a place, with nothing but scrub brush and a few solitary date palms dotting the forbidding landscape. To the more imaginative, the ground itself seemed holy. The expedition's logisticians, however, had reason to worry for they knew that they would have difficulty finding water and forage in those arid surroundings. Where, they wondered, were the fabled cedars of Lebanon and the land of milk and honey? Richard, too, knew that they could not tarry on that beachhead, that they would have to move on and join forces with the Crusaders already besieging Acre.

Saladin had swept down from Turkey almost four years earlier, conquering Syria and Egypt and most of the towns south of Tripoli, including Jerusalem. The defeated King Guy of Jerusalem had gathered a few stragglers to besiege the port city of Acre. He was later joined by Duke Leopold of Austria's Crusaders, a handful of Dutch and Scandinavian Templars and, the latest arrivals, the French hosts under King Philip. But Acre remained impregnable, its defenders stubborn and unyielding. It would take Richard's charismatic leadership to turn the tide.

Richard had Berenguela and his sister Joanna remain on board the ship, considered safer and more comfortably appointed than any tent on shore, until they could move into better quarters on land. Actually, he would have much preferred sending the two women back to England, away from harm's way, but he was stuck with them now and had to add their safety to his many other concerns. He had to assign a trusted knight and several men-at-arms to protect the ship's precious cargo. After Richard consulted with Sancho, Iñaki was chosen for the task. His trustworthiness and unswerving loyalty to Berenguela made him her ideal safeguard and escort. Though Sancho would miss his loyal knight during the assault of Acre, he had to agree with Richard that Agorreta was the best choice for the task.

Iñaki was of two minds about the assignment. He was devoted to Berenguela and had vowed to defend her life and her honor. But he was in a quandary: he had come to the Holy Land to fight the Saracens, not while his time away doing guard duty aboard some ship, anchored offshore. Fighting in a Crusade had been his most fervent vow. He was torn between these two conflicting pledges. Another vow, however, finally settled his dilemma: he had sworn to defend his lord and obey his every wish. And Sancho had asked him to be his sister's guardian. There was small solace in the thought that Jerusalem still lay ahead. The conquest of that Holy City remained his most cherished goal in this Crusade. Not even the horses of Pharaoh could hold him back from that appointed rendezvous when the time came. Meanwhile Iñaki had to resign himself to staying behind while the others proceeded to assault Acre.

"Mother sure got us into a fine pickle this time!" grumbled Joanna to Berenguela at dinner that first evening offshore. From their anchorage, they could see the lights of the Crusaders' campfires, not far from the city they were getting ready to assault. Being a few years older than Berenguela and having recently been a queen, herself, Joanna could take certain liberties with her sister-in-law, expressing her thoughts with frankness when they were alone. The queen allowed such familiarities from Joanna; they had shared more adventures in one month than other women had in a lifetime and had grown fond of each other during that brief interval.

"Let's face it, dear Joanna," responded Berenguela, refusing to feel guilty for having dragged her sister-in-law around the Mediterranean. "Your life would have been a crashing bore in Messina. You didn't belong there after your husband died. You know that and I know that." After a brief pause, she added: "Besides, this way, you can claim to be a Crusader."

"Some Crusader!" sniffed Joanna despondently. "I wonder if that brother of mine will let us join him when he enters Jerusalem."

"They have to take Acre first," responded Berenguela equably. "One thing at a time. Iñaki says that every one of those Muslims guarding those parapets is a religious fanatic, actually praying to die defending the city against us "infidels," as they call us. They get to go straight to heaven, that way. Strange people, these Saracens."

"No stranger than the martyrs in the Colosseum," remarked Joanna morosely. She was determined to feel bored aboard ship, no matter what the excitement around her. Only Berenguela's mention of Iñaki seemed to relieve her ennui. She had been making subtle overtures to the Vascon during the trip, advances which the young innocent had either totally misread or simply ignored, and which only served to redouble her thrill of the hunt. The dowager queen was Iñaki's age but infinitely wiser in the ways of the world. Not in vain had she been brought up in the courts of Aquitaine by a mother who was, herself, the master of intrigue and the courtly tryst. Iñaki did not have a chance against her daughter's equally devious wiles.

Despite his ostensible aloofness, Iñaki had not been totally unaware of her veiled advances. Joanna's graceful figure and striking good looks had not gone unnoticed. Yet, he did not want to get romantically involved with someone of such high station who was, besides, his queen's constant companion and confidante. Though in no way related, he fancied a certain physical resemblance between her and Berenguela; they were equally svelte, both of fair complexion and soulful blue eyes. But the resemblance ended there, for while the queen was demure and circumspect to a fault, Joanna was vital and outspoken, decidedly bubbly and extroverted. She was usually surrounded by a crowd of young men eager for her company. He could not help being intrigued by this Aquitainean woman. She had her mother's vitality and self-assurance and, like her, was coquettish and teasing, a born flirt.

He had never met anyone like her in Navarre, where women spoke only when addressed and, even then, answered only guardedly and with modest propriety.

But this Aquitainean beauty was different. She was like a free earth spirit, her tantalizing laughter like clinking glass to a thirsty man's ear. He was intrigued by the way she would toss her hair about, sensing it was simply an excuse to turn her head around and sneak a furtive glance at men she knew were ogling her behind her back. There was nothing coy or demure about the way she cut her eyes at him or brushed herself against his body when they crossed paths in the ship's narrow passageways. The chance encounters sent pleasurable shivers coursing up and down Iñaki's spine. He had become increasingly aware of an animal magnetism in her that was starting to challenge his chivalrous thoughts. This woman reminded him of a Biblical Jezebel, a Greek Helen, dangerously seductive, a brazen hussy in regal trappings.

One night, while standing solitary guard on the forecastle of the ship during the pre-dawn hours, Iñaki heard a sudden rustling of clothes behind him. Turning around, he was startled to find Joanna standing there only a few feet away from him. By the tenuous light of the moon, he could see that she was wearing a flimsy nightgown, its plunging neckline revealing the deep cleft of her young, impertinent breasts, nipples hard against the transparent gown. Her golden hair was tousled, lovely curls cascading over her bare, milk-white shoulders. Without uttering a word, she approached Iñaki and pressed herself gently against him. Lifting her face up to his, she eyed him meaningfully, lips slightly parted in a silent, eloquent plea. In that look there came to him a knowing, a yearning that would never grow old. Her beauty and her forwardness caught his breath, stirred something deep inside him.

Though already in his mid-twenties, Iñaki had known only a few women in his life, a quick one-night stand here, there a tryst, passing and forgotten fancies, all. Now, suddenly, he found himself holding a real woman in his arms. She had reached up with her hand and was running her fingers up and down the back of his neck. Then, suddenly, relinquishing her earlier limpness, she began to arch and sinuate her body against his, ever so slowly and rhythmically. He was now torn between his better instincts and the passion he suddenly felt for this enticing woman, a lonesome, widowed queen, begging to be taken. From his innermost being he wanted to touch her. Stilling his nobler instincts, Iñaki rationalized that this would qualify as a woman in distress, needing a man's affection and the warmth of human companionship. Scruples thus allayed, he talked himself into believing that the consolation of distraught widows was but a simple act of knightly charity. The next thing he knew, he was holding her in his arms, closer and closer to him until, finally, in a fit of passion, he leaned over and kissed her parted lips, feeling as he did the soaring lightness of desire.

A night of tumultuous lovemaking followed in the dowager's stateroom, with all the erotic sensuality of youth redoubled by the thrill of forbidden fruit. Her scent reminded him of the warm, gentle breezes that hovered over the meadows of Navarre in the summertime, sweet with the smell of thyme and poppies and new-mown hay. They nuzzled and touched and kissed with all the carnality of youth, arousing what once slumbered into full and splendid bloom. His soul soared until finally, when he came into her, it was from some aroused and exquisite void in him, hidden long ago in some haunted convolution of the brain. The swelling in parts of him was soon followed by a tingling warmth rushing from his belly to his spine and then, finally, to his medulla, where it exploded in some ancient limbic sunburst. She drew his seed into her being, exhausted, placidly content. They lay there, limp, for what seemed an eternity, rocking to the gentle swells of the bountiful Mediterranean, listening to the tranquil slapping of the waves around them, to the soft creaking and groaning of the ship's planks under them. They said nothing, felt everything. There was little to add to love.

When Iñaki woke up the next morning, the light of dawn felt heavy, the world seemed older and there was little song in his heart. Unlike his hero, Ulysses, he knew that the greatest voyage a man can make is in his own mind. He felt like a cheated hunter who never really possessed the prey he thought he had caught. Even before surfacing into full consciousness he was already struggling to identify the source of his malaise, an odd feeling of a labored crossing with the heavy ballast of wrong.

As he left Joanna in her stateroom, still deep in slumber, he felt little joy in the reminiscence of their lovemaking. He felt soiled inside. A sense of peace evaded him. He did not love this woman and yet he had debased himself by falling for her wiles. He was going to have a hard time facing her or Berenguela after the brief liaison. All that day Iñaki's conscience gnawed at him, relentlessly poking an accusing finger in the wound of his transgression. To add to his misery, he now began to feel regret for having betrayed his vows of chivalry so soon after taking them.

He felt despondent all that day, slinking away from Joanna, ashamed to face her after the affair. Iñaki was taking his failing rather poorly. He felt uneasy under his own skin and longed to escape. He wanted out of this awkward arrangement, desperately trying to find a way to relieve himself of his nursemaid duties, redeem himself in the field of honor. He felt a need to cleanse his soul in battle, in the company of hounds and hawks and men, anywhere but in that damnably constraining ship.

His wish was granted earlier than he expected.

Sancho, who needed him desperately at his side under the walls of Acre, had sent a messenger to relieve him of his duties and to hurry him to his side. He was too valuable to be lingering aboard ship, playing chess and backgammon with the ladies. Geoffrey de Montagú, a trusted Aquitainean knight, was sent to relieve him. Though he tried hard to hide his elation from the ladies, Iñaki could not have been more pleased. He packed his few belongings and, with the help of his squire, unloaded his gear onto a small skiff and eagerly sailed off to battle. The ladies were disconsolate, especially Joanna, who had enjoyed the pleasure of his company more than she let on to her queen.

"*C'était beau mais c'était triste,*" she murmured plaintively to herself, as she saw him sail off. He struck such a handsome figure!

Chapter 30

The Third Crusade

Richard managed to breathe new life into the floundering siege after only a few weeks at the walls of Acre. His arrival had been received with a joy bordering on delirium, the Christian hosts thankful for finally having a renowned leader guide them in their mired enterprise. King Philip's disgruntled mood was not assuaged by the jubilant cheers and boisterous acclaim that his own French troops accorded Richard when he took charge of the siege.

A full head shorter than Richard, Philip had never grown used to the Englishman's bluster. He now slunk into the background, busying himself with his hobby of designing siege machines. Giant catapults soon started heaving boulders at the fortress while trebuchets showered the defenders with sharp flint stones. Wheeled mangonneau and spring-loaded espringales rained rocks and burning, tar-soaked bales of straw on the defenders and their residences. Monstrous, sixty-foot assault towers with ample space for archers and battering rams on their various platforms, were rolled up to the battlements. But despite the ingenious equipment, the attempts to take Acre were repeatedly repulsed by the Saracens. The frontal attack was definitely not working against such determined opposition.

Sitting on a promontory overlooking the city one afternoon, Richard and Sancho studied the lay of the fortress, probing for weak points. Three enormous walls protected the city; the barbican, with its powerful keep and fortified gatehouses enfiladed all approaches. The main, fifteen foot-thick, curtain wall was surrounded by towers bristling with determined defenders behind arrow loops, portcullises and machicolations. The deep moat surrounding the fort would be hard to span. Sancho had seen many such massive Moorish castles in his own land, knew the blood and the guts it took to assail and take them.

"They've been under siege for four years now," commented Richard abjectly, "and still there's no sign of flagging in their ranks. And there's probably no more than a few thousand men defending it!"

"A garrison with that determination can hold out against an attacking force ten times its number," remarked Sancho. "Surely they have all the well water they need. Besides, it's easier to feed a handful of men with a well-stocked granary and a few cows and chickens than it is to feed an army the size of ours. We're going to have more of a supply problem than they unless we come up with a quick way to breech those walls."

"The French sappers have tried tunneling under the wall to set Greek fire under it," remarked Richard. "They only managed to crack it slightly, not enough of a breech to allow penetration. The Turks just laughed at their effort."

"The side facing the sea appears to be its most vulnerable," Sancho observed. "The engineers who built those walls and towers never expected a serious threat from the sea. I don't see many enfilading towers along the stunted wall facing to seaward. We could probably surprise them with a naval assault while they're distracted by the frontal attack from the mainland."

"It's not going to be easy," responded Richard. "There's a heavy chain strung across the seaport's entrance to prevent just such an attack."

Sancho mulled over the problem. "We could use flat-bottomed landing craft to sail over the sunken part of the chain," he suggested.

"Good idea!" remarked Richard, slapping Sancho on the back. "I should have thought of that myself! You're thinking more like a leader of a maritime power than a landlocked kingdom!"

"We're not quite landlocked yet, milord," commented Sancho. "I know Alfonso of Castile is trying hard to take over our outlying Basque counties and their ports, but we won't let them, will we?"

It was Sancho's shrewd assay at a power play. His father, Sancho the Wise, had always worried about Navarre's tenuous hold of the ultra-Pyrenean Gascon Viscounties, presently under Richard's suzerainty. As their overlord, the British king had been under some pressure to cede them to his brother-in-law, Alfonso of Castile, as dowry for Alionor, Richard's elder sister and the Castilian's wife. It was only because of his mother Eleanor's reservations that the promised dowry had never been honored. Berenguela's marriage to Richard now almost ensured that

Navarre would hold sway over those Viscounties, assuring an outlet to the sea should Castile gobble up the outlying Basque ports of Biscaye and Guipuzcoa.

Richard did not rise to the bait. His mind was busy figuring out the combined land and naval assault of Acre. He could order special landing craft built to carry out the amphibious raid; it would only be a question of surreptitiously landing a few troops with assault ladders, without being observed by the defenders. The element of surprise would be of the essence.

"You're right, Sancho. The fortifications are flawed," admitted Richard. "They were built with a land threat in mind. The town is surrounded by soaring masonry walls except where it faces the sea. Though shoal-strewn and rugged, there is enough of a shoreline there to establish a quick beachhead at low tide. The stunted sea walls would allow our troops to go over them without need for clumsy assault towers."

It was a cunning plan, Sancho thought. Richard may have had his peculiar sexual preferences but he was a brilliant strategist. "We will create a distraction on the land side," suggested Sancho, now caught up in the excitement of the plan. "Then," he added: "under cover of darkness, we can land a few of our best troops on the lightly protected beach and the city will fall like Troy to the Achaeans in their wooden horse."

Richard smiled at Sancho's simile. "It pays to know one's Homer, doesn't it," he remarked. "One never knows when the Classics will come in handy."

It was four weeks after Richard's arrival in Acre that the walled city finally fell to the Christians. Iñaki had joined the elite commando group that stormed ashore at midnight. At a signal from a bonfire lit on the mainland, two-hundred hand-picked knights were put ashore on flat-bottomed boats expressly designed for the amphibious operation. The group waded onto a narrow strip of rocky shoreline directly under the city's western breastworks, undetected and unopposed. Like the other knights, Iñaki felt ill at ease going into battle on foot, without the benefit of horse or heavy armor. Even their coats of mail had to be left behind for fear their clatter would compromise the surprise element of the operation.

The assault turned out like clockwork. The defenders had been distracted by the unusual midnight activity at the curtain walls near one of the fort's towers. Several assault towers had been moved up to the northern battlements while projectile-throwing machines hurled stones at close range. The din of thousands of voices shouting "*Dieu et monjoi!*" enervated the defenders. The combined frontal and diversionary tactics allowed the commandos to overpower the few startled guards manning the sea wall. The amphibious assailants quickly spread out along the walkway, heading towards the main gate. After a furious skirmish with its surprised defenders, the assault party succeeded in unwinding the windlasses and throwing open the gates. When the drawbridge was lowered, the besieging army negotiated the body-strewn moat and stormed into the city like a flash flood.

It was a rout. Only their commanders' strict orders prevented the wholesale massacre of defenders and the civilian population. Though the lives of the Saracens were spared, the Crusaders were not to be denied their spoils. Homes were ransacked, women abused, overzealous defenders cut down mercilessly. Considered fair targets in the heat of a religious war, mosques and minarets were systematically torched, while the Imam and his muezzins were disrobed and flayed in the main square. Thousands of civilians cringed in terror as the drunken Crusaders laid waste the town and desecrated its temples. Richard held the entire population hostage demanding, in exchange, the release of Christian soldiers captured earlier by Saladin's forces.

In the flush of victory, the commanders of all three victorious armies ordered their banners flown on flagpoles atop the castle's keep. Richard went into a paroxysm of rage when he spotted the Austrian ensign flying alongside his English flag. Furious at what he took to be Duke Leopold's effrontery at glory-grabbing, Richard ordered the Austrian emblem lowered and dumped into the muddy moat. Not taking kindly to the desecration of his flag, Duke William gathered his troops and abandoned Acre and the Holy Land in a huff a day later.

A typhus epidemic broke out in town shortly after the invasion, exacerbating the endemic malarial plague already afflicting conqueror and conquered alike. Both Richard and Philip Augustus came down with the chills, incapacitating them momentarily. Philip, whose hair and fingernails had mysteriously started to fall off, suspected foul play. It was the straw that broke his crusading resolve. Disgusted by Richard's assertiveness and appalled by his mean-spirited treatment of the Duke of Austria, the French monarch saw little future in lingering in the Holy Land with the grandstanding Englishman.

Three weeks after the fall of Acre, Philip Augustus pulled up stakes and sailed for France. Richard turned apoplectic at the Frenchman's withdrawal. Though part of Philip's army remained behind, under Coeur de Lion's command, Richard worried about the mischief Philip was likely to stir back home. For some time now, the French king had been eyeing Normandy, hoping to recapture it from the English. With Richard absent from his dominions, there was no telling what rascality the Frenchman could wreak on England's continental possessions. Philip's hurried departure was a troubling prospect indeed.

Berenguela and her ladies-in-waiting settled in the captured palace's quarters, in what had once been the Sultan's harem. They were spacious and ornate and exquisitely appointed but the queen never laid eyes on her husband, who persisted in his own deviant obsession. It was ironic, she thought, that that seraglio, which had seen so much love squandered within its walls, was now filled with such crashing monastic silence. It had started to dawn on her that Richard's extramarital interests would continue unabated, driving a spike deeper into the very heart of their marriage. A gnawing fear started to worm its way into her heart: how could she ever give him a son if he never shared her bed? Here she was, in her twenty-first year, living a nun's life! Her despair was so dark and bottomless that she could not even consider confiding it to Joanna, let alone Iñaki, her childhood friend and confidant. It was too intimate a subject to broach, too hurtful to share. She would have to bear her cross alone and in silence.

His wife was not the only object of the king's churlishness. His short-fused temper exploded when one of Saladin's messengers galloped up one day to inform him that the hostage exchange and its agreed-upon ransom had to be delayed. Incensed by the suspected breech of contract, Richard ordered three-thousand of the city's citizens put to the sword. Though ostensibly executed to strike fear in Saladin's heart, it was a senseless massacre to salve his own personal pique. Many in his court were appalled by the heinous cruelty but no voices were raised to challenge the order.

"The man's deranged!" remarked Sancho to Iñaki. "I forbid any Navarran from participating in the slaughter."

In his God-fearing mind, the end never justified the means. He condoned the plunder of a city by an invading army, but the massacre of innocent non-combatants went beyond the pale. Though aware of Sancho's refusal to follow his orders, Richard looked the other way. He respected the Navarran's pious qualms and said nothing. An irate religious zealot was tricky enough to handle but one a full head taller than he, and a disgruntled Vascon, to boot, would be foolhardy. It was best to let the scowling Navarran giant alone.

In the middle of August, Richard gathered his army and marched down the coast to Jerusalem, leaving his wife and sister behind to while away the days in the castle of Acre. Though it was hot and muggy, the knights rode in full armor for fear the infidels would surprise them along the way. Alerted to the Christians' approach, Saladin intercepted them in the open fields outside Arsouf. It was a tactical error. The terrain, flat and unobstructed, was ideal for a knights' charge.

Observing his opponent's straggling disposition, Richard split up his men in a three-pronged attack. Two light cavalry wings engaged the enemy's flanks in a fast, enveloping movement, pushing them towards the center, directly in the path of the heavily mounted shock force of Norman and Angevinian knights in the center column.

Sancho, with Iñaki riding escort, led the western prong of the pincer movement, made up of a thousand-knight contingent of Aquitaineans, Gascons and his handful of hardy Navarrans. There was a certain *esprit-de-corps* among those who, millennia earlier, had shared a common language, worshipped the same earth spirits, buried their dead in similar dolmens. They had once all been Basques.

Saladin's men rode swift Arabian steeds whose quick, evasive movements were of little avail against the Christian knights' long lances. Unhorsed after the first charge, most infidels fell easy prey to the ensuing broadsword attack. The battle was over in a few hours, survivors slain on the spot. Only a handful of prisoners were spared and sent back to Jerusalem to inform Saladin of the debacle and the Christian wrath awaiting him.

The Christians were flush with victory. As they sat around the campfires that evening, drinking wine and stale mead, they distributed the recovered booty among themselves, allotting the pickings according to rank and standing. Sancho won a magnificent scimitar with bejeweled handle that must have belonged to some high-ranking Bey. Iñaki's modest spoils consisted of a small golden amulet in the shape of a half moon. He would hang it from a gold chain and give it as an engagement gift to the maiden who would, one day, become his wife. Although he had drawn Saracen blood before, he would claim that it was from his baptism of blood against the Muslims in the Holy Land. It was earned near Jerusalem, making the token that much more valuable.

They did not tarry in Arsouf. No more than a few dozen miles away, Jerusalem waited. The main objective of this Crusade was now within grasp. But foraging for food in the countryside was fruitless. There was not much to begin with, and the little that remained had been burned by the farmers in a scorched earth tactic ordered by Saladin. Grumbling was rife, particularly among the French troops, unaccustomed to such privation. "Are we barbarians?" one of their leaders was overheard to complain.

"The walls of Jerusalem are formidable," remarked Richard to Sancho, as they approached the city. "My mother used to tell me about them. She was here during the last Crusade." He remained silent for a moment before adding: "I'm starting to have second thoughts about being able to hold it, even if we succeed in taking it."

"That makes two of us," Sancho agreed. "Philip's withdrawal with half his French forces may be telling." A dark shadow fell across the Navarran's face. "Besides, I don't like the way those Frenchmen he left behind are whining. It's not good for morale. You should talk to them."

Richard reflected on his friend's remarks, offered no comment, almost as if resenting being told how to run a Crusade. Instead, the moody Englishman came up with one of his non-sequiturs: "Damn!" he said, sniffing the air as he eyed the sky above him. He had noticed cranes flying over the marshlands nearby and the sound of their flapping wings and wild, vacant calls became irresistible. "I'd sure love to do a little hawking right about now, wouldn't you?"

It was so like Richard, thought Sancho, taking off on one of his wild goose chases, searching for solace in some inner, greener world of his, completely relaxed, oblivious to the most important fray in his life now facing him. But it really wasn't a bad idea, the prince agreed.

While the army rested at their next rest stop, the king and the prince, with a handful of noblemen, went off hawking. Iñaki was, needless to say, invited to join the party. He had become a fixture in royal falconry circles, always riding with his prince, holding a spare falcon for him. The hawking turned out to be very good, abundant wildfowl flying out of the marshes over a rolling countryside where one could ride in any direction for as long and as far as one pleased. And, as in previous hawking events, Sancho, with Iñaki's subtle help and guidance, managed to bag more fowl than any of the other falconers, much to Richard's chagrin.

After a short ride the next day, Jerusalem finally loomed into view. Reflecting shards of late afternoon sunlight, its honey-colored walls wrapped themselves around the city of God in a dumb embrace. Closer inspection revealed an incongruity: interspersed among cupolas and bell towers of Christian temples were the needle-sharp minarets of another persuasion. Otherwise, the city looked as it must have looked during the time of Christ. It exuded an awesome sense of something timeless and enduring, massively iconic.

It even looked like a holy city. Its grandeur overwhelmed the thousands of knights and men-of-arms who beheld it from the top of a hill. It was the hallowed place in whose streets, only a dozen centuries earlier, their God had walked and preached and died for all so that they could be redeemed from eternal damnation. Without anyone's giving a signal or bellowing an order, the knights dismounted as one and, together with the foot soldiers, knelt before the sight of Jerusalem, thankful for the happy culmination of a long and arduous pilgrimage.

"You will never hold that city," whispered King Guy, who was standing by Richard's side. Guy was the counselor par excellence. Having ruled Jerusalem for a number of years, he was familiar with the city's nooks and crannies, knew every sinuous street and hidden alley better than anyone else in the expedition, Richard's own reservations now turned into full-blown anxiety. Here stood a man whose judgment he trusted, voicing his own worst premonitions and unspoken fears.

"What makes you say that, Sire?" asked Richard, pretending disinterest. He knew the answer all too well but wanted to hear it from someone who had had a brush with the Saracens behind those very walls—and lost.

"Those walls you see before you are nigh impregnable. Even if you succeed in vaulting over them or breaching those doors, your men will be sorely outnumbered by Saladin's forces inside. These are not your run-of-the-mill Saracens inside those walls; these are Islam's best and most fanatic warriors. Horses are no good in narrow streets or in house-to-house combat. And if you think your knights have the inspiration of the Holy Sepulcher to drive them on, the Muslims have Abraham's tomb to motivate them as well. You see, that too, is a holy place in Jerusalem." He paused to let Richard absorb his advice before adding: "And one last thing; your knights are only fighting to retrieve the Holy Sepulcher. The Moslems are panting to die because that way they'll get to go to heaven."

Richard remained pensive. The arguments he had just finished hearing felt like a series of body blows, telling in their forcefulness, merciless in their delivery, lucid in their logic. He, who considered himself a master strategist, had just received a lesson from a peer, perhaps even his better. Richard was depressed and humbled, feelings both unfamiliar to him. After all these many years of preparation, after all these preliminary skirmishes, after all this pain and suffering, he had to abandon his mission. But what hurt most was that the object of his quest was right there in front of him, teasing, tantalizing, unreachable.

"Damn that Philip!" he muttered under his breath.

It was not easy for him to order his army to turn around and abandon its prize, being within striking distance of it. His men were sullen and heartbroken but dimly understood their Commander's arguments. There was no point in getting killed just trying to get into the city. They had long suspected that although their hearts were brave and their mission holy, their numbers had fallen woefully short of the task. There was resentment against the turn-tail Austrians and Frenchmen, who could have probably made a difference. Even those who stayed behind after Philip abandoned the fray had turned mutinous, claiming exhaustion from shortage of food and water. There were recriminations and sour feelings among the disillusioned ranks. The old esprit was gone.

With heavy heart, Richard ordered a retreat. Morale was low. It was only the memory of their last victory that held the men together. Marching west toward the coast, they came upon Jaffa, a town defended by Saladin's forces. After a brief siege, they took it and held the population hostage. Sensing that Richard's Crusade was foundering, Saladin offered one last treaty. In exchange for the cessation of hostilities, he was willing to let the Crusaders keep all the territory they had captured and, for the next three years, guaranteed the rights of all Christian pilgrims to visit their holy places in Jerusalem, unarmed, of course. It was the best deal Richard could extract from Saladin under the circumstances. It would be the only pathetic achievement of his Third Crusade.

A messenger from Eleanor had alerted Richard of trouble brewing back home. In a foul conspiracy with Philip, his brother John had made his first overt move; he promised to return Normandy to France in exchange for Philip's support of his own quest for the English crown. It was almost, word for word, what his mother had warned would happen in his absence. It was time to disband his army and head for home. Many Crusaders chose to settle in Syria and Egypt. Others, empty-handed, were in no rush to return to fiefs strapped with debts, contemplating the unhappy prospect of having to mortgage their lands to pay for their romantic fling in the Holy Land.

Sancho and his Navarran contingent had been away from home long enough, too. There were still many battles to be fought and lands to be wrested from the Moors back home. Outremer had been a nice little practice run but they had their own Crusade to worry about. The Iberian *Reconquest* was only halfway accomplished and King Sancho the Wise was waiting. They had come to escort Berenguela to her wedding and that mission had been accomplished. After Jaffa had been secured and Richard officially announced the disbanding of his Crusade, Sancho rode up to Acre to see his sister one last time before sailing. He asked Iñaki to accompany him.

They found Berenguela, Joanna and their ladies-in-waiting pining away in the castle they had been occupying for over a year. Richard had not visited them once during all that time. Iñaki felt an ineffable pity for the lonely and abandoned women. Berenguela had taken her seclusion stoically enough. Joanna, on the other hand, was fit to be tied, perfectly furious at having been ignored all this time. Her brother got an earful when he finally turned up to tell them he had arranged passage for their return trip to France.

In an aside to Sancho, Iñaki confided: "I know Agotes in the valley of Baztán who are treated more humanely," referring to a group of untouchables living in the valley of Baztán. "And they aren't even lepers!" he added scornfully.

Sancho was aggrieved by the way his sister was being treated, but there was little he could do except sympathize with her.

"My dear Bery," he said. "I know how bored you must have been, waiting all this time."

"I would have loved to have gone with you," she admitted, smiling her sweet, wan smile. She had lost some weight in their absence and looked a little pale. But she was the same dear, uncomplicated Berenguela. She should have been a nun, reflected Sancho, as her mother had once suggested. She had flatly turned down the proposition, sensing that there was more to life than joining a nunnery, as her sister Constanza had contemplated doing.

"It would have been dangerous, certainly uncomfortable for you to have come along with us," replied Sancho, trying to convince her that she had not missed much. "Besides," he added, "we never even got to enter Jerusalem, never visited the Holy Sepulcher, nothing! It was all an exercise in futility."

"At least we can say we were in the Holy Land," she observed, resignedly. "There must have been some indulgence gained just for that!" She was reaching, it was painfully obvious. Sancho felt for her. She not only married the wrong man, she would now have to live away from home in a strange land with people whose language and customs she did not fully understand. He was at a loss for words of sympathy.

"Has Richard made arrangements for your return?" asked Sancho, trying to change the subject.

"Yes. I understand we, Joanna and I and the ladies, are sailing shortly for Brindisi, and from there on to Marseilles, where someone will escort us to Poitiers. Eleanor will host us in her palace there before we go our separate ways. I don't know what other plans Richard has for me. Perhaps we'll go to England. After all, I am their queen."

Iñaki was summoned to her receiving room after Sancho bade her farewell. Though happy to see each other again after a year's absence, the meeting was awkward. They both sensed that this could be their last encounter.

"Be good to Sancho," she counseled. "He needs your help and good judgment. You have been friends these many years. He'll need your company even more when he becomes king. The life of a king is a lonely one." Iñaki's eyes moistened at the thought of her saying it. No truer words had been uttered by anyone who knew anything about the loneliness of leadership. And Berenguela, young as she was, had already learned that bitter lesson.

Iñaki kissed the queen's extended hand and left the room, closing the door behind him.

Chapter 31

A Wobbly Legacy

1199

The third Crusade had fizzled out with a whimper. While Berenguela and Joanna made their way safely back to Poitiers, Richard was not so fortunate. Blown aground by a storm in Venice and fearful of the city's intrigues and civil unrest, he tried continuing his journey on land, disguised as a merchant. His masquerade uncovered, he was apprehended by moneylenders who sold him to the Leopold, Duke of Austria, who had old accounts to settle with him. He was whisked off to Germany where, for the next two years, he was to remain under the custody of the Holy Roman Emperor. The thirty tons of silver demanded for his ransom were eventually collected from hobbling taxes back home before Richard regained his freedom. The desecration of that Austrian flag in Acre had cost his country a pretty penny.

Prince Sancho, meanwhile, had returned to a kingdom mired in turmoil. His father, Sancho the Wise, now an ailing monarch of sixty, had just about run out of wisdom trying to put out local fires. Castile and Aragon, Navarre's two unfriendly neighbors, were intent on splitting her up among themselves.

Complicating matters, king Sancho's western Basque domains of Guipuzcoa and Vizcaya had developed a cozy *entente cordiale* with Castile. The unhealthy compact promised Castile an outlet to the sea for her wool exports in exchange for handsome profits to the dissident Basques. Álava, another outlying Basque province under Sancho's suzerainty, also shared a border with Castile. Lying fully athwart her path to the sea, Castile had been slowly nibbling at Álava's edges, intent on gobbling her up.

The tug of war between Castile and Navarre was becoming increasingly threatening to the smaller, much weaker Vascon kingdom. Richard I of England could have lent his father-in-law, Sancho the Wise, a helping hand but his captivity in Germany had prevented that. Still, Sancho felt that it would be to his kingdom's best interest to help defend Richard's threatened possessions in southern France. Strapped for money, Sancho could ill afford to contribute to Richard's ransom but he could, instead, send his son, *el Fuerte,* to help Richard's seneschals hold on to England's Gascon territories. Stirred by John Lackland's open sedition, the discontented Count of Perigord and Viscount of Brosse had turned restive, smelling a quick profit in the troubled waters of Gascogne.

Shortly after prince Sancho returned from the Crusades, his father sent him off to defend Richard's threatened lands in the Gascogne. With Iñaki in tow, the prince marched off at the head of a small contingent of eight hundred lances. Bayonne was their first destination, its citizens having turned edgy. On their way there and at Iñaki's insistence, the commanders of the expedition stopped in Agorreta for the night. Alerted to her son's and the prince's arrival, Iñaki's aging mother was waiting in Jaureguizar to greet the commanders of the *chevauchée.*

As he stepped into the Great Hall, Iñaki was flooded with memories of younger years. It struck him, for the first time, how deeply his roots sank into this, his native lair. There seemed to be an air of permanence about the house and everything in it, nothing ever seemed to change. His mother had aged noticeably. Her hair had turned the color of fresh-fallen snow yet she remained the same *grande dame* he had always remembered and loved. Despite her simple attire, Doña Laura looked stately, almost regal. Wrapped in a plain black shawl, her only visible jewelry was a small, pearl-studded brooch pinned to her black neckband and two wedding rings, one hers, the other her deceased husband's.

"*Amatxo!*" whispered Iñaki in her ear as he hugged her. Tears of joy rolled down his cheeks as he bent over, kissing her repeatedly. Her scent of lavender brought back memories from some hallowed nook of forgotten childhood. He had not seen her for several years now and the meeting touched something very deep in him.

"*Gure mutiko ederra!*" she whispered in his ear. She had called him 'my handsome boy' many times before, always considered him her beloved Benjamin. And now, here he was, all dressed up in knightly attire, stronger and more handsome than ever, with his father's square jaw and kind blue eyes.

"Mother," said Iñaki in a low, almost reverent voice. "I would like for you to meet my liege lord, the prince of Navarre." Turning to Sancho, who stood behind him, he said: "My lord, this is my mother, Lady Laura of Agorreta."

The old woman turned to the Prince, looked him in the eye and curtsied ever so slightly, a sign of obeisance to her future king. "You are welcome in my humble abode, milord" she said in a voice stronger than anyone expected from a lady of such slight and fragile build. In a flash of *dèja-vu,* Iñaki remembered how his father had uttered those very same words when he welcomed the Lionheart, the time the Englishman dropped in on his way to the tourney in Pamplona years earlier. Strange, he reflected, how sounds and smells and phrases rush back unbidden from the warm folds of memory.

Being early November and already into the first frosts, the prince and his retinue of knights had arrived just in time for the *matacherri,* the ritual yearly celebration of the slaughter of the pigs. Several enormous, fatted sows had been butchered in the shed that morning and an entire crew of household women and serfs had congregated in the sprawling kitchen to transform the porcine meat and entrails into sausages and chops, hams and loin strips, snouts and pigs' feet. Someone was sent to nearby Orbaiceta for fresh trout, someone else to nearby Roncevaux, for several rounds of cheese from the Collegiate's sheep farm.

By nightfall, the feast was in full swing. Trestled tables laden with food had been spread out along the Great Hall. The fires of the huge hearth and the firebrands hanging from the walls lit up the hall, filling it with a pleasant, smoky haze, which lent an even cozier atmosphere to the gathering. There was little ceremony; the maids filled the men's cups with red Tiebas wine, while the squires cut the meat and laid it out in trenchers for the prince and his knights. The hounds wagged their tails as they picked on bones and tidbits the guests tossed at them over their shoulders. The unexpected visit had not allowed time to arrange for any formal entertainment and so the knights provided their own amusement after the meal. The wine flowed more copiously as the evening wore on, the tales of their exploits in Terra Sancta growing increasingly improbable.

But there was one story prince Sancho wanted to relate before Lady Laura retired to her chambers. Someone who had seen it firsthand had to tell her about her son's deeds in the Holy Land.

"I can sit here all night talking about your son's exploits, milady," said Sancho in his usual blustery voice, "but I couldn't tell it all. And so, for the sake of brevity, I will limit my account to only a few of his more unusual ones." He then proceeded to recount Iñaki's feat of arms at the tourney in Pamplona, years earlier, when he unhorsed King Richard's squire. He went on to describe his participation in the daring commando assault on Acre, which turned that battle's tide. He concluded by describing the epic battle of Arsouf, where her son single-handedly slew a dozen Saracens. "I know," explained the prince, noticing Lady Laura's incredulity, "I was right there, fighting by his side."

"If I had to choose one knight from among the many brave who fought in the Holy Land, milady," concluded Sancho, "I would choose your son, hands down."

"Hear, hear!" proclaimed the gathering of intoxicated knights, banging their cups on the table in inebriated approval. The din died down a bit, silence descending upon the Great Hall. It was almost as if they were expecting the Lady of Agorreta to say something in acknowledgment of the paeans to her son. As in all her pronouncements, she was brief.

"We have always bred them brave and strong in this high country, milord," she remarked, beaming proudly at Iñaki. "Being an Agorreta," she added, after a brief pause, "my son could not have done otherwise."

There was a roar of applause. It was good to hear a proud mother chime in with her own praise, thought Iñaki, now choked for words. She may have been old and infirm but her mind was still keen-edged, her words, as always, pithy. She was the very salt and essence of the Navarran earth, he thought. She reminded him of one of those Spartan mothers he'd read about, who would vow to see their warrior sons return from battle only as victors or honorably dead.

Early the next morning, after a good night's rest and a hearty breakfast, the prince and his small force struck out for France. Though the Pyrenees were still to see their first heavy snows, the weather had turned blustery, the going arduous. It would take them the better part of two days to reach Bayonne. On their way there, they stopped at Roncevaux to say a prayer at the chapel of Charlemagne. Sancho, a deeply religious man, took note of the Abbot's concerns about having to feed the avalanche of pilgrims now spilling over the mountains on their way to Santiago, in the northwestern tip of the Peninsula. The discovery of the Apostle James' remains there, several centuries earlier, had been slow to attract pilgrims, what with the Moors' occasional forays and the local bandits' maltreatment of pilgrims.

But things were now starting to look up. The Moors had been pushed back to their southern enclaves of *al-Andalus* and the battling monks of Roncevaux had neutralized the bandit threat and now gave succor to the pilgrims. Sancho the Wise, had encouraged the influx of Frankish artisans and Jewish bankers into Navarre, offering them special dispensations and property tax exemptions, hoping they would settle and bring with them their arts, their crafts and their guilds. It was a farsighted move on the part of the Wise king, one that would allow Navarre to emerge from a backwoods kingdom into the budding European arena of trade and commerce. A new world order was dawning beyond the Pyrenees and King Sancho wanted his kingdom to be part of it.

After a brief show of force in Bayonne, prince Sancho rode around the Gascon countryside, showing his and his brother-in-law's colors, clashing with rebellious barons and reasoning with others. Sancho's fame as a gallant Crusader had preceded him and many lords grudgingly opened their castle doors to him, promising to return to Richard's fold. He was in the middle of this *chevauchée* when Sancho heard of Richard's release from prison. Weary of English rule, some of the more refractory Gascon warlords were not elated by the news. But the English king was soon back on his throne and the dissidents returned to their fawning ways.

It was during a joint operation between Richard's and Sancho's forces in Aquitaine, executing a pincer movement to retake the castle of Loches, south of the Loire, that Sancho learned about his father's death. Gathering his small army, he hurried back to Pamplona to take the reins of power. He had a lot to think about on his ride back, inheriting, as he had, a seriously threatened kingdom. As always, in times of turmoil, he turned to his friend and confidant.

"Iñaki," he said, speaking guardedly in Basque. "I have just turned forty. I'm getting too old for this sort of life, riding around the countryside tilting at someone else's quintains. You and I have been to the Crusades. No one can aspire to more glory or more adventure. I wish I could just sit back and do what I really enjoy doing."

"And what would that be, your Highness?" Both Iñaki and Sancho were surprised by the form of address. It was the first time Iñaki had used it to address his liege lord.

"Well, you know my passion for hawking. I could do a little more of that."

Iñaki nodded. "And what else, milord?" he asked. "Even too much of a good thing can be boring, you know. What about other more serious endeavors?"

"Well, I've thought about those, too. I wouldn't mind spending a little more time taking care of my kingdom's finances," he answered without hesitation. "You know my weakness for real estate. It's the only sure investment in unsettled times. People have to live in houses and live off of the land, you know. And if you hadn't noticed," he said, the way he always did when he was about to say something pithy, "the more one owns, the nobler his title."

It was a maladroit comment, coming from a king to a subordinate, but then kings could say anything they wanted, especially to their best friends. "You are only a knight because you have but one fief, the one I granted you last year," he continued, pursuing his insensitive line of thought. "Your father, on the other hand, was a baron–a petty one, but a baron no less–because he was lord of Agorreta and had fairly sizable landholdings in Narbart, Santesteban and Azcayn, if memory serves." Pausing to gather his thoughts, he continued: "Now, Lehet, for instance, is a Count because he owns large towns, like Peralta, and Count Rada owns Aibar and Funes. And so, you see, a king must own a goodly part of his kingdom's lands, not to mention a few choice properties in rich towns. That's the only way he can control the barons and maintain peace with them."

Iñaki had heard his king's financial dissertations before. Everyone knew of his penchant for profitable business deals, some, purportedly, a bit on the shady side. 'Prince Midas,' they called him behind his back. He had also been dubbed 'banker of kings', lately.

"I'm afraid you have other more important things to worry about than counting Sanchetes right now," Iñaki made bold to suggest, referring to the Navarran currency of the day, first minted by the king's father. "Castile and Aragon have plans in mind other than business deals with you."

"I know," said Sancho pensively. "Pedro can be bought with loans and grants. The Aragonese pauper seems to be in perpetual debt, poor devil. He is no great threat. Alfonso is the one I worry about. He seems determined to gobble up my kingdom all by himself. I've got to find a way to stop him."

Sancho's crowning ceremony took place with great solemnity in the Cathedral of Pamplona. *El Fuerte* had inherited a sprawling kingdom, delimited, on the east by Aragon, and on the west by Vizcaya, with Rioja and Álava, to the south and Basse Navarre to the north, beyond the Pyrenees. He would have to emulate his father's shrewd diplomacy and nimble footwork to hold on to the young kingdom he had inherited from him. His own succession had taken on a sudden and pressing importance. Like his brother-in-law, Richard, he was getting on in years and was still to sire a legitimate heir. And so it came as no surprise that, shortly after his coronation, a marriage to princess Constanza, daughter of Raymond VI of Toulouse, was quickly arranged. As in most such marriages of convenience, the bride and groom had never met before nor greatly cared for each other once they did. She would eventually produce a son who would never reach adulthood.

Sancho's hold on his border possessions was growing increasingly tenuous. His nemesis, Alfonso of Castile, had started nibbling at Navarre's southern border, a castle one day, a fortified town the next. Soria fell, followed soon after by Logroño. Sancho was learning, firsthand, the depth of his father's anguish as he stood by, helplessly watching his kingdom shrink before his very eyes. He had run out of allies to ask for help. The Church, too, had turned a deaf ear to his entreaties. The kingdom of Leon had its own problems with Castile. Even Richard, his brother-in-law, hobbled by the staggering taxes with which he had saddled England to pay for his outrageous ransom, was of little help. Sancho *el Fuerte* was now on his own. Diplomacy had been exhausted. He had to look for help elsewhere.

Providentially, he received an odd diplomatic visit from an emissary of Abu Yusuf Yaquib, the Caliph of the Almohades Moors, requesting his presence in Morocco, in a military advisory role. From Castile's and Aragon's resident ambassadors at his court, the Caliph was aware of Sancho's political and financial straits. Sancho, whose fame as a strategist had preceded him, was now being invited to visit North Africa to help the Caliph organize his defenses against hostile local warlords. A large reward, including dazzling treasures and the transfer of several important Moorish landholdings in the Iberian Peninsula, was dangled in front of Sancho as inducement.

Sancho was sorely tempted to accept the astounding offer offhand. His shrewd business mind raced with visions of mercenary armies raised with these windfall profits. He could recruit knights from all over Christendom, Europe crawling as it was with unemployed and debt-ridden Crusaders. He could literally overrun Alfonso's forces until the Castilian would have to scream for peace, restore all the lands he had usurped from Sancho, and then some. Sancho was literally salivating, thinking of the possibilities of these unforeseen riches.

His counselors were quick to dash cold water on his fantasies. "How long does Your Majesty think it would take the Pope to react to such an outrageous alliance?" asked his palace Seneschal. "Here's the man trying to drum up another Crusade against the Almohades Moors and you're proposing to sidle up to the enemy? You are flirting with Excommunication, Your Majesty. Perhaps even a General Interdict on your kingdom!"

Sancho was in a terrible quandary, dammed if he went, lose his kingdom if he didn't. He could live with the threat from Rome for a while, perhaps, but what really worried him most was leaving his kingdom at a time of such great peril, perhaps in pursuit of a chimera. At wits end, he summoned Iñaki to his private quarters one evening. His Vascon friend was the only one he could bare his soul to in moments of profound personal crisis. He trusted his down-to-earth wisdom, born of his mountain people's centuries of strife and survival. Iñaki would offer him sensible advice, he knew.

"Alfonso is at Álava's doors," bemoaned Sancho. "His armies are poised to overrun Vitoria. How can I absent myself from my kingdom under such straits?"

"The Lionheart did," responded Iñaki without hesitation. "And for a lot more time than you'll be absent. They're only asking you to visit there a few weeks. In and out, that's it. Besides," added Iñaki, pursuing his line of thought, "the Caliph is not asking for your armies, just your military advice. You can leave your field commanders to handle Alfonso for a brief spell. You don't have to be in Álava to defend it, but you *do* have to be in Morocco to reap the benefits. Then you can come back to face the headaches of Alfonso. They'll keep, I'm sure. But when you return from Africa you'll weigh into Alfonso's and Pedro's armies with the weight of a heavy purse. It will buy you the army you need to stop them."

"What if it's only a ruse?" persisted Sancho, trying to poke holes in Iñaki's logic. "I'd lose everything, kingdom, subjects, perhaps even my life!"

"It's a gamble you'll have to take, milord," responded Iñaki unswervingly. "Without the trip, your kingdom is lost. Without your kingdom, your life as a king is finished."

"You put it bluntly, my friend, but wisely," said Sancho, thankful of Iñaki's candid advise. "You mince few words with me. I appreciate that. You're the only one who tells me the unvarnished truth."

"Yes, your Highness. That's because I love both you and this land of ours."

Sancho smiled. It was a fitting remark. Iñaki had come through once again with sound advice. Deep down, Sancho sensed that he would eventually have arrived at the same conclusion, more tortuously perhaps, but with the same outcome. He looked at Iñaki impishly. "You will come with me to Morocco. You'll have to put your life where your mouth is." They both laughed.

Chapter 32

An African Adventure

1200

Although Sancho did not know it at the time, the Caliph's invitation was partly due to his daughter's instigation. Having heard of Sancho's rugged good looks and prowess in battle, the fair Zoraida had fallen madly in love with her idea of the Navarran king. She would have no one else for a husband, she assured her father. Such was her infatuation that she even threatened to take her own life if her wishes were not granted. Yusuf Yaquib loved his daughter dearly and knew that, being as headstrong as her mother, she was not given to idle threats.

Yaquib, whose mind worked in devious ways, thought he'd kill two birds with one stone: he would grant Zoraida's wishes and then pick the Navarran's brains for ways to outmaneuver the rebellious chieftains in the Rif Mountains. Always a testy lot, the Berbers in that mountain redoubt had been trying to undermine his Caliphate for some time now. He did not really intend to honor his promise to hand over to Sancho sizable Muslim-held territories in Iberia, but he had riches to spare and could shower him with enough gold to help him fend off his encroaching neighbors. And then, of course, there was Zoraida. She'd be thrown into the bargain. The scheme had great possibilities and, in the Oriental's mind, perfectly fair.

Preparations for the journey were tedious and convoluted. There was a need for utmost secrecy, for Sancho's enemies were sure to strike the moment they learned of his escapade. And it was this secrecy that complicated the whole enterprise. Only a few trusted officials were informed of the trip and plans had to be carried out surreptitiously. Not even the Bishop of Pamplona was let in on the trip since he was likely to be the first to sound the alarm. All preparations were made in the royal palace of Tudela, where, like his father, he had always preferred to live and hold court, away from the scheming magnates and pompous church officials in Pamplona. The trip, it was agreed, would have to be by sea since traveling incognito across Castilian territory would have been too risky. Sancho named a triumvirate of trusted Counts to run the affairs of state in his absence. Safe-conducts were arranged for him and the two dozen knights who would escort him. Finally, in early March, they were ready.

Under cover of darkness, the small expedition headed north to Bayonne, where they boarded a galley that would transport them to Morocco. After a rough crossing, they put into the bustling North African port of Rabat, where a mounted guard of a hundred turbaned horsemen with shiny lances awaited to escort them to the Caliph's palace in Marrakech. The Christians were a little nervous, surrounded as they were by a throng of curious Moors lining the streets to the Caliph's palace. Sancho's and Iñaki's uncommon stature and powerful build were the object of awed curiosity among the sea of gawking Moroccans. They must have wondered how their own people had ever managed to hold on to their Iberian possessions, faced with such formidable Christian warriors.

"It's strange, isn't it," commented Iñaki, as they trotted down the main thoroughfare of Marrakech, amazed by the slight build and apparent frailty of their swarthy onlookers. "I can't figure out how such undernourished people could have ever conquered our land. I could see the Turks of Outremer doing it, but these runts?"

"Turmoil, my dear Iñaki, internal turmoil," responded Sancho enigmatically. "A house divided falls by merely puffing on it. These people caught our Visigoth rulers with their guard down, bickering among themselves. We're still trying to recover from that ineptitude, half a millennium later!"

Iñaki thought about that for a moment. "Aren't you just a bit worried about ever getting out of here alive?" he inquired sheepishly. He was already feeling a little guilty about having advised his king to embark on this daft adventure.

"You will soon learn that hospitality among these people is a paramount virtue, an inviolate rule of conduct. No harm ever befalls a guest of theirs, no matter how humble, or foreign—or bellicose. Besides, we are their Caliph's guests. You will soon see the warm reception that awaits us. We will be offered the best rooms in our host's palace, fed his choicest morsels, offered the fairest maidens in his household."

Iñaki's eyes bulged in disbelief. This was shaping up to be a jolly good adventure, after all.

They were in for a rude surprise.

Upon arriving at the palace, they learned of Caliph Yaquib Nasir's sudden and unexpected demise several weeks earlier. His young son, Al-Nasir, popularly known as Boya Miramamolin, had taken over the reins of power and would honor his father's promises only under certain conditions. Sancho and his men would have to actively join forces with him in an imminent military operation planned against the Berbers, who had turned even more belligerent following the Caliph's death. It was an awkward situation from which Sancho would have difficulty extricating himself, seeing that he could leave Morocco only by the good graces of the young Caliph. All he could hope for now was to end this visit as quickly as possible and return to his pressing problems back home.

In the confusion, Zoraida's wishes had been overlooked. Not one to be lightly sidetracked, however, she slipped into Sancho's rooms that night with amorous intent. Though startled at first, he soon realized, from his visitor's retinue, that the young lady had to be a high ranking member of the royal family. From her youngish features and self-assured demeanor, he quickly guessed that he was in the presence of a member of the deceased Caliph's family, perhaps a daughter. He watched her imperiously dismiss her entourage, close the door behind her and glide into his quarters with supreme confidence, acting almost as if she owned the place. She was a beautiful woman in her late teens, lithe and of graceful movement. The faint fragrance of an exotic perfume trailed behind her as she walked past him. The veil that partially covered her raven hair also hid from view the lower part of her face. Her warm brown eyes looked at him with the confidence of one sizing up her prey.

"I am Zoraida," she pronounced with confidence as she reclined languorously on a lounger. With a quick whisk of the hand, she pulled off her veil, slid off her gold-lamée sandals and propped up her bare feet on a cushion, like one getting comfortable for an intimate tryst. Sancho was a little flustered by her forwardness. A Muslim woman never bared her feet in public, let alone lifted her veil in front of a stranger. So much for notions of modest and retiring Muslim women, he thought.

"You are in Morocco because of me," said the young lady with cool aplomb. Sancho raised his eyebrows in surprise. She continued: "I asked my father for your hand in marriage and he gave it to me."

The news hit Sancho like a mace. He knew right away that he was in a predicament, for, as a host was honor-bound to be gracious to his guest in this cultured land, the guest did not mar that welcome with an unpardonable faux pas. Reciprocity was the code of the desert, the handshake of the Bedouin that ensured peace among strangers.

"I am honored by your interest in me, milady," stuttered Sancho when he finally recovered from his surprise, "but my hand is no longer mine, or anyone else's, to give. You see, I already am a married man." Sancho tried not to sound prudish but polygamy was not something he wanted to add to his many pressing problems. "I am sorry to put you through this embarrassment but unlike yours, my religion does not allow a man to have more than one wife." After a brief pause, he added: "And I happen to be a religious man."

Zoraida looked crestfallen. She remained speechless for a long time, her lower lip trembling as she tried to repress a sob, her soulful brown eyes now brimming with tears. Sancho was devastated by the sight of a crying maiden. This went against the code of chivalry he had sworn to uphold; one succored ladies in distress, not made them weep. He was at a loss for words, watching this beautiful maiden, now weeping uncontrollably in front of him.

"My dear Zoraida," said Sancho soothingly, holding her hand. "Please do not cry. Even if I were not already married, you can see that I am getting on in years. I must be at least a score of years older than you. You may already have noticed that the girth of my waistline is about to catch up with that of my shoulders. I am growing fat!" He hesitated a moment to see the effect of his self-deprecating remark. She remained disconsolate.

In his helplessness, he was suddenly struck by an idea that, he hoped, would relieve the awkward tension. He, personally, might not be available but there was one in his company who was still a bachelor. Iñaki was always looking for new adventures and other sources of wealth to support his new station in life. Here was his chance.

"Look," he said finally, "there is one in my retinue who will be more to your liking. He is young like you, handsome and strong. He is as valiant a warrior as I and will give you strong sons. Best of all, he is single. You may have noticed him among my men. He is as tall as I and a good ten years younger."

Zoraida had, by now, risen from the reclining lounger. She hastily slipped on her sandals and arranged her veil the way she had worn it when she first walked into the room. She was still unwilling to look at him as she walked past him towards the door. Her feelings had been bruised as never before in her short, pampered life. A woman rejected, thought Sancho, can be a formidable opponent. He had to alert Iñaki of the awkward situation. The Vascon would get him out of this scrape.

Boya Miramamolin had little time for niceties. There was a war going on in the Rif Mountains and little time left to resolve the festering tribal rebellion. Sancho and his score of knights and as many squires rode off with the young Caliph and his generals at the head of a large Moorish troupe of hardy horsemen. Sancho was shocked by the young Caliph's inexperience in the field. His commanders were no better. Perhaps, thought Sancho, the Almohades' best warriors were away manning the ramparts in Iberia, and only green reserves remained at the home front. That was probably why Boya's father had sent for him in the first place. But it was too late to start a training program for these inexperienced troops; they were already on the move. He had to wait and observe the disposition of the enemy's forces before deciding on his plan of action. He could only hope that superior tactics could make up for the Caliph's troops' inexperience. At least, he rationalized, they seemed to be good horsemen.

The Rif Mountains were definitely not for the faint-hearted, Sancho soon discovered. The landscape was stern and sober for leagues on end, until suddenly, off on some distant cliff, some whitewashed village would loom, splashed with a whiteness that hurt the eye and startled the imagination. Occasionally, off on a slanting slope, a solitary goatherd stood outlined with his dung-colored herd against a weightless, unforgiving sky. Otherwise, there was only sheer, hurting emptiness. Far off in the distance, the jagged heights beckoning them appeared steep and forbidding, unapproachable by a surprise attack. To make matters worse, cavalry would be of little use in those steep hills and deep gullies. Sancho also knew that Berbers were a hardy, ferocious lot when threatened.

"These mountain people remind me of the Vascons from your upland country," remarked Sancho to Iñaki during a bivouac rest. "Tough barbarians, both!"

"That's what Julius Caesar and Abd-el-Raman once said of us," answered Iñaki with a smile. "We prevailed, they didn't! We mountain Vascons esteem our toughness, even if it sometimes verges on the foolhardy."

Sancho did not comment on what he knew was a truism. Perhaps thinking like one of these mountain people, Iñaki could anticipate the Berbers' moves, but he seriously doubted it. Looking at the rocky, cactus-strewn landscape around him, he remarked: "I don't think we'll be doing much good here. We can pillage and burn a few hamlets, but that's it. They'll fade into their mountains and then come back when we're gone. Only way to stop these people is to capture their leader and I don't think our hosts have a clue where he could be hiding."

"Nor the guts to do anything about it, if they did," agreed Iñaki. After a thoughtful pause, he remarked brightly: "Perhaps we can encourage them to do it. Remember that large, whitewashed settlement up on the side of the mountain we rode past early this morning? It looked like a village of some importance, a place where warlords live. It looked impregnable from below but perhaps we could sneak up around it and swoop down on it from above."

"Possible," said Sancho noncommittally. "But how do we get these inept goons up above the village without being detected?"

"That's where we come in," proposed Iñaki confidently. "There're three dozen of us, right? We'll spread our men out and quietly subdue their lookouts in the heights, one at a time. There are some pretty sharp bow-and-arrow marksmen among our men. Not too shabby crossbow handlers, either. Kill at a distance, swiftly, quietly."

"Sounds plausible," commented Sancho, warming up to the idea. "It's probably worth a try." He trusted Iñaki's instincts blindly. There had always been something cunning and untamed about him, ever since he was a boy. "We could feign an attack from below with a small part of our forces," continued Sancho. "That should distract them. We'll bring the bulk of our forces up to the heights after the lookouts have been eliminated and then conduct the main attack from above!"

"And if we kill or capture their leader," remarked Iñaki, warming up to the plan, "that'll be the end of their resistance. That should earn us our return passage home."

Boya Miramamolin and his generals embraced the Christians' plan enthusiastically. To ensure the element of surprise, one of the generals suggested, they'd leave their horses behind, wrap their men's boots with cloth and secure their scabbards to their thighs to eliminate the clatter of their approach. The timing between neutralizing the lookouts and controlling the heights was critical; too long an interval without signals from their pickets could alert the enemy below that something was amiss.

The midnight attack went like clockwork. A full moon helped Iñaki and his advance scouts clamber up the rugged cliffs from several rear approaches, stealthily and with dispatch. There were only five Berber lookouts in all, it turned out, most of whom dozed under fig trees, except one who was busy picking cactus pears. Their end was silent and swift. When Iñaki's owl-hoot signal sounded, the rest of the force scaled the heights furtively, leaving a Company of men behind. From the crest, they had a commanding view of the town as it slept peacefully in that midnight hour. Boya had split his army into three groups; two would swoop down on the town from above along two different mountain paths, while a third would remain hidden in the narrow pass at the bottom of the gorge, directly below the settlement.

When the second owl hoot sounded, the group that had remained below started to howl vociferously, creating an ungodly din to distract the enemy. The settlement stirred to wakefulness on hearing the racket, embers quickly fanned into roaring fires, unwittingly lighting up their positions. All their defenses faced the valley below, from where enemy assaults had always threatened. Led by the score of Navarrans, Boya's men came howling down the mountainside, making an enormous fracas. Sancho and Boya remained on the heights with a handful of men, observing the assault's progress.

The inhabitants of the town were caught completely by surprise. Never expecting an attack from above, they raced around the village, bumping into each other. The panic and chaos that ensued only hastened their defeat. Those who attempted to escape down the mountain path to the valley below were cut down by the company of men waiting in ambush at the bottom of the hill. The battle lasted a little over an hour. No mercy was shown by Boya's troops, no prisoners taken. Only an old woman was spared to identify the village's chieftain. Weeping disconsolately, she pointed to a young warrior who lay dead, surrounded by the bodies of a dozen of Boya's men. He must have put up a good fight, dying, as brave men do, with no wounds on his back. The old woman wept as she confessed that Amal, the dead young warrior, had led the Berbers' against the Almohades ever since his father died years earlier. He had been the tribe's leader, she avowed.

Having no other witnesses, the young Caliph would never be able to confirm the old woman's story, but whatever the identity of that fallen warrior, an uneasy peace ensued following the military operation. And so, Boya's Moors conjectured, they had, by dint of sheer luck, decapitated the niggling Berber opposition. Young Miramamolin became a hero among his people overnight. The operation's success buttressed Boya's standing among his local chieftains, ensuring the continuation of his Caliphate. Boya felt deeply indebted to Sancho for his brilliant generalship. His clever stratagem had brought them victory and the consolidation of his power among the Almohades Moors. He proposed to reward him handsomely for his effort.

Several days after their victorious return from the Rif Mountains, Sancho found a tall pile of sturdy wooden boxes stacked high in the middle of his palace living quarters. Cracking one of them open, he was surprised to discover it brimming with gold and silver coins. Although he had expected some recompense for his trip to Africa, he was stunned by Miramamolin's largesse. There, lying in front of him, was at least half a ton of precious metals and assorted jewelry. Awed by such staggering wealth, his thoughts flew home to his abandoned kingdom. At last, he reflected, he would be able to handle Castile's armies knocking at his doors if it was not already too late.

But that was not the last of his pleasant surprises. Sancho had, long since, given up hope that Caliph Yaquib's promised restitution of certain Moorish-held lands in the Peninsula would ever be honored, surmising that it had been just an idle pledge. On the eve of their departure, the young Boya handed him a sheepskin scroll containing a decree deeding him, Sancho, King of Navarre, several large Moorish landholdings in Iberian Valencia and Almería. Sancho was nonplused. He had become rich beyond all imagining overnight. These people may have been Muslims but their promises were as good as gold. A father's oath had to be honored by his son. These were, indeed, men of honor. After all was said and done, the hazardous trip to Morocco had been well worth the trouble and the risk.

Before leaving Morocco, Sancho signed a new peace treaty with the Almohades. He was not alone among Christian kings to sign such treaties for he later discovered that Castile's and Aragon's Ambassadors to the Caliph's court had only recently renewed similar treaties with the North Africans. Strange, he pondered, how war could be waged against the Saracens in the eastern shores of the Mediterranean while peace treaties were signed with Moors by Christian kings at its western shores.

The jilted Zoraida, meanwhile, had been evasive ever since they returned from the Rif. Sancho's rejection must have hurt her deeply and while she had time to pout and nurse her wounds in their absence, she had started wondering about the other tall knight in his retinue. This other one may not own a kingdom but she had noticed that he was good-looking, indeed quite a bit better looking than Sancho himself. And younger too. He was probably well worth a tryst. These Christians, she had heard, were good lovers.

Zoraida had not escaped Iñaki's attention, either. Even before Sancho asked him to divert her amorous advances away from him, the Vascon had already noticed that the young Caliph's sister was a delectable woman of exotic beauty. She was everything a young man fancied. She reminded him a little of some mythical nymph, alluring and unapproachable. But what really captivated him were those liquid, soft-brown eyes of hers, doe-like almost, open windows to a generous soul.

Ever since he returned from the Rif Mountains, he had noticed that she had been making subtle overtures to him, casting longing glances in his direction, fluttering her eyelashes, smiling her beguiling smile at him for no reason at all. He had seen all these subtle signals before but the innocence, the inexperience of Zoraida's come-on captivated him. She was, he thought, a true ingénue.

The night before they sailed for home, Iñaki discovered someone occupying his bed when he slipped into it. He knew, without saying, who it was; her faint exotic jasmine perfume, subtly wafting over the room when he walked in, gave Zoraida's presence away.

He lay down next to her, saying nothing, feeling her warmth, smelling her wonderful fragrance. Turning to her, he kissed her eyes tentatively, and then her lips, softly caressing her face and running his fingers through her pliant, lustrous hair. Then he started exploring the exuberant terseness of her youthful form, bewitched by the pleasurable groans his gentlest touch elicited, the sudden catching of breath in innocent awkwardness on feeling his hard, warm edges. He knew that she had never known man before. She was uncharted territory, a beach unmarked by others' footprints. He couldn't help wondering how so unlike the sophisticated Joannas and all those other Jezebels he had known, this young princess was.

Iñaki tried to be gentle with her, caressing her subtly, unhurriedly, softly pulling her young, terse nipples with trembling lips. His fingers groped down her body, slowly, tentatively, in joyful pilgrimage, hearing, in ageless wonder, surprised, muted groans of sheer delight as she felt the probing fingers, stumbling, like errant Bedouins, into the warm folds of her secret oasis. And when she was aroused almost to the threshold of ecstasy, Iñaki came into her, with slow, rhythmic movements at first, then more urgently, until finally, they both reached the summit of feeling, he flowing like a mighty river, spilling his life-giving waters into her secluded glen.

They lay awake after the lovemaking, side by side, in silence, still listening to strains of the spent rhapsody.

Finally, Iñaki spoke:

"I must leave with my lord tomorrow. There is trouble in our land," he said, caressing her face with infinite tenderness. "I am sorry we did not meet before, under different circumstances. Our cultures and religions may be different, our classes chasms apart, but I will cherish this night forever." He leaned over and kissed her softly on her lips.

Zoraida said nothing for the longest time. She was thinking about how men sowed their seed and then left for the hunt, while women stayed behind to nourish their essence and bring forth new life. It, somehow, seemed unfair; the hunter, cavalier and nonchalant, the gatherer, eager, long-suffering. But it had been the unwritten compact between man and woman since the beginning of time, he to provide and protect, she to nourish and perpetuate. It was always thus, and always would be.

She climbed out of bed and silently dressed. As she was about to leave the room, she turned to him and said, in her delightfully faltering Castilian: "You are a kind and gentle man," she said softly. "You have given me great pleasure and I will sorely miss you. Someday, perhaps, our paths will cross again."

She then raised her head, and kissed him one last time. "I wish you long life and Godspeed, fair knight."

Noticing the tears on her cheeks, he bent over and kissed them away.

CHAPTER 33

▼

A Nostalgic Reunion

While Sancho was reaping a financial windfall in Morocco, Castile had been busy gnawing at his kingdom's edges. Having drawn Guipuzcoa under his aegis, Alfonso VIII's armies overran Álava and captured Vitoria, its only fortified city. Richard the Lionheart's untimely death in a minor scuffle in the Limousin, emboldened Alfonso to invade southern France, forcibly taking several Gascon Viscounties promised him as his wife's dowry by Richard's father years earlier.

Having lost almost a fourth of his kingdom during his brief escapade to Africa, the prospects facing Sancho could not have been gloomier. His deceased father, Sancho the Wise, would have grieved to see the kingdom he had so painstakingly sewn together, now dwindled into a mere shadow of its former glory. All *el Fuerte* could hope for now was to contain the damage. The loss of San Sebastián, his kingdom's principal outlet to the sea, was a serious blow. He had to ensure that the same fate did not befall Bayonne, his last remaining opening to the sea. With England's blessing, Sancho mounted a brief expedition to Bayonne to stiffen the Gascons' resolve and reinforce their defenses. On his way there, he took possession of St. Jean Pied de Port and Chateau Rochebrune, both of which had been dowered by the Lionheart to Berenguela. An uneasy truce between Castile and Navarre ensued.

It was during this lull in hostilities that Iñaki one day overheard the English ambassador to Sancho's court mention Lionheart's sister, Joanna. Memories of their torrid night aboard a ship anchored off Acre came flooding back to Iñaki like a ghost from the past. He could still see her, with her tantalizingly whimsical moods and irreverent ways. She had inherited her mother's *cachet*, and like her, expressed it charmingly, with unaffected grace and elegance, unaware of the spell she cast about her or the charm she squandered as she went through life. She was so unlike anyone else he had ever known.

As he escorted the English diplomat out of the Royal Palace grounds in Pamplona, Iñaki made bold to inquire: "Is she still living with Eleanor?"

"No," answered the puzzled Ambassador. "Joanna now lives in Poitiers." The envoy was intrigued by a lowly knight's interest in ladies of such high rank, even referring to the queen mother by her first name. "Queen Eleanor has been living in Fontevrault, where she cloistered herself a few years back. She's been feeling rather poorly, lately. They don't expect her to live much longer. Even so, she's managed to arrange a wedding for her daughter Joanna, who is now betrothed to Count Raymond VI of Toulouse."

Iñaki was not really surprised that Eleanor, already in her seventies, was still busy making marriage arrangements even from behind the walls of some Abbey. It was so like her! He could not help thinking how the marriage she had arranged for her son Richard had ended poorly for, despite all her scheming, Richard never sired any progeny with Berenguela. It struck Iñaki as odd at first that Eleanor would have any dealings with the house of her avowed rivals, the lords of Toulouse, whose ancestors had seized a sizable chunk of her father's rightful dukedom of Aquitaine. But Eleanor's all-too-transparent scheme soon dawned on Iñaki: she was going to get someone in her family back holding the reins in Toulouse. Though belated and somewhat contrived, it would in the end be her stab at poetic justice.

"How about Berenguela?" persisted Iñaki. "Where is she now?" The Ambassador was growing increasingly intrigued by the way this giant of a knight hobnobbed in high places until Iñaki explained his long-standing friendship with, and service to the latest English dowager queen.

"The dowager queen of England now resides in her estates in Maine," he answered stiffly. "That's just north of Anjou, on the Loire," he explained gratuitously. The Ambassador did not volunteer the information that the dowager queen of England had still to set foot on her own erstwhile kingdom. It was all too odd even for a proper Englishman to acknowledge, let alone try to explain away.

Iñaki had heard through the grapevine that, months before his death, Richard's bout with some life-threatening illness had prompted him to summon his confessor. Aware of his checkered past and his fast-dwindling chances of siring any progeny, the friar had refused him absolution unless he promised to mend his pederast ways, summon his estranged wife, and share his bed with her. Though Richard meekly complied, the awkward liaison yielded no issue. Poor Berenguela, commiserated Iñaki. She had been living the life of a widow from the day she married in Limassol. She did not deserve such backhanded treatment.

He was not the only one who remembered Berenguela fondly. Sancho, too, thought about his sister often. He had not seen her since they parted ways in Acre, and he missed her, being as she was his favorite sibling. Occasionally some messenger would drop in with bits of news about her stranded up there in the Maine, pining her days away. He'd send her the occasional missive inviting her to come visit. But she had never accepted. It was almost as if she'd made some vow to cut herself off from the outside world.

Hawking with Iñaki one afternoon, the king brought up the subject of Berenguela. In a recent visit, the English Ambassador had informed Sancho of Eleanor's eightieth birthday celebration at Fontevrault. It was a splendid party, he reported. He'd never seen so much royalty gathered under one roof to pay their respects. Even her son, John Lackland, was there with all his regal retinue, as were Joanna and Berenguela. Inquiring about his sister's health, Sancho was informed that she had looked pale and listless, a bit under the weather, perhaps.

"How would you like to go to Maine and pay Berenguela a visit?" asked Sancho. He would have liked to go himself, he said, but could not risk another absence from his kingdom, after what happened during his last adventure abroad. "Your visit would do her a world of good," he added. He knew Iñaki's devotion to his sister. She was probably lonely, cooped up in some cold French castle, ignored by her late husband's subjects, bereft of friends she could trust. She was not the type to pick up the pieces and start a new life. Hers was probably pretty much a cloistered existence. What a waste of a life, Sancho thought with a pang of sibling sympathy.

"Ask her if she'd consider coming back to live in her own country," said Sancho. "She belongs here. Tell her I'll be happy to take care of her, perhaps even scare up a new husband for her. The English wouldn't mind that. Happy to get her off their hands, I'm sure!"

It took Iñaki and his two squires a little over a fortnight to reach the Loire country. The beauty of the countryside and the green, lush farmland he rode through impressed him. Small wonder these Frenchmen were so prosperous and sophisticated in their ways, he reflected. He saw little of his country's pastoral way of life here, just one castle after another surrounded by vast vineyards and huge luxuriant farms. "La douce France," they called it, and with good reason. This was the birthplace of chivalry, where noblemen could afford the luxury of daily hawking and hunting outings, frequent tournaments and all manner of frivolous entertainment. Even Pamplona looked provincial, compared to some of the cities he rode through, like Bordeaux and Angoulem and Poitiers.

He wasn't quite sure what prompted him to tarry in Poitiers and inquire about Joanna at the inn. Perhaps it was mere curiosity or simply the desire to look up old acquaintances in a beautiful, but unfriendly land. She must now be approaching forty, he figured, certainly past her prime. And so there was little of the sensual appeal that induced him to turn back to this dog-eared leaf in his life. The innkeeper informed him that Lady Joanna just happened to be at the palace that week, making final arrangements for her wedding in Toulouse. Her marriage was set for the following week, he was informed.

He approached the palace in the heart of town with some trepidation. Would she snub him and turn him out on his ear or would she share his curiosity about how the other had fared since that torrid night aboard the Dauntless off Acre so long ago now, it seemed. His imposing stature and fine garb caught the palace steward's attention. The foreign name must have struck him as appropriately distinguished, but it was not until Iñaki produced the scroll with the lacquered seal bearing the royal Navarran eagle that the steward agreed to announce his presence to the dowager queen of Sicily, soon-to-be Countess of Toulouse. After the seneschal announced his presence to Joanna, Iñaki was ushered into a small anteroom in the private quarters of the palace.

"My dear Iñaki," Joanna said, emerging from her quarters and walking breezily up to him. Iñaki held her proffered hand in his, kissing it deferentially. "Milady," he said in his deep, baritone voice. She looked stunningly beautiful in her pale blue, embroidered gown. Her hair was done up like a Roman patrician's, held up by a golden coronet, curls bouncing down the back of her neck in studied neglect. The warmth of her blue eyes had changed little, barely perceptible wrinkles now gracefully framing them. They still had that same sparkle he remembered, crinkling, laughing in the same salacious way, looking up at him from under fluttering eyelashes. She was still the inveterate flirt, he could see.

Except for a more buxom figure and an ever so slightly fuller waist, she had hardly changed.

"You're as enormous as I remembered!" she said, looking up at him fondly, "and just as handsome, I can see." Something inside Iñaki blushed; he was not used to such facile compliments. This woman was the same incorrigible coquette he remembered. She could beguile a stone with her charm! She was such a delightful seducer.

"And you, milady, look younger and more radiant than I remembered," said Iñaki. He, too, could play at her suave game. Well, not quite, but at least with as much gallantry as any Navarran provincial could muster. Though he sensed he was hopelessly outclassed in this rarefied, cosmopolitan milieu, he was bolstered by the thought that these sophisticates were usually charmed by someone's rough edges. And he knew he had a few of those left in him.

"I hear," she said, "that you and your king have been trying to keep the lid on those cauldrons of restless Béarnaise and Gascon malcontents." Iñaki was surprised at her informed interest in political affairs. "You're setting a fine example for those fidgety barons around Toulouse. My future husband will be pleased." She smiled her bewitching smile and added: "You know, of course, we're marrying shortly, don't you?"

Iñaki nodded. She would make Raymond a happy man, probably twirl him around her little finger as her mother Eleanor had done with this Count's grandfather eons ago in the Lebanon. Joanna was one piece of work, he reflected. Her mother had done well by her.

"I was happy to hear your mother's doing passably well," said Iñaki. "I'll never forget our first encounter at King Sancho the Wise's table years ago. I was so taken by her strength of character, her wit, her *je-ne-sais-quoi*. But above all by her courage. I can still see her, a sexagenarian dowager queen, trampling up those Alps, determined to force your brother Richard to marry the girl she was carrying in tow across the snowy passes." Iñaki paused a moment before adding, "I have never met the likes of her. You, perhaps, come closest."

"Coming from you, my dear Iñaki, that is the highest compliment. Thank you. We all dearly love her."

The conversation gradually shifted to Berenguela. "I'm on my way to visit her. I haven't seen her since Acre," explained Iñaki. "I bring her a message from her brother."

"Lucky girl!" commented Joanna, casually. Iñaki didn't know how to take her remark, but then one seldom knew how to interpret Joanna's witticisms and *double-entendres*. He paused a moment before asking, "What do you hear from her?"

"She looked a bit pinched at *maman*'s party," said Joanna, trying not to sound too concerned. "She didn't admit anything was amiss. Perhaps it was just the garb she was wearing that day. Dark clothes do tend to bleach one's color a little, you know." Joanna paused before proceeding. "She did mention that she missed the excitement of old. I'm afraid her confessor must be leaching all the fun out of her. Not that she had great reserves of it, to begin with. She never much cared for parties."

"And you," said Iñaki, changing the subject, "are on your way to marry the Count of Toulouse." He thought he saw her wince almost imperceptibly at the mention of marriage. From his many years of talking with animals, Iñaki knew a thing or two about the subtle nuances of body language. Joanna, he sensed, was not exhilarated by the prospects of her upcoming wedding. She had been a widow for almost fifteen years—no doubt a merry one—and though now approaching forty, she was probably not quite ready to settle down. Not in vain had she inherited her mother's free-wheeling *joie de vivre*.

"Yes," she answered brightly. "I will be in the corridors of power again!" For someone who had once been a queen, becoming a Count's wife must seem a bit of a letdown, thought Iñaki. Although she was loathe to admit it, this marriage was obviously one of convenience; it would bring back the respect she once enjoyed, perhaps even scare up new acquaintances to sate her insatiable thirst for companionship. After all, Toulouse, like Poitiers, was home to troubadours and other merry men.

"I wish you well, milady," said Iñaki. "I only hope Berenguela could one day be so lucky."

"She may be happy where she is," remarked Joanna philosophically. "She always had a bit of a contemplative streak in her. Her life behind those castle walls in Chateau Gontier may be just what she desires. Look at my own mother! She chose to live behind the walls of Fontevrault all these many years. Some people enjoy a little peace and solitude, you know. God knows Berenguela got a good whiff of that during her marriage!"

It was the first time Joanna let slip her brother's neglect of his wife. She knew, better than anyone else, that he had treated her more like an untouchable than a wife.

"She is too young to shut herself up," admitted Iñaki. "She's only thirty-four! That's less than half your mother's age. Why, Eleanor was that age when she bore you!"

"Yes, I agree. Any age is too young to go into seclusion, especially in the prime of one's life." An impish twinkle suddenly lit up her eyes. "Perhaps she's got a friend she hasn't told us about." She was now grinning broadly. "You'll find out soon enough."

Iñaki took his leave, wishing Joanna a happy life in Toulouse. They parted ways promising to visit each other again some day. After all, Toulouse wasn't that far from Pamplona.

In contrast to the many pretentious castles along the Loire, Chateau Gontier was a pretty little palace sitting placidly on the banks of the Mayenne, almost effeminate in architecture. Iñaki found Berenguela pruning roses in the flower garden of her castle's bailey when he walked up to her.

"Hello, Bery," he said brightly, coming up from behind to surprise her. The greeting startled her. Only two people in the whole world had ever called her by that name and they both were in far-off Navarre. Spinning her head around, she caught sight of her tall Vascon friend.

"Well, if it isn't my dear Iñaki!" she cried gleefully. Dropping her pruning shears, she rose from her gardening and gave him a warm welcoming hug. She looked far more radiant and in better health than he had been led to expect by the Ambassador's or Joanna's comments. In fact, he thought, she looked prettier than ever, a bit more mature and appealing, if anything. This was no longer the giggling adolescent whose pigtails he pulled or played backgammon with, the teenager who would shriek in girlish delight watching her falcon bring a crane to ground. This was a regal woman, in every sense of the word.

"What brings you here?" she asked, still holding both of his hands. She was looking up at him admiringly, having noticed that he now sported a close-cropped beard and looked more mature than she remembered. There was still that earnest look about him, she thought. Dear, predictable Iñaki! She could read his face like an open book. He would never change, that way.

"'Heard you were out here waiting for me," he answered teasingly. She laughed her haunting, crystalline laughter. Grabbing him by the arm, she led him through the maze of rose bushes toward the castle's keep.

"You've learned to jest, I see," she said, letting go of his arm. "Well, as a matter of fact, I wasn't waiting for you. I've thought a lot about you, I'll admit, even missed your company a little. But I was most assuredly not expecting your visit! I hope you're here for more than just a few days. I hate in-and-out social calls. Doctor's visits, I call them!"

Iñaki took the hint and stayed a week. It was a glorious holiday for both of them. They wasted little time reverting to their younger years, crowding their hours with all the playful jesting and teasing of earlier, more carefree days. They laughed with unrepressed mirth at their respective foibles, filling their days with innocent, happy banter, all in their native Basque so no one around could eavesdrop or wag their tongues. It was like jumping back into their adolescence, uninhibited by the many little thou-shalt-not's of royal propriety, gleefully young and insouciant again. It was a magical week for both of them.

Hawking in the fields outside the castle grounds one afternoon, Berenguela confessed to Iñaki: "I sometimes miss the olden days. You know I've always been a romantic at heart. I've always believed that the days gone by were always better than the present ones. I have still to find true happiness in France. I keep busy doing little inconsequential things, like gardening and watching over my estates' finances and other equally prosaic chores. I've even picked up bird watching lately. Very English, you know." Then, turning pensive, she said: "But I feel I missed the boat somewhere back there."

Iñaki knew the confession must have pained her. It was a sign of the depth of their friendship that they could bare their souls to each other like that. They seldom held anything back from each other. "Of course there was nothing I could have done about it," she added fatalistically. "It is not for queens to choose their kings."

There it was, out in the open, like a gaping wound: the anguish of rejection, the unrequited love, the unsatisfied hunger for companionship. She could not have expressed it more succinctly or less painfully. Poor dear Bery! He reached over and held her hand, tucking it comfortably in both of his. Noticing her tears, he reached over and gave her a brotherly hug, cradling her head on his shoulder. He ran his fingers through her flaxen hair, wiping the tears off her cheeks with trembling fingers.

"My dear Bery," he said soothingly, "Nothing I can say will ease your pain. We all have to fight our own inner demons. You've been dealt a bad hand in the game of life. You deserved better. But you are young and life must go on for you.

When one's favorite hawk dies, one goes out and trains another one. Forget the past. Look at what's ahead. It's full of promise, I assure you. You have a full life ahead of you. *Carpe diem!*"

She was sobbing openly now. Consolingly, he held her against him for the longest time, saying nothing, letting her pain flow out of her. When she had cried herself out and calmed down enough to talk, she said:

"My dear Iñaki, you've always been my best friend. I've trusted your judgment, admired your strength ever since I was a little girl. You are, and always will be, my noble Vascon. Would that I had been born a knight's daughter instead of a king's! Things might have turned out differently."

Iñaki was struck by the depth of her feeling. There was a time when they had flirted with the idea of being more than mere friends. For her it had been like a game, a playful sort of divertissement, something similar to puppy love. But he had always been dutiful and courteous when she tried to make it more than an adolescent fancy. He had lived by the tenets of chivalry long before he was dubbed. And she loved him the more for it. He always reminded her of Sir Galahad of Arthurian legend, gallant, noble, pure of heart. Dear, dear Iñaki! He would have been such a kind and loving consort! But there were impossible dreams in life, certain unreachable islands of happiness. She had, indeed, been dealt a rotten hand in the game of life, as Iñaki himself had admitted.

"Your brother wants you to come back and live in Navarre," said Iñaki finally, wiping her remaining tears away. "He misses you very much. And so do I," he added softly. "I miss losing at backgammon!"

She smiled wanly. "That is sweet of you to say," she said softly. "I may visit Tudela someday but I can never abandon Maine. This is my life, this is my land now. My subjects here depend on me for guidance and leadership. As you can see, it is a fair land and I have grown to love it. I have the best of both worlds, really; privacy when I crave it, fun when I need it. Much as I love and dream of Navarre, I belong in this country now. Tell my brother that I have made my peace in Maine."

Iñaki wanted to believe her but couldn't. He sensed she was saying that just so her brother and he would stop feeling sorry for her. That generous streak had been her trademark since she was a little girl. She was always too transparent to fib credibly. But Iñaki could not say or do anything that would change her mind, and so he dropped the subject, pretending he believed her brave invention. People can sometimes talk themselves into believing their own imaginings, he reflected. It was just as well, for her pretense would probably assuage the pain of exile.

During the week he spent at Chateau Gontier in Berenguela's company, they relived the old days, pretending they were young and carefree again. They rode with the hounds and flew their falcons, they played chess and backgammon and *Mus*, and, as in the olden days, he lingered in her hands more than he had to when they played cat's cradle.

Riding in a forest of her vast domains one afternoon, they were caught in a sudden summer squall and had to duck for cover in a hunter's lodge. Iñaki built a fire and they sat in front of it to dry. It was a sweet and quiet time, a time to reminisce and renew their fondness for each other. He confessed that he too would have liked to have been born a duke or a prince so he could have offered her more than just a knight's vow to defend her honor or to merely express his courtly love. She held his hand and kissed it and he did likewise with hers. And that was all they needed to confirm their deep, abiding affection for each other. They had gone through this sort of ritual before, when they were young, pretending it was a secret pact between them, a mutual promise, an impossibly-plighted troth.

The time for Iñaki to leave Chateau Gontier arrived all too soon. It had been an amiable, bittersweet kind of a visit, a sentimental journey that served only to convince them both that one could not really go home again. They parted ways wistfully, promising to keep in touch, sensing, with a pang of sadness, that they would never see each other again.

Chapter 34

Navas de Tolosa

1212

Sancho was in Tudela when Iñaki came back from his trip abroad. He was relieved to learn that his sister was in good health and, though regretting her decision to remain in her estates in Maine, he was immensely proud of her high sense of duty and noble determination to live her life as the dowager queen of England.

Sancho, on the other hand, had troubling news for Iñaki. The ten-year peace treaty with the Almohades Moors had just expired and Alfonso VIII of Castile was anxious to resume hostilities with them. Fresh from military failures that would have daunted a wiser man, the Castilian monarch managed to marshal the support of the Church to sanction his latest attempt to expel the Moors from Iberia. Alfonso, who now fancied himself an emperor, was named leader of the Crusade. Other peninsular and European monarchs were invited to join him in Toledo and mass for battle. The response was tepid. Of all the ultra-Pyrenean knights who promised to join the Crusade, only the Bishop of Narbonne turned up with a handful of French knights. Initially reluctant to join the Crusade, the king of Leon came around only after he was promised a sizeable cut of the booty and a hefty share of the Moorish lands to be conquered.

No one expected the king of Navarre to join the fray. Castile and Aragon had harassed him for too long, cudgeled him out of a fourth of his kingdom, threatened to gobble up the rest at the slightest show of weakness. Nevertheless, prodded by Alfonso, Pope Innocent III implored Sancho to join the Crusade, appealing to his valor as a warrior-king and his duty as a Christian. The Bishop of Pamplona shrewdly added his own nudge, subtly hinting that the failure of the last Crusade in Outremer had to be avenged. The Bishop's astute reminder of that inglorious effort touched a raw nerve with Sancho, finally goading him to bury the hatchet with Castile and join the Christian forces against the common enemy. He would show them how it should be done this time around. Neither the Lionheart, before, nor Alfonso, now, could teach him how to go about trouncing Muslims.

The Christian hosts gathered in Toledo in early July, under a blazing Castilian sun. Alfonso, who bore the financial brunt of the Crusade, commanded the largest contingent of warriors. Sancho turned up with two hundred lances while the king of Leon came up with a handful of reluctant warriors, as did Pedro II of Aragon, who, with Alfonso's financial support, managed to assemble a small number of knights and foot soldiers. In all, the Christians mustered an army approaching eighteen thousand-strong, twelve thousand infantry, the rest mounted knights.

They had never fought as a unit before, indeed, had only fought against each other in the past. Leading the Vizcayan contingent was Diego Lopez de Haro, whose earlier command of the Vitoria siege still rankled with the Navarrans. This lack of cohesion and memories of old animosities only added to their skittishness of the others' proximity. The armies bivouacked in separate camps, making it a point to keep their distance during their marches. To Sancho's experienced eye, this lack of *esprit-de-corps* boded ill for the disjointed alliance.

They marched out of Toledo, along the sere, flat countryside of La Mancha. The desolate landscape was pocked with villages whose shimmering, whitewashed dwellings hurt the naked eye, lending a certain surreal quality to the godforsaken landscape. Having eked out a miserable existence under the harsh rule of the North Africans for four centuries running, the suspicious inhabitants eyed the Christian warriors with a mixture of relief and concern, cheered by the promise of a better life, afraid of the wrath of an aroused, slumbering North African giant.

The first signs of discord among the Crusaders surfaced a week out of Toledo. Alfonso summoned Sancho and Pedro of Aragon to his tent, pointedly snubbing the king of Leon. Purportedly slated as an operational meeting, Alfonso, instead, proposed that they turn on the Leonese. They were in this Crusade merely for lucre, he grumbled, not to fight Moors. He begrudged their having commandeered several Moorish castles that had fallen along the way, spoils, which, he claimed, rightly belonged to Castile.

Sancho bristled at Alfonso's petty scheming.

"I did not join this force to quibble," declared Sancho. "I came to fight the heathen, not to cross swords with other Christians." Subdued by the Navarran's righteous indignation, Alfonso relented. This was not the time to alienate the edgy Vascon giant.

Alfonso's advance scouts returned a few days later with news that the Moors had amassed a force of a hundred thousand men along a narrow valley nestled in the southern foothills of the Sierra Morena Mountains of *al-Andalus,* about a day's march away. To reach them, the Christians would have to negotiate *Despeñaperros,* or Dogslip Pass, that opened onto the valley known locally as Navas de Tolosa. Sancho and Iñaki were surprised to learn that the Moors' leader was no other than Al Nasir, the same boy-Caliph, nicknamed Miramamolín, alongside whom they had fought in the Atlas mountains of Morocco a dozen years earlier, the very brother of Iñaki's once-ardent lover, Zoraida. Strange, the twists and turns of fate, mused the Vascon knight.

Alfonso was puzzled that the Moors had not bothered to defend the pass itself, an obviously flawed military tactic.

"Hubris!" volunteered Sancho. "He knows that his force is so superior to ours—and, numerically, it is—that he believes he can afford a head-on encounter in the open. Indeed," he added, "he seems to be looking forward to it."

"Well," said Alfonso, "if he doesn't get any closer to the foothills than he is right now we'll be able to deploy our forces once we've negotiated Dogslip Pass. That'll give our heavy cavalry room to deploy." Some of the Captains thought the tactic risky and voiced their concern to that effect. Alfonso ignored their anxiety and proceeded to brief them on his order of battle.

The attack would be carried out by three groups. The central one, spearheaded by Lopez de Haro's Vizcayan shock troops, would be followed by knights of the Orders of St. John, Santiago, Uclés and Calatrava, all heavily armed and mounted on powerful war-horses. Flanking the Vizcayan vanguard would be two cavalry units, Sancho's Navarran knights on the right and Pedro's Aragonese on his left. The bulk of the Castilian infantry would follow directly behind the two cavalry wings, in a mopping up operation after the frontal assault. Alfonso, accompanied by Archbishop Ximenez de Rada of Toledo, would remain behind this formidable triple-columned formation to direct the battle from a commanding height.

From the beginning, Sancho knew that the plan was flawed. It seemed to him almost a carbon copy of the ill-fated battle of Alarcos, where Alfonso had barely managed to escape with his life, a year earlier. He didn't seem to have learned that the odds of winning a face-to-face encounter with a force ten times larger were negligibly small. But Alfonso was a headstrong man; it would take time and many casualties to convince him of his folly. They were quickly running out of both.

"We must end-run them," Sancho told Iñaki that evening. "That's our only hope. We've got to outflank them. Outsmart them, like we did in Acre and the Rif. Hit them where they least expect us."

"Fancy you suggesting that," said Iñaki. "I was scouting the countryside all day yesterday and only this morning I came across a young shepherd tending sheep near a gully not far from here. He told me about a narrow opening in the canyon, west of Dogslip Pass, that winds around the foothills and empties onto the valley just south of where Miramamolín's forces are deployed. Pass of Muradál, he called it. Said it's hard to find. Only shepherds around here know its whereabouts."

"Can cavalry negotiate it, or is it just some goat path?" asked Sancho, intrigued by the possibility of outflanking the Moors. Assured that it was passable on horseback, he inquired further: "If it's so hard to find, how are we going to find it ourselves?"

"I asked him the same question. He said he'd clearly mark its entrance with a *cabeza de vaca*. He said we couldn't possibly miss the cow's skull.

"I want you to find this Muradál pass this very afternoon and confirm the shepherd's information. Follow it to make sure horses can negotiate the canyon floor beyond, that it's hidden from view from the valley and that it, indeed, leads around to Miramamolín's camp. This might be the breakthrough we've been looking for!"

Iñaki had no difficulty finding the shepherd's cow's skull, bleached white by the merciless sun of *al-Andalus*. An ancient rockslide had hidden the passageway's narrow entrance from view. The seldom-used path twisted its tortuous way around fallen boulders, descending gradually to the canyon floor below, where the sun thinned, its shadows elongating, as one descended. The path broadened gradually into a dry, widening arroyo meandering between steep canyon walls. It had been aptly named *muradál*, a walled-in place, a concealed byway winding its way around the valley floor behind narrow, upright folds of towering granite drapery, which provided excellent cover for miles. Light slanted down the canyon walls like gold on rock, accentuating the harsh broken perfection of the cliffs above. Several miles south of its entrance, the curtain walls finally melted away as the dry arroyo bed emptied onto the valley. A bird chirped in the willows, startled by Iñaki's presence.

He could not believe his eyes. There, only a few hundred yards in front of him, sitting on a small rise surrounded by a palisade of heavy iron chains, was a scarlet tent, pennants flying the crescent moon atop its support poles. It was the only gaudily adorned tent around. The camel-mounted Berber warriors standing guard around the palisade convinced Iñaki that this had to be Miramamolín's quarters and command post. It was too well protected to be anything else.

Hurrying back to camp, Iñaki couldn't wait to relay the news of his discovery to King Sancho, who, in turn, conveyed the news to Alfonso. The Castilian did not share Sancho's enthusiasm nor was he too keen on the Navarran's suggestion of pulling his small force out of formation and venturing off, half-cocked, along some concealed passage to engage the Moors' rear. It would, Alfonso muttered, leave a gap in Castile's right flank.

"I hate to tell you this, Sire," said Sancho, an edge of impatience creeping into his voice, "but this may be our only hope of winning this battle. The Achaeans took Troy with a similar subterfuge. We took Acre using an analogous ploy. Unless we quickly decapitate the enemy's leadership in a surprise move such as I propose, we stand little chance of winning against such enormous odds. Capture Miramamolín and the battle is over. Think about it!"

Sancho was getting increasingly frustrated with his strong-headed, short-sighted leader. He was ready to go it alone, with or without Alfonso's authorization.

Sensing the Navarran's incipient rebellion, Alfonso relented. "Very well," he finally agreed. "You will take your two hundred knights on a flanking movement through this Muradál Pass you've discovered and attack Miramamolín's headquarters directly. But only after Lopez de Haro's men have closed with the enemy," he added. "You can leave your Segovian and Ávilan detachments behind so they can fill in your void on Lopez de Haro's right flank."

The Christian armies attacked at dawn. Streaming down Dogslip Pass unopposed, they quickly amassed their forces into the planned formations, wondering, all the time, why the Moors were allowing them to deploy without any harassing action. The reason became clear as the Christians started marching south, towards the Hollow of Tolosa, in full battle order. The Moors were thick upon the horizon, as far as the eye could see. Their crescent formation gave Alfonso and his Commanders pause; it was, they realized with some trepidation, a classic deployment of forces with a built-in enveloping potential. Alfonso's narrow columns would be hopelessly engulfed the farther they advanced. They were literally walking into a trap and it was now too late to pull back. The crescent's pincers had started to close in on them.

The shock troops in Lopez de Haro's spearhead took the brunt of the first encounter. Although the Vizcayan foot soldiers fought valiantly, they were soon overwhelmed by sheer numbers. Scores of Vizcayans fell during the first few moments of combat before any knights could come to their rescue. The Aragonese cavalry on the left flank and the Ávilan and Segovian cavalry detachments on the right were desperately trying to keep the horns of the enemy's crescent formations from closing in on the Christian army in the center.

From atop a hill, Alfonso observed the gathering debacle with mounting dismay. Turning to his aide, Ximenez de Rada, he cried hopelessly: "All is lost. You and I will die here today!" to which the feisty cleric responded: "Not at all, Your Majesty!" So saying, he spurred his mount and hurled himself into the thick of battle, like some latter-day Turpin, leaving the cowering Alfonso to stew in his own fears.

Sancho and his two hundred lances, had by now traversed the length of the Muradál pass and reached its southern opening. Taking it all in, Sancho's mind began to weave a web of meaning around the spectacle before him. He watched as the Vizcayan center crumbled under a wall of Muslim humanity while the knights behind them began to falter, confronted by a crushing number of enemy warriors. It was now or never.

Swords raised on high and shouting "*Santiago y cierra España!*" Sancho and his *irrintzi*-howling knights charged the palisades surrounding the purple tent on the small hillock. Encouraged by their King's voice and example, the Navarran forces lunged forward, the dust of so many palfreys darkening the skies. The superior weight and strength of the Navarran knights' warhorses bore down on the Africans' light cavalry like scythes through wheat, the fury of the encounter taking horses and men to ground. The tumult and the confusion of battle cries drowned the groans of the fallen and the trampled, the knights' once-resplendent armor soon smudged by dust and blood, crest plumages shorn. Slowly, inexorably, the tide of battle flowed towards the scarlet tent, on which they were now closing fast.

Turning and wheeling with his customary agility, Iñaki cut a swath through the masses of Moors in front of him, dealing sweeping blows first with his mace, then with his battle-ax, and finally with his sword, parrying every blow aimed at him. Slashing through the perimeter troops, the Navarrans lunged at Miramamolín's elite, camel-mounted cavalry guarding the chain fence encircling the palisade. The original height advantage enjoyed by the Africans sitting atop their tall beasts was quickly leveled when the Navarrans switched from swords to maces with which they bludgeoned the camels' legs with telling blows.

Sancho was the first to reach the perimeter chain. It was a joy to behold, the stalwart Navarran galloping forward into the sunlight on his black Andalusian charger, hair streaming in the wind, mouth set. With powerful mace blows, he severed the chain links, opening a pathway to Miramamolín's tent. Iñaki was not far behind.

Afraid that the Christians were about to breech his innermost line of defense, the young Miramamolín panicked. Observing in consternation his elite Berbers' defensive wall crumble, the Caliph jumped onto his swift Arabian steed and abandoned the fray, fleeing south, first to Bailén, then to far-off Jaén, by nightfall. Had he looked back as he sped off, he might have recognized the assailants leading the charge as the two Navarran giants who had once helped him defeat the rebels in his Rif Mountains only a dozen years earlier.

With their leader's flight, the formidable Almohades force crumbled. When word that their leader had abandoned the field spread among the Moorish ranks, they tried to disengage. So disorganized and chaotic was their retreat that the Christians succeeded in utterly destroying the once-invincible force.

That valiant Navarran flanking charge at Navas de Tolosa was to be the defining moment in the Iberian Peninsula's long, drawn-out Reconquest of their land. Everything after that battle would be an anticlimax. In a missive to Sancho's sister, Blanca, Alfonso's wife would later acknowledge that the victory was, in large measure, due to Sancho's gallant effort. As for personal booty, Sancho asked for only one thing: the links of the chain that had surrounded Miramamolín's tent, which he had breached on his final assault. He would take them back with him and hang them from the walls of the Chapter Chapel of Roncevaux, a memento of the single, most glorious feat of arms in Iberia's eight hundred-year Crusade to push the Moors back to Africa. Those chains would henceforth replace the double-headed eagle in Navarre's coat-of-arms.

Besides their share of the booty, Sancho granted each and every one of his battling knights the privilege of incorporating an inverted crescent on their family coat-of-arms in commemoration of their gallant contribution to Islam's resounding defeat at Navas de Tolosa. Iñaki was granted the privilege of sporting not one but two inverted crescents on his arms, one for his brave intervention at Navas de Tolosa, the other at Acre, in the Holy Land. Iñaki would eventually earn several fiefdoms that would make him a rich man.

The young shepherd who had revealed to Iñaki the secret Muradal passage was not forgotten when the glory and the booty were being parceled out. Following Sancho's suggestion, Alfonso granted the shepherd the noble title of 'Cabeza de Vaca' in memory of the cow's skull he had used to show the Navarrans the concealed entrance to the Muradal Pass, of such signal importance to the battle. Three centuries later, a descendant of that very shepherd would become one of the most daring Conquistadors of the New World.

BOOK III
THE WANING KINGDOM

"The present of past things is the memory."

—St. Augustine
Confessions

Chapter 35

A Gentleman Farmer

1343

"We've about run out of room for any more inverted crescents in our escutcheon!" commented Fortún lightheartedly to his wife. "So I brought you these, instead," said the young lord of Agorreta, upending a knapsack full of jewels, gold coins and other silver artifacts on their bedspread. "The booty was grand this time, as you can see," he said, beaming at Arantxa. "It turned out to be a good war, after all."

Already in his mid twenties, the lanky, broad-shouldered man had inherited his father's Basque features, complete with a prominent nose, a square, jutting jaw and a bowlegged stance epitomizing the archetypal dare of his defiant race.

Arantxa, buried her hands in the spoils and tossed them up in the air gleefully, dazzled by the trove. She could just see herself wearing the glittering jewelry at Count Lacarra's Christmas ball in Pamplona, the cynosure of envious eyes. It would be a delightful stroke of one-upmanship, she reflected, as she tried on a heavy gold necklace of fanciful Damascene design. More gratifying, still, she could now boast of being married to a man who had earned his knighthood in battle like so many of his forebears.

"I'm so proud of you!" she said, embracing her husband. "First the knighting, now this!" Between repeated kisses, she managed to add: "But most of all, my love, I'm thankful that you've come home unscathed."

Fortún had just returned from the latest Crusade in *al-Andalus*, fighting Moors under the banner of Philip d'Evreux, his liege lord and king. He had been knighted on the eve of the final assault on Algeciras, being the first to scale the

Moorish ramparts and hoist the Navarran emblem on the flagpole of the fortress' highest tower. It seemed to run in the family, this getting there in time to reap the glory and the laurels. Alfonso of Castile was not overjoyed to recognize the emblematic chains of Navarre fluttering in the muggy Andalusian breeze. Evreux could only gloat at his peer's discomfiture.

Philip d'Evreux had been the latest in a long line of French monarchs to rule Navarre. What Charlemagne could not achieve by force of arms six centuries earlier had been accomplished by dint of diplomacy. When Sancho el Fuerte died without an heir, the Navarran scepter passed on to his sister Blanca, whose marriage to the Count of Champagne and Brie marked the beginning of a long and unfulfilling dalliance between Navarre and France that was to last several rudderless centuries. Resenting the French encroachment, the lords of Navarre managed to enforce their ancient *Fueros* rights, franchises not unlike those of their coeval Magna Carta in England. The Navarran *ricos-homes* proudly proclaimed that "each one of them was equal to the king and that, together, they could achieve more than he." They offered grudging obeisance to the French monarch on condition that he maintain and respect their liberties and privileges. "And if not, not!" read the brazen *Fueros* document.

A century had already elapsed since Sancho el Fuerte's death when the Valois inherited the French scepter from the Capets. The lords of Navarre demanded some measure of autonomy from the throne of St. Louis, requesting that Juana II, a direct descendant of their beloved Blanca, inherit the Navarran scepter. Her consort, Philip d'Evreux, appealed to them as well, for he, too, was descended from the revered Navarran queen.

Though his Capetien predecessors had treated the Vascon kingdom with benign neglect, Evreux took to Navarre with gracious good nature, taking a keen interest in cultivating his new domain. He succeeded in goading and cajoling it into the Fourteenth Century, injecting the knightly ideals of French chivalry into the Iberian Crusade, dubbed the "*Reconquest*" by the locals. Backed by several hundred Navarran knights, King Evreux organized a small expedition of Norman, English, French, and Bohemian men-at-arms to come to the aid of Castile in her latest attempt to dislodge the Africans from southern Iberia. But the Moors were still too well entrenched to be budged from their enclaves in *al-Andalus* just yet and, like so many earlier attempts, this one, too, fizzled out with a whimper. Philip d'Evreux gloried all too briefly in the sight of Fortún's flying banner in the Algeciras fortress, for he was struck down shortly after by an early strain of the Black Death.

Fortún and most of the mountain men-at-arms and foot soldiers in his small mesnie were luckier than their king, managing to survive both plague and scimitar during their brief adventure in *al-Andalus*. They returned home to an exuberant welcome in late October, unscathed and weighed down with handsome booty. A short pilgrimage to nearby Roncevaux was organized, attended by the inhabitants of the mountain valleys around Esteribar. On their way to the shrine, the returning warriors paused at the foot of Roland's cross, where they laid wreaths in honor of their fallen king. After a *Te Deum* Mass at the Royal Collegiate, the combatants laid their arms at the foot of the altar under the Virgin's benign gaze. Religious ceremonies thus concluded, the warriors gathered round the hearth at Gasteluzar for three days of festivities and merrymaking, in celebration of their safe return. Brief and unavailing though the war against the Moors had been, it had turned out to be a good one with negligible casualties and ample booty.

"The views from Algeciras are grand," Fortún was explaining to Arantxa after the revelers had left for their homes. With the Great Hall all to themselves, they lay on a huge bearskin rug in front of the fire, surrounded by half a dozen sleeping hounds. "It's across the bay from that huge rock they call Gibraltar. On a clear day, you can even see Africa across the strait from there," he elaborated. "But I'd sure hate to live there. I dislike that southern climate," commented Fortún with a grimace. "With that heat and that humidity, I'm not surprised people contract those awful diseases. You should have seen the king's body all covered with black, festering sores. And the stench! It was unbearable! Even the priests were reluctant to come near him in his agony. It was ghastly!" Fortún shuddered at the reminiscence.

Arantxa stroked Fortún's hair, occasionally leaning over to kiss him. "It is all over now, my love," she said softly, threading her fingers through his long brown locks, streaked auburn by the reflected firelight. "Get it all out of your mind. You are back home now, safe and sound. You won't have to leave again for a long, long time."

"I hope you're right," he answered idly. "There are too many things to do around the manor. I noticed some of the barn roofs and fences need mending. And the meadows cry out for a good scything. Amazing, what a month without farmhands will do!"

"You have other reasons to want to stay home, my love," she said softly, looking deep into his eyes. She had been trying to keep the secret for the right moment. Feeling it had now finally come, she said. "You will soon become a father," she whispered in his ear. "I'll need you by my side when the child arrives."

Fortún sat bolt upright, his face gleaming in the reflection of the flames. He had noticed a special glow about Arantxa the moment he walked in the house. Something about the sparkle in her eyes, the luster of her hair, he wasn't quite sure what. At first he attributed it to the heightened fondness that wells up in one's heart after a long absence from a loved one.

He had first met her on a visit to the lord of Roncal's palace a year earlier and remembered being swept off his feet by Arantxa's charm and rare beauty. Their lightning courtship, uncommon those days, was followed by a fabulous ceremony which was still the talk of the valleys a year later. They made the ideal couple, everyone agreed; he, a handsome, well-heeled *gentilhombre*, she the daughter of the highly regarded lord of Roncal. The young lord of Agorreta had chosen well indeed, winning the hand of the fairest in the mountain valleys and adding, while at it, a smart dowry to his already considerable landholdings.

He was madly in love with this fair, winsome woman, adored her youthful, innocent smile and the adoration he could read in her eyes. He kept pinching himself to make sure it was not a dream, feeling wholly undeserving of such a jewel. And now, to top it all off, she was about to give him the greatest gift of all– an heir! The continuation of the Agorreta lineage would be assured. His joy was boundless. For the longest time he remained speechless, holding her in his arms, kissing and caressing her with infinite tenderness. Finally, he spoke:

"We shall name him Sancho, after Navarre's most illustrious king. Our Sancho, too, will grow up to be a great warrior!"

Arantxa smiled. "But you don't even know if it's going to be a boy!"

"Oh, but I do!" he answered with conviction. "Men can sense these things," he added, gently resting his hand on her stomach, caressing it with ineffable pride and tenderness.

The familiar sounds of the manor woke Fortún up early the next morning. Somewhere in a nearby courtyard, a cock crowed irresolutely at the gathering dawn. Through the open window, Fortún could see that the fogbank that had enveloped the Pyrenean foothills the night before still swaddled the manor of Agorreta in a dream of mists. Somewhere beyond the little stream at the foot of the hill several cowbells tolled their muffled notes in the early meadow, plaintively reminding the dairymaid that it was past milking time. A dog of nameless breed barked at someone riding an ox-drawn cart up the hill along the rutted footpath behind Jaureguizar and now almost directly under the master bedroom window. Still wrapped in slumber, Fortún was happy to hear Basque voices wafting up through the open window. He knew that he was back home again.

When the smell of fried eggs and *txistorra* sausage drifted up from the kitchen, Fortún knew it was time to get up. Alberto, the steward of the manor, was already sitting at the table when Fortún came down for breakfast.

"Mornin', Sire," mumbled the steward. "I hope you had a good night's rest." Alberto was Fortún's head administrator, seneschal of his several manors scattered around Baztán and Labourd. He was a stocky, powerfully-built man with thin, mousy hair and a ready smile. For years now, Alberto had looked after the Agorretas' properties and livestock, upholding the family's rights, defending their franchises.

"*Egun on,*" responded Fortún, returning the greeting. He noticed that his steward had been busily adding numbers scribbled on a translucent sheepskin, preparing to give his lord an accounting of the manor's finances during his absence. Fortún could not help noticing Alberto's hands. Like callused, unfeeling mallets, they bespoke a lifetime of glove-less handball matches. In his younger years he had been that sport's champion in the Esteribar and Erro valleys. Fortún remembered watching him bite his swollen fingers, trying to keep the inflammation down so he could finish the game. There was something stoic about ignoring pain, never complaining, not even grimacing. It was so Vascon, he thought.

"How is Leonor?" asked Fortún solicitously. The steward's wife had taken ill on the eve of his Algeciras expedition and they had to whisk her off to Pamplona for medical attention after the village barber's potion of wormwood and foxglove nearly did her in.

"As you may recall, she was suffering from fierce headaches, but she's recovered now. Some Jewish physic in Iruñea prescribed a draught of beech and willow bark that seemed to ease her pain. She's alright now," he said. Then he added, "I'm afraid I can't say the same for the bailiff's youngest son, Sire."

"What's wrong with him?" asked Fortún. The bailiff was Fortun's trusted deputy, whose ability to read and write inevitably made him the chief law officer of the manor.

"He died, Sire. Bitten by a rabid dog," explained Alberto. "It was dreadful," he added, grimacing. "They tried everything the barber suggested, wiped his wound with cobwebs, soaked it with elm-bark juice, even hung holly branches from the corners of his room, like they do with calves when they come down with black spots. Nothing seemed to work" Alberto was obviously distressed by the memory. "The hiccups started soon after, then the convulsions. When he developed a horror for water they dunked his head in the river to force him to drink. Nearly drowned the poor chap. Ghastly! The frothing at the mouth and the madness followed soon after. They had to restrain him to prevent any further misfortune. It was a horrible death."

Fortún was shaken by the report and made a mental note to offer his condolences to the bailiff. He'd palliate his loss by raising his salary twelve Sanchetes a year. He'd also allot him extra fodder for his horse for good measure. Then, come Christmastime, he'd present his wife with a new fur coat or something.

"Any other important happenings during my absence?" asked Fortún, hesitantly.

"Well," said Alberto reluctantly, "other than the Arteaga girl being fined for premarital sex and Tiburcio's bricking up his wife alive, things were otherwise calm and uneventful during your absence."

"Bricked her up?" blurted Fortún, incredulous.

"Yes, Sire. He caught her cheating on him with one of the Ulzama farmhands during the hay harvest. Caught them *in flagrante delicto*, he did, up in his *sabaiao* hayloft. I had to refer the case to the Royal Courts in Iruñea for high justice. Last I heard, it's still pending consideration. You know how slowly the wheels of justice turn in that city."

There was something sober and imperturbable about Alberto that Fortún found inestimable. He was the perfect steward, efficient, unflappable. He ran a good Hallmote, presiding equitably over the manorial court. He was also a trustworthy collector of fees and dues, an effective enforcer of labor services and handler of inheritance legalities. Above all, he was honest and quite effective at reaping profits, doing everything in his power to increase his lord's patrimony.

Fortún was glad to get back to his chores as lord of the manor, happy to resume the life of a gentleman farmer. He took great pride in husbanding his considerable resources, looking over his steward's shoulder, overseeing the wheat harvest and the sale of timber from his forests, planning the transhumance of his large flocks of sheep and cattle, the exploitation of his grain mills. He loved the land, loved to occasionally dirty his hands in the rich, loamy soil, smell the sweet scent of the Navarran heath in the summertime. The earth may not have been quite as rich as that of Gascogne across the mountains, but this was his earth, this his native land. It had belonged to his family since God knew when. Long before Roland was defeated in these very mountains, long before the Romans came, his forefathers had already settled in them. And, like his forebears before him, he was fiercely proud of being an Agorreta. His beautiful young wife was now with child, *his* son, an Agorreta. Fortún's eyes would mist over as he lay awake in bed, nights, overwhelmed by the joy of onrushing fatherhood.

The child's arrival only added to the familial bliss and bustle. It turned out to be a fine, healthy boy as Fortún had predicted. The manor's midwife had commented on the good looks of the child, inappropriately remarking that the child was too good looking to be a boy. Fortún would lean over the child's crib for hours on end, watching him make gurgling noises, which, he was sure, were the first signs of paternal recognition. He was amused by Arantxa's motherly concern and hawk-eyed vigilance, and made a game of timing her response every time the child stirred. He couldn't wait to teach him the fine arts of hawking and hunting, and, of course, the arts of war too. He would need those if he wanted to get around in the world.

Life in the manor rolled on as placidly as the little brook that flowed along the bottom of the hill, below Gasteluzar, the manor's fortress-home. As it had been since time beyond memory, the cycles and rhythms of planting and gathering were still guided by the moon's waxing and waning. The slaughter of the fatted sows still came with the first frost, in late October, also the time when the doves flew over the mountain passes, on their migration south. Lambing in early spring was followed by shearing around St. John's and, at the drop of a hat, there would be hawking and hunting. And woe to the villein who overused the forest mast and deprived the lord's favorite hunting quarry, the wild boar.

But despite all those earthly pleasures, Fortún soon began to weary of the humdrum, predictable life of the manor. Hawking and hunting were fun but there were things in life other than pastimes and hobbies. He had been in so many wars and skirmishes that he was beginning to miss the thrill of danger, the thunder of hooves, the sound of maces clanging on armor. A warrior without a good fray was like a summer squall without lightning, unfulfilling. Without wars to fight or ransoms to secure, the life of a gentleman farmer was starting to weigh on Fortún's spirit.

He was not alone in his restlessness. The lords of some of the other mountain valleys around were starting to get restless as well. They would come to visit and sit around the fire, play *Mus* over a bottle of hard cider, recount stories about the good old rough-and-tumble days, turn nostalgic when recounting increasingly improbable war stories.

Rumors were rife about companies of rogue French and English knights who, equally bored by the inactivity of peace, had banded together to maraud the French countryside, ravaging and pillaging the land for sport and lucre. These Free Companies, as they came to be named, were led by men like the Norman Bertrand duGuesclin, and the Englishman Hugh Calverley, restless knights both who had fought gallantly in past Crusades and local skirmishes and were now wearied by the drudgery of peace. It was their twisted belief that if it was peace one sought, then, by God, there had to be tumult first, that it may die. Life without war, Fortún's friends concurred between sips of stout mead and heady hard cider, was becoming dull and tiresome. To make matters worse, they were not getting any younger.

Peace for other knights was not only dull; it was penurious, as well. Fortún, who had inherited the family lands and titles, was fortunate enough to garner all the resources needed to live comfortably as lord of his several manors, able to keep his wife in the style to which she had grown accustomed. But deep down, the humdrum life of a gentleman farmer with its bland duties and tedious chores had started to bore him. His restless spirit stirred inside him; he even briefly considered joining the Free Companies. But he brushed the tempting thought aside on sober reflection. He knew he would never stoop to join those ruffians in their wanton ways although some of his friends were now seriously considering it. Surely there had to be other more noble and chivalrous endeavors, especially now that he was a father. There was something sobering about fatherhood, he reflected, a new and awesome responsibility, a sacred trust with one's own progeny.

CHAPTER 36

CRECY

1346

It had been two years since the battle of Algeciras. Having reached an entente with the Moors, Castile and Aragon had turned on each other, leaving Navarre in an unusual state of suspended quiescence. Across the Pyrenees, however, relations between England and France had soured. While soaring cathedrals were going up, the basest of political intrigues were being hatched. The transition of French power from the Capets to the Valois finally lit the fuse of the Hundred-Year war. Edward III of England laid claim to the throne of France, invoking his mother's primogeniture. Citing the Salic law, the French disabused him of his pretensions and prepared for war.

Weary of France's threatening to recapture his Aquitainean and Angevinian possessions in the Continent, Edward decided to take matters into his own hands. In July of 1346, he landed a formidable army near Cherbourg, with the avowed intention of taking Paris and claiming the throne of France. Finding strong opposition along the way, the English army veered north toward Calais instead.

The tension could be felt as far south as Gascogne, then controlled by the English. Fortún's tenants in his ultra-Pyrenean possessions of Azcain felt uneasy, wondering how long it would take Navarre to be sucked into the maelstrom. The burning question, if that were to happen, was towards whose side their queen would tilt. Fortún did not have long to find out.

It was the end of July when Queen Juana's governor in Pamplona summoned all able-bodied knights and their mesnies to arms. The Queen's possessions in

Normandy were being overrun and pillaged by the English juggernaut and, after much soul-searching, she gave in to the insistent entreaties of King Philippe, her French cousin and neighbor. In a moment of weakness and misplaced loyalty, she decided to commit her Norman and Navarran forces to the French cause.

His fief's feudal contract left Fortún little choice but to obey his queen's orders. He had misgivings about fighting the English, but duty called. Besides, he reasoned, bearing arms was more fun than counting sheep any time. Though he would hardly admit it to Arantxa, he was simply itching to get back in the saddle again, don full armor and lead his men into battle, this time in a real, honest-to-goodness war. Bidding his family farewell, he rode off with his mesnie of a dozen mounted men-at-arms and twice that many foot soldiers, all recruited from his lands in Esteribar, Baztan and Labourd. That was what was expected of feudal lords, he reflected.

It was late August when the opposing armies closed near the forest of Crecy, on the outskirts of Ponthieu, across the Somme. The French had gathered an army of unruly mercenaries, bands of rustic militia and feudal nobles with their disgruntled bumpkins in tow. As bad luck would have it, Fortún's mesnie was thrown in with a group of mismatched Savoyard mercenaries and rebellious Genoese crossbowmen, all hastily thrown together to form the shock division of the French army's vanguard. There had been no thought of matching skills or coordinating efforts, certainly no time for joint operations to train troops of such disparate origin, language and disposition. It was the proverbial foul-up and the results would soon show it.

The French three-to-one numerical advantage over the English boded ill for England's Edward III's hosts. It turned out to be, however, not numbers but tactics and discipline that ultimately carried the day. Crecy was a disaster of magnificent proportions for the French. The panache and dazzling valor of French chivalry was no match for the discipline and superb generalship of the English. Edward, the young Prince of Wales, who had just turned sixteen and been recently knighted by his father, fought with a gallantry that did his father and countrymen proud. The young warrior, fondly known as the Black Prince for the color of his armor, was to bathe in the glory of England henceforth. His later exploits in France would only enhance his already exalted standing.

It was the first time in the annals of chivalry that a group of lowly foot soldiers, albeit armed with powerful longbows, would devastate a superbly armed force of mounted men-at-arms. Those, like Fortún, who had their horses shot out from under them early in the fray, were the lucky ones. If they were fortunate enough to be captured alive for ransom, some of them would live to tell the tale. After his mount had been brought down by a Welshman's arrow, Fortún continued fighting valiantly on foot for a while, managing to bring down several Englishmen with his swinging sword before being, himself, struck down by a mail-rending sword stroke.

As he lay on the ground, agonizing over a broken ribcage, bleeding profusely from a gash over his left eye, he happened to look up at his assailant. Embossed on his adversary's black leather shield, he detected the royal arms of England. In a flash of *déjà-vu*, Fortún's feverish thoughts turned to a story his father loved to tell about an ancestor of his who had once crossed lances with English knights in a tournament in Pamplona. Fortún marvelled at how history repeated itself as he lay there in pain, waiting to be finished off.

He was lucky to come away from Crecy with his life. His valor and seriously damaged condition had moved the Prince to spare his life, granting him the grace of another day. Fortún passed out from loss of blood shortly after. It was not hard for him to play dead when, in the aftermath of battle, Welsh foot soldiers came rummaging for valuables among the dead and dying. He almost lost a finger when one of them forcibly ripped his wedding ring from it. When evening fell and the battlefield had quieted down to the pitiful groans of dying men around him, Fortún struggled to open his eyes.

Everything was a blur; the blood that had caked over his good eye prevented him from seeing. He was convinced that he'd lost his eyesight altogether. The thought was almost as devastating as the crushing weight on his chest. He knew that he was in a bad way. With great effort, he managed to wipe the dried blood off of his good eye, only to witness the death and spoliation around him. The looters had abandoned the field, leaving behind a pitiful dirge of death groans and lamentations. He decided it was safe to move on. With great difficulty, he wobbled up onto his feet and started groping his way in the dark, stumbling over broken bodies and dismembered limbs, wading through all the gore around him. Thirsty and disoriented from loss of blood, he wandered aimlessly in the moonlit night, across fields crisscrossed by intimidating hedgerows. It was almost dawn when he finally stumbled into a farmhouse on the outskirts of a small village. A broken sign at a crossroads proclaimed it to be Abbeville.

Alerted by his hounds' frantic barking, an elderly farmer emerged from behind a shed, wielding a menacing pitchfork. Fortún, exhausted and near shock, collapsed on the ground at his feet. Seeing the knight's sorry condition, the farmer took pity on him and dragged him into the farmhouse, laying him on a straw pallet by the hearth. After being awakened by the commotion, his wife, a rotund country woman with a kindly face, started cleaning and dressing his wounds as best she could, then fed him a hot broth, which brought Fortún halfway back to consciousness. Fortún could only express his gratitude with a weak smile.

He had noticed that the couple spoke a different French dialect than the one in Gascogne. Through their rattled utterances, he slowly, dimly perceived the drift of their conversation. A few days passed before he could manage to communicate with them in his own dreadful French. "*Il parle comme une vache iberienne,*" he overheard the angular woman jocosely whispering to her husband one day. Fortún was amused by her comment about his abominable French accent. Villeins, like children, always seem to speak their mind, he noticed, without beating around the bush.

It was during his convalescence that he learned about the French king's narrow escape from the battlefield. Philippe had fled, leaving behind eighty banners, the bodies of several princes, countless knights and an appalling number of common fighting men. "It was an unmitigated disaster," the farmer admitted ruefully. There was a tinge of shame and reproach in his admission. Trying to commiserate with him, Fortún commented: "Kings sometimes start frivolous wars so future generations of schoolchildren can memorize the names of famous Generals." The sarcasm went over the farmer's head. Seeing the blank expression on his host's face, Fortún pressed on with his reflections: "It was a battle to end all battles. With Crecy, Edward and Philippe will have left their scent in the history books."

Fortún remained with the kindly couple until his chest had stopped hurting when he sneezed and there was no further need for poultices. He discovered that wearing a patch over his left eye relieved the annoying double vision that the blow to the head had occasioned. The eye patch, he realized, affected his depth perception but he didn't have to go hawking or jousting anytime soon, so that would only be a small inconvenience.

When it came time to leave, Fortún borrowed a nag from his farmer friend, promising to repay him for it just as soon as he got home. The Welsh robbers had stripped him of his purse, leaving him in the awkward predicament of having to borrow a few sous from his compassionate hosts to get him started on his long journey home. Since he had to travel through unfriendly territory to get home, he wisely chose to leave his armor behind, as collateral for his debt, donning instead a frayed woolen jerkin, some patched woolen trousers and a pair of wooden shoes that the farmer gave him. Completing his rustic attire was a knapsack containing a loaf of hard bread and a slab of dry sheep cheese. A goatskin wine bag filled with slightly rancid wine completed his baggage. He must have looked a fright, he thought to himself, but the disguise would get him through the unfriendly territory ahead. After embracing his hosts warmly and promising to keep in touch, Fortún mounted his nag and spurred it on its way. As he turned to wave one last farewell he saw the couple waving back at him and was struck by the thought that kindness and generosity must be universal human traits, and that country folk, like this pair from Abbeville, had to be the very salt of the earth.

News of the Crecy disaster traveled far and fast, and Arantxa was greatly distressed on hearing about the rout. She felt a wrenching loneliness on realizing that she might now be a widow. Some wives never found out with certainty the fate of their loved ones; they simply never returned. That was the worst part of it, the not knowing. Arantxa despaired of ever seeing Fortún again, worrying about how she'd manage his estates, how she would bring up young Sancho all by herself without a father's love and guidance. Any day now she would have to arrange for a funeral Mass and don mourning black, the dreary garb she would have to wear for the rest of her life. She knew she would never marry again. It was not the done thing. Widowhood was a grim and cruel fate at any time in a young woman's life, but in Navarre it was appallingly permanent and irreversible.

One gray fall afternoon, three months after he had left, Fortún rode into his manor of Agorreta. His vassals eyed him shiftily as they watched him ride into the village on his swayback nag and beggar's attire. The suspicious lot thought they were seeing an apparition as they ogled their lord's homely attire and the dark patch over his eye. Their gawking made him uncomfortable, arousing in him the half-forgotten feeling of inadequacy he had felt as he lay sprawled out on the wet moss in the forest of Crecy.

But he was not really concerned about his appearance; others bore such scars as badges of honor. He would go back to the life of a gentleman farmer, sit back and watch his family grow. This was not the time for self-pity, he tried to reassure himself. But as his nag cantered up the rise to the fortified manor house of Gasteluzar, he became keenly aware that, though only thirty-five, he would probably never again ride into battle with that damnable double vision. The thought depressed him. For him, the battlefield had always been the crucible and ultimate measure of manhood. The thought of not being able to wield a lance or swing a sword again hit him, making him feel that he was now but half a man.

He entered the main gate, still trying to push the emasculating thought aside. When Arantxa saw him struggling up the steps to the Great Hall she rushed to him, clasping him tightly to her breast.

"Oh, thank God you're alive!" she cried with irrepressible emotion. She had noticed the patch over his eye, knew what had happened without the asking. But he was alive and that was what counted.

"We had all given you up for dead," she said, eyes still wide with wonder and disbelief. "I even ordered votive masses for your soul!" She was crying uncontrollably now, tears of joy streaming down her cheeks. Wracked by the same emotion, Fortún held her against him, burying his head on her shoulder lest she notice the moistness in his eyes. Her effusive welcome had been as heart-warming as he had dreamed it would be, all those miserable months in France. He could not help noticing her svelte figure, her waist still almost as slim as when they first met in Roncál. He had married one attractive woman, he thought. She looked beautiful even in mourning black.

"Where is my son?" he asked, pulling away from her embrace momentarily. He was almost afraid to ask lest some misfortune had befallen him during his absence. "Is everything all right?"

"Sancho is just fine," Arantxa answered reassuringly, a gleam of motherly pride lighting up her face. "He is getting to be a fine looking boy, big and strong like his father." Arantxa paused before adding: "Mother came to keep me company while you were away. She's been such a comfort and solace to me in your absence!"

Fortún was greatly relieved. "Can I see him now?"

She led him into their chambers on the far end of the daised platform of the Great Hall. There, in a small bed set up beside the large canopied master bed, lay a pink-cheeked boy sleeping peaceably under a quilt bearing the embroidered arms of Agorreta. Fortún leaned over and kissed the child's broad forehead peeking from under his blond tousled hair. "You will be a strong Agorreta, my son," he whispered to the sleeping child, as if pronouncing an oracle. "You will pick up where your father left off," he added almost inaudibly. Arantxa felt a sudden twinge of sadness in her heart on overhearing the self-pitying remark.

After gazing at his son for a long time, Fortún straightened up, held Arantxa in his arms. "Thank you, sweet wife," he whispered, looking deep into her blue eyes. "You made me the happiest man on earth when you gave me this son!"

Fortún withdrew into his manor and his inner world those first few years after Crecy. The scourge that had claimed the Navarran kings' life in Algeciras several years earlier had spread throughout Europe with a vengeance. The Black Plague, as it was being called, had gripped the land with dreadful virulence two years after Crecy and was to remain for several years to come, wiping out a full third of Europe's population, indiscriminately scything rich and poor alike. Unbeknownst to Fortún and Arantxa—or anyone else, for that matter—the coolness of their mountain retreat would hold the Black Death at bay. Following the horror of the plague itself, an unspeakable hunger and famine desolated the European countryside. In such pathetic straits, few even thought about warfare, the instinct of survival overwhelming whatever petty squabbling their kings may have had among themselves.

Chapter 37

Besieged

1366

In 1349, three years after the battle of Crecy, the queen of Navarre relinquished her scepter to her son, Charles II, a king soon to earn the dubious sobriquet of *le Mauvais*, "the evil one." Slight of build and quick of wit, his sensuous mouth could just as quickly curl into a smile as tighten into a thin, cruel line. Equally disconcerting, his gray-blue eyes could one moment come alive with a jovial sparkle, then abruptly darken to a withering gaze. There was never a unexciting moment in Navarre during his reign, his twisted character contriving to embroil her in every European conflict of the day. Charles' gauche complicity in the murder of the Constable of France earned him the French King's enmity and his incarceration in the Louvre. His detainment triggered a secret accord of mutual defense between England and Navarre, reigniting the spark that rekindled the smoldering hostilities between England and France.

"It's a good thing our king is cooling his heels in some French dungeon," commented a relieved Fortún to his wife, on first hearing about the massive army the Black Prince had landed in Bordeaux in the summer of 1356. "He'd surely have gotten us involved in another of his harebrained scuffles!"

News of the subsequent French disaster at Poitiers was soon to follow. Fighting with the same resplendent incompetence as at Crecy, the French knights seemed intent on forgetting about their armor's vulnerability to English longbow arrows. The losses at Poitiers turned out to be even more appalling than at Crecy, the English dealing French chivalry a nigh-mortal blow. The French King was captured by the Black Prince and unceremoniously whisked off to England.

Things simply fell apart after that. More ruinous even than the king's ransom of three million gold crowns was the treaty of Bretigny itself, which surrendered over a quarter of France's western lands to England, territory extending from the Loire to the Pyrenees. France paid a heavy price indeed for her delirium of *grandeur* at Poitiers.

During that debacle, Charles of Navarre managed to slip out of prison unnoticed. Foiling his jailers after eighteen months of prison spoke volumes about his devious and cunning ways. On learning of his king's escape, Fortún sarcastically remarked to his wife: "*Hierba mala nunca muere,*" reminded of the old Iberian aphorism that crabgrass never dies.

"You should be thankful he was in jail all this time," Arantxa reminded him. "That kept him from entangling you in the Poitiers disaster!" she added, shuddering at the reminiscence of her husband's earlier nasty experience at Crecy.

Settled in his Navarran eyrie, Fortún de Agorreta had long since recovered from his despondency after the Crecy calamity. His double vision still bothered him but he was too much of a stoic to let that impediment turn him into a recluse. He learned to enjoy the peaceable life of landed gentry, busied himself with the administration of his fief, dispensed justice in the Hallmotes of his several manors, made the occasional trip to the king's Court in Pamplona to settle his fiefs' accounts. It would have struck him odd to have overheard his wife's prayers thanking God for his marred vision. She considered his impairment a godsend, having kept him grounded all those years, helping with their son's upbringing. She knew that a father's admonitions and good example were critical in molding a son's character, for a woman could bring forth any number of sons into the world but it took a father to make men out of them.

Fortún never lost hope of one day recovering his normal vision and reverting to a more normal life. Miracles did happen sometimes, he reflected, and one was bound to visit him one of these days. Until that occurred, however, he would have to bear his cross like a man and make do with his handicap. He did not need perfect vision to pass his knowledge on to his son. Young Sancho, already a strapping lad of ten, would take over the lordship of the manor someday but he still had a wealth of things to learn besides Latin and numbers. There were other more pleasurable things in life such as hunting and falconry, of which father and son were equally fond. Their outings were slowly cementing a bond between them that would grow stronger with each passing year.

It was on one such outing in the fall of 1361 that Fortún's life would take a dramatic change. Father and son had gone hawking to Lindux, a peak overlooking Roncevaux. Fortún had been itching to try out the young peregrine he had been training for the last several months, and doves made better prey than crane at this stage of its instruction. It was the peak of the dove migrating season, when the birds abandoned their European haunts and came streaming across the Pyrenean passes in droves, on their yearly flight south. Fortún had ordered a blind set up on the eastern slope of Lindux, directly below the doves' main flight path.

"They're expecting a lot of doves this year," remarked Fortún. "Hawking will be as effortless as falling asleep. It won't be very challenging." His son failed to grasp the nuance of sportsmanship in his father's remark.

Fortún's hawk, which had cost him a small fortune, had not quite mastered the art of delivering its prey properly, dropping it, instead, willy-nilly around its owner, like so many random projectiles. Fortún was determined to break the bird of its distracting habit. They had been hawking nearly all day and the pile of dead doves at their feet attested to a successful hunt. It was getting on late afternoon and the heavy mists had started to swirl around them, impeding visibility. Fortún was waiting for the two hawks to return with their last kill before calling it a day.

Immensely proud of the way his son had handled his gyrfalcon, Fortún was admiring its power stoop into a blur of dove feathers when something suddenly slammed against his upturned face, tearing his eye patch loose. His peregrine had dropped its prey on him, blindsiding him. It took him several seconds to recover from the stinging blow, muttering his displeasure as he looked around for his missing eye patch. Still smarting from the impact, Fortún became gradually aware that there was something different about his vision. Incredulous at first, it slowly dawned on him that his double vision had miraculously vanished; no longer working at cross purposes, his eyes had regained their focus. It was almost as if a second blow were needed to undo the damage of the first.

There was much jubilation atop Lindux that afternoon. With raucous whoops and joyous *irrintzis,* father and son danced around the stack of dead doves, rejoicing on the bald mountaintop like two demented warlocks celebrating a midsummer night's rite in Sorogain. There was even greater jubilation that evening in Gasteluzar, where an impromptu celebration was organized by Arantxa to celebrate her husband's miraculous recovery. A banquet of doves was prepared in every conceivable fashion, accompanied with generous jugs of the best Campanas wine in the buttery. The merrymaking in the Great Hall lasted till the wee hours; it was not every day one was given back the gift of normal sight.

The fortuitous accident on the mountaintop of Lindux was to change their lives in ways they could never have foreseen. Though Fortún had never openly admitted it all those many years, he had sorely missed the active, rough-and-tumble life of a knight. It took the recovery of his normal eyesight for all that pent-up ennui to surface. The time for a change in life could not have come at a more propitious moment, it turned out, for the peaceful interlude Navarre had been enjoying was about to come to an abrupt end. The dormant Hundred-Year War was about to yawn back into wakefulness, its battlefield dramatically shifting from France to Iberia.

In the year 1360, during one of his fits of schizoid rage, Pedro *el Cruel,* king of Castile, ordered his French wife, Blanche de Bourbon, imprisoned and subsequently murdered. Outraged, the King of France decided to lean in favor of Pedro's bastard half brother, Henry of Trastamara, who had been angling for the throne of Castile all along. Eager to rid his country of the scourge of the Free Companies, the French monarch was only too happy to volunteer their services to the king of Aragon and his ally, Trastamara, helping in one fell swoop the Aragonese monarch to repel Pedro *el Cruel's* latest offensive, and enhancing the bastard's chances of usurping the crown of Castile. Promised a handsome booty, the Free Company ruffians were only too happy to oblige. Because of this unhealthy allegiance, England's King Edward opted to side with Pedro *el Cruel,* considering him Castile's legitimate monarch, warts and all. The stage was set for a confrontation in the Peninsula.

Charles *le Mauvais,* who was worried about the renewed hostilities brewing between Castile and Aragon, ordered a general mobilization in Navarre. There was a certain urgency to the call to arms since the long peaceful interlude Navarre had enjoyed had dulled her knights' proverbial battle fever. The shrunken pool of warriors had to be replenished, enticed back to duty with sweetened offerings.

When the position of Seneschal to the king's castle in Cascante came available in the spring of 1362, Fortún took notice; he knew a good thing when one turned up. The castle's location in southern Navarre was particularly appealing to him. Bordering, as it did, on the fluid and uneasy Castilian frontier, it promised all the excitement he had secretly longed for. There would be enough action to revive in him the old fighting spirit. Hazards would be minimal, perhaps nothing riskier than repulsing the occasional siege, maybe even sallying forth on the odd skirmish, no more. Besides, there was an undeniable prestige attached to the position, for though his main responsibility would be the castle's defense, he would have to preside over the castle's Council of Knights and act as their deputy to the

Royal Court in Pamplona. Because of his having to report directly to his realm's counselors, perhaps even hobnob with his monarch and go hawking with him when he came visiting, Cascante sounded like the perfect position for an eager knight.

"The offer is too good to pass up," he explained to Arantxa when he finally made up his mind to accept it. "I am honor-bound to answer the king's call; I might as well choose the best position available."

Arantxa remained skeptical. She disliked the idea of his being involved in anything remotely connected with armed conflict. There had been unfortunate consequences the last time he got mixed up in that business. Besides, she had serious reservations about leaving the idyllic little valley of Esteribar for the hot, humid climate of southern Navarre. She racked her brain for a good argument against the move.

"Who is going to tend to your manorial responsibilities while you're gone?" she queried, trying, somewhat unsubtly, to discourage her obstinate husband with practical, down-to-earth arguments.

"My steward, Alberto, will be delighted to take over that responsibility," replied Fortún. "He can do it in his sleep! You know he's honest to a fault." Seeing through her obfuscation, he went on with his original argument. "What's at issue here is our family," he continued, bringing the discussion back to the subject of home. "Young Sancho is quickly outgrowing Gasteluzar. He is ten now and fast running out of lessons to learn. I can teach him all the horsemanship and falconry he will ever need but there are finer things in life he must pick up. You and I and the village priest have pretty much scraped the bottom of the barrel with our Latin and our Astronomy and our numbers. He will have a chance for a better education in the king's castle, more friends his age. The king might even get to meet him personally one day. Who knows, he may even knight him when he grows up, or grant him some privileged position in his administration, a judgeship, perhaps. One never knows about these things."

Fortún paused for her reply. With none forthcoming, he continued: "To court the Court, one must be either near it or *in* it. That, my dear Arantxa, is a fact of life. Miracles don't just happen. One must work at them. As the saying goes, "*A Dios rogando y con el mazo dando,*" reminding her of the old adage that prayer needed to be complemented with hard work.

Arantxa knew it was useless to pursue the subject any further. Like all Agorretas, her husband was headstrong and unswerving once his mind was made up. Her only consolation was that his eagerness to return to a knight's life was an unmistakable sign that he had fully regained his confidence and self-esteem. He was his old self again.

"Even if you have to get involved in a conflict, surely it'll be only against some brigands, not Pedro *el Cruel's* Castilian army, or Pedro *el Ceremonioso's* Aragonese forces," she said, with more hope than conviction. On further reflection, she added: "Then again, the way *le Mauvais* shifts allegiances these days, only God knows who you'll have to end up fighting!"

Fortún's distinguished military career against the Moors in *al-Andalus,* which earned him his knighthood a dozen years earlier, and his subsequent seasoning at Crecy, were ample credentials to land him the position. His stint as seneschal of the king's castle in Cascante promised to be a rewarding experience. Even Arantxa began to warm up to the idea. Being the spouse of the highest-ranking officer in the castle's staff appealed to her. More importantly, after several miscarriages, she was again growing big with child and had started worrying about potions and midwives. Cascante promised to be a good birthing place for the baby, considering the castle's owner, its facilities and professional help from the king's own Jewish physics, if needed.

They settled in a large apartment in the castle's keep when they arrived in Cascante. The nearby frontiers with Castile and Aragon seemed oddly quiet at first. In his inimitable fashion, *le Mauvais* had been tiptoeing around his neighbors' sensitivities, promising to Castile unstinting loyalty one day, to Aragon the next, keeping both parties off balance, never committing himself to one or the other. But his fence straddling was bound to come to an end sooner or later. Reminded of the French debacles at Crecy and Poitiers at the hand of the English, *le Mauvais* wisely decided to join the English-Castilian coalition. With epithets like "*le mauvais*" and "*el Cruel,*" the agreement finally signed between the Navarran and the Castilian seemed like a pact made in hell. Navarre was about to be swept into the maelstrom swirling anew between England and France, Castile and Aragon.

In his struggle against Aragon, Pedro *el Cruel* was delighted to gain a new and unexpected ally in Navarre. *Le Mauvais'* alliance with Castile had momentarily removed the pressure on Navarre's southern frontier, temporarily relieving her border castles of their original defensive mission. But events were about to change all that. Early in 1363, Pedro *el Cruel* decided to mount an offensive against Aragon, in hopes of preventing his half-brother, Trastamara, from crossing the Pyrenees with his dreaded Free Companies. A pincer movement around Zaragoza was planned: Castilian forces would thrust north, while *Le Mauvais'* Navarrans would sweep east, across their common frontier with Aragon.

Fortún had hardly settled in Cascante when he received his marching orders. The call to arms happened so fast that he barely had time to unpack or bid his family a proper farewell. Arantxa and young Sancho saw him part with deep foreboding. Leaving a small detachment behind, he moved out with a dozen knights and as many men-at-arms to join the siege of Sos, a fortified Aragonese town several dozen miles north of Cascante.

After a brief and successful siege, Fortún's force was ordered to take Ejea, along the road to Zaragoza. Seeing his capital threatened by the approaching Navarrans, the king of Aragon sent an urgent plea to the king of France to expedite the crossing of Trastamara-led Free Companies across the Pyrenees. The French monarch cunningly offered *le Mauvais* a recently-vacated Burgundian dukedom, on condition that he sever Navarre's ties with Castile and pull out of Aragon. The ruse worked. Unprincipled by nature, *le Mauvais* reneged on his treaty with *el Cruel* and pulled back his army. He then signed a treaty with Aragon, his erstwhile foe, and proposed to partition the Castilian lion's skin even before it had been slain.

Disengaging from the Ejean siege, *le Mauvais* ordered his lances to return post-haste to their forts and castles and prepare to meet the consequences of the wrath of the jilted *el Cruel*. Though the Castilian threat never materialized, a more pressing worry lurked. Trastamara and ten-thousand lawless soldiers-of-fortune led by duGuesclin and Calverley had just come streaming across the Pyrenean passes of Aragon.

"I fear for us," Arantxa confided to Fortún, as they sat in front of the fire, one blustery evening in January. They had heard rumors of the Companies' devastating progress across northern Aragon on their march south.

"Fear not, my love," comforted Fortún. "I know it's confusing but this time Navarre is on Aragon's side. There's no reason for the Companies to attack us. It's Pedro *el Cruel* they're after, and we're no longer his allies."

Fortún spoke with hesitant conviction. He, too, was worried about what this rampaging horde of freebooters was capable of wreaking, even on their own 'allies'. Like all mercenaries, they were in it for booty. Besides, it was hard for them to tell whose side the shifty *le Mauvais* took on any given day. Their king's allegiance was hard to fathom by Navarrans themselves, let alone these barbarians.

"What about the atrocities in nearby Barbastro and Borja?" persisted Arantxa plaintively. "They're Aragonese towns, aren't they? And isn't Aragon this horde's ally?" Seldom concerned, her voice now had a slightly distraught edge to it. She was a fearless Navarran, endowed with the inner strength of frontier women. And they were, indeed, living on a frontier at the moment. Yet conditions were different now. For one thing, there were the children to worry about. When Fortún applied for the job, they never expected having to contend with the Free Companies.

"Our buttery maid tells me they've ravaged her parents' home in Barbastro," she continued balefully. "The butcher, who's from Borja, heard troubling news about the Companies there, too. If they behave that way with their own main allies, I dread to think what they'll do to us!"

They did not have long to find out.

Charles *le Mauvais* had also been concerned about the Companies' comportment in neighboring Aragon. The brigands were a law unto themselves and he had to prepare his kingdom against them, just in case, making sure it was on a proper war footing. Financed by Jewish moneylenders, he ordered large caches of food and supplies sent to his frontier strongholds. Moats were dug around Pamplona and the Muladi ward of Tudela; travel in or out of Navarre proscribed without his explicit permission; orders sent out to his border castles to remain on full alert.

Sire Martin Enriquez de Lacarra dropped in to visit Fortún's castle in late February. The king's standard bearer and recently appointed Commander of the Southern Marches of Navarre was on an inspection tour of the frontier strongholds when he turned up at the king's castle of Cascante and requested overnight lodgings.

"What do you think about our king's latest alliance with the Aragonese?" asked Arantxa during dinner that evening. She was referring to *le Mauvais'* recent startling turnabout, switching allegiances from Pedro *el Cruel* to Aragon's *el Cermonioso*. "It's all very confusing to us," she bemoaned. "I thought Castile was our friend for a change!" Arantxa, who had a knack for going to the heart of the matter, did so sometimes with maladroit bluntness. Fortún darted her a reproving glance for opening up that pot of worms.

"It's a bit of an embarrassment if you ask me," confessed the Commander, who like Fortún, was a good soldier but a reluctant diplomat. But that was all he would volunteer on the prickly subject. Still, it struck Fortún odd that the *Alferez* should be making unflattering remarks about his lord's knack for playing with two decks. "We should worry about the Companies," added the *Alferez*, trying to change the subject of *le Mauvais'* shameless fence-straddling. "From what I saw this afternoon, your stocks of food and arms are adequate to counter a determined siege," he observed approvingly. "How is the morale of the troops?"

"Excellent, sire," responded Fortún, with more than a hint of pride. "After the successful Sos and Ejea operations, they're fully prepared to withstand a siege if it comes to that. They are in top shape and ready for any contingency." As an afterthought, he added, "Nevertheless, it'd be nice to have a few more men-at-arms. Those Free Companies are a tough lot, I hear."

"Commanders are always asking for more soldiers," commented the *Alferez* impatiently. "We all end up shorthanded at one time or another. One has to remember that a determined defender is worth ten attackers if his heart is in the right place."

"Then it'll take a thousand to take this castle!" answered Fortún, who had made a quick mental calculation of what his twenty knights and thrice that many sergeants and squires could handle. Arantxa winced at her husband's glib response. She did not relish the thought of undergoing a siege, successfully repulsed or not.

"You must remember that these Companies are here to support the bastard Trastamara in his quest for the throne of Castile, not loll about in long sieges of bothersome frontier castles," remarked Lacarra cooly. "I'm not so sure about the town but the castle will stand if they have a mind to cause trouble in your area. Hungry wolves usually do, you know. They have a hard time telling friend from foe."

His comment turned out to be all too prophetic.

After crossing the Pyrenees, Trastamara's hordes proceeded south along Aragon's western border before swinging west on their march to Burgos, where the usurper intended to be crowned. The army of brigands, who had no bone to pick with *le Mauvais*, was pointedly trying to skirt Navarre. Not far from Fortún's castle in neighboring Aragon lay Borja, a town Pedro *el Ceremonioso* had granted to the Breton Captain duGuesclin in payment for his troubles. After a brief scuffle to take possession of it, the undisciplined rabble proceeded west following the Ebro River. Cascante was now fully athwart the Free Companies' path.

Rumors had been flying about the devastation they were leaving in their wake. Having bivouacked in nearby Ablitas the previous day, the invaders had plundered and leveled the town before marching on. Fearing a similar fate, Fortún ordered the townsfolk of Cascante to gather inside the castle's bailey for safety. It was a wise decision for shortly after dusk that day, a deputation of foreign knights came riding up to the moat, demanding entrance to the castle.

At the head of the group of mounted men was a stumpy knight sitting astride an enormous horse. "I am Bertrand duGuesclin," he announced in a deep, stentorian voice, clearly accustomed to command. "We need lodgings for the night." It sounded more like a command than a request.

Fortún, who was standing in the tower overlooking the drawbridge, looked down on the group, eyeing them warily. Even from his height, he could sense that there was something odd about the man addressing him. He had heard about duGuesclin's exploits in Britanny, where he had earlier humiliated *le Mauvais'* Norman forces at Cocherel. Fortún had imagined the brave Breton to have cut a more gallant figure than the thick-necked, heavy-set man sitting awkwardly astride his oversized charger. The snub nose and chinless jaw on the dark-complexioned face did not mark him as a nobleman in Fortún's book of chivalrous attributes.

Fortún ordered the drawbridge to remain raised, looked down on the group, responded in his own deep, carrying voice:

"I have standing orders to prevent any foreign forces from entering the king's castle." After the echoes of his voice had subsided, he added, now in a more conciliatory tone, "I suggest you seek lodgings elsewhere, Sire."

It hurt Fortún to have to deny hospitality to anyone, let alone a brother knight, ignoble though this one's bearing was. Any stranger had a right to room and board. That was the code of chivalry. But enough foul news had preceded this motley group of thugs to warrant caution. There were limits even to chivalry, for, as some famous Greek general once wryly noted, a lion should not be let into one's house unless one was ready to humor it. Besides, reflected Fortún, looking down on his visitor, this was one mean-looking excuse for a knight.

The group of horsemen galloped off in a huff, raising puffs of dust as they disappeared in the town's narrow alleys. Fortún saw the first smudges of smoke rising from the town shortly after. Cascante had been set to the torch. There was consternation among the townsfolk huddling behind the castle walls as they watched their homes go up in flames. Fortún knew that only the oncoming darkness had postponed the assault on his castle. That evening, he ordered a redoubling of the guard, exhorted his men to be ready to repulse an attack at dawn. Bonfires were lit in the bailey to start heating up cauldrons of oil and pitch to pour on the assailants from the machicolations if the attackers attempted to climb the ramparts with assault ladders the next morning. Men donned their hauberks and honed their weapons; women prepared bandages and set up straw pallets in the bailey's sheds for the wounded. No one slept that night, dreading the worst.

Dawn broke cool and crisp the next morning. The castle Chaplain, a doddering Dominican, celebrated Mass in the open bailey and gave a general absolution to the people gathered around him. To lift their spirits for the impending battle, extra rations of *aguardiente* spirits were passed around to the troops at breakfast. The men-at-arms, sergeants and squires had been on the delivery end of siege machines before and knew where their own castle's weaknesses lay. Fortún gave orders to redouble the guard at the barbican in the rear of the castle, considering its shallow curtain walls particularly vulnerable.

They waited nervously as the sun rose higher in the sky. The deathly stillness blanketing the countryside was shattered only by the occasional howls of a stray dog in the distance. Even the usual daybreak chirps of mockingbirds and the caws of magpies were strangely absent. It was as if the dawn had failed to arouse the countryside. Everything remained still, both that day and the next. They could detect no enemy movement whatsoever, only the lingering pall from the previous night's fires. The men were puzzled, the women relieved.

"Where are they?" asked Arantxa when her husband finally crept up to their living quarters for a few winks, the second night. "Have they really gone?"

"They may well have," he responded wearily. "Lacarra was right; they wouldn't bother with us. The scouts I sent out this morning returned empty-handed. No trace of them except for a swath of destruction all along the road to the Ebro. You heard about Ablitas the other day and saw what they did to Cascante night before last. They did the same to Monteagudo and Murchante, up a ways. Both plundered and razed."

"Barbarians!" remarked Arantxa, covering her mouth in shocked disbelief. "They could have killed us all! Why do they do this to Navarre? Aren't we their allies?"

"Yes," responded Fortún wearily. "Neither the bastard Trastamara nor *el Ceremonioso* have any bone to pick with our king this time. But commanders sometimes have to let their troops run loose to let off steam. These are, after all, mercenaries and the lust for booty is what keeps them going. It doesn't matter to them whether it belongs to friend or foe."

"I will never understand men's passion for war!" remarked Arantxa, shaking her head. "Thank God they're gone!"

Chapter 38

Nájera

1367

Fortún de Agorreta's contract as seneschal in the king's castle of Cascante had been recently renewed. His gallantry in the sieges of Sos and Ejea and subsequent defiance of duGuesclin's demand had earned him the king's personal commendation and the title of Royal Steward, a far more prestigious designation than that of seneschal, with a remuneration to match. Although the title promised to open new doors for Fortún, he was happy enough with his lot. He had left his manor to fulfill his fief's duty to defend Navarre and her king. The Lord of Agorreta felt no desire to develop closer ties with the Court in Pamplona. His ancestors had frowned upon the devious ways of politics and he was not about to go down that path. Recognition for his chivalry was enough reward and the best legacy he could bequeath his progeny, something they would someday look back on and be proud of.

But his king would not let him long savor his new title in peace and quiet. *Le Mauvais* had signed almost simultaneous pacts with both Edward of England and Trastamara of Castile, granting the former's army authorization to cross the Pyrenees at Roncevaux, while, at the same time, assuring the bastard king that he would disallow just such a crossing. More duplicitous still was his collecting the same fee from each contending party.

During an inspection tour of his king's domains in southern Navarre, Lord Martinez de Lacarra, now Supreme Commander of *le Mauvais'* army, dropped in on Fortún's castle one afternoon to check up on its defenses. Fortún had come up a few notches in Lacarra's appreciation after his brazen face-off with duGuesclin.

"So, then," asked Fortún over a beaker of sweet Cariñena during the postprandial *sobremesa*, "who shall Navarre side with this time around?"

"Well," answered the *Alferez* cagily, "if history is any guide, we'll side with Pedro *el Cruel* simply because the English are backing him this time. From all I can gather, fighting the Black Prince is a losing proposition."

"Yes," said Fortún pensively. "I know." He needed little convincing on that point, recalling his unpleasant encounter with the Black Prince at Crecy years earlier. Noticing his involuntary wince, Arantxa reached over and cupped his hand in hers. She remembered all too well how he had agonized over that eye patch all those many years.

"Castile has been nothing but trouble for Navarre all along," commented Fortún. "It looks like we'll have to get involved in the squabbles between those unsavory Castilian half-brothers. I hear the English are already massing their forces across the mountains in St. Jean de Pied Port. I'm sure our king will be calling us to arms before long."

"He will, indeed," responded Sire Lacarra. "I didn't want to bring it up during supper but my real mission here today is to order your castle company to prepare for an engagement. You are to report to the Pamplona garrison with your men as soon as possible. Our king, as we speak, is in Tudela reviewing the town's fortifications there."

They would have both been shocked to learn that *le Mauvais* was, at that very moment, holding secret talks in Tudela with a Breton relative of Bertrand duGuesclin, in other words, the enemy. They were scheming to stage a kidnapping of the Navarran king during an upcoming hawking outing. *Le Mauvais* would sit out the fray at duGuesclin's recently-acquired castle in Borja in neighboring Aragon until the conflict was settled, one way or the other, when it would be safe to be released and join the victor. This was not the first time *le Mauvais* would pull such a stunt. During the battle of Poitiers, when he was conveniently incarcerated at the Louvre, he had discovered an expedient excuse for not being shot at in someone else's war.

A week after the *Alferez*'s visit to Cascante, Fortún heard of the English army's crossing the Pyrenees at Roncevaux. A messenger from the Constable of Navarre arrived with orders that Fortún and his complement of castle knights leave immediately to join the five-hundred Navarran lances already assembling in Pamplona to join the English force. That was *le Mauvais'* token contribution to the allied effort. The Navarrans would support the Black Prince during his advance on Burgos, where Pedro *el Cruel*, who would be tagging along, would reclaim the crown of Castile, lost earlier to his bastard brother, Trastamara.

"Alferez Lacarra was correct, after all," commented Fortún to his wife that evening. "Navarre *will* side with the English."

"I find it a little ironical that you'll be fighting alongside the Black Prince this time, instead of against him," remarked Arantxa.

"Safer that way, I'm sure," observed her husband wryly. "I'll have to remind him of our previous encounter if I get a chance," he added with a grin. Fortún enjoyed the anticipation of meeting the gallant prince again, this time close-up and on his feet. "This Black Prince has become quite a legend in his own time. Did you know that he was only sixteen when he flattened me at Crecy?"

"He must have been a strong boy," commented Arantxa lightheartedly. "He certainly crowned himself with glory in those battles at Crecy and Poitiers. I suppose the French never pardoned him for capturing their king. I'd be mortified, if I were they!"

"There's never been much love lost between those two people," remarked Fortún thoughtfully. "Cousin Antxon in Azcayn tells me that they really love and admire this prince in the Gascogne. He must be the epitome of chivalry, from all I hear. He'll make a good king, someday."

It must have been an awesome spectacle to behold, thirty thousand disciplined troops tramping over the frozen, windy *Summo Pyreneo* pass above Roncevaux. A stronger, better-equipped army had never before marched on Iberian soil, an army far more formidable than the one that had come through six centuries earlier under the banners of Charlemagne. In three separate groups they came, led by such stalwarts as the Black Prince and John of Gaunt, the kings of Castile, Navarre and Majorca, and notables such as the Gascons Count d'Armagnac and Sire d'Albret.

The allied army milled around Pamplona for over a month, showing little urgency to get on with their military mission. It was almost as if the Black Prince were trying to give the bastard king a chance to reconsider the lunacy of waging war against him and reflect on the wisdom of giving back the kingdom he had usurped. The bastard Trastamara, on his part, remained adamant. It was precisely all the innocent blood his half brother Pedro had spilled in Castile during his infamous reign of terror that underscored this conflict. Nothing short of *el Cruel's* blood could erase that blot. No amount of psychological warfare would change the bastard's mind.

Fortún had billeted his twenty lances in the crowded barracks of the city's Citadel during the allied army's stay in Pamplona. They shared the cramped quarters with five hundred other Navarran knights and their squires. All of them had been selected to participate in the allied expedition on the merits both of their gallantry and their familiarity with French, the *lingua franca* of the expedition.

Fortún had always enjoyed visiting Pamplona, particularly its friendly inhabitants living in the district of Navarreria near the soberly Romanesque cathedral. Basque was still spoken there and Fortún felt at home among the hard-working, hard-drinking guild members who spoke his mother tongue.

Strolling along the hanging gardens of La Taconera one cold spring afternoon, accompanied by several of his Cascante knights, Fortún happened to notice a group of foreign noblemen strolling in a parallel lane, headed toward the balustrade which overlooked the lush, emerald-green valley below. The foreigners' rich attire and fancy headwear bespoke their high rank and nobility. The group of armed attendants, discretely following the small cortege at a distance, convinced Fortún of his hunch. As the two groups approached within earshot, Fortún overheard their spirited conversation in French.

The center of the others' obsequious attention was a tall, broad-shouldered nobleman walking with graceful, athletic stride. Though only in his mid thirties and obviously the youngest in the group, his strong chin, sharp features and penetrating blue eyes revealed an unmistakable air of command. There was something vaguely familiar about his youthful good looks and bearing. As Fortún strained to recall where he had seen that face before, he suddenly remembered. It was in a clearing in the forest of Crecy, twenty-odd years earlier. It was the Black Prince!

Fortún remained speechless as old memories came flooding over him. He remembered, just as if it were yesterday, how he had looked up at those same blue eyes in silent supplication, before passing out from loss of blood. An insane urge suddenly overcame him: he had to thank this man for having once spared his life. He had dreamed of doing so all these many years and was not about to let the opportunity pass by now.

Leaving his perplexed friends behind, he jumped over the low hedge separating the two groups and approached the prince. Suspicious of the stranger's intentions, the noblemen's guards suddenly closed in on Fortún, restraining him. The startled group of noblemen looked on in puzzlement. The stranger did not look menacing and yet he had approached them, unbidden and with dubious intent.

The prince raised his hand signaling the Captain of his guard to release the intruder.

"What is the meaning of this?" he asked Fortún in perfect French. "Speak up, my man." Though his voice had the unmistakable ring of authority, it was not harsh, not even peremptory. It was almost a friendly request.

"Milord," responded Fortún with a slight bow of the head. "I apologize for my brashness but I had to address your lordship. I have an old debt to settle with you. You spared my life at Crecy many years ago and I never had a chance to thank you for it."

"And how, pray, was that?" asked the prince, visibly baffled. Here was a man who claimed to have once fought against him and was now, obviously, a friend, else he would not be there on his odd errand. His first thought was that it was one of those Free Company turncoats now allied to him, but this man's accent was neither French nor English. Indeed, he sounded more like a local trying to make himself understood in poor French.

"My name is Fortún de Agorreta, milord. I fought at Crecy under the banners of Navarre in obeisance to my then-queen Juana. My men were in the vanguard with the Savoyard lances and the Genoese crossbowmen, in the glen below the forest. I lost my horse to one of your Welshmen's arrows and was fighting on foot when you came along and cut me down with a sword stroke, Sire. I recognized you by your black armor. I knew you spared my life because I saw you hesitate at the very last moment." Fortún was on one knee by now, head bowed in homage to his benefactor. "It is time that I thanked you for your kind gesture, milord."

The prince continued to look perplexed. Leaning over, he helped Fortún to his feet. "You must forgive me for not recalling the incident," he replied apologetically. "I unhorsed a few knights that day." There was no swagger in his voice, merely a statement of fact. "But I'm glad I have one good Navarran ready to fight with me now. For you will fight under my banner, will you not?"

"Yes, milord," he said. "And it won't be the first time my family has done so," he added.

"Oh?" responded the prince, now thoroughly puzzled. This enigmatic person was full of surprises.

"It was a long time ago, milord," said Fortún hesitantly. "One of my ancestors fought with one of yours in the Holy Land."

"Really?" said the prince, his curiosity now piqued. "And when, pray, was that?" he pursued.

"During the Third Crusade, milord. He fought with Sancho *el Fuerte*, who fought with Richard the Lionheart."

There was a look of pleasant surprise in the prince's face. Here was a local knight boasting a warrior heritage almost as old as his! Having lived in the Aquitaine all those many years, he had heard of these Vascons' indomitable fighting spirit. It was always good to have them on one's side. Pity, *le Mauvais* had offered him only five hundred Navarran lances for the campaign.

"And you said your name was Fortún?"

"Fortún de Agorreta, milord, at your service," he answered. "My company will fight under Lord Lacarra's command."

"A good man, I hear. I wish you the best of luck, Fortún de Agorreta," said the prince in parting. "I'm glad we're fighting on the same side this time around," he quipped. "We may meet again in the battlefield."

Fortún would brag about the encounter for days to come. Not everyone got a chance to converse with the Black Prince. Not many had lived to tell after crossing swords with him, either. Strange how their paths had crossed and intertwined! Stranger still, how the Agorretas had had these chance encounters with the Plantagenets over the generations.

Word soon spread at the Citadel that one of theirs had chanced upon and actually conversed with the Black Prince, himself. Details of their encounter were sketchy but the fact that the meeting had been congenial added an undeniable luster to the small contingent of Navarran lances. When the king's standard bearer, Lord Martinez de Lacarra, heard about the encounter, he summoned Fortún to his headquarters to hear the account firsthand. He was pleased that one of his numbers was in good standing with the leader of the expedition. It might come in handy one day.

The allied army, which had dawdled around Pamplona for over a month now, was finally ready to move out against Trastamara's hosts. The plan was to march south and west, across the fertile Navarran plains, cross the Ebro and continue on to Burgos, there to reinstate Pedro on his rightful throne. On the eve of the departure from Pamplona, the prince was informed that, while hawking with friends in Tudela, *le Mauvais* had been kidnapped by a French Captain of the Free Companies loyal to King Henry of Trastamara. Appalled by the news at first, the Black Prince gave his marching orders, nonetheless, leaving the wayward king to his own devices.

Distressed by her husband's abduction, the queen of Navarre convoked the Council of the Realm to come up with a plan of action. Nonplused by their sovereign's mysterious disappearance, the assembly of Navarran lords came up with a desperate and bizarre proposal: they would ask the Prince of Wales to act as Viceroy of Navarre, hoping he'd order the search and rescue of their missing king. As commander of the Navarran contingent, Alferez Lacarra was designated to convey the request. Remembering Fortún's recent friendly encounter with the prince, the Alferez summoned Fortún to accompany him on his awkward errand.

As they sat in the Great Hall of the prince's palace waiting for the hearing, Fortún and Lord Lacarra shared serious reservations about their embassy. Fortún was mortified by the whole charade. And with good reason, for no sooner had the Alferez relayed his message than the prince, politely but firmly, turned down the queen's request, arguing that on the eve of battle, he neither had the resources to spare nor the time to delay the offensive any longer. The prince had the delicacy of not disclosing his awareness of the Navarran king's penchant for skirting confrontation. Indeed, he had a growing suspicion that the scoundrel had arranged for his own pretended kidnapping.

The citizens of Pamplona were relieved to see the allied hosts finally move out of town. An army thirty thousand-strong could quickly deplete a land's patience and resources. Lacarra's five-hundred Navarran lances, among whom were Fortún's, were attached to Sire d'Albret's Gascon forces. The congenial relations between Gascons and Vascons and their similar fighting tactics argued for such a grouping. Albret, who had exchanged sour words with the Prince before leaving France, had been relegated to the rearguard under the command of the King of Majorca. In a sense Fortún was glad not to be on the army's leading edge this time. He had promised Arantxa that he would come home soon and without physical impairments. The rearguard was a good place to keep that promise if one forgot that Charlemagne's rearguard once got hammered by Fortun's own ancestors.

It was already the end of March when the Black Prince's army finally marched out of Pamplona, heading southwest, towards Logroño. Trastamara's scouts started shadowing them, trying to anticipate where the prince would cross the Ebro. Bertrand duGuesclin, the usurper's ally, had advised Trastamara of the folly of confronting the Black Prince head-on, suggesting instead that he merely harass and starve the enemy into submission or retreat. Trastamara, however, was fast running out of patience. He worried that delaying a confrontation would only further thin his ranks. The number of desertions was growing with every passing day.

The two armies finally closed in the early spring of 1367. The allies had just finished crossing the Ebro River at Logroño when Trastamara's troops engaged the oncoming army on the outskirts of Nájera. John of Gaunt's dismounted spearhead confronted the Castilian vanguard, led by Bertrand duGuesclin and Marechal d'Audreheim. A strong contingent of archers supported each frontal group, longbow men in the allied army, crossbowmen in the Castilian, both intent on inflicting damage at long range on cavalry and foot soldiers alike. Riding in each army's central group were their respective, heavily armed commanders with cavalry battalions covering their wings. The King of Majorca brought up the rear, with the Count of Armagnac, Sire d'Albret and Lord Lacarra, who was leading their Gascons and Navarrans.

What followed was a painful reenactment of Crecy and Poitiers. Positioned to protect the Black Prince's left flank, the Gascon Captal de Buch and his battalion of mounted lancers executed a brilliant flanking maneuver around duGuesclin. Supported by the Welsh longbow men's deadly barrage, de Buch's move turned the tide of battle. Trastamara's vanguard held momentarily but his center collapsed behind it, forcing the usurper king and his palace guard to flee. In the rout that ensued, many fleeing Castilians drowned attempting to cross the Najerilla, relentlessly pursued by the English, the Gascons and the Navarrans. DuGuesclin and his vanguard troops eventually surrendered but Trastamara managed to escape with his life. The final tally was lopsidedly gruesome; hundreds of Castilian knights and thousands of foot soldiers perished at Nájera, while only a handful of allied knights succumbed in the encounter. The battle of Nájera would stand out as a monument to folly, a senseless fray that should never have been fought.

No sooner had he recovered his crown than Pedro *el Cruel* returned to his ignoble ways. In a bitter and long-drawn argument with the Black Prince, the Castilian monarch ultimately reneged on his promise to foot the expedition's expenses. Embittered and sick with the dropsy, the Black Prince returned to Aquitaine empty-handed.

Pedro *el Cruel's* continued atrocities in his recovered kingdom led to his final undoing. Scarcely a year after Nájera, Trastamara returned to the Peninsula from his refuge in France, where he had fled. Starting out with only several hundred lances, his army soon began to swell with disgruntled Castilian knights and partisans as he advanced south, determined to oust Pedro once and for all. Having by now lost all his foreign allies, *el Cruel* had to ignominiously appeal for help to the Moors of Granada to stave off his half brother's relentless press. But even the Moors eventually abandoned him. While trying to flee from a siege, *el Cruel* was tricked into a trap outside the castle of Montiél, finally falling into the hands of his bastard brother.

His end was as unedifying as his life had been. Tussling with Trastamara when they finally came face to face, Pedro tried to stab his half brother but was constrained by Trastamara's knights. His foe thus hamstrung, Trastamara drove his own poignard into Pedro's heart. It was a fitting end to a lifelong brawl between two brothers who epitomized the ignorance and savagery of a crumbling feudal system darkly groping for nationhood.

CHAPTER 39

Rubbing Elbows with Royalty

1450s

Miguel de Agorreta was born the same day *le Mauvais'* granddaughter, Blanca, married Juan II, heir to the throne of Aragon. Miguel's father, a squire in the court of Pamplona, had married into nobility when Maria de Chesnes, Queen Blanca's favorite lady-in-waiting, became infatuated with the raw-boned hidalgo and sweet-talked him to the altar. Nurtured by his mother's genteel, high-born ways, young Miguel grew up rubbing elbows with royalty. He was fond enough of queen Blanca, who was kind and well disposed towards him, but tended to shy away from her consort, King Juan, whom young Miguel considered a pompous man with scant reason to be so, and a bit of a popinjay, to boot. As he was growing up, the young lad felt increasingly ill at ease in the king's presence, perhaps because, from the youth's perspective, he had little difficulty seeing through the king's new clothes.

Being the same age, Miguel befriended the shy and retiring heir, Carlos, Prince of Viana, early on. Mollycoddled by his mother, Blanca, and cosseted by a covey of doting ladies-in-waiting, the frail, soft-spoken prince had trouble growing up in a man's world, a fact which probably explained why he so enjoyed young Miguel's company. The prince tried to emulate the rapscallion's impish ways and earthy turns of phrase, but only earned both boys scowling reprimands from Don Alfonso de la Torre, the prince's stern, straight-laced preceptor.

Finding Latin terminally boring, it took the least excuse for the two boys to skip classes on a hot summer day and sneak out for a game of handball against the cathedral's back wall, or take a dip in the Arga nearby. Their favorite watering hole was under the bridge of *Los Franceses,* where they enjoyed splashing about in the river's cool, slow-flowing waters far from their teacher's watchful eye. Sometimes playing make-believe knights pretending to be assaulting some Moorish encampment, they would chance upon some unsuspecting group of gypsy children camped nearby. On occasion, they would sneak into a napping farmer's orchard in the plains of La Rochapea at the foot of Pamplona's ramparts to pick forbidden cherries or lie under some gnarled old vine and gorge themselves sick on luscious red grapes.

The male bonding between the two boys grew stronger with the passage of time but as they approached adolescence, the chasm between their social stations and the rigid court protocol put a gradual end to their shared lessons and truant outings. They remained good friends, however, despite this parting of the ways, exchanging laughs on the odd chance encounter in palace halls or garden paths, reminiscing about old pranks and devilment. And though these meetings grew more infrequent with time, the two were to remain good friends for the rest of their lives. In the years to come, that friendship would stand Miguel in good stead. It also would get him into a lot of trouble.

Miguel's strict upbringing and the elite company he kept during his growing-up years at palace gradually built a veneer of propriety over his innately picaresque spirit. He was growing up to be a well-bred gentleman of quiet ways and proper demeanor, with an affable manner that belied the adventuresome spirit within. There was a forthrightness about him and, save for his friend the prince, his other palace acquaintances had always seemed a little foppish and obsequious. As he grew older, the vacuous courtly life started to lose its allure for him. He sensed that there had to be a deeper meaning and purpose to life than trading pleasantries and exchanging hollow banter with empty-minded courtiers.

He always enjoyed visiting the family haunts in Agorreta whenever he got a chance. He was particularly fond of his grandmother's hearty country fare, especially the wild strawberries of summer, sprinkled over dollops of thick, yellow-fresh cream. He delighted in helping his cousin's villeins with the farm chores and though it could be back-breaking work at times, he felt there was something honest and wholesome about going to bed bone-tired with dirt under his fingernails and hay in his hair. He loved the wholesome, cleansing smell of pine resin in the early spring mornings, even the smell of dung that rose up as his hoe turned the rich, loamy Navarran soil. It was all so plebeian, so honest, and so down-to-earth!

But much as he enjoyed these occasional escapades to his ancestral home, he would never tarry there. He knew that cousin Otxoa would eventually inherit the family properties and titles. Otxoa, who had been slaving in the manor all his life, had a solid claim to these lands and their perquisites. Miguel did not begrudge it. He had been having fun in Pamplona, leading the sophisticate's life while his cousin had been helping his grandmother run the manor, doing all that backbreaking work. Otxoa had earned his birthright, fair and square.

Miguel would have to seek his fortune elsewhere. He had turned his back on the life of arms and chivalry early on and was now left with only a few career options. There was always the old standby life of the cloth, of course. Traditionally, there was always one in every Navarran family who followed the religious calling. He had rather enjoyed his experience as an acolyte at St. Cernin's as an adolescent, having, at one point, even toyed with the idea of joining some monastic order. It would not have been too shabby a choice, he once reflected, recalling old stories about his great-uncle Guillemot de Agorreta, who had risen to the exalted rank of chaplain to the *Alferez* of Navarre, the kingdom's military Commander. The *padre's* exploits during the siege of Coimbra, in Portugal, had always intrigued him and fed his feverish imagination as a child. Archbishop Turpin had done as much for Roland and much good it had done both, he mused.

No, Miguel's heart was not quite into asceticism, even when spiced with an occasional feat of arms. He felt he had other more worldly talents to exploit. Miguel ruminated on the thought that he could put his knack for knocking heads together to good use. He had always been good at making peace out of discord among his friends. "The peacemaker," they jokingly called him sometimes, but he did not mind. After all, what nobler calling was there than an advocate's, perhaps even a judge's?

He got to spend less and less time at court especially after Queen Blanca passed on and his mother lost her position in Court. After mulling it over, Miguel reached what would turn out to be the most important decision in his life: he would spend the next few years vigorously pursuing legal studies under the tutelage of a friendly court magistrate in Pamplona. Several years of hard work followed, living off of his father's meager allowance, lodging in dreary flophouses in the run-down district of Navarreria, forever shrinking away from his snobbish court acquaintances. Miguel eventually overcame his penuries, achieved his Advocate's degree, earning his barrister's diploma with high honors. He proudly nailed his professional shingle outside his dingy walkup apartment in the town's central square and started practicing law in earnest. He had just turned thirty.

Though his first few cases were mundane and unrewarding, Miguel learned from each lawsuit, polishing the fine arts of polemics and legal discourse as he went. The "peacemaker's" pithy arguments soon earned him another flattering sobriquet, *Boquita de Oro*, the golden-tongued one, a moniker that secretly pleased him. His growing success at the bar soon started to attract a higher class of clientele and Don Miguel's standing started to rise, even in aristocratic circles. His litigation gradually grew in importance, moving up from suits of petty larceny and fisticuffs to property disputes between feuding gentry. The magistrates of the court secretly enjoyed Miguel's cogent, well-marshaled defense arguments as well as his adroit handling of evidence or, sometimes, lack thereof. He was quickly earning a name for himself in the halls of Navarran justice.

Already in his mid thirties, Miguel's thoughts finally turned to marriage. He had had his share of dalliances during his growing-up years but it was getting time to start casting about for a wife. Being a man of fastidious tastes, he had to find a special wife, preferably one a cut above his station. Spoiled by his courtly upbringing, he had grown partial to women of high breeding, especially those with cultivated tastes and aristocratic features. Though not pertaining to the most exalted ranks, Miguel considered himself a member of the minor gentry. After all, he thought, did he not come from one of the oldest lordships of the high mountain valleys of Navarre? Had not his ancestors rubbed elbows with—indeed, fought alongside—kings and princes? Yes, there was no reason he shouldn't aspire to the hand of some lady in the higher levels of society.

His search for a partner did not take long. Miguel's growing celebrity had come to the attention of Juan de Beaumont, the Count of Lerín, leader of one of the more powerful families in Navarre. The case involved a nasty lawsuit concerning an inheritance squabble between the Beaumonts and the Peraltas, the latter, members of the equally powerful faction of the Gramonts.

While taking a deposition at the Beaumont palace in Pamplona one afternoon, Miguel chanced upon the Count's young niece, Sabina de Beaumont, who happened to be visiting with her aunt and uncle at the time. Her warm brown eyes and sunny disposition bowled Miguel over; it was love at first sight. Swept off her feet, herself, Sabina reciprocated Miguel's attentions and began meeting with the gallant advocate in discrete rendezvous. Once a week, at dusk, the two would slip past the lax vigilance of Sabina's maid and meet in their favorite spot, the hanging Half Moon gardens overlooking the Arga there to profess their love for each other.

"My uncle Juan will throw an apoplectic fit if he ever finds out we're meeting like this," remarked Sabina one evening, smiling mischievously. "He intends to marry me into the Gramont family," she confessed, visibly unsettled at the prospects. "He keeps mentioning bringing the two warring families together with our union. Can you believe it?"

The fires of dissension between the two powerful families had been smoldering since the days of Charles *le Mauvais*. Named Viceroy of Navarre, his brother, Louis de Beaumont, had managed to alienate the Gramont faction in Basse Navarre with arbitrary rulings and self-serving decisions. Their feud remained as raw as ever two generations later.

"My dear Sabina," said Miguel, smiling lovingly at her. "I shouldn't be saying this but I love you too dearly to remain silent. You shouldn't throw your life away by accepting the role of a sacrificial lamb. Intelligent and beautiful though you are, you would only be sucked into that fire storm. There is too much bad blood running between the Beaumonts and the Gramonts for even a pretty face like yours to stem."

"Yes," responded the young woman, "my very same feelings."

"Besides," pursued Miguel, "now is not the time for peace offerings. Our scheming monarch is making a mockery of our sacred, primeval laws, our *Fueros*. He's determined to have Fernando, his offspring from that second wife of his, succeed him to the throne of Navarre instead of Carlos, his firstborn and true heir."

"Poor Carlos!" said Sabina, referring to Miguel's boyhood friend, the hapless heir-apparent, Prince of Viana. "He'll never inherit the scepter with that conniving father of his!"

"I'm afraid you're right," agreed Miguel. "You can already see the writing on the wall. The two ruling bands are hopelessly polarized, what with the Beaumonts supporting the prince; the Gramonts, his father King Juan."

"He's not our king!" said Sabina with emphasis, her Beaumont blood rising. "He was a mere consort and now a shameless usurper!"

Miguel loved the spunk of this lovely young Beaumont. She would make a good wife, despite the formidable obstacles to overcome. But love conquers all, he reflected, holding her in his arms. He looked deeply into her eyes then kissed her passionately as he had never done before.

"Will you be my wife?" he proposed.

"Yes!" she answered without hesitation, "with all my heart!"

Before anybody knew it, their courtship had blossomed into wedding plans. There were loud protestations from her uncle, the Count, who had more substantial marriage prospects in mind for his beautiful and vivacious young niece. But as in all such plans love's blind and bumbling ways would prevail. It was only prince Carlos' friendship and advocacy that eventually gained Miguel the Count of Lerín's grudging consent to their wedding. Miguel's intelligence and personal charm did the rest.

Chapter 40

The Wages of Friendship

The wedding took place in Roncevaux in the little shrine the locals romantically referred to as Charlemagne's Chapel. While most of Miguel's friends and family were present, only a smattering of Sabina's illustrious relatives showed up. Her uncle, the Count of Lerín and Constable of Navarre, deigned to honor the wedding with his presence only because Prince Carlos himself was in attendance, acting as Miguel's best man and chief witness. The Beaumonts sat stiffly on the hard pews on the right side of the aisle while the sizable contingent of Agorretas occupied the left side of the chapel. As he waited for his bride's arrival, Miguel faced the congregation from the foot of the altar. He could not help noticing the contrast between the two families' attire and demeanor, one noisy and homespun, almost rough-hewn, the other elegant and restrained, verging on the arrogant. He was comforted by the thought that his own earthy people had lorded it over the land on which they now stood eons before these other *parvenus* slipped across the passes to grab the reins of power. Grandeur, he reflected philosophically, lay in the heart.

Joyful, fecund years followed their marriage, Sabina, busy with child-rearing, her husband working late nights, preparing briefs, defending increasingly important cases, all the while garnering a growing reputation. For Miguel, the joys of fatherhood were underscored by a gradual rise to prominence in the world of the

Law. Several years into his practice he was awarded the coveted title of *Merino de las Montañas*, Chief Justice of all the mountain valleys of Navarre. The title was handed down by royal decree for meritorious judicial service in an increasingly contentious political atmosphere.

The honorific title, however, would come at a price. His new assignment and broadened responsibilities demanded that he establish residence in Aoiz, the seat of the judicial district of the northern counties. Miguel would have preferred to remain in his beloved Pamplona. Sabina, likewise, was reluctant to abandon her friends and the life of high society that she had grown accustomed to. But her husband's professional priorities came first. And so, when it came time to move, she followed him submissively to the small, unpretentious town wedged among the foothills of the Pyrenees. Pamplona was really not that far away, she reflected, and they could visit relatives and friends, or go shopping there whenever the spirit moved and work allowed.

Miguel had a busy schedule ahead of him what with the growing number of incidents between the Beaumont and Gramont factions who held sway in Navarre. Flouting the Fueros' rules of succession, Juan II, the widower and unloved Regent, persisted in preventing his firstborn, Carlos, prince of Viana, from occupying his rightful throne. He was impudently subverting Navarran statutes, conniving to have Fernando, his son from a second wife, named heir to the throne of Navarre. His underhanded scheming did not sit well with the Beaumonts, the opposing political faction.

There was no dearth of lawsuits in this volatile atmosphere seething with hatred and distrust. Miguel had his hands full trying to keep the internecine battles from flaring up into open warfare. But it would take more than the gallant efforts of the *Merino de las Montañas* to avert escalating discord. His long-standing friendship with the Prince of Viana and his marriage to a Beaumont made it increasingly awkward for him to be impartial in fractious court cases pitting the Beaumonts against the Gramonts. The gathering storm that finally broke would relieve him of such conflicts of interest and civil niceties.

Weary of the mockery his father was making of his hereditary rights to the throne, Carlos, Prince of Viana, signed a treaty of allegiance with Castile and ordered his usurping father expelled from Navarre. Having festered for years, the revolt was now out in the open and in full swing. The battle lines were drawn: the Beaumonts, who controlled the northern cities and mountain valleys, sided with the prince, while the south, lorded by the Agramont faction, supported the obstinate king Juan. The smoldering, age-old animosities between the Vascons of the ancient *Saltus Vasconum* and the inhabitants of the *Ager Vasconum* finally erupted in open, fratricidal conflict.

Like all civil wars, this one, too, was brutal and unremitting. The conflict's first blood was drawn in the battle of Aibar, where King Juan's victorious forces captured and subsequently imprisoned Prince Carlos. Even that appalling development failed to put an end to hostilities. Frustrated by the Beaumonts' refusal to acknowledge his son, Fernando, heir to the crown, King Juan tried brute force instead. He tried to nip Carlos' followers' rebellion in the bud by soliciting support from his powerful Bearnaise son-in-law, Viscount Gaston de Foix. Married to the Prince of Viana's willful sister, Leonor, the Bearnaise viscount was only too happy to accommodate his father-in-law, who dangled the crown of Navarre in front of him.

From his Bearnaise stronghold in southern France, Gaston de Foix's forces crossed the Pyrenees at Roncevaux and romped over northern Navarre, crushing Beaumont units near Lumbier and Esparza, before laying siege to Aoiz, where Miguel de Agorreta held court.

Already angered by the capture and imprisonment of his friend and rightful heir, the prince of Viana, Miguel was further outraged by King Juan's inviting a foreign army to do his dirty work for him. Abandoning all civilities, the judge decided to take up arms against the interlopers. The warrior blood in him was too thick for him to sit idly by and watch foreigners overrun his land. The time for platitudes and civil discourse was now past. It was time to act.

There was much serious discussion between Miguel and Sabina when he first broached the subject of his active participation in the defense of the town, but the judge's logic and consummate rhetoric won the hour. His ultimate argument was that if Bishops, like his uncle Guillemot and the Carolingian Turpin could wield swords, then, by St. Fermín, so could a magistrate!

"Besides, I have no other option," he argued earnestly, trying not to add to his wife's mounting concern. "There's no love lost between the Foix and the Beaumont families. You know that better than I. Gaston de Foix's wife, Leonor, simply shakes with hatred toward her brother, the prince of Viana. I can see her salivating at the very thought of inheriting his rightful throne. Now, not only is this town of Aoiz in grave peril of being overrun by her husband's forces but the two of us and our children are particularly at risk. They're bound to discover, sooner or later, that we're part of the Beaumont clan. We must prevent them from taking the town at all costs. I must help defend it."

Sabina was sobbing softly now. Civil wars were bad enough but the presence of foreign troops nearby was a real cause for concern. She knew that mercenaries were in it only for adventure and booty. News of their plundering and raping in the nearby village of Esparza was common. "What shall we do about the children?" she asked pitiably. Elena, the eldest, had just turned two.

"You will take yourselves to the castle on the hill. I have arranged for your lodgings there. I'll join you shortly. The Clarisa sisters are also moving there. They have agreed to lend you a nun's habit, just in case." Noticing her startled look, he decided to try a little levity: "You'll look attractive in a wimple!" Sabina failed to see the humor in his remark. "Even barbarians refrain from inflicting harm on the religious," he reasoned. "They have so far respected the safe haven of holy places. You should be safe there."

It was not easy for Miguel to uproot his family from their comfortable home in the heart of town and move them to the cold, cramped, impersonal lodgings in the hilltop castle. But he had little choice; the enemy was practically at the gates. After escorting his wife and children to the castle, he discarded his robes of office, donned a borrowed, ill-fitting hauberk, slipped an old sword into the scabbard hanging from his belt and proceeded to join the brave citizens already manning the castle's ramparts. A cheer arose from the defenders when they saw the *Merino* himself attired as one of them. Vascons were used to such heroic measures; they had displayed them for countless ages. Deeply ingrained in tribal memory, the code of honor was still a way of life with them.

The meadows around the city walls were alive with enemy soldiers, their colorful battle banners fluttering in the breeze, artillery pieces ominously in place, assault machines and ladders at the ready. The attack was imminent. As he surveyed the enemy encampments around the besieged town, Miguel felt a sudden shiver of pride. He had not felt anything like it since the time he subdued the neighborhood bully many years ago for some now-forgotten effrontery. He could even feel the surge of adrenaline coursing through his veins again, flooding him with an indefinable sense of courage and daring. Totally conscious of his surroundings, he became keenly aware of the impending danger and his eagerness to do battle. The strange perception mystified and exhilarated him at the same time; it was almost as if he'd felt this urge before, in some previous reincarnation. It must be the Agorreta in him, he reflected, stilling an *irrintzi* now swelling irrepressibly in his breast.

Deep in the recesses of his mind he pondered on a world littered with mistaken vocations, one of them his own. He should have been a knight instead of a judge, he reflected. He knew the strange revelation was not far off the mark when he became aware that his right hand was clutching the handle of his sword in a white-knuckled grip. The sudden realization that he was ready and eager to do battle brought a smile to his face.

The town's defense turned out to be a gallant but vain effort. Running out of supplies and ammunition, the stalwart defenders were soon overwhelmed by Gaston de Foix's superior force. After a determined artillery attack on the city gates and ramparts with their half dozen culverins, the Bearnaise soldiery and supporting mercenaries from Bigorre and Foix, assaulted the walls with their siege machines and ladders, spilling over onto the concourse and quickly neutralizing the towers' defenses. Shortly after, the city gates were flung open, letting the others in. Bursting through the portals with savage howls, the main body of the invaders overwhelmed the town's crumbling resistance in short order. For a few awful moments a deadly silence hung over the city as its frightened citizens retreated into basements and attics, trying to escape the inevitable. A few dozen quick-thinking citizens fled to the castle overlooking the town, to join its last-ditch defenders.

The mercenaries crawled all over town, sacking and looting, laying everything waste. Smoke from their torched buildings routed the inhabitants out of their hiding places and onto the streets, where they soon met their death. Young women were spared to satisfy the soldiery's lust while men, young and old alike, were mercilessly cut down, even as they pleaded for their lives. Only the fortunate few who had managed to flee to the castle would survive. Heinous atrocities against loathed political opponents were commonplace. It was the Gramonts' turn to repay an ancient blood debt with the Beaumonts, no more, no less. The name of Foix would forever live in infamy in the town of Aoiz after the events of that day.

After Foix's rabble had had its fill of rape and plunder in the town, Gaston turned his attention to the hilltop castle dominating the town; he could not leave Aoiz without eliminating that threat to his rear. Surrounding the fortress with his sizable army, he proceeded to subject it to a relentless artillery barrage. For days on end the obstinate defenders held their ground, ignoring the shells, repulsing persistent sapper assaults. Their refusal to surrender promised a long and bloody siege. The defenders fought valiantly on, hoping that the onset of winter would weaken the Bearnais' resolve. They would have continued to resist had not a critical shortage of food and water developed, threatening their very survival. When they had slaughtered their last lamb and emptied the brackish water from their last cistern, they sent an emissary to the enemy camp, offering an honorable capitulation.

Amazed at the valiant effort of this handful of defenders, Gaston de Foix accepted their surrender terms, promising to spare their lives on condition that they allow a garrison of Bearnaise soldiers to remain behind and occupy the castle, unmolested. Being the least of many evils, the offer was accepted outright by the Captain of the fortress.

Miguel was not present when the surrender talks took place. He had been seriously wounded by an artillery round that crashed into the tower he was defending on the very last day of the assault. All around him lay shattered rafters and broken slate tiles from a gaping hole in the roof above him. As he lay there, bleeding profusely from a head wound, only half conscious and in shock, he realized that his comrades around him were either dead or dying and wondered if he himself would survive. For almost a day he lay there in shock, slipping in and out of consciousness. In one of his lucid moments he thought he heard voices. They were enemy soldiers speaking an odd French-Basque dialect, searching for booty. As his grandfather in Crecy a century earlier, Miguel instinctively knew the importance of remaining motionless, holding one's breath, hoping to pass for dead. He had heard gruesome tales about mutilations to pry rings off fingers and other ghastly acts in the aftermath of battle. After what seemed an eternity, the soldiers finally vacated the small enclosure to rummage for booty elsewhere.

Spent from nervous exhaustion and loss of blood, Miguel passed out once again, this time with a vague sense of relief. When he regained consciousness hours later, he realized he'd die of exposure if he didn't start looking for help. Sensing that the coast was clear, he wriggled out from under the tower's debris and onto the wall-walk, where, weakened by the effort, he passed out once again. His last sensation was that of a feeble Navarran sun beating down on his shivering body. It was good to feel its warmth again.

The nuns did not recognize Miguel when he was brought into the castle's infirmary, wrapped in a soiled blanket. The blood from his head wound had caked over his face, effectively masking his identity. Sabina, who had been helping the Sisters dress the survivors' wounds and ministering to them, was the first to recognize him. The unfamiliar hauberk had thrown her off momentarily but the distinctive boyhood scar on his right hand caught her eye. She almost fainted when she recognized her husband.

She was looking down at him hours later when he finally groped his way back to consciousness.

"Is this heaven?" he asked weakly. A glance at his surroundings slowly disabused him of the happy notion. Reassured by her familiar smile, he added, almost inaudibly: "I had always hoped my guardian angel would be as pretty as you."

Overwhelmed, her warm brown eyes misted over with tears of joy. "I'm sorry to tell you," she said, "you've got a few more years left down here." Bending over, she kissed him softly on his parched lips. "And probably," she added with a smile, "if you're good to me, you may someday get to know that other angel of yours, but not any time soon."

"Have they gone yet?" he asked.

She knew to whom he was referring. "Yes and no," she answered enigmatically. "Gaston de Foix and his main force left yesterday but he left a platoon of Bearnaise soldiers manning the castle. You may catch a glimpse of their sentries walking about now and then, making the rounds. The barbarians devastated the town. They killed many of the town folk. These Bearnaise soldiers tell us that Foix spared our lives only because of the gallant defense put up against them. 'Brave men!' they quoted him as saying. We have the good Lord to thank for that, and also you, of course." After a brief pause, she added: "Word is that Foix's army is now heading for Sangüesa. I feel sorry for those poor people."

"Do they have any idea who you are?" asked Miguel, a note of concern creeping into his voice. He knew full well that the name of Beaumont was anathema to the victors.

"Not yet," she answered with a worried look. "But there'll be some charitable soul who'll volunteer the information sooner or later, I'm sure."

The following day Miguel remarked: "I don't think this is a safe place anymore. We must leave as soon as my wounds heal."

"But where shall we go?" asked Sabina, her furrowed brow revealing deep concern. "Pamplona is no longer safe. The Beaumonts have been taking a beating ever since this civil war started."

Miguel considered the alternatives. There was always the family manor house in Agorreta. His cousin Otxoa had recently passed away after a lingering sickness and he, Miguel, had become the rightful lord of the manor. He would have to put his judicial practice in abeyance and lie low in his mountain lair while things simmered down. Neither the Beaumont nor the Gramont factions had any interest in the forests and pasturelands of Esteribar valley's high country. It would be an ideal place to repair to and keep a low profile for the moment.

"We shall move to Agorreta," Miguel said with a finality that surprised and pleased her. "The family manor house is comfortable," he continued. "Life there is simple, the food wholesome and plentiful. More importantly, it will be a safe haven. Nobody cares about Beaumonts or Gramonts up there, or vice versa. You may miss the niceties of select society and may have to give up rubbing elbows with educated people for a while, but in a civil war, life in the country is healthier. Besides, it will be a good, wholesome place for the children to grow up."

Sabina was relieved by the decision. The children's safety was her main concern and she'd go anywhere to ensure their wellbeing. It would be a nice change for her, too. Country life had always intrigued and attracted her. She romanticized about unaffected country folk, the smells and sounds of their fields, the simplicity of life around them. The few times she had visited the Agorreta manor, she had loved waking up in the morning to the sound of cowbells and crowing roosters, the bleating of sheep, the grunting of pigs. She'd have to deal with farm hands now, instead of sophisticates and others of her husband's self-important friends, but that was all right by her.

"Yes, I think I'd like that," she admitted, warming up to the idea. "It'll be good to be the wife of a gentleman farmer," she added, half in jest. "We can tutor the children ourselves and when they grow a little older we'll send them to St. Jean de Pied de Port. I hear they have good schools in Basse Navarre."

Chapter 41

Majordomo to a would-be King

The servants, who had lived and worked in the manor house of Agorreta, some for generations, stayed on after Miguel's cousin, Otxoa, passed on, hoping to someday serve the new lord of the manor. The staff of twelve serfs—from Antonio, the administrator, to young Imelda, the milkmaid and laundry woman—was an eclectic group. Except for the literate Antonio, who was allowed to share his new lords' roof in the fortress-castle of Gasteluzar, the rest of the help resided in Jaureguizar, the dilapidated old manor house standing stolidly on the hamlet's square, a mere stone's throw away from the castle. The help was impressed with their new lord's title, "Merino de las Montañas," and his genteel ways were a far cry from their late oafish lord's. They were not exactly sure at first whether they could get used to the difference.

The hamlet's inhabitants eyed the new lord with characteristic reservations, Vascons being notorious for taking their time warming up to strangers. Although they outwardly accepted him as their new lord, in their private thoughts he remained an outsider. Some even questioned his motives for wanting to move back to their humble village after having lived in high places. Others suspected that he may have run afoul of the law he had sworn to uphold, probably even fallen into disgrace. *Piensa mal y acertarás*, went the old adage, suggesting that one guesses right when suspecting the worst about others. It would take a thicker veneer of Christian charity, perhaps a millennial leap's worth, to prove that aphorism wrong.

"Distrustful lot, these mountain folk," commented Sabina, a week into her new surroundings. She was having trouble drawing a smile from the half-witted buttery maid or having her instructions understood by the cook. Even Antonio took his sweet time mulling over her requests before acting on them.

"Perhaps that's why they've survived these many eons," volunteered Miguel equably. "A little miserably, perhaps, but here they are, still alive and kicking. And their kind will probably outlive ours. They're survivors. No doubt about it."

"Dreary prospects," reflected his wife, resignedly.

Homecoming was bittersweet for Miguel. It was good, on the one hand, to feel safe behind the sturdy walls of Gasteluzar, in the relative anonymity of the countryside. The small hamlet, on the other hand, was a far cry from the bustling community of Aoiz. But it didn't take Miguel long to get used to the trappings of lordship of the manor. Always good at numbers, he soon came up with new ideas to improve the land's productivity and the husbanding of its ample resources. Antonio, his administrator, was a quick study, swiftly picking up on his lord's every suggestion, implementing them "*ipso facto*", a phrase he picked up somewhere and mysteriously employed whenever he meant "right away". Of all Miguel's new duties as lord of the manor, meting out justice was his favorite. He was, after all, still the Chief Justice of all the mountain valleys around, at least until someone in Pamplona ruled otherwise.

Several months into his new life as a landlord, Miguel was admiring his estate from his balcony one day when he was startled by the sight of endless columns of foreign troops marching up the steep road that wound around the foot of the hill past the manor. His surprise turned to delight when he recognized units of Gaston de Foix's *chevauché* marching past on their way back to southern France after having left nothing but desolation behind. As he watched in somber silence, Miguel earnestly prayed that it would be the last he saw of them.

A brief and uneasy peace descended upon the land. Miguel had heard rumors that his friend the Prince of Viana had managed to evade his jailers and escape from his Tudela prison. There was consternation among the Gramonts and a great deal of finger-pointing between the Peralta and the Navarra factions of that family, each blaming the other for the escape. The trump card they had held in the high-stakes game of the succession to the throne had suddenly evanesced. God only knew what devilment the runaway prince could wreak on Juan II's best-laid plans of sovereign succession. A general mobilization was ordered to smoke out and capture the princely fugitive.

Miguel had just retired to his quarters one evening when he heard an unusual clatter of horseshoes on the flagstones outside Gasteluzar, followed, moments later, by a loud banging of the clapper on the front door. As he reached the bottom of the stairs of the Great Hall, his steward was ushering several strangers into the hallway. Even in the dim light of the dying rushlights hanging from the walls, Miguel could see that these were no ordinary visitors. Though dusty and disheveled, something about their attire and demeanor bespoke their highborn station. As he approached the group, he noticed three of the gentlemen speaking deferentially to the fourth, a balding, slightly built man whose serene demeanor exuded an authority at odds with his unimposing stature. As Miguel approached them, his eyes focused on the enigmatic figure. Despite his unkempt appearance and soiled attire, Miguel suddenly recognized the visitors' leader.

"My prince and my lord," he said, dropping on one knee, as he reached for Prince Carlos' hand to kiss it. "You do me great honor with your presence. Welcome to my humble home."

Pulling Miguel up to his feet, Prince Carlos gave him a warm, heartfelt embrace. "My dear Miguel," said the prince, holding his friend at arm's length to better study his face. "This is almost like old times!" he said nostalgically. "You'll always remind me of all that trouble you got us into, playing hooky from de la Torre's Latin classes!"

"Yes, milord," answered Miguel, grinning broadly. "I, too, remember those truancies with fondness."

"You look well, my friend" commented the prince expansively. "This mountain air must do wonders for one's health." Even in the dim torchlight, Miguel could see that he could not say the same for the prince, whose sunken eyes and sallow coloring reflected failing health. It had always been fragile and his recent harsh imprisonment must have only worsened his condition.

"It is good to see you again, milord," said Miguel, trying to steer the conversation away from the subject of health. "I wonder if you recall that we last met at my wedding in Roncevaux. It is not far from here, you know."

"How can I forget!" said the prince. "I got pretty tipsy on your heady Liédena wine at the wedding feast, as I recall!" He was now holding Miguel by the arm, slowly steering him away from the others, as if seeking privacy for what he was about to discuss with his host. Sitting on a bench by the hearth's dying fire, the prince said:

"As you probably know," he began, "I've been held captive in the dungeon of the castle of Tudela ever since the battle of Aibar. It was by sheer good luck that my Commander-in-Chief, Juan de Beaumont, plotted my escape and brought me here." Noticing Miguel's surprise on hearing the name of his wife's uncle, the prince added: "Yes, the Count of Lerín is here in my small retinue tonight. You did not recognize him under his cape's hood. Your wife will be happy to see him again if she's here."

Miguel was dumbfounded. Sabina's uncle, who had thrown up so many roadblocks to their engagement and given him such a hard time during his courtship, was here, under his roof. Small world!

"She will indeed, milord!" responded Miguel, elated at the unexpected family reunion. "And so will I," he added, reflecting ironically on the strange twists of fate. "I am embarrassed for not having recognized him when he came in. I hope he will pardon me."

"He will," said the prince confidently, in the same kind voice that Miguel remembered so well. He could scarcely believe that he was exchanging pleasantries with his liege lord, the Prince of Viana, soon to be king of Navarre, or so he hoped. "And now to business," continued the prince. "We will need someone to help us slip past my father's troops guarding the frontier. We are on our way to France. I have business there with their King Charles, whom I hope to meet shortly. I trust he can help me regain my kingdom. Wish me luck, my friend."

"I hope he will, Sire," responded Miguel with feeling, despite serious misgivings about the outcome of that meeting. Not in vain, he reflected, was the French king the cousin and mentor of the infamous Gaston de Foix, whom he would dearly love to see on the Navarran throne. It appeared to Miguel that the prince of Viana was on a desperate and impossible errand but he had always been a little out of touch with reality.

"I will be happy to guide you across the Pyrenees and into friendly territory in Ultrapuertos," continued Miguel, referring to the trans-Pyrenean lands of Basse Navarre. "I am familiar with all those goat paths and un-traveled mountain passes. I've hawked in them often. And after we've negotiated the mountains, you will lodge in my cousin's manor house in Elizaldea, which they now call 'Valcarlos'. He used to be the administrator of my manor in Azcain, a good and loyal subject. He will keep you out of harm's way and be your personal guide in your travels in France. He knows the country well, speaks the language like a native. You will be in good hands, milord."

"Thank you, my friend," said the prince, obviously relieved. "I knew I had come to the right place. I was lucky I remembered where it was!"

Sabina's reunion with her uncle, Juan de Beaumont, was joyous and affectionate. They had much to catch up on and sat chatting by the hearth into the wee hours, long after the others had retired to their chambers. They had always been close to one another, especially after Sabina's mother passed away at an early age and her aunt, the Countess, had taken her under her wing. As a child, she had always been a little intimidated by her uncle's gruff ways but eventually learned to see through him and realize that under all that bluster and gruff demeanor lay a charming softness. They caught up with each other's lives, he, pleased to see her happy and radiant in her new role as lady of the manor, she, worried about his uncertain future as Commander-in-Chief of the prince's ghost army.

The next day dawned crisp and clear. It was one of those rare late winter mornings in the western Pyrenees when the skies were blue and cloudless and even the farm animals sensed that a glory day was on the way. After a hearty breakfast of *magras con tomate*—a Navarran version of ham and eggs, served with a rich tomato sauce—Miguel and his royal retinue struck out towards Roncevaux. As they were about to leave the plain of Errozabal, they veered off the main road and followed a footpath towards Menditxuri to avoid encountering any of the king's troops believed to be guarding the pass above Roncevaux. From the skirts of Menditxuri, they wended their way up the shoulders of Lindux until they reached its summit.

It was a breathtaking view. From there, on a clear day, one could literally see forever. Below them and to the east, they could see through the winter-bare limbs of the birch forest the gray rooftops of the Collegiate of Roncevaux. On the esplanade at the foot of the Hospice, they could see moving dots in the distance—pilgrims striking out for Santiago, in quest of indulgence for their souls. Not far to the east, and across the gap, stood Ibañeta, topped by a giant cross. Under its shadow, the small hermitage's bell tolled at irregular intervals, guiding the pilgrims over the pass.

"This is where my ancestors crushed the Franks," said Miguel, making a sweeping motion with his hand over the valley below him. He did not have to explain the allusion to Charlemagne's debacle in those very chasms. They both knew; everyone had learned *La Chanson de Roland* by heart as a child. Juan de Beaumont remained silent despite a twinge at the mention of his ancestors' defeat in that very pass, seven centuries earlier.

"They were brave Vascons then," said the prince wistfully. "They were focused against a foreign foe. Brother fought alongside brother, not against him."

Miguel felt a pang of pity for the prince, so desperately longing for a kingdom. He sensed, deep down, that he would never find it.

It was almost dark when they descended into the valley of Luzaide. Miguel, who was riding point, went ahead to reconnoiter the village of Valcarlos to make sure there were no Gramont troops around. The king's forces had recently taken

St. Jean Pied de Port, a fortified town only a few miles up the road, and Valcarlos was too close to it for comfort. Finding the village unoccupied, Miguel arranged lodgings for the prince's retinue in a small manor house owned by his cousin, Ramón de Urculu, a loyal sympathizer of the Prince of Viana. Under cover of darkness, the group rode into the village and was warmly welcomed by Miguel's cousin. The hidalgo outdid himself that evening, regaling his illustrious guests with his finest viands and choicest wines. Ramón was profoundly grateful to Miguel for allowing him the distinct honor of hosting his prince and future king.

For his troubles that day and for providing him with a guide and escort in his quest for a royal audience with the French king, Miguel was bestowed the title of Royal Majordomo. The title was to remain only honorific for he was never to exercise the exalted duties of royal steward to a prince destined never to wear the crown.

Almost two years after that ultra-Pyrenean adventure, Miguel came across his cousin Ramón at a country fair in Valcarlos. The two caught up with each other's lives over cups of hearty Bordeaux wine and *tapas* of *txistorra* sausage and chatted at great length about their recent experiences.

"I traipsed all over France with him and his retinue," Ramón explained. "We almost stumbled on some of Gramont's supporters in Pau and then, several weeks later, we barely managed to sneak past Foix's allies near Toulouse. That was close. We had to cross the length of the Languedoc because someone told us that the French king was summering in Lyon. What a nightmare that trip turned out to be!"

"Sounds dreadful," commented Miguel, impressed by his cousin's tour-de-force with his prince. "How did the interview go in Lyon?"

"Poorly," said Ramón somberly. "All that ghastly trip for naught! The French king was gracious enough during the interview but, in the end, he was unwilling to commit himself to help Prince Carlos regain his throne. You know how kings stick by one another. Thick as thieves, they are! There was no way he would undermine another's royal authority. Juan II is, after all, still officially king of Navarre. Besides, King Charles would like for the prince's sister, Leonor, to inherit the crown of Navarre. She's married to a cousin of his, Gaston de Foix, you know."

"How can I forget!" remarked Miguel balefully. "I was wounded by one of his culverin missiles in Aoiz several years ago." After a thoughtful pause, Miguel said: "Leonor would make a dreadful Navarran queen and her husband an even more unsavory consort king!" Miguel was distressed by the depressing prospects. "Where did the prince go after that royal rebuff?"

"We sailed down the Rhone and on to Italy. It was not a pleasant trip. I wanted to come back home but the prince insisted I remain in his company. He pleaded his case with Pope Calixtus in Rome but got as cool a reception from him as he had from the king of France. Dislodging a sitting king is not a very politic move, even for a Pope. Anyway, the prince was one dejected man. Then, on top of everything else, his cough seemed to worsen. Must have been all that traveling and all that disappointment. He is not a well man, you know."

"I am aware of his delicate health," said Miguel. "It was always brittle, even when he was a boy. He caught colds easily, I remember. The court physic even suspected him to have a touch of consumption at one point."

"Well," continued Ramón, "he struggled with his coughing bouts until we left the inclement northern clime and headed south to balmy Naples. His uncle, King Alfonso, the one they called the Magnanimous, invited him to stay at his court in Naples until things cleared up a bit. The prince was just beginning to enjoy his stay there when his uncle up and died! It was a terrible blow. Here was the prince, already in frail health and in a foreign country, with nowhere to go. I had been planning to come back home that second winter. I'd been away from home for over a year, you know. But I couldn't abandon the hapless prince. So I hung on to his dwindling entourage."

"I'm sure he appreciated that," remarked Miguel. "He, more than anyone else, understands the rare value of loyalty."

"He did, indeed. I really earned my keep as his majordomo during that trip. It was a relief when he received an invitation to the court of Sicily. But his economic situation, like his health, was fast deteriorating. He had used up his resources and had trouble making ends meet. I know; my stipend was put on hold. It was during our brief stay in Sicily that his father, King Juan, sent an ambassador inviting him to return to Iberia and let bygones be bygones. I think his father was a little worried about the enthusiastic reception the Sicilians had given the prince when he arrived in Palermo."

"Did he accept the invitation?" asked Miguel, fearing the answer. No good could possibly come from accepting an offer from that conniving rogue-king of Navarre.

"He did," said Ramón, mournfully. "He had few other remaining options. He was sick and penniless. The worst part was that he had to sign an agreement relinquishing his claim to the throne of Navarre until his father died. Worse yet, he had to agree never to set foot in Navarre during that interlude. Appalling agreement, wouldn't you say?"

"Poor Carlos!" remarked Miguel, feeling for his ill-starred friend. "That contract he signed is worthless, you know. It violates every single tenet and clause of the *Fueros* of Navarre." Miguel knew every arcane codicil and obscure legal statute of Navarran law better than almost anyone in the realm. The covenant would be indefensible in any court of law in the land. And yet he knew that there were powerful forces conspiring against the Prince of Viana's chances of ever occupying the throne of Navarre.

In the spring of 1460, sick at heart and spirit, the prince sailed into Barcelona, to a clamorous reception by the Catalans, who saw in him the rightful king of Navarre and Aragon, some even of Catalonia. The tumultuous welcome worried his father, who saw in it a threat to his carefully laid plans for his hegemony and succession. He was quick to foil the prince's feeble pretensions to the hand of Isabella of Castile by hurriedly arranging her marriage to his other son, Carlos' half-brother, Ferdinand, a couple shortly destined to rule Spain under the grand title of "the Catholic Monarchs". The hapless prince did not have long to mourn his circumstances. A sick and dejected man, the Prince of Viana passed away at the young age of forty without ever setting eyes on his Navarre again. His father, Juan II, outlived him by a dozen years.

Ill winds were blowing over Navarre.

Chapter 42

A Pilgrimage to Santiago

1500s

The early 1500s were years heady with rebellious ferment, the Renaissance about to tear the fabric of Christianity asunder. The Beaumonts and Gramonts were still at each other's throats, their petty dissensions slowly dragging the storied kingdom of Navarre to its ineluctable end. The tragi-comical French connection that had begun two centuries earlier with Sancho el Fuerte's heirless death was about to come to an end.

Juan II's son, Ferdinand, had married the formidable Isabella of Castile and had just overrun the last Moorish stronghold in the Peninsula. Free at last of the centuries-old Islamic yoke, he turned his attention to the more pressing business of administering a recently discovered New World. Wary of the Humanistic inroads into her kingdom, Isabella encouraged the Inquisition to drum out any challenge to Catholic dogma. The Moors and the Jews were the first to fall in the heresy hunt. Offered the choice between embracing Christianity or leaving the country, many opted for the latter, stripping Spain of a vital financial infrastructure just at the time she would need it most, when the gold from the colonies began to pour in.

Juan de Aguirre was as boisterous and unruly as the times into which he was born. He was only dimly aware of the political and religious turmoil swirling around him during his youth. Occasionally, some bizarre event would come along to pique his curiosity, like the time an Italian teenager by the name of Cesare Borgia was named Bishop of Pamplona. The village was abuzz with the extraordinary news. It was odd enough for a sixteen year-old to earn a Bishopric, thought Juan, but for the peach-fuzzed adolescent to be the illegitimate son of a Cardinal was, to say the least, surprising. Only a year into his Bishopric, Borgia was named Archbishop of Valencia and anointed Cardinal and Primate of Spain, all at the tender age of seventeen. That, it turned out, was not the last time Juan would hear about the precocious young Italian, who was one day to inspire Machiavelli to write his *Prince*.

Nestled in the folds of the Esteribar valley, hard by the western Pyrenean foothills, the sleepy village of Agorreta remained largely untouched by the turmoil swirling around it. The only excitement visited on its villagers was the occasional comings and goings of kings and queens traveling along the sinuous road that wound past the family home on their way to and from France. Young Juan, who had just turned twenty, had recently inherited the lordship of Agorreta on his father's death. His grandfather, the judge, had managed to enlarge the family estate during his lifetime by adding several manors to its assets which in earlier days would have earned him a petty baronage.

Juan was not much into the privileges of nobility nor did he particularly enjoy the company of noblemen who dropped in occasionally out of the wintry blast. Chivalry and its increasingly archaic code of ethics did not have much allure for him. He was perfectly content to be lord of his several manors, happy to sport no more prepossessing title than *hidalgo* in the smug conviction that his family's arms and blazons were proof enough of his nobility. His grandfather, the "Merino de las Montañas," had managed to raise the family's status in the ranks of Navarran gentry, earning for it the signal distinction of "Cabo de Armeria" with its privilege to assign heraldic blazons to families worthy of joining the ranks of the Navarran gentry. That was something that would appeal to a Chief Justice of the Realm, thought Juan. He, personally, could care less.

His life was more down to earth. Slender and auburn-haired, his neatly trimmed beard and sharp features added to his pleasing but rakish air. His Rabelaisian bent was a thorn in his mother's side, who considered his wayward and irreverent ways an affront to her romantic notions of chivalry. She was particularly mortified by his inclination to mock every solemn occasion. Religion had long lost its allure for him. Only the pagan Mari, the archaic Mother Earth goddess of his ancestors, seemed to retain any appeal for him.

On occasion, he would trundle off on a moonlit night to the hillock overlooking Sorogain, the place of witches. There, he would sit in the center of the *arrespil*, the ring of the ancient cromlech's upright stones, hoping to catch a glimpse of the goddess herself, or simply listen to the strains of her plaintive song, lost in the breeze that stirred the evening fog. He was seldom fazed by the fact that she never actually manifested herself, content to sense her presence in the damp, cold wind blowing down the mountainside, whispering her lament in the branches of the lofty beech trees towering above, whispering to him that men knew nothing, that Mari knew everything.

Juan had a thing about women of flesh and blood, as well. His good looks and devil-may-care temperament made him irresistible to the opposite sex. Eyes always lit with the suggestion of mischief, the young Agorreta was not unlike a *basajaun* forest genie set loose amidst a flock of sheep. Women were attracted to a certain wildness in him. On their way to Saturday confession, the town lasses would cast longing glances at his manor home, hoping to hear his siren calls tempting them to come add a little something to their stale litany of innocent venial sins. Lured by his enticements, there was always some wench in the group of giggly lasses who would succumb to the invitation for a tumble in the hay in Jaureguizar's *sabaiao* hayloft. A man can learn much between the thighs of a good woman, Juan always said.

It had come to the village priest's attention that Juan and his ne'er-do-well friends liked to sneak out of church at the start of his sermons, slinking back to their pews at the Offertory, just as Mass resumed. The snub to his homilies so unsettled the priest that he threatened to cast an interdiction on the young truants if they persisted in their wayward habits.

Juan ignored the threat with casual insouciance, reminding the pastor that the Agorretas built and owned the manor church, paid for his studies at Seminary and subsequent ordination expenses, and were now paying his wages. The priest was, in other words, serving in the manor's chapel by the grace and bidding of the lord of Agorreta, that was to say, Juan. Still rankling from that reminder, the young priest scurried off to his Bishop in Pamplona for moral support. The Bishop stepped in shortly after to un-ruffle feathers and settle differences between Church and Gentry. Meanwhile, Juan and the priest continued to circle warily around each other, like two young hounds sniffing for the odor of hesitation in the other.

A no less traumatic incident occurred during this uneasy truce. Telesforo, Juan's bailiff's reeve, came down with some mysterious ailment that left him incapacitated with excruciating abdominal pains. The barber, who doubled as village doctor and veterinarian, was summoned to apply his usual poultices and leeches to thin the patient's blood and chase the bad humors away. The barber's ministrations only aggravated Telesforo's condition and shortly after, the priest was called in to administer the oils of Extreme Unction. The surpliced Padre walked into the sickroom, preceded by his lantern-bearing, bell-ringing server. The apparition startled Telesforo who, fearing that penance for his sins would entail sexual abstinence, underwent a sudden and miraculous recovery.

His cure, unfortunately, was short-lived. Telesforo died shortly after from something the barber unctuously identified as "*miserere* colic," a blanket diagnosis ascribed to any and all mysterious ailments of the digestive track. There was much lamentation among the villagers because Telesforo had been a kind and decent reeve, who tended to overlook delays in their rent-payments, pardoned their fines when accused of shoddy workmanship for the lord of the manor and looked the other way when their cattle strayed into the lord's demesne. Juan and his bailiff knew about this kind-hearted reeve of theirs but overlooked his weaknesses because he was such a decent and honest man otherwise. Besides, he always made a good fourth at *mus*, their favorite card game. Juan even suspected that the good reeve had thrown an occasional game or two, just to ingratiate himself to his lord. Now, *that*, in Juan's book, was true nobility of spirit.

There were the usual attendees at the wake the night Telesforo died. A handful of his best friends offered to stay up all night watching over the cadaver, praying for his soul's happy and unimpeded passage into paradise. More times than not, however, friends had been known to turn a wake into an evening of drinking and merriment. One can pray for only so long, they rationalized. Sensing that this wake would be no different, the parish priest reminded Juan and his dissolute friends that morning after Mass that a wake was a sorrowful event that should not be turned into an occasion for revelry.

Telesforo's widow, who had nagged and bedeviled the poor man all his life, was aware of the irreverent practice and had admonished the 'wakers' to refrain from their usual shenanigans in her house. When she retired to her quarters that evening, she was comforted by the men's mumbled prayers and the soft, clicking sound of rosary beads around the bier in the room next door.

The drinking started soon after. Well into their cups, the men started looking around for a table on which to play *mus*. They owed Telesforo one last *órdago*, the ultimate all-or-nothing bet. Not finding a card table on which to play, they decided to pick up the now stiff Telesforo, stuff him in the armoire by the wall, straighten out the bed sheets and use his bed as a makeshift card table. As the party grew rowdier and the *órdago* bets started flying, Telesforo's now-suspicious widow suddenly burst onto the scene and discovered that her dead husband was missing. Apprised of his whereabouts, she opened the armoire door to find him inside, propped up among the pillows, a vacant look on his face.

That was the end of the wake. Picking up a firebrand from the hearth, Telesforo's wife chased the drunken lot out of her house, spouting vituperations. Word of the profanation soon spread around the village. Apoplectic, the village priest lit into Juan and his good-for-nothing friends with choice, un-pious expletives, once again threatening excommunication. The incident further eroded the uneasy truce between Church and Fief in Agorreta.

The lord of the manor had other quirks that the *padre* found even more reprehensible than his customary pranks. Although the feudal *derecho de pernada*, or first night's right, had long since fallen into disuse, Juan insisted on keeping the rite alive much to his villeins' dismay. Though he sensed their displeasure, Juan refused to give up the pleasurable tradition of *Ius primae noctis*, his only concession being to exercise the dubious privilege sparingly.

"It is high time you took a wife," his aging mother, Elena, told him one day, aware of the priest's and villagers' grumbling. Widowed several years earlier and, having had no progeny other than the *bon-vivant* Juan, she had grown increasingly doubtful about his legitimate perpetuation of the Agorreta line. "I have heard of a nice, marriageable young lady in Aoiz." she told him one day. "She's the granddaughter of one of your grandfather's old associates there. Her father owns great tracts of land in the suburbs of town. Our village pastor, who, as you know, comes from there, tells me that the lord of Larangoz is considering dowering his daughter with all of his lands when she marries. And the groom can't be just anybody, either. The lord of Larangoz has to approve the union himself."

"Is she pretty?" queried Juan, pretending interest. Unlike his mother, he was not much of an entrepreneur. He had always taken real estate for granted, having been generously endowed with it. Not too keen on the institution of marriage either, he would have to up the ante on his mother with some outrageous pre-condition, such as the candidate's physical charm. He knew, of course, that people did not marry for grace or beauty—or love, for that matter. It always boiled down to some hard-nosed business deal like the one his mother now seemed to be getting ready to close.

Seeing through her son's subterfuge, Elena huffed: "What does it matter?" barely able to hide her irritation. "From what I hear, Pilar is a nice, pious young lady. And that's the most important virtue in a young maiden, isn't it." She sensed right off that piety was the wrong argument to use with a son who always seemed to have other more earthy female attributes in mind.

"Oh, so now it turns out you even know her name!" he chided. He was now worried that this whole conversation only presaged a noose-tightening on his carefree bachelor's days. But he also knew the rules: parents traditionally arranged marriages for their children. And from the sounds of it, his freedom was about to end.

"Of course!" responded Elena. "And her father's too." Pausing a moment to let the revelation sink in, she proceeded, now in a less imperious tone: "I have asked them over for Michelmas. You will meet her then. Her father and I will discuss terms and make the final arrangements at that time."

"But, mother," protested Juan. "I'm not even twenty-two yet!" Just as the words tumbled out of his mouth he knew he had put forth the wrong argument.

"Your father was only twenty when we married," she retorted huffily. "And he was not even the lord of Agorreta at the time! You already are!" Leveling him with a reproving gaze, she added: "Enough said!" And that was the end of the discussion. Officially, the Navarran family may not have been considered a matriarchy but that was just an oversight; it had been one from time immemorial and would remain so. Not by happenstance had the Salic law so utterly failed to take root in the land.

Juan sulked. He had tried hard to prolong his free-wheeling days but he knew that they would soon end. Marriage was a pretty sobering proposition even if it were not rammed down one's throat.

He was pleasantly surprised by the young woman's good looks and demure demeanor when he first set eyes on her at the Michelmas reunion in Agorreta. Pilar's blue eyes and flaxen hair bespoke a Visigothic strain she shared with many mountain women. But her gentle disposition belied her barbarian ancestry. Juan was immediately taken by her arresting smile and melodious voice so unlike the local wenches' hoarse, throaty utterances. But it was her modesty, the way she averted her eyes when addressed, that truly captivated him. He had never met such a delightfully shy and decorous woman in his entire life. In a charming, un-self conscious sort of way, she was challenging his boorishness with an innocent grace and understated poise that entranced him.

But Juan was not one to indulge in romantic musings for long. Some deep-rooted defensive mechanism in him always prompted him to search for the dross, any kind of dross, behind the luster. Having come back down to earth, he now observed this woman with a cold, analytic eye. The first thing he noticed about her was her baffling study in contrasts: though graced by the comeliness of youth, her figure was not voluptuous. In fact, try as he might, his roving eye read few signs of fecundity in her small breasts and narrow hips.

In that dark corner of his mind where options were weighed and choices made, he started pondering this candidate's procreative potential. She was no buxom Mari, not by any stretch of the imagination. But, then again, he reflected, some women are sometimes full of surprises. Take Imelda, next door, for instance, skinny as a knitting needle and yet the mother of ten! Besides, a wife was not some sort of art object for all to admire and drool over. She was supposed to be modestly tucked away in the house. That's why they were called housewives, in the first place. As if to reinforce his convictions, strains of the Aragonese *jota "Las mujeres pa'l fogn"* came wafting out from under some back door of memory, chauvinistically proclaiming a woman's place to be in the hearth, with her pots and pans.

When his mind finally came to rest, Juan had reached his decision: She would do just fine. Pilar's real assets, he decided, were her meekness and docility. A pliant wife would cut him all the slack he needed to do his own thing.

The decision was not his to make, anyway. It was his mother who had to close the deal. Pilar's grandfather, the lord of Larangoz, a comrade-at-arms of Miguel de Agorreta during the siege of Aoiz, had maintained close ties with the *merino* during his lifetime, a friendship passed on and nurtured by their progeny. Now an aging and infirm widower, Larangoz' son, Andrés, was turning over his lands as dowry to his only daughter, Pilar. Her marriage to Juan would thus effectively join the houses of Agorreta and Larangoz, making for a very handsome estate, by any landed gentry's standards.

The wedding took place in early spring the following year at Roncevaux, where all the Agorretas had traditionally married. There was little argument about the choice of shrine; Aoiz had no comparable sanctuary. Besides, the young couple had planned to strike out on a pilgrimage immediately after the nuptials, and Roncevaux seemed an appropriate place for that.

It had been Pilar's idea to visit Santiago on their honeymoon. Juan was not too keen on such religious adventures, let alone one entailing a round trip of several months, but he was so taken by his new bride that he succumbed to her entreaties, humoring her with her pious request. More unusual, though, was her proposition to refrain from consummating their connubial union until after they had kissed the feet of the Apostle's statue in Santiago. They would offer that sacrifice to the saint, she explained. Flatly refusing to go along with this highly irregular celibate hiatus, Juan started to worry about such bizarre notions. Reassured by her eventual relenting, however, he allowed their marriage plans to proceed without further surprises.

The nuptials were followed by a huge wedding feast in Burguete, a hamlet near Roncevaux, with an inn famous for its repasts. After spending several days in Gasteluzar, the newlyweds set off for Santiago, leaning on their ash staffs, displaying the emblematic pilgrim's scallop-shell stitched on their coarse pilgrim cloaks. They would acquire the real scallop shells when they got to Santiago.

The weather was crisp and clear that early spring morning, a blessing for any pilgrim starting on a three-month trek. They could have traveled faster and more comfortably on horseback but Pilar refused, believing it would detract from the sacrifice, which was, after all, the whole object of the pilgrimage.

They followed the traditional Jacobean route, first south to Pamplona, then on to Puente la Reina, where they joined other pilgrims who had negotiated the Pyrenees farther east. Crossing the town's Roman Bridge, they proceeded westward along the rolling, vine-dotted hills of La Rioja, following the fertile Ebro valley into Logroño. They averaged fifteen miles a day, sometimes having to duck into some shepherd's shelter to get out of a rain shower. They stopped at free hostels and modest inns that catered to pilgrims, but sometimes, when the hostelries were full, they would night in some monastery, sleeping in bug-ridden straw pallets, sharing the humble country fare with fellow pilgrims. Their host stamped the safe-conduct certificates which they would later have to produce to prove that they had passed through that place. Pilar prayed endless rosaries along the way while Juan grumbled about sore feet. They had to stop at a Benedictine monastery in Sahagún to have the friars tend to Juan's blisters.

Always, on arriving at a large town, they would seek out some lively tavern, frequented by other friendly, boisterous fellow travelers. They would treat themselves to local delicacies such as dried venison with cheese-stuffed peppers in

León, or crisp, tangy blood sausages in Burgos, all washed down with an invigorating Tempranillo Rioja red. Those were meals fit for kings. But mostly, it was shepherd's fare.

After Burgos, the road wound through tedious plateaus and desolate, wind-blown wastelands, where the surrounding silence and appalling absence of people played havoc with the mind and tested the spirit. Ahead and to the north, they caught the first glimpse of the snow-capped Cantabrian Mountains rising high above the wheat fields. They knew then that they were closing in on their journey's goal.

"We're lucky we don't have to travel all the way to Jerusalem to earn this plenary indulgence," commented Pilar, as they approached Villafranca del Bierzo, trying to soothe her husband's increasingly irascible mood. Mention of Jerusalem brought memories of childhood stories to Juan.

"There's an old family tradition," he said, remembering one of his mother's bedtime stories, "about one of our ancestors who lived centuries ago. Tall as a five-year beech sapling, they said he was. He went to Jerusalem on a Crusade. I think he also fought at Navas de Tolosa. 'Moor slayer' they called him." Pausing a moment, he continued. "Did you notice those inverted crescent moons in our family's armorial bearings carved into the large stone slab in the floor of the front hall?"

"Yes," answered Pilar. "I often wondered why they were inverted."

"Well, an inverted anything is about as useful as an upturned pail; holds about as much water, too! In this case an inverted moon stands for a Moorish defeat. It seems this giant ancestor of ours earned those blazons by defeating Muslims in a couple of battles."

Pilar was impressed. She loved to hear snippets of her husband's family lore. The Agorretas, she thought, had such an interesting family history, much more so than the Larangoz. Traveling together like this was a wonderful way to get acquainted with each other's quirks and foibles, too. As the days grew into weeks, Juan's first impressions about his bride were confirmed; she may have seemed frail of body but there was nothing feeble about her spirit. And her mind was remarkably keen. She was a good woman. He had chosen well.

Pilar, on the other hand, was sometimes shocked by Juan's earthy, rough-hewn edges. But then, she reasoned, that was the way mountain men were brought up to be. There was much bluster and scant subtlety about his pronouncements. Yet despite the swagger, he was kind and gentle with her and, as she discovered, extremely protective. At an inn at Astorga, a local bumpkin had addressed her disrespectfully and, incensed by the slight, Juan put up a fight defending her honor.

The stark, tawny plains gradually changed into a wooded, rain-drenched mountain landscape, all gray and green. This was the last bastion in the Peninsula's northwest to which the Celts had retreated. Juan and Pilar started seeing more granite crosses and odd-looking stone buildings standing on stilts, which the locals called *horreos,* ancient Celtic dwellings now used as granaries. The farmers and townsfolk displayed a flinty independence, not unlike that of their Navarran counterparts, thought Juan. But they looked different. The women were broad-shouldered and big-bosomed, the men fair-haired and light-complexioned, unlike the swarthier Castilians to the south. They knew they were in Galicia when they heard the haunting music from the *gaita* bagpipes, whose shrill notes reminded them of their own *txistu* flutes back home.

It had taken five weeks to reach Santiago but the breathtaking scene now before their eyes made it all worthwhile. From atop an outlying hill they espied a large, sprawling city enveloped in mists. Like fingers reaching up to heaven in supplication, the spires of a dozen churches attested to the holiness of the place. Peering through the haze, they saw the city walls breached by several portals opening onto the inner city. As they wound their way down from the hills, they were soon lost in a maze of streets lined with plantain trees draped in the young green of spring. A series of narrow streets radiated from what appeared to be a large central square, surrounded by a jumble of smaller squares. On their approach to the heart of town, they had to duck under the arches of porticoed passageways to escape the drizzle. Village life in Agorreta had not prepared them for this architectural marvel.

"Not even Pamplona can compare with this!" thrilled Juan, awed by the magnificence of the city's architecture. "Must be all these French pilgrims bringing in their wealth and craftsmanship." His guess was not far off the mark.

Threading their way through narrow back streets, they entered a medieval world of stately squares over which honey-colored granite palaces brooded, proudly displaying coats-of-arms atop their lintels. Eventually, they stumbled onto the Plaza Mayor, a vast, bustling central square dominated by an immense Romanesque cathedral. Its stunning facade reminded Juan of a forest of granite, its columns, polished by the insistent drizzle of ages, now shining golden in the setting sun.

They stood transfixed at the Portal of Glory, a massive, triple-arched main entrance laden with carved statues of saints and prophets, each with his lifelike smile and exquisitely chiseled tunic folds. They easily recognized Jeremiah and his luxuriant beard, Moses' thoughtful frown, Isaiah's pensive brow and Daniel's youngish smile, even Esther's feminine grace. And the trumpeting angels were so lifelike that Juan could almost hear their clarion peals.

Entering the cathedral, they were greeted by the sweet scent of pungent incense barely masking the stale, sour smell of the sweat of ages. They searched long and hard for what they had traveled so far to see until a kindly friar pointed them in the right direction. Following the aisle under the central apse, they climbed down a spiral staircase to a crypt where they came upon a silver urn resting under what appeared to be a Roman mausoleum. It contained the remains of the apostle James. As they knelt to pray on their reclinatories, Juan and Pilar felt a mystical release, as if they had been suddenly relieved of a lifetime baggage of un-forgiven sins. Tears of joy streamed down Pilar's cheeks and even the flint-hearted Juan felt his eyes moisten with emotion. In that moving instant, their plenary indulgence was gained. They could almost feel its timeless grace flowing over them.

Everything else after that could have been an anticlimax, but it wasn't. The town was full of surprises. The pilgrim's Hospice, recently inaugurated by the Catholic Monarchs, had opened its gates to pilgrims who could produce safe-conducts appropriately stamped along their way. As bona-fide pilgrims, Juan and Pilar had earned three days of free room and board in the magnificent Hospice. A sense of awe swept over Pilar when she discovered that both St. Francis of Assisi and St. Dominique had visited there, centuries earlier. A fledgling University had recently been inaugurated nearby. Even more amazing, they heard stories about a fabled ship called La Pinta, which some Italian navigator had recently sailed into the nearby port of Bayona after discovering a new world across the sea.

It drizzled every single day during their stay in Santiago but the locals didn't seem to mind. The market stalls under the colonnaded porticoes caught Pilar's eye. There were women selling wonderful vegetables and fruits, rabbits and chickens, even delicious breast-shaped cheeses, amusingly called *tetilla*. But best of all was the wonderful seafood that Pilar could seldom find in Pamplona, let alone Agorreta. Heaped on trestle tables were piles of still-writhing salmon and trout, lamprey eels and langoustines, shrimp and oysters, and a hundred other crustaceans she had never even seen nor heard of before. And, of course, *vieiras*, the delicious scallops found only in Galicia, whose shells had come to symbolize the pilgrimage to Santiago itself.

The day of parting came all too soon. It had been a memorable experience, full of religious fervor, impressive sights, interesting people and, yes, wonderful seafood. Certain images stood out from the rest, like the awe-inspiring reliquary of the Apostle James' remains, and the enormous *botafumeiro* censer hanging over the main altar, which the six little friars swung like a mighty pendulum across the breadth of the wide transepts, spewing incense to mask the foul smell of a thousand unwashed bodies. They were memories to be tucked away and treasured for a lifetime.

More important yet for Pilar was the certainty that the plenary indulgence thus earned had cleansed the dross of a lifetime of sins, assuring her of a non-stop passage to heaven upon her death, bypassing the dire stopover in Purgatory. Juan's thoughts were not as lofty but he was quite proud of the trekking exploit itself. He would brag about it to his cronies back home for a long time to come.

Chapter 43

The Last Act

"You are ordered by the King to report immediately to Pamplona with your armed retinue," read the peremptory order scribbled on a scrolled parchment and secured with the royal seal. The courier, a young squire from the king's court, had been galloping up and down the high mountain valleys of Navarre, handing out summons to the lords of the different manors.

Juan, who had just returned from his pilgrimage, was dumbfounded. On his return from Santiago, he thought he sensed a certain political unrest simmering just under the surface but the possibility of full-blown hostilities breaking out was not something he had considered. Ferdinand, the recently widowed Catholic king of Castile, had married Germaine de Foix in hopes that her uncle Louis XII of France would name her queen of Navarre, despite the fact that Navarre already had a legitimate king. The peremptory missive Juan was now holding in his hands informed him that his king, Jean d'Albret, was not going to take the Castilian's scheming lying down.

"And what, pray, is the reason for this summons?" demanded Juan de Aguirre after going over the document a second time. Although his fiefly duties included rendering military service to his king when summoned, active duty could sometimes be bargained away, depending on the emergency. A footnote in the document he had just finished reading explicitly ruled out such an option.

"I don't know the exact reason for the summons, milord," responded the messenger respectfully. "But I suspect it may have something to do with a planned assault on Viana. Count Louis de Beaumont, as you may know, has taken control of the castle there and is holding it in Castile's name."

"I see," said Juan, momentarily distracted by the thought of having to call his men to arms. After a moment's reflection he muttered: "Louis de Beaumont!" with undisguised contempt. Although Beaumont blood ran in his veins, Juan cordially despised the Count of Lerín, the clan's latest leader, for having sided with Ferdinand of Castile in the latter's running feud with the king of Navarre. That, in Juan's book, was treason. The opportunistic little despot was doing untold damage to Navarre by sleeping with the enemy. Juan's loathing for this "dwarf", as he sometimes referred to the Count, suddenly made the inconvenience of suiting up for battle against him almost welcome.

"Who will command this expedition?" inquired Juan.

"Cesare Borgia, milord. The king has just named him Commander-in-Chief of Navarre's forces in the Castilian frontier."

The name rang a distant bell with Juan. "You don't mean our one-time peach-fuzzed Bishop of Pamplona, do you?" Juan was trying to probe the young messenger's political leanings. He knew full well that the Pope's son had hung up his clerical robes soon after being named Cardinal and Primate of Spain years earlier but he had lost track of him since.

"Yes, milord," responded the messenger noncommittally. "You know, of course, he married our king's sister, Charlotte d'Albret, not too long ago. I believe it was for that reason that he was imprisoned by the Castilian king in Medina del Campo. But he somehow managed to escape to Pamplona, where his brother-in-law, our king, promptly named him military Commander of the southern Marches."

"So, we'll be led into battle by a defrocked cleric!" snorted Juan, unable to hide his contempt any longer. "Sounds like a promising campaign!" he added sarcastically.

Being but a messenger, the squire judiciously kept his thoughts to himself. Then, as if to soothe the lord's petulance, he added: "*Condottieri*, they call Captains like him in Italy, I hear."

That last piece of gratuitous information only served to intensify Juan's irascible mood.

"Bah! A bunch of be-plumed toy soldiers, those Italians are!" retorted Juan, who had often wondered what ever happened to the stalwart legionnaires they once bred in Italy. "Never hear about any of those *condottieri* ever dying in battle!" he declared disgustedly.

All his grumbling was, of course, for naught. Three days after receiving the summons, Juan trotted up to the Citadel in Pamplona with a dozen mounted men-at-arms, his fief's allocation. They were a sorry looking lot, twelve country bumpkins mounted on swayback nags, who could barely hold a steady lance or shoot a straight arrow. Their training exercises during the course of the year had been haphazard and lackadaisical. Neither Juan nor his villeins had taken the practice sessions too seriously: a quintain charged here, a crossbow target practice held there, an occasional harquebus shot gone awry, nothing too strenuous or fruitful. Juan only hoped that they would not rue the desultory training.

The Captain of the Guard at the Citadel stifled a chuckle as he watched them dismount their hacks before assigning them to quarters in the already-cramped military barracks.

Juan's first encounter with Commander Borgia, several days later, filled him with a deep sense of foreboding. Noticing the Italian's aristocratic and, in his opinion, somewhat effete features, Juan regarded him with arch disapproval, felt grave reservations about the outcome of this whole operation. He, along with six-thousand other fighting men, stood stiffly at attention in the parade grounds outside the barracks. It was a gray, blustery morning in February. A cold wind whistled down the slopes of San Cristobal, making everyone in the formation hope that the swearing-in ceremony would be brief. Standing uncomfortably on a raised platform in the center of the parade grounds, were Captain General Borgia and several of his aides. Holding the regimental flag was his good friend and aide-de-camp, Count of Benavente, who had helped him escape from Medina del Campo.

After the call to attention had been sounded and the obligatory salutes exchanged, the knights, *hidalgos* and *infanzones* dismounted and marched up in line to the platform's steps to kiss the battle banner in the act of swearing allegiance to Navarre. Juan was one of the few present who knew what the emblematic chains embroidered on the flag stood for and whence they came. Countless times before, he had seen the original ones hanging from the Chapter Chapel in Roncevaux, dimly remembering that one of his ancestors, the giant, had helped his king seize them from the Moors and personally hung them there. After kissing the embroidered cloth with reverence, Juan looked up and, for the first time, faced his commander close up. Juan's scrutiny was cold, almost contemptuous, failing the cardinal military requirement of respect for one's commander. It boded ill, Juan sensed.

Swelled by the ranks of Austrian reinforcements sent him by Philip the Handsome, Borgia's army marched out of Pamplona in early March of 1507, heading south and west, to the fortified town of Viana, some fifty miles distant. A strong artillery contingent supported the force of a thousand knights, several hundred men-at-arms and some five thousand foot soldiers.

Although they arrived shortly after, the ensuing siege of Viana dragged on unavailingly for days. Louis de Beaumont was frustrating Borgia's siege by sneaking provisions into his fortified town through a secret entrance, under cover of darkness.

Hearing about it, Cesare decided on the spur of the moment to personally investigate the concealed gap one stormy night. With characteristic panache, he took off to scout the breach, unescorted. He paid dearly for his foolhardiness, falling prey to an ambush laid by Beaumont's men in a ravine close by the city walls. It cost Borgia his life, his armor, even his undergarments.

Apprized of the tragic event, King d'Albret rushed to Viana to confirm the death of his brother-in-law, who was still lying there, naked and battered, at the foot of the ravine where he had been surprised the night before. Grieved and outraged by the appalling incident, the king ordered the Count of Benavente to storm the Viana defenses, take the town and have Cesare's body buried with full military honors in the local church's cemetery.

Furious at Louis de Beaumont's dastardly act, King d'Albret ordered the Count's possessions in Navarre obliterated, making sure every mansion in the Count's town of Lerín was razed, every vineyard uprooted, every neighboring forest cut down. It was a heavy price to pay for siding with Castille.

Juan de Agorreta and his men, who never had their hearts in the ill-planned Viana operation, were only too happy to return home shortly after the siege was concluded, un-bloodied and unbruised.

"The spoiled son of a Pope had no business leading an army into battle," he confessed to his wife, Pilar, when he arrived home. "It only confirmed my worst premonitions about Borgia's generalship."

Several years had passed since the Pyrrhic victory at Viana. Matters in Navarre had deteriorated visibly, to the point where even Vascons in the isolated mountain valleys of Vasconia were starting to feel queasy about their unsettled future.

"This king of ours always seems to get mixed up with the wrong allies," commented Juan dejectedly to Pilar. "Here he is, alienating France, squabbling with Castille, being wishy-washy about the Pope! He seems bound and determined to bring Navarre to her knees!"

He was understandably concerned about Castille's latest attempt to muscle the spineless Navarran king out of office. Ferdinand had recently cooked up a "Holy League" to depose the then-reigning Pope Jules II from office on grounds of simony. The Navarran king's tepid response to the power play did not bode well; King Jean d'Albret was bucking a powerful international plot.

"I hear Ferdinand has even sweet-talked the King of England into joining his 'unholy' League!" remarked Pilar, who had been brushing up on the latest scuttlebutt. "I understand the Castilian has even offered to help his son-in-law, Henry VIII, recapture Aquitaine from the French!" Reflecting on the English bullheadedness, she remarked contemptuously: *"Kaskagogor!"* chiding them for persisting in the fantasy of recapturing their long-lost Continental possessions.

"That's all we needed," bemoaned Juan, his crumpled face a picture of despair. "Castile overrunning Navarre so she can take over Ultrapuertos for Henry! What a contrived excuse!"

The remark was more prophetic than the lord of Agorreta could ever have imagined.

Used to fishing in troubled waters, Ferdinand finally saw his chance to grab Navarre's scepter. When his brother-in-law, Gaston de Foix, succumbed in the battle of Ravenna, Ferdinand was quick to ascribe Foix's questionable hereditary rights to the Navarran throne to Gaston's sister, Germaine, who was at the time Ferdinand's wife.

There was only one catch: Jean d'Albret, the current reigning monarch of Navarre, had to be dislodged.

Digging, once more, into his bottomless bag of tricks, Ferdinand came up with a trumped-up charge that the Navarran king's opposition to his "Holy

League" amounted to heresy. With a nod from Rome, the stage was set for Castile's final takeover of Navarre.

There was still the little matter of France, which could hardly be expected to stand idly by and watch Castile gobble up Navarre, an old jewel in the crown of Valois. A tawdry deal was struck whereby France would look the other way in exchange for being allowed to share sovereignty with Castile over Naples, Milan and Venice. The thirty thousand Castilian ducats offered to sweeten the pot made the deal baser still.

The pieces of the puzzle were now in place.

With the excuse of helping Henry VIII, Ferdinand's army burst through Alava in July of 1512, and swept north toward Pamplona. Led by the Duke of Alba, a force of ten thousand men, supported by heavy artillery, overran Pamplona before proceeding toward southern France.

Seeing the gathering storm, King Jean d'Albret fled to Bearn, in ultra-Pyrenean Basse Navarre, there to lick his wounds for the duration.

Navarre was now without a king.

From their balcony of Gasteluzar, several weeks later, Juan and Pilar watched despondently as long Castilian columns marched past on their way to Roncevaux and beyond.

"It never ends," whispered Pilar despairingly. "We never seem to learn that Navarre's most serious threats always come from the south!"

"You're right," agreed Juan somberly. "There're no mountains there to hold them back."

Truer words had not been spoken by a Vascon about his kingdom's Achiles' heel: its southern exposure. An ancestor of his, the Visigoth Edilbert, had pronounced something equally pithy, centuries earlier, but, of course, Juan had no way of knowing it.

The violation of their kingdom's sovereignty was met with strange indifference by the lords of Navarre, who would, shortly after, abjectly swear allegiance to the king of Castile-Aragon. Grown lethargic from centuries of absentee French rule, old Vasconia had been slowly rent asunder by the internecine struggle between the Beaumonts and the Gramonts only to be finally subjugated by their inveterate foe, Castile.

"It's all been downhill since *el Fuerte*," remarked Juan philosophically.

Several French attempts to dislodge Ferdinand from Navarre failed; he was too well installed and stood his ground. Finally, in 1515, Ferdinand convoked the Cortes in Burgos and drove the last nail into the heart of Navarre's sovereignty, officially incorporating her in the crown of Castile-Aragon.

It was as if, having written the last page of his incunabulum, some monk had closed its goatskin cover on a thousand years of Vascon history, musing, as he did, on the birth pangs, the fleeting glory and the final thunderous silence of a fabled kingdom that was no more.

In the centuries that followed, successive generations of Agorretas continued to be born and to die in an ever changing yet strangely continuing pattern. Although different political administrations would come and go, the family endured, some of them spreading even to the far reaches of the world. They, the wanderers, never forgot the rugged mountains that were once theirs and, for a few, the timeless urge of *querencia* sharpened their hunger for homecoming.

Chapter 44

Querencia[1]

~2000 A.D.

The haunting, beech-lined lane between Burguete and Roncevaux was once the main artery between France and Spain across the western Pyrenees. Hostile armies and peaceful migrations trudged along this narrow road to clash with Basques or invade the peninsula farther south. The lane is now eerily quiet with its dreams of fern, velvety moss and patches of wild strawberries growing along its shallow ditches in the early summer. Unexpected shafts of sunlight punch through the canopy of beech and silver fir, dappling the lichen-stained Pilgrims' Cross that guards the southern approaches to Roncevaux. At times the only sounds that intrude are the wind in the tall dark trees and the occasional call of a bird. In a rare moment of quiet epiphany, I am swept by a feeling of déjà vu, uncannily reminded that I was there centuries ago marching shoulder-to-shoulder with kindred Vascon warriors on our way to punish the Franks.

The dark woods end abruptly in a small esplanade at the foot of the lofty mountain the Romans called *Summo Pyreneo*. Huddled around the sunny clearing is an odd assortment of buildings of patently ancient architecture. The sign on the side of the hamlet's first building reads *Orreaga,* a place of thorns. The French also call it *Roncevaux,* valleys of thorns. The flower of their knighthood once fought there and lost a battle which minstrels and troubadours immortalized in the medieval *chanson de geste,* the Song of Roland.

---

1. Spanish: Inclination of man or beast to return to the place where they were bred and raised.

Just beyond the inn stands a squat building of strikingly Romanesque features bearing the evocative name of "Charlemagne's Silo". A wobbly cross teeters precariously above the galvanized sheet metal of its odd, polygonal roof. Low squat arches punctuate the building's walls, giving it an unmistakable sense of sturdiness and age. Local lore says that the Frankish king ordered Roland and his noble paladins to be buried there where they fell in 778.

Adjoining the pantheon stands a small, narrow stone church of equally primitive design dating back to the early 1200s. Gracing its façade is a simple rosette window topped by a small belfry in which a brass bell hangs. One can still hear its snow-muffled chimes carrying over the fog-bound mountains, guiding pilgrims out of the dark forests and over treacherous passes into the welcome warmth and safety of the Hospice of Roncevaux.

Just beyond the Pilgrims' Church is a tangle of medieval buildings housing the pilgrims' Hospital of the Royal Collegiate. The unmistakable sound of Gregorian chant wafts out of what appears to be a Thirteenth Century church sitting at the end of a flagstone path. Pushing the reluctant door ajar, I let myself into a dimly lit, incense-choked gothic interior of simple yet striking elegance. Its airy arches and ribbed vaulting remind me of a miniature Notre Dame de Paris.

Varicolored shafts of early morning sunlight stream into the penumbra through stained glass windows teeming with saints. Inlaid in the marble floor of the central aisle is the emblem of the monastic-military Order of Roncevaux, cleverly combining the symbols of the Abbey's religious and military charters. Arching over the altar is a tall silver canopy under which rests a statue of the Virgin of Roncevaux holding the Christ child. The sweet, slightly Oriental expression on her face is vaguely reminiscent of French religious statuary of the early middle Ages.

Arranged along the wall behind the incense-choked altar are ornately-carved armchairs on which seven sleepy-eyed Canons are ensconced, singing an ancient homophonic Latin chant that reverberates off the stark granite walls. A handful of pilgrims, both local and foreign, occupies the pews on the right. They have lodged in and been fed at the Hospice, and now await the Canons' farewell blessing at the end of the service. On the pews to the left, kneeling all by themselves, half a dozen local elderly women dressed in mourning black, thumb their rosary beads in silent prayer.

When Mass is over, I approach a side altar and collar one of the Canons before he can disappear into the refectory. As luck would have it, I have detained Don Agapito Martinez Alegría, the Royal Collegiate's official historian. After the introductions, I ask him if he could spare a few moments to show me around the Royal Collegiate and acquaint me with the place's history.

"Anything for the Agorretas!" remarks the jovial Canon, patting me on the shoulder as one would a long-lost friend. His friendship with my grandmother's family dates back some time. Taking me by the arm, he leads me up a dark, winding stairwell, through a long corridor and into a large, ill-lit room. It has the musty feel of a small, private museum, incunabula and reliquaries untidily strewn about on a long oak table. Queried about an ancient mace hanging inside a glass showcase, the curate explains that Sancho *el Fuerte* once used it to break the chains that encircled Miramamolin's tent during the epic battle of Navas de Tolosa. Its worm-bitten handle and rusty, spiked iron ball lend some credence to its purported age.

The Canon motions me to sit in one of the comfortable leather armchairs directly across from his cluttered desk. Only his bald pate is visible from behind a pile of manuscripts. Making himself comfortable in his own leather chair, he shoves a few documents aside to better view his visitor. With slow, deliberate twirls of his nicotine-stained fingers, he deftly rolls a cigarette and lights it, his jocund face disappearing momentarily behind a cloud of smoke. After a few deep puffs, he puts the lumpy cigarette out in a brimming ashtray, folds his arms over his belly and holds forth, as one speaking *ex-cathedra*.

"We'll start with the battle of Roncevaux," he says, as way of introduction. "Everyone's interested in Roland, the noble knight. Then we'll go over the Hospice's history and its role as anchor of pilgrimage over the last nine centuries. Then, if we have time, I'll show you around the grounds."

After delving into the background of the famous eighth-century fray and the politics behind it, he plunges directly into the battle itself, citing the number of troops involved, their disposition and maneuvers. "It all started in Atzobiskar, the tallest peak of the Cissa range and eventually spilled down the southern slopes of Ibañeta, Girizu and the Arranosín gully, to end right about where the Collegiate now stands." He goes on to explain how and why the *chanson* misconstrued history.

"The French balladeer of *La Chanson de Roland* not only romanticized a battle that had taken place several centuries earlier," he explains, "but erroneously injected the Moors into the fray. It was a face-saving device on the part of the chauvinistic Breton monk who wrote it, trying to invent a foe more formidable than a rustic mountain rabble to trounce his beloved Roland. You see, Roland, too, was a Breton. The romanticized chronicle was patently inaccurate and self-serving."

"It's not always that the victors get to write the history of famous battles," I commiserate. "I suppose the winners of that particular battle weren't much into writing ballads at the time."

The conversation drifts forward several centuries to the pilgrims and their rugged trek to Santiago, in northwestern Spain. The curate explains how the Hospital of Roncevaux was once held in the same high esteem as those of Jerusalem, Rome and Santiago, how it was manned by the first monastic Military-Hospitalier Order in Christendom. "Their charter," he explains, "was to care for the pilgrims during their hazardous Pyrenean crossing, protecting them from bears, wolves, even marauding bandits."

Asked to explain the phenomenon of Santiago, the Canon waxes eloquent.

"Legend has it that a ninth-Century hermit witnessed strange lights and melodious strains coming out of a forest near Iria Flavia, in far-off Galicia. That's in northwestern Spain, you know," he clarifies. "Alerted to the strange goings-on, the local Bishop went and unearthed a Roman sarcophagus containing the remains of the Apostle James, the 'Son of Thunder', and those of two of his followers."

"How could they identify the remains, nine centuries after the fact?" I inquire, trying not to sound skeptical. Unfazed, the curate responds: "For those who believe, no explanation is necessary." The historian in him appears to wince a little at his own facile reply. Without missing a beat, he drones on: "Christian warriors adopted Santiago as their patron Saint. They nicknamed him '*Mata-moros,*' the Moor-slayer. A famous battle cry during Spain's Reconquest was '*Santiago y cierra España*', which may not make much sense today but once inspired Christian Crusaders to invoke the Saint's help in 'shutting Spain's doors' to the North Africans."

Aware of my interest in the topic, the curate turns to the subject of the Basques. Being the Collegiate's historian and author of several learned tracts on Navarran lore, he mentions an on-going archeological dig in nearby Espinál, where the remains of the northernmost Roman necropolis in Navarre have recently been unearthed. He sounds impressed by the discovery.

"So, why are these remains so important?" I inquire. "I picked up several Roman coins and a couple of ivory needles from between the flagstones of ancient Itálica, near Seville, not too long ago. They're fairly common down there."

"It doesn't surprise me," he admits. "Itálica is a good site for Roman relics, being, as it was, the birthplace of Hadrian and Trajan. But northern Navarre is quite another story. We know that the Romans used this road and the pass above

Roncevaux to move their armies back and forth from Gaul, chasing after Celts. The word 'Cissa' describing this Cissa Range is a corruption of the word 'Caesar'. But there's really no hard evidence that the Romans ever settled anywhere north of Pamplona."

"The Romans," he continues, "left only their dead in these mountain valleys they called the *Saltus Vasconum*, perhaps a mute reminder of the unfriendly welcome they received here. They never subjugated the mountain *Vascones*, as they called us. These fierce, warlike people here were expert at guerrilla tactics; probably invented that kind of warfare! The Romans had a great respect for them. Indeed, the short Roman sword was copied from our *ezpata*," he explains with a hint of pride.

"Here, let me show you what Julius Caesar himself had to say about them. This may interest you."

From a sagging bookstall behind his desk, he pulls down an old leather-bound volume on whose front cover is the faded, gold-embossed inscription: *De Bello Civili, Libro I,* and under it: *J. Caesar*. Opening it to a dog-eared page, he starts reading, translating from Latin to Spanish as he goes:

> "Vascon men wear their hair long and flowing, like women, but when they go to war, they restrain it with a leather thong tied around their forehead. They are as skillful at ambushing others as at avoiding enemy ambuscades, moving with an alacrity proverbial in them. They conduct their military operations with great ease and order.
>
> "Their peculiar tactics consist in launching impetuous attacks from advantageous positions, with dispersed platoons, without distinction of position or rank. When obliged to cede to numerically superior forces, they retreat and escape, not in a rout but in an orderly fashion, to regroup again in a different place determined by their chieftains, so that from there they can once again swoop down on their pursuers.
>
> "They fight without helmets or coats of mail and are armed with a short, double-edged sword, an offensive weapon which we Romans have copied from them and adopted as our own. Others carry iron-tipped arrows and brass-tipped spears, which they launch with formidable accuracy."

"I wonder if they threw those spears the way my friend Quadra-Salcedo once proposed to launch his javelin in the Olympics," I volunteer.

"How was that?"

"Well, he claimed that's how Basque shepherds have been doing it for centuries whenever wolves threaten their flock. Instead of hurling it from over the shoulder, as javelins have been launched at the games since Greek times, these shepherds grab their short *güecias*, as they call their barb-tipped steel rods, palm down, thumb facing forward. Holding the spear at arm's length, they start whirling their whole body around, faster and faster. When they've attained maximum momentum, they hurl the spear great distances and with deadly accuracy. Quadra could hurl his javelin a full five meters farther than the Olympic javelin record of the day!"

"He must have won a gold medal in the event!"

"No. Actually, the Olympic Committee banned the unusual technique claiming it was too dangerous. Some neophyte could release the javelin a second too early or too late and end up skewering some unsuspecting spectator in the stands. My friend Quadra was crushed by the ruling. But anyway, back to Caesar, that's probably the spear-launching technique he was referring to!"

"It may well be! 'Sounds plausible, anyway." After making a note on the margin of the page, he continues translating:

> *"They wear no defensive gear other than a small concave shield measuring two feet in diameter. Only some chieftains cover their heads with helmets, woven from animal sinews and adorned with three feathers.*
>
> *"The horses of their cavalry are adept at climbing mountains and know how to bend their knees when needed. Usually, in battle, two riders mount each horse, so that, if required, one can jump off to fight on foot while the other remains mounted, a tactic that offers quite positive advantages.*
>
> *"They have an absolute disdain for death and are prodigal with their lives in combat. Neither hunger nor thirst bothers them, nor cold confines them, nor heat fatigues them. Their only regret is to reach a useless old age."*

He closes the book and returns it to the bookshelf. "How do you like that!" he comments brightly.

"That's a remarkable first-hand report! And by Caesar, no less! You were saying earlier that the Romans never subjugated the mountain Vascons. Do you mean those living north of Pamplona?"

"That's correct. The fact that no remains of any permanent Roman settlements have ever been discovered in this mountain region of northern Navarre suggests a tenuous political control, at best. But there was really no deep-seated animosity between them and the Basques. Indeed, they recruited these mountain tribesmen as volunteers to serve in their Roman legions as auxiliaries. Tacitus wrote about Basque cohorts fighting gallantly in the Rhine against the Germans. They were recruited to defend Hadrian's Wall in Britain as well."

"Did the Basques ever have a kingdom of their own during the Dark Ages?" I ask.

"Not a kingdom but a dukedom, in the late Seventh Century. It extended from the Loire to the Pyrenees. Lupus, the first Duke, established a hereditary line from which the future kings of Navarre were to descend."

"The name 'Lupus' doesn't sound Basque. Doesn't it mean 'wolf' in Latin?"

"It surely does!" he replies, lighting up. "Basques used to adopt names of animals as personal cognomen, a custom probably dating back to the days when, as hunters during the last Ice Age, they were given nicknames of the animals they killed and brought back to the cave and painted on their walls. Take *Otxoa*, a fairly common Basque name today. It means 'wolf'. The same with *artza*, which means 'bear' and later evolved into Garcia. These names were sometimes translated to Latin during the Roman Era, so that *Otxoa* became *Lupus*, which eventually evolved into Lope, or Lopez."

"These Basques must be pretty ancient folk, then, if they were associated with cave paintings," I remark. "I knew they were an ancient people but not from that far back!"

"They are an ancient people indeed. Their language predates the Neolithic. Their current word for 'ax' is still *aitzkorra*, while the word for 'knife' is *aitzoa*, both derivatives of the root word *aitz*, which literally means 'stone'. Pretty archaic, really. Some geneticists believe Basques are relic Cro-Magnon. The oldest cave paintings date to the time when the Cro-Magnon took over from the Neanderthal, some thirty five thousand years ago."

"Remarkable! But how do you suppose they managed to remain in place these many millennia, probably even speaking the same language?"

"Nobody is really sure. But there are a few plausible theories. You already know about the unknown roots of the Basque language. You may also have heard about the astonishingly high incidence of blood type O-negative among us. The highest in the world is found in this little corner of the Pyrenees! This feature alone underscores our 'other-ness', or at least our 'apart-ness'. We're different from all other Europeans, not only linguistically but biologically as well. This is, indeed, a relic race. Think about it!"

The Canon glances at his watch, a signal that the interview is coming to an end. "I have to leave shortly, but before I do, I'd like to show you the Chapter Hall on your way out."

Walking back down to the first floor, Don Agapito opens an enormous door near the eastern corner of the cloister and leads the way into a large, square chamber. Its magnificent vault rises some eighty feet above the granite floor, supported by an elaborate gothic ribbing. Light streams into the hall from a huge, rosette window that frames a magnificent stained-glass rendition of a medieval battle. In it, a crowned horseman with sword drawn rides a white warhorse charging an encampment of cowering Moors. In the middle of the hall is an impressive alabaster sarcophagus, a band of Latin inscriptions carved around its four sides.

"This," says the curate with reverence, "is the pantheon of King Sancho *el Fuerte* of Navarre." His voice echoes through the enclosure's vault with startling acoustic resonance. "He defeated the Moors in the battle of Navas de Tolosa in the year 1212. That's what the stained glass window above you portrays. The recumbent statue you see here on this sarcophagus is a faithful replica of *el Fuerte*. He was, as you can see, a veritable giant, measuring some two and a quarter meters in height. That's over seven and a half feet tall!"

"He must have been awesome in battle!" I remark.

"He was," he replies matter-of-factly. "And those," he adds, pointing at a set of long, rusty chains hanging over a massive granite altar shoved against the enclosure's northern wall, "are the very chains that once ringed the tent of the Moorish Caliph Miramamolin, whom Sancho defeated in that battle. They have been the symbol of Navarre ever since and are now part of Spain's coat-of-arms."

I remain silent, awed by the realization that all this was part of my own heritage.

I know that the tour has come to an end when Don Agapito starts for the door. I thank him for his time and his enlightening lecture and bid him farewell:

"God be with you, pilgrim," he says, as he disappears into a dark hall.

Returning to my car, I drive past rolling hills and green pastures, headed for my ancestral home in the town of Agorreta, some twelve miles farther south. Grandmother Amatxi, has made arrangements for the caretaker to show me around her ancestral home. The winding road dips in and out of beech and oak forests, dappled by occasional stands of chestnuts and black poplar. I drive past quaint, geranium-splashed whitewashed towns on whose communal meadows sit large rolls of hay waiting to be stored for winter feed. There is a fresh, clean scent in the air, an aroma that pervades the Navarran countryside in the summertime, a blend of new-mown hay and red poppies, perhaps a whiff of cattle. It is the smell of fertile mountain pastures.

The hamlet of Agorreta perches atop a wide shelf above the road. My first thought is that it would have been easy to defend, perhaps the reason why they built it there in the first place. Turning off the main road, I maneuver the car up the narrow rise, inching the vehicle toward the hamlet's square. Half a dozen Basque *caserios* huddle around the plaza's cracked flagstones. I park the car directly in front of a large house that absolutely reeks of age. This, I've been told, would be *Jaureguizar*, the old palace. A few dozen paces up the rise and to my right, sits a massive granite building brooding over the others. That, judging by its fortress-like appearance, has to be *Gasteluzar*, the old castle. Breaking the monotony of its four walls are narrow slits from which arrows must have once been shot in self-defense. I can still see the townsfolk retreating behind its walls in times of peril.

I have seen many manorial fortresses like *Gasteluzar* before, but *Jaureguizar* simply takes my breath away. It is a grand old edifice, simple as all first ideas, primitive like all rough drafts. Its coarsely-hewn stones give the house a certain unpretentious nobility and grandeur. Distinctly Basque in architecture, the large two-story building with its swayback roof just sits there with a pained look of age about it, almost as if each stone's once-fond affection for its neighboring stone has waned, wearied of the weight and togetherness of eons. A feeling of age clings to everything about it as if Time in a moment of weakness has chosen to spare it, tucking it away in one of its cobwebbed back rooms. Though not a ruin, the building flirts dangerously with the possibility.

A moldering coat of arms is sculpted on the facade of the house, just above the brass-studded front door. Gracing its second and third quadrants are two inverted crescent moons, heraldic arms earned fighting Moors in separate battles centuries ago. I feel a shiver of pride on realizing that I have just touched the sarcophagus of the stalwart king with whom one of my ancestors is said to have fought in those battles. Gracing the escutcheon's two other quadrants is a field of nine leaves, which family lore improbably attributes to Agorreta's lordship over one of the nine Vascon prefectures of Roman Novempopulania.

Lost among the brass studs driven into the garish green door is a brass hand-shaped knocker. Banging it resolutely against the metal doorplate, I hear a sonorous echo bouncing around the walls of some large interior. After what seems an interminable wait, Doña Filomena, the old caretaker, cracks the door inquisitively, then lets me in after the introductions.

Uncompromisingly somber, the foyer and its adjoining basement are illuminated by shafts of light streaming through slits cut at irregular intervals along the massive, three-foot thick stone walls. Embedded among the uneven flagstones at my feet is the same family coat-of-arms painstakingly chiseled in a granite slab worn smooth with age. A large enclosure beyond the heavy oak door at the end of the hallway must have once served as stables for a herd of cows and horses. As in most Basque *caserios,* animals winter on the ground floor, providing warmth for the living quarters directly above the stables.

There is a smell of age about the place, as we stumble around kicking up fine dust, disturbing ancient cobwebs in the semi darkness of the relic's basement. Extending from one end of the ceiling to the other are enormous beams of dark, coarsely hewn oak, visibly bowed with age. In one corner of the stables is a chute down which hay must have been delivered from the *sabaiao* hayloft in the attic. In my mind's eye I can almost see a dozen men-at-arms being outfitted for battle in that huge basement, receiving their final marching orders from the lord of the manor.

Limping visibly, Doña Filomena leads me up the main switch-back stairway to the second floor, which really is the first, considering that the house is built on a steep, slanted hill. Blinding sunlight pours in from a dozen open bedroom doors along both sides of the long hallway. The rooms are empty now but their tall ceilings and wainscoted walls are mute reminders of the manorial wealth the owners must have once enjoyed.

At the end of the long hallway is a huge dining room extending the width of the building. This must have once been the Great Hall. I can almost hear the now-stilled voices of the many festive receptions held there, whispered love avowals of long-ago trysts, even sobs for loved ones lost in battle, all haunting the place, wrapping themselves around me. The room is bare now except for a bookshelf along one of the walls, sagging with ancient, leather-bound books and rolled parchments. Walking over to it, I pull down a dusty red leather folder from the top of a teetering pile of papers stacked on one of the shelves. After asking permission, I untie the red ribbon binding the folder and open it to discover several time-mottled parchments inside.

Gingerly, I pick up the brittle document. The folded, two-paged manuscript has torn edges and two gaping holes in the middle where a binding ribbon must have once held the document together. The medieval calligraphy looks convoluted, almost foreign, like something one would find in the Library of the Indies, in Seville, were one searching for treasure manifests of galleons sunk in the Spanish Main. The documents could, after all, have been coeval. From the lacquered seal affixed to the back page, I realize that I am looking at the first and last pages of a legal document.

It suddenly dawns on me that I have stumbled upon the famous 'Bastard document', the one my grandmother and her daughters used to talk about in hushes referring to one of our ancestor's illegitimate sons, who had sued for, and won, the right to inherit his deceased natural father's palaces, lands, even noble titles.

After briefly studying the document, I am able to decipher some of the cryptic abbreviations and shorthand flourishes of the ancient handwriting. Though garbled and mutilated, I manage to work out the first paragraph:

"Don Carlos, by divine clemency, Holy Roman Empe(ror,)...King of Germany, son, by the same grace of God, of Doña Juana and Felipe, King of Castile, Toledo, Seville, Jerusalem, Granada, the Mallorcas and the Menorcas, Sardinia, Murcia and Jaen, the Algarbes, Algeciras, the Indies Islands of firm land in the sea of the Caribbean,..."

The familiar grandiloquent preamble hints at the authenticity of the document, most Royal Court records of the time starting in the same long-winded way. The document then proceeds to list the different Agorreta palaces in Navarre and Labourd, seven in all, describing their individual coats-of-arms in painstaking detail. I am intrigued by the family title of "Cabo de Armeria", which, I later learn, identifies the house as the heraldic registrar of families seeking to join the ranks of Navarran gentry. Other titles listed are those of Majordomo and Royal Cupbearer, confirming an old family tradition that an Agorreta once hosted a Navarran king at one of his palaces. Also cited were such earned privileges as "the right to walk with kings, reside in royal residences, attend royal councils and coronations".

Skipping to the second page I come across a quaint segment, which reads:

"The Palace and House of Agorreta, the principal head of so many noble and illustrious palaces of this Kingdom, has, from time immemorial to this day, possessed and owned the palaces of Azcayn, in the land of Labourd, Kingdom of France, diocese of Bayonne, known by the name of Azcayn Nansegna and by other names, as well as other manors and palaces in Narbart and Gaztelu, and Santesteban de Lerin. It has had, and still has, many of its own servants and vassals who, every year, owe the lords of the palace, vassalage money or wheat, honey, apples, chickens or other services of greater worth, in return for defense..."

This feudal exchange of apples for security is the quaintest description of feudalism I have ever come across. But what really impresses me is that even as far back as September of 1552, the date scribbled at the end of the document, just above the signatures and lacquered seal, the house of Agorreta had already existed "since time immemorial". These people, I reflect, could easily have been in place even before Caesar crossed the Summo Pyreneo!

"I see you've stumbled on the 'bastard' document," says Doña Filomena, plucking me out of my musings. "Iñigo," she volunteered, "that was his name."

Noticing my curiosity, she elaborates: "I understand he turned out to be some kind of a hero in the wars of the Low Countries, years later. They did that a lot, those days, *plantar la pica en Flandes*."

The colorful expression of "planting one's pike in Flanders" to describe someone's noteworthy feats amused me. Intrigued by her story, I continue:

"I notice here that his father's name was Juan de Aguirre, Lord of Agorreta. Why do you suppose a son out of wedlock would have to go to court to inherit his forebear's lands and titles?"

"Probably his wife was sterile, *quien sabe*?" she reasons with shattering feminine logic. "This bastard Iñigo probably had to fight to keep the family lands from reverting to the government. After all, he probably had some claim to them, seeing he was the acknowledged fruit of his natural father's *prima nocte* gallivanting!" As if to wrap up her judgment, she adds a parting swipe: "They were one randy lot, those folks, you know."

I cannot repress a smile, listening to her quaint explanation of an ancient lawsuit nor help wondering how much history has been written over the years, based on much less sagacious *post facto* psychoanalysis than Dona Filomena's.

Satisfied with her own insightful explanation, Doña Filomena comes back down to earth with a thud: "It's getting late. Let me show you the rest of the house."

She leads me out of the library and onto a long balcony stretching the length of the house's eastern exposure. Waving her hand in an encompassing sweep, she pronounces: "All these forested lands you see before you belong to the Agorretas." Below me is a grand view of an oak and pine-covered valley with a stream running through it. I can still vividly remember my mother's stories about how her grandfather, don Serapio, still ruled the roost in these mountains, living comfortably off of his wooded landholdings, his mills, his large flocks of sheep.

"Let me show you the oldest part of the house," offers the caretaker, leading me down the opposite end of the hallway toward the kitchen.

Yawning darkly in a corner of the large room is a huge, beehive-shaped oven. Two ancient torch loops frame the peculiar structure. The ceiling directly above them is smudged with the smoke of countless firebrands. Not far from the oven is an open hearth from which hangs a huge copper kettle, punctured by countless pinholes of age. I can still remember my grandmother reminiscing about how she would sit around the hearth in the long winter evenings, listening to stories about wolves and griffins, as they watched the turnips for pig slop, probably cooking in that very same kettle.

A massive, four-foot tall cylindrical block of solid granite sits opposite the oven. It has a concave cavity hollowed out on its top and a small spout sticking out from the bottom.

"This was their washbasin," volunteers Doña Filomena, anticipating my question. "They used ashes for soap, letting the clothes steep in them in hot water for hours, then rinsing them several times."

Prodded about my great-grandfather Serapio, the caretaker suddenly waxes eloquent. She explains how he ran the town like the *Gran Señor* that he was, acting as both Mayor and Judge. "Sunday Mass would never start before he arrived and knelt down in his personal kneeler," she states, awed by her lord's importance. "And from his balcony," she continues, "he'd light the rocket that signaled the start of the town's festivities every year."

Encouraged by my interest, she continues: "The first electric light bulb in the valley was installed right here, in Jaureguizar," she gushes. "You should have seen the visitors from all over the valley come touch the newfangled bulb! 'Witchcraft!' they'd mumble as they licked their singed fingers." She chuckles at the memory. "Don Serapio was so influential in the government of Navarre that he even had the road to France re-routed to run right past Gazteluzar."

"Tell me more about this house," I ask, trying to steer the conversation from Don Serapio to more ancient history. "How old is it?"

"*Uy, uy ama!*" she exclaims in Basque, shaking her hand, like someone waggling her fingers dry. "Before God was God, Agorreta was Agorreta," she says without hesitation, parroting some local irreverence. "There are such old documents in the attic that not even the experts have been able to decipher them. People around here say there's always been a house here. Some even say that the first lord descended from Aitor himself! That's the father of the Basques, in case you didn't know," she offers gratuitously. "Only God knows where *he* came from! Probably from *ultramar*, beyond the seas, thousands of years ago."

It is getting on late afternoon and I have one more place to visit. I thank Doña Filomena for showing me around my ancestral home. Eager to get back to her chores, she smiles a toothless grin, happy to be done with the interruption. Hopping back into the car, I wave good-bye and head back up the road toward Burguete. I wonder if anyone else has visited Jaureguizar in the last dozen years. I feel a pang of sadness thinking that it will one day just collapse and that that will be the end of all that history, the endless brushes with the Celts and the Romans, the Goths and the Moors...and the Castilians.

Heading north, I turn off the main road halfway between the villages of Viscarrét and Espinál and proceed west down a narrow country lane. It is a quiet place where only the soft sounds of nature intrude. Standing in the middle of a brook flowing alongside the road, is a solitary fisherman, casting his fly line, deftly avoiding the dense overhang. A little farther on, painted on the side of a hill, some Basque graffiti denounces the planned flooding of the pretty little valley, threatening to turn it into a reservoir.

Several miles farther on, the paved road ends abruptly in front of a solitary *caserío*. On its façade a chipped enamel plaque proudly proclaims that this is Sorogain. It is the first one-house town I have ever seen. With the caretaker's permission, I unhitch the chain guarding the path, climb back in the car and cautiously advance up a deeply rutted cart path, precariously wending my way up the side of the mountain. Several cows graze on a slanted meadow above me, their bells echoing peacefully in the narrow valley.

Halfway up the mountain a soft drizzle begins to fall, turning the dirt path into a slippery slide. I consider abandoning my mission but find no room to turn the car around, and shifting it into reverse on that slick slope would be hazardous. Committed to following the trail, I proceed more cautiously now, occasionally skidding and slipping as I inch my way up, gritting my teeth every time the car's undercarriage scrapes against the deep cart ruts.

As I proceed up the narrow path, muttering in disgust, I notice the road suddenly widening just enough to allow turning the car around. As I get ready to execute the maneuver, I happen to look up and see what I have been looking for: there, directly in front of me, sitting on a small promontory overlooking the path, is an odd circular arrangement of grayish granite stones sticking out of the ground like a miniature Stonehenge, but without the lintels. It is the cromlech!

I hop out of the car and clamber up the slippery bank, clawing my way up to the center of the *arrespil*. In a circular pattern, some twenty feet in diameter, stand a score of roughly hewn, two-foot tall granite uprights, protruding from the ground. Circumscribed in the center of the arrangement is an almost imperceptible grassy knoll. The light drizzle and the mists roiling over the weird circle of monoliths give me a strange feeling that I am not alone.

An inscription on a historic marker by the side of the cromlech proclaims that the late Iron-Age monument, presumed to be religious in nature, dates from two-and-a-half millennia ago. The chromlech being pre-Christian, I surmise that the rites must have been pagan since sorcery, witchcraft and goat idolatry were prevalent among the mountain Basques long after the flatland Vascons had adopted Christianity. In my mind's eye I can see witches dancing in that very cromlech on a moonlit summer solstice. The thought gives me a slight shiver, suddenly remembering that Sorogain, means 'the place of witches' in Basque. There is a distinct presence of something surreal in that ghostly place that is making me uncomfortable. I know it is time to leave.

The sun sinks behind the mountains as I slip and slide down the hill towards the *caserio* of Sorogain. As I drive the last few miles north to my grandmother's place in Burguete, I try to relive the blurring events of that day, from the clash of arms at Roncevaux, to the staggering millennial age of Jaureguizar, and finally the unearthly feel of Sorogain, each speaking, in its own hauntingly quiet way of the timeless mystery and fleeting splendor that was once Vasconia.

0-595-31148-2

Printed in Great Britain
by Amazon